Mary Higgins Clark is the author of twenty-two
worldwide bestselling novels and a memoir.
She lives with her husband in Saddle River,
New Jersey

Also by Mary Higgins Clark

Second Time Around
Daddy's Little Girl
On the Street Where You Live
Before I Say Goodbye
We'll Meet Again
All Through the Night
You Belong to Me
Pretend You Don't See Her
My Gal Sunday
Moonlight Becomes You
Silent Night
Let Me Call You Sweetheart
Remember Me
Weep No More, My Lady
Stillwatch
A Cry in the Night
A Stranger is Watching
Where are the Children?

Non-fiction
Kitchen Privileges

With Carol Higgins Clark
He Sees You When You're Sleeping
Deck the Halls

MARY HIGGINS CLARK

THE CRADLE WILL FALL

POCKET
BOOKS

LONDON • SYDNEY • NEW YORK • TORONTO

First published in Great Britain by Collins, 1980
This edition published by Pocket Books, 2003
An imprint of Simon & Schuster UK Ltd

A CBS COMPANY

Copyright © Mary Higgins Clark, 1980

Simon & Schuster UK Ltd
Africa House
64–78 Kingsway
London WC2B 6AH

Simon & Schuster Australia
Sydney

www.simonsays.co.uk

A CIP catalogue record for this book is available from
the British Library

1 3 5 7 9 10 8 6 4 2

ISBN 0-7434-8427-4

Printed and bound in Great Britain by
Cox & Wyman Ltd, Reading, Berkshire

In Tender Memory of
Laura Mary Higgins
May 4, 1961–August 30, 1962

". . . for some patients, though conscious that their condition is perilous, recover their health simply through their contentment with the goodness of the physician."

—Hippocrates

◆ 1 ◆

If her mind had not been on the case she had won, Katie might not have taken the curve so fast, but the intense satisfaction of the guilty verdict was still absorbing her. It had been a close one. Roy O'Connor was one of the top defense attorneys in New Jersey. The defendant's confession had been suppressed by the court, a major blow for the prosecution. But still she had managed to convince the jury that Teddy Copeland was the man who had viciously murdered eighty-year-old Abigail Rawlings during a robbery.

Miss Rawlings' sister, Margaret, was in court to hear the verdict and afterward had come up to Katie. "You were wonderful, Mrs. DeMaio," she'd said. "You look like a young college girl. I never would have thought you could, but when you talked, you *proved* every point; you made them *feel* what he did to Abby. What will happen now?"

"With his record, let's hope the judge decides to send him to prison for the rest of his life," Katie answered.

"Thank God," Margaret Rawlings had said. Her eyes, already moist and faded with age, filled with tears. Quietly she brushed them away as she said, "I miss Abby so. There was just the two of us left. And I keep thinking how frightened she must have been. It would have been awful if he'd gotten away with it."

"He didn't get away with it!" The memory of that reassurance distracted Katie now, made her press her foot harder on the accelerator. The sudden increase in speed as she rounded the curve made the car fishtail on the sleet-covered road.

"Oh . . . no!" She gripped the wheel frantically. The county road was dark. The car raced across the divider and spun around. From the distance she saw headlights approaching.

She turned the wheel into the skid but could not control the car. It careened onto the shoulder of the road, but the shoulder too was a sheet of ice. Like a skier about to jump, the car poised for an instant at the edge of the shoulder, its wheels lifting as it slammed down the steep embankment into the wooded fields.

A dark shape loomed ahead: a tree. Katie felt the sickening crunch as metal tore into bark. The car shuddered. Her body was flung forward against the wheel, then slammed backward. She raised her arms in front of her face, trying to protect it from the splinters of flying glass that exploded from the windshield. Sharp, biting pain attacked her wrists and knees. The headlights and panel lights went out. Dark, velvety blackness was closing over her as from somewhere off in the distance she heard a siren.

The sound of the car door opening; a blast of cold air. "My God, it's Katie DeMaio!"

A voice she knew. Tom Coughlin, that nice young cop. He testified at a trial last week.

"She's unconscious."

She tried to protest, but her lips wouldn't form words. She couldn't open her eyes.

"The blood's coming from her arm. Looks like she's cut an artery."

Her arm was being held; something tight was pressing against it.

A different voice: "She may have internal injuries, Tom. Westlake's right down the road. I'll call for an ambulance. You stay with her."

Floating. Floating. I'm all right. It's just that I can't reach you.

Hands lifting her onto a stretcher; she felt a blanket covering her, sleet pelting her face.

She was being carried. A car was moving. No, it was an ambulance. Doors opening and closing. If only she could make them understand. I can hear you. I'm not unconscious.

Tom was giving her name. "Kathleen DeMaio, lives in Abbington. She's an assistant prosecutor. No, she's not married. She's a widow. Judge DeMaio's widow."

John's widow. A terrible sense of aloneness. The blackness was starting to recede. A light was shining in her eyes. "She's coming around. How old are you, Mrs. DeMaio?"

The question, so practical, so easy to answer. At last she could speak. "Twenty-eight."

The tourniquet Tom had wrapped around her arm was being removed. Her arm was being stitched. She tried not to wince at the needles of pain.

X-rays. The emergency-room doctor. "You're quite fortunate, Mrs. DeMaio. Some pretty severe bruises. No fractures. I've ordered a transfusion. Your blood count is pretty low. Don't be frightened. You'll be all right."

"It's just . . ." She bit her lip. She was coming back into focus and managed to stop herself before she blurted out that terrible, unreasoning, childish fear of hospitals.

Tom asking, "Do you want us to call your sister? They're going to keep you here overnight."

"No. Molly's just over the flu. They've all had it." Her voice sounded so weak. Tom had to bend over to hear her.

"All right, Katie. Don't worry about anything. I'll have your car hauled out."

She was wheeled into a curtained-off section of the emergency room. Blood began dripping through a tube inserted into her right arm. Her head was clearing now.

Her left arm and knees hurt so much. Everything hurt. She was in a hospital. She was alone.

A nurse was smoothing her hair back from her forehead. "You're going to be fine, Mrs. DeMaio. Why are you crying?"

"I'm *not* crying." But she was.

She was wheeled into a room. The nurse handed her a paper cup of water and a pill. "This will help you rest, Mrs. DeMaio."

Katie was sure this must be a sleeping pill. She didn't want it. It would give her nightmares. But it was so much easier not to argue.

The nurse turned off the light. Her footsteps made soft padding sounds as she left the room. The room was cold. The sheets were cold and coarse. Did hospital sheets always feel like this? Katie slid into sleep knowing the nightmare was inevitable.

But this time it took a different form. She was on a roller coaster. It kept climbing higher and higher, steeper and steeper, and she couldn't get control of it. She was trying to get control. Then it went around a curve and off the tracks and it was falling. She woke up trembling just before it hit the ground.

Sleet rapped on the window. She pulled herself up unsteadily. The window was open a crack and making the shade rattle. That was why the room was so drafty. She'd close the window and raise the shade and then maybe she'd be able to sleep. In the morning she could go home. She hated hospitals.

Unsteadily she walked over to the window. The hospital gown they'd given her barely came to her

4

knees. Her legs were cold. And that sleet. It was mixed with more rain now. She leaned against the window-sill, looked out.

The parking lot was turning into streams of gushing water.

Katie gripped the shade and stared down into the lot two stories below.

The trunk lid of a car was going up slowly. She was so dizzy now. She swayed, let go of the shade, and it snapped up. She grabbed the windowsill. She stared down into the trunk. Was something white floating down into it? A blanket? A large bundle?

She must be dreaming this, she thought, then Katie pushed her hand over her mouth to muffle the shriek that tore at her throat. She was staring down into the trunk of the car. The trunk light was on. Through the waves of sleet-filled rain that slapped against the window, she watched the white substance part. As the trunk closed she saw a face—the face of a woman grotesque in the uncaring abandon of death.

♦ 2 ♦

The alarm woke him promptly at two o'clock. Long years of learning to awake to urgency made him instantly alert. Getting up, he went over to the examining-room sink, splashed cold water on his face, pulled his tie into a smooth knot, combed his hair. His socks were still wet. They felt cold and clammy when he took them off the barely warm radiator. Grimac-ing, he pulled them on and slipped his feet into his shoes.

He reached for his overcoat, touched it and winced. It was still soaked through. Hanging it near the radiator had been useless. He'd end up with pneumonia if he wore it. Beyond that, the white fibers of the blanket might cling to the dark blue. That would be something to explain.

The old Burberry he kept in the closet. He'd wear that, leave the wet coat here, drop it off at the cleaner's tomorrow. The raincoat was unlined. He'd freeze, but it was the only thing to do. Besides, it was so ordinary—a drab olive green, outsized now that he'd lost weight. If anyone saw the car, saw him *in* the car, there was less chance of being recognized.

He hurried to the clothes closet, pulled the raincoat from the wire hanger where it was unevenly draped and hung the heavy wet Chesterfield in the back of the closet. The raincoat smelled unused—a dusty, irritating smell that assailed his nostrils. Frowning with distaste, he pulled it on and buttoned it.

He went over to the window and pulled the shade back an inch. There were still enough cars in the parking lot so that the presence or absence of his would hardly be noticed. He bit his lip as he realized that the broken light that always made the far section of the lot satisfactorily dark had been replaced. The back of his car was silhouetted by it. He would have to walk in the shadows of the other cars and get the body into the trunk as quickly as possible.

It was time.

Opening the medical supply closet, he bent down. With expert hands he felt the contours of the body under the blanket. Grunting slightly, he slipped a hand under the neck, the other under the knees, and picked up the body. In life she had weighed somewhere around one hundred ten pounds, but she had gained weight during her pregnancy. His muscles felt every ounce of that weight as he carried her to the examining table. There, working only from the light of the small flashlight propped on the table, he wrapped the blanket around her.

He studied the floor of the medical supply closet carefully and relocked it. Noiselessly opening the door to the parking lot, he grasped the trunk key of the car in two fingers. Quietly he moved to the examining table and picked up the dead woman. Now for the twenty seconds that could destroy him.

Eighteen seconds later he was at the car. Sleet pelted his cheek; the blanket-covered burden strained his arms. Shifting the weight so that most of it rested on one arm, he tried to insert the key into the trunk lock. Sleet had glazed over the lock. Impatiently he scraped it off. An instant later the key was in the lock and the trunk door rose slowly. He glanced up at the hospital windows. From the center room on the second floor a shade snapped up. Was anyone looking out? His impatience to lay the blanketed figure in the trunk, to have it out of his arms, made him move too quickly. The instant his left hand let go of the blanket, the wind blew it apart, revealing her face. Wincing, he dropped the body and slammed the trunk closed.

The light had been on the face. Had anyone seen? He looked up again at the window where the shade had been raised. Was someone there? He couldn't be sure. How much could be seen from that window? Later he would find out who was in that room.

He was at the driver's door, turning the key in the car. He drove swiftly from the lot without turning on the headlights until he was well along the county road.

Incredible that this was his second trip to Chapin River tonight. Suppose he hadn't been leaving the hospital when she burst out of Fukhito's office and hailed him.

Vangie had been close to hysteria, favoring her right

leg as she limped down the covered portico to him. "Doctor, I can't make an appointment with you this week. I'm going to Minneapolis tomorrow. I'm going to see the doctor I used to have, Dr. Salem. Maybe I'll even stay there and let him deliver the baby."

If he had missed her, everything would have been ruined.

Instead he persuaded her to come into the office with him, talked to her, calmed her down, offered her a glass of water. At the last minute she'd suspected, tried to brush past him. That beautiful, petulant face had filled with fear.

And then the horror of knowing that even though he'd managed to silence her, the chance of discovery was still so great. He locked her body in the medical supply closet and tried to think.

Her bright red car had been the immediate danger. It was vital to get it out of the hospital parking lot. It would surely have been noticed there after visiting hours ended—top-of-the-line Lincoln Continental with its aggressive chrome front, every arrogant line demanding attention.

He knew exactly where she lived in Chapin River. She'd told him that her husband, a United Airlines pilot, wasn't due home until tomorrow. He decided to get the car onto her property, to leave her handbag in the house, make it seem as though she'd come home.

It had been unexpectedly easy. There was so little traffic because of the vile weather. The zoning ordinance in Chapin River called for homesites with a minimum of two acres. The houses were placed far back from the road and reached by winding driveways. He opened her garage door with the automatic device on the dashboard of the Lincoln and parked the car in the garage.

He found the door key on the ring with the car keys, but did not need it; the interior door from the garage to the den was unlocked. There were lamps on throughout the house, probably on a timing device. He'd hurried through the den down the hall into the bedroom wing, looking for the master bedroom. It was the last one on the right and no mistaking it. There were two other bedrooms, one fitted as a nursery, with colorful elves and lambs smiling out from freshly applied wallpaper and an obviously new crib and chest.

That was when he realized he might be able to make her death look like a suicide. If she'd begun to furnish the nursery three months before the baby was expected, the threatened loss of that baby was a powerful motive for suicide.

He'd gone into the master bedroom. The king-sized bed was carelessly made, with the heavy white chenille bedspread thrown unevenly over the blankets. Her nightgown and robe were on a chaise longue near it. If he only could get her body back here, put it on top of her own bed! It was dangerous, but not as dangerous as dumping her body in the woods somewhere. That would have meant an intensive police investigation.

He left her handbag on the chaise longue. With the car in the garage and the handbag here, at least it would look as though she'd returned home from the hospital.

Then he walked the four miles back to the hospital. It had been dangerous—suppose a police car had come down the road of that expensive area and stopped him? He had absolutely no excuse for being there. But he'd made the trip in less than an hour, skirted the main entrance to the hospital and let himself into the office through the back door that led from the parking lot. It was just ten o'clock when he got back.

His coat and shoes and socks were soaked. He was

shivering. He realized it would be too dangerous to try to carry the body out until there was a minimal chance of encountering anyone. The late nursing shift came on at midnight. He decided to wait until well after midnight before going out again. The emergency entrance was on the east side of the hospital. At least he didn't have to worry about being observed by emergency patients or a police car rushing a patient in.

He'd set the alarm for two o'clock and lain down on the examining table. He managed to sleep until the alarm went off.

Now he was turning off the wooden bridge onto Winding Brook Lane. Her house was on the right.

Turn off the headlights; turn into the driveway; circle behind the house; back the car against the garage door; pull off driving gloves; put on surgical gloves; open the garage door; open the trunk; carry the wrapped form past the storage shelves to the inside door. He stepped into the den. The house was silent. In a few minutes he'd be safe.

He hurried down the hall to the master bedroom, straining under the weight of the body. He laid the body on the bed, pulling the blanket free.

In the bathroom off the bedroom he shook crystals of cyanide into the flowered blue tumbler, added water and poured most of the contents down the sink. He rinsed the sink carefully and returned to the bedroom. Placing the glass next to the dead woman's hand, he allowed the last drops of the mixture to spill on the spread. Her fingerprints were sure to be on the glass. Rigor mortis was setting in. The hands were cold. He folded the white blanket carefully.

The body was sprawled face up on the bed, eyes staring, lips contorted, the expression an agony of protest. That was all right. Most suicides changed their minds when it was too late.

Had he missed anything? No. Her handbag with the keys was on the chaise; there was a residue of the cyanide in the glass. Coat on or off? He'd leave it on. The less he handled her the better.

Shoes off or on? Would she have kicked them off?

He lifted the long caftan she was wearing and felt the blood drain from his face. The swollen right foot wore a battered moccasin. Her left foot was covered only by her stocking.

The other moccasin must have fallen off. Where? In the parking lot, the office, this house? He ran from the bedroom, searching, retracing his steps to the garage. The shoe was not in the house or garage. Frantic at the waste of time, he ran out to the car and looked in the trunk. The shoe was not there.

It had probably come off when he was carrying her in the parking lot. He'd have heard it fall in the office, and it wasn't in the medicine closet. He was positive of that.

Because of that swollen foot she'd been wearing those moccasins constantly. He'd heard the receptionist joke with her about them.

He would have to go back, search the parking lot, find that shoe. Suppose someone picked it up who had seen her wearing it? There would be talk about her death when her body was discovered. Suppose someone said, "Why, I saw the moccasin she was wearing lying in the parking lot. She must have lost it on her way home Monday night"? But if she had walked even a few feet in the parking lot without a shoe, the sole of her stocking would be badly soiled. The police would notice that. He had to go back to the parking lot and find that shoe.

But now, rushing back to the bedroom, he opened the door of the walk-in closet. A jumble of women's shoes were scattered on the floor. Most of them had impossible high heels. Ridiculous that anyone would believe she had been wearing them in her condition and in this weather. There were three or four pairs of boots, but he'd never be able to zip a boot over that swollen leg.

Then he saw them. A pair of low-heeled shoes, sensible-looking, the kind most pregnant women wore. They looked fairly new, but had been worn at least once. Relieved, he grabbed them. Hurrying back to the bed, he pulled the one shoe from the dead woman's foot and slipped her feet into the shoes he had just taken from the closet. The right one was tight, but he managed to lace it. Jamming the moccasin she had been wearing into the wide loose pocket of his raincoat, he reached for the white blanket. With it under his arm he strode from the room, down the hall, through the den and out into the night.

By the time he drove into the hospital parking lot, the sleet and rain had stopped falling but it was windy and very cold. Driving to the farthermost corner of the area, he parked the car. If the security guard happened to come by and spoke to him, he'd simply say that he'd received a call to meet one of his patients here; that she was in labor. If for any reason that story was checked, he'd act outraged, say it was obviously a crank call.

But it would be much safer not to be seen. Keeping in the shadow of the shrubbery that outlined the divider island of the lot, he hurried to retrace his steps from the space where he'd kept the car to the door of the office. Logically the shoe might have fallen off when he'd shifted the body to open the trunk. Crouching, he searched the ground. Quietly he worked his way closer to the hospital. All the patients' rooms in this wing were dark now. He glanced up to the center window on the second floor. The shade was securely down. Someone had adjusted it. Bending forward, he slowly made his way across the macadam. If anyone saw him! Rage and frustration made him unaware of the bitter cold. Where was that shoe? He had to find it.

Headlights came around the bend into the parking lot. A car screeched to a halt. The driver, probably heading for the emergency room, must have realized he'd taken the wrong turn. He made a U-turn and raced out of the lot.

He had to get out of here. It was no use. He fell forward as he tried to straighten up. His hand slid across the slippery macadam. And then he felt it: the leather under his fingers. He grabbed it, held it up. Even in the dim light he could still be sure. It was the moccasin. He had found it.

Fifteen minutes later, he was turning the key in the lock of his home. Peeling off the raincoat, he hung it in the foyer closet. The full-length mirror on the door reflected his image. Shocked, he realized that his trouser knees were wet and dirty. His hair was badly disheveled. His hands were soiled. His cheeks were flushed, and his eyes, always prominent, were bulging and wide-lensed. He looked like a man in emotional shock, a caricature of himself.

Rushing upstairs, he disrobed, sorted his clothing into the hamper and cleaning bag, bathed and got into pajamas and a robe. He was far too keyed up to sleep, and besides, he was savagely hungry.

The housekeeper had left slices of lamb on a plate. There was a fresh wedge of Brie on the cheese board on the kitchen table. Crisp, tart apples were in the fruit bin of the refrigerator. Carefully he prepared a tray and carried it into the library. From the bar he poured a generous whiskey and sat at his desk. As he ate, he reviewed the happenings of the night. If he had not stopped to check his calendar he would have missed her. She would have been gone and it would have been too late to stop her.

Unlocking his desk, he opened the large center

drawer and slid back the false bottom where he always kept his current special file. A single manila expansion file was there. He reached for a fresh sheet of paper and made a final entry:

February 15

At 8:40 P.M. this physician was locking the rear door of his office. Subject patient had just left Fukhito. Subject patient came over to this physician and said that she was going home to Minneapolis and would have her former doctor, Emmet Salem, deliver her baby. Patient was hysterical and was persuaded to come inside. Obviously patient could not be allowed to leave. Regretting the necessity, this physician prepared to eliminate patient. Under the excuse of getting her a glass of water, this physician dissolved cyanide crystals into the glass and forced patient to swallow the poison. Patient expired at precisely 9:15 P.M. The fetus was 26 weeks old. It is the opinion of this physician that had it been born it might have been viable. The full and accurate medical records are in this file and should replace and nullify the records at the Westlake Hospital office.

Sighing, he laid down the pen, slipped the final entry into the manila envelope and sealed the file. Getting up, he walked over to the last panel on the bookcase. Reaching behind a book, he touched a button, and the panel swung open on hinges, revealing a wall safe. Quickly he opened the safe and inserted the file, subconsciously noting the growing number of envelopes. He could have recited the names of them by heart: Elizabeth Berkeley, Anna Horan, Maureen Crowley, Linda Evans—over six dozen of them: the successes and failures of his medical genius.

He closed the safe and snapped the bookcase back

into place, then went upstairs slowly. He took off his bathrobe, got into the massive four-poster bed and closed his eyes.

Now that he was finished with it, he felt exhausted to the point of sickness. Had he overlooked anything, forgotten anything? He'd put the vial of cyanide in the safe. The moccasins. He'd get rid of them somewhere tomorrow night. The events of the last hours whirled furiously through his mind. When he had been doing what must be done, he'd been calm. Now that it was over, like the other times, his nervous system was screaming in protest.

He'd drop his own cleaning off on the way to the hospital tomorrow morning. Hilda was an unimaginative housekeeper, but she'd notice the mud and dampness of his trouser knees. He'd find out what patient was in the center room on the second floor of the east wing, what the patient could have seen. Don't think about it now. Now he must sleep. Leaning on one elbow, he opened the drawer of his night table and took out a small pillbox. The mild sedative was what he needed. With it he'd be able to sleep for two hours.

His fingers groped for and closed over a small capsule. Swallowing it without water, he leaned back and closed his eyes. While he waited for it to take effect, he tried to reassure himself that he was safe. But no matter how hard he tried, he could not push back the thought that the most damning proof of his guilt was inaccessible to him.

♦ 3 ♦

"If you don't mind, we'd like you to leave through the back entrance," the nurse said. "The front driveway froze over terribly, and the workmen are trying to clear it. The cab will be waiting there."

"I don't care if I climb out the window, just as long as I can get home," Katie said fervently. "And the misery is that I have to come back here Friday. I'm having minor surgery on Saturday."

"Oh." The nurse looked at her chart. "What's wrong?"

"I seem to have inherited a problem my mother used to have. I practically hemorrhage every month during my period."

"That must have been why your blood count was so low when you came in. Don't worry about it. A D-and-C is no big deal. Who's your doctor?"

"Dr. Highley."

"Oh, he's the best. But you'll be over in the west wing. All his patients go there. It's like a luxury hotel. He's top man in this place, you know." She was still looking at Katie's chart. "You didn't sleep much, did you?"

"Not really." Katie wrinkled her nose with distaste as she buttoned her blouse. It was spattered with blood, and she let the left sleeve hang loosely over her bandaged arm. The nurse helped her with her coat.

The morning was cloudy and bitterly cold. Katie decided that February was getting to be her least-favorite month. She shivered as she stepped out into

16

the parking lot, remembering her nightmare. This was the area she had been looking at from her room. The cab pulled up. Gratefully she walked over to it, wincing at the pain in her knees. The nurse helped her in, said good-bye and closed the door. The cabdriver pressed his foot on the accelerator. "Where to, lady?"

From the window of the second-floor room that Katie had just left, a man was observing her departure. The chart the nurse had left on the desk was in his hand. *Kathleen N. DeMaio, 10 Woodfield Way, Abbington. Place of Business: Prosecutor's office, Valley County.*

He felt a thrill of fear go through him. *Katie DeMaio.*

The chart showed she had been given a strong sleeping pill.

According to her medical history, she took no medication regularly, including sleeping pills or tranquilizers. So she'd have no tolerance for them and would have been pretty groggy from what they'd given her last night.

There was a note on the chart that the night nurse had found her sitting on the edge of the bed at 2:08 A.M. in an agitated state and complaining about nightmares.

The shade in the room had snapped up. She must have been at the window. How much had she seen? If she'd observed anything, even if she thought she'd been having a nightmare, her professional training would nag at her. She was a risk, an unacceptable one.

◆ 4 ◆

Shoulders touching, they sat in the end booth of the Eighty-seventh Street drugstore. Uneaten English muffins had been pushed away, and somberly they sipped coffee. The arm of her teal-blue uniform jacket rested on the gold braid on his sleeve. The fingers of his right hand were entwined with those of her left hand.

"I've missed you," he said carefully.

"I've missed you too, Chris. That's why I'm sorry you met me this morning. It just makes it worse."

"Joan, give me a little time. I swear to God we'll work this out. We've got to."

She shook her head. He turned to her and with a wrench noticed how unhappy she looked. Her hazel eyes were cloudy. Her light brown hair, pulled back this morning in a chignon, revealed the paleness of her usually smooth, clear skin.

For the thousandth time he asked himself why he hadn't made the clean break with Vangie when he was transferred to New York last year. Why had he responded to her plea to try just a little longer to make a go of their marriage when ten years of trying hadn't done it? And now a baby coming. He thought of the ugly quarrel he'd had with Vangie before he left. Should he tell Joan about that? No, it wouldn't do any good.

"How did you like China?" he asked.

She brightened. "Fascinating, completely fascinat-

18

ing." She was a flight attendant with Pan American. They'd met six months ago in Hawaii when one of the other United captains, Jack Lane, threw a party.

Joan was based in New York and shared an apartment in Manhattan with two other Pan Am attendants.

Crazy, incredible, how right some people are together from the first minute. He'd told her he was married, but also was able to say honestly that when he transferred from the Minneapolis base to New York he had wanted to break with Vangie. The last-ditch attempt to save the marriage wasn't working. No one's fault. The marriage was something that never should have happened in the first place.

And then Vangie had told him about the baby.

Joan was saying, "You got in last night."

"Yes. We had engine trouble in Chicago and the rest of the flight was cancelled. We deadheaded back. Got in around six and I checked into the Holiday Inn on Fifty-seventh Street."

"Why didn't you go home?"

"Because I haven't seen you for two weeks and I wanted to see you, *had* to see you. Vangie doesn't expect me till about eleven. So don't worry."

"Chris, I told you I put in an application to transfer to the Latin American Division. It's been approved. I'll be moving to Miami next week."

"Joan, no!"

"It's the only way. Look, Chris, I'm sorry, but it's not my nature to be an available lady for a married man. I'm not a home wrecker."

"Our relationship has been totally innocent."

"In today's world who would ever believe that? The very fact that in an hour you'll be lying to your wife about when you got in says a lot, doesn't it? And don't forget, I'm the daughter of a Presbyterian minister. I can just see Dad's reaction if I tell him that I'm in love with a man who not only is married but whose wife is finally expecting the baby she's prayed for for ten years. He'd be real proud of me, let me tell you."

She finished the coffee. "And no matter what you say, Chris, I still feel that if I'm not around, there's the chance that you and your wife will grow closer. I'm occupying your thoughts when you should be concerned about her. And you'll be amazed how a baby has a way of creating a bond between people."

Gently she withdrew her fingers from his. "I'd better get home, Chris. It was a long flight and I'm tired. You'd better get home too."

They looked directly at each other. She touched his face, wanting to smooth away the deep, unhappy creases in his forehead. "We really could have been awfully good together." Then she added, "You look terribly tired, Chris."

"I didn't sleep very much last night." He tried to smile. "I'm not giving up, Joan. I swear to you that I'm coming to Miami for you, and when I get there I'll be free."

♦ 5 ♦

The cab dropped Katie off. She hurried painfully up the porch steps, thrust her key into the lock, opened the door and murmured, "Thank God to be home." She felt that she'd been away weeks rather than overnight and with fresh eyes appreciated the soothing, restful earth tones of the foyer and living room, the hanging plants that had caught her eye when she'd visited this house for the first time.

She picked up the bowl of African violets and inhaled the pungent perfume of their leaves. The odors of antiseptics and medicines were trapped in her nostrils. Her body was aching and stiff, even more now than it had been when she got out of bed this morning.

But at least she was home.

John. If he were alive, if he had been here to call last night . . .

Katie hung up her coat and sank down on the apricot velvet couch in the living room. She looked up at John's portrait over the mantel. John Anthony DeMaio, the youngest judge in Essex County. She could remember so clearly the first time she'd seen him. He'd come to lecture to her Torts class at Seton Hall Law School.

When the class ended, the students clustered around him. "Judge DeMaio, I hope the Supreme Court turns down the appeal on the *Collins* case."

"Judge DeMaio, I agree with your decision on *Reicher versus Reicher.*"

And then it had been Katie's turn. "Judge, I have to tell you I don't agree with your decision in the *Kipling* case."

John had smiled. "That obviously is your privilege, Miss . . ."

"Katie . . . Kathleen Callahan."

She never understood why at the moment she'd dragged up the Kathleen. But he'd always called her that, Kathleen Noel.

That day they'd gone out for coffee. The next night he'd taken her to the Monsignor II restaurant in New York for dinner. When the violinists came to their table, he'd asked them to play "Vienna, City of My

Dreams." He'd sung it softly with them: *"Wien, Wien, nur Du allein ..."* When they finished he asked, "Have you ever been to Vienna, Kathleen?"

"I've never been out of the country except for the school trip to Bermuda. It rained for four days."

"I'd like to take you abroad someday. But I'd show you Italy first. Now, there's a beautiful country."

When he dropped her off that night he'd said, "You have the loveliest blue eyes I've ever had the pleasure of looking into. I don't think a twelve-year age difference is too much, do you, Kathleen?"

Three months later, when she was graduated from law school, they married.

This house. John had been raised in it, had inherited it from his parents.

"I'm pretty attached to it, Kathleen, but be sure you are. Maybe you want something smaller."

"John, I was raised in a three-room apartment in Queens. I slept on a daybed in the living room. 'Privacy' was a word I had to look up in the dictionary. I *love* this house."

"I'm glad, Kathleen."

They loved each other so much—but besides that, they were such good friends. She'd told him about the nightmare. "I warn you that every once in a while, I'll wake up screaming like a banshee. It started when I was eight years old after my father died. He'd been in the hospital recovering from a heart attack and then he had a second attack. Apparently the old man in the room with him kept pressing the buzzer for the nurse, but no one came. By the time someone got around to answering the buzzer, it was too late."

"And then you started having nightmares."

"I guess I heard the story so much it made an awful impression on me. In the nightmare I'm in a hospital going from bed to bed, looking for Daddy. I keep seeing faces of people I know in the beds. They're all asleep. Sometimes it would be girls from school, or cousins—or just anybody. But I'd be trying to find Daddy. I knew he needed me. Finally I see a nurse and run up to her and ask her where he is. And she smiles and says, 'Oh, he's dead. All these people are dead. You're going to die in here too.'"

"You poor kid."

"Oh, John, intellectually I know it's nonsense not to get over it. But I swear to you I'm scared silly at the thought of ever being a patient in a hospital."

"I'll help you get over that."

She'd been able to tell him how it really was after her father died. "I missed him so much, John. I was always such a daddy's girl. Molly was sixteen and already going around with Bill, so I don't think it hit her as hard. But all through school, I kept thinking what fun it would be if he were at the plays and the graduations. I used to dread the Father and Daughter Dinner every spring."

"Didn't you have an uncle or someone who could have gone with you?"

"Just one. It would have taken too long to sober him up."

"Oh, Kathleen!" The two of them laughing. John saying, "Well, darling, I'm going to uproot that core of sadness in you."

"You already have, Judge."

They'd spent their honeymoon traveling through Italy. The pain had begun on that trip. They'd come back in time for the opening of court. John presided on the bench in Essex County. She'd been hired to clerk for a criminal judge in Valley County.

John went for a checkup a month after they got home. The overnight stay at Mt. Sinai stretched into three days of additional tests. Then one evening he'd been waiting for her at the elevator, impeccably elegant in the dark red velour robe, a wan smile on his face. She'd run over to him, aware as always of the glances the other elevator passengers threw at him, thinking how even in pajamas and a robe, John looked impressive. She'd been about to tell him that when he said, "We've got trouble, darling."

Even then, just the way he said, *"We've* got trouble." In those few short months, in every way, they had become one. Back in his room he'd told her. "It's a malignant tumor. Both lungs, apparently. And for God's sake, Kathleen, I don't even smoke."

Incredulously they had laughed together in a paroxysm of grief and irony. John Anthony DeMaio, Superior Court Judge of Essex County, Past President of the New Jersey Bar Association, not thirty-eight years old, had been condemned to an indeterminate sentence of Six Months to Life. For him there would be no parole board, no appeal.

He'd gone back on the bench. "Die with your robes on—why not?" he'd shrugged.

"Promise me you'll remarry, Kathleen."

"Someday, but you'll be a hard act to follow."

"I'm glad you think so. We'll make every minute we have count."

Even in the midst of it, knowing their time was slipping away, they'd had fun.

One day he came home from court and said, "I think that's about it for the bench."

The cancer had spread. The pain got steadily worse. At first he'd go to the hospital for a few days at a time for chemotherapy. Her nightmare began again; it came regularly. But John would come home and they'd have more time. She resigned her clerkship. She wanted every minute with him.

Toward the end, he asked, "Would you want to have your mother come up from Florida and live with you?"

"Good Lord, no. Mama's great, but we lived together until I went to college. That was enough. But anyhow, she loves Florida."

"Well, I'm glad Molly and Bill live nearby. They'll look out for you. And you enjoy the children."

They'd both been silent then. Bill Kennedy was an orthopedic surgeon. He and Molly had six kids and lived two towns away in Chapin River. The day Katie and John were married, they'd bragged to Bill and Molly that they were going to beat their record. "We'll have seven offspring," John had declared.

The last time he went in for chemotherapy, he didn't come back. He was so weak they had him stay overnight. He was talking to her when he slipped into the coma. They'd both hoped that the end would come at home, but he died in the hospital that night.

The next week Katie applied to the Prosecutor's office for a job and was accepted. It was a good decision. The office was chronically shorthanded, and she always had more cases than she could reasonably handle. There wasn't any time for introspection. All day, every day, even on many weekends, she'd had to concentrate on her case load.

And in another way it was good therapy. That anger which had accompanied the grief, the sense of being cheated, the fury that John had been cheated out of so much of life, she directed into the cases she tried. When she prosecuted a serious crime, she felt as though she were tangibly fighting at least one kind of evil that destroyed lives.

She'd kept the house. John had willed her all of his very considerable assets, but even so, she knew it was silly for a twenty-eight-year-old woman on a twenty-two-thousand-dollar salary to live in a home worth a quarter of a million dollars with five acres surrounding it.

Molly and Bill were always urging her to sell it.

"You'll never put your life with John behind you until you do," Bill had told her.

He was probably right. Now Katie shook herself and got up from the couch. She was getting downright maudlin. She'd better call Molly. If Molly had tried to get her last night and not received an answer she'd have been delighted. She was always making a novena that Katie would "meet someone." But she didn't want Molly to try to reach her at the office and find out that way that she'd been in an accident.

Maybe Molly would come over and they'd have lunch together. She had salad makings and Bloody Mary ingredients. Molly was perpetually on a diet, but would not give up her lunchtime Bloody Mary. "For God's sake, Kate, how could anyone with six kids *not* have a belt at lunch?" Molly's cheerful presence would quickly dispel the sense of isolation and sadness.

Katie became aware of the bloodstained blouse she was wearing. After she'd talked to Molly, while she was waiting for her to come over, she'd bathe and change.

Glancing into the mirror over the couch, she saw that the bruise under her right eye was assuming a brilliant purple color. Her naturally olive complexion, which Mama called the "Black Irish" look from her father's side, was a sickly yellow. Her collar-length dark brown hair, which usually bounced full and luxuriant in a natural wave, was matted against her face and neck.

"You should see the other guy," she murmured ruefully.

The doctor had told her not to get her arm wet. She'd wrap the bandage in a Baggie and keep it dry. Before she could pick up the phone, it began to ring. Molly, she thought. I swear she's a witch.

But it was Richard Carroll, the Medical Examiner.

"Katie, how are you? Just heard that you'd been in some kind of accident."

"Nothing much. I took a little detour off the road. The trouble is there was a tree in the way."

"When did it happen?"

"About ten last night. I was on my way home from the office. I'd worked late to catch up on some files. Spent the night in the hospital and just got home. I look a mess, but I'm really okay."

"Who picked you up? Molly?"

"No. She doesn't know yet. I called a cab."

"Always the Lone Ranger, aren't you?" Richard asked. "Why the blazes didn't you call *me?*"

Katie laughed. The concern in Richard's voice was both flattering and threatening. Richard and Molly's husband were good friends. Several times in the last six months Molly had pointedly invited Katie and Richard to small dinner parties. But Richard was so blunt and cynical. She always felt somewhat unsettled around him. Anyhow, she simply wasn't looking to get involved with anyone, and especially anyone she worked with so frequently. "Next time I run into a tree I'll remember," she said.

"You're going to take a couple of days off, aren't you?"

"Oh, no," she said. "I'm going to see if Molly's free for a quick lunch; then I'll get in to the office. I've got at least ten files to work on, and I'm trying an important case on Friday."

"There's no use telling you you're crazy. Okay. Gotta go. My other phone's ringing. I'll poke my head in your office around five-thirty and catch you for a drink." He hung up before she could reply.

Katie dialed Molly's number. When her sister answered, her voice was shaken. "Katie, I guess you've heard about it."

"Heard about what?"

"People from your office are just getting there."

"Getting where?"

"Next door. The Lewises. That couple who moved in last summer. Katie, that poor man; he just came home from an overnight flight and found her—his wife, Vangie. She's killed herself. Katie, she was six months pregnant!"

The Lewises. *The Lewises.* Katie had met them at Molly and Bill's New Year's Day open house. Vangie a very pretty blonde. Chris an airline pilot.

Numbly she heard Molly's shocked voice: "Katie, why would a girl who wanted a baby so desperately kill herself?"

The question hung in the air. Cold chills washed over Katie. That long blond hair spilling over shoulders. Her nightmare. Crazy the tricks the mind plays. As soon as Molly said the name, last night's nightmare had come back. The face she'd glimpsed through the hospital window was Vangie Lewis'.

♦ 6 ♦

Richard Carroll parked his car within the police lines on Winding Brook Lane. He was shocked to realize that the Lewises lived next door to Bill and Molly Kennedy. Bill had been a resident when Richard interned at St. Vincent's. Later he'd specialized in forensic medicine and Bill in orthopedics. They'd been pleasantly surprised to bump into each other in the Valley County courthouse when Bill was appearing as an expert witness in a malpractice trial. The friendship that had been casual in the St. Vincent's days had become close. Now he and Bill golfed together frequently, and Richard often stopped back to their house for a drink after the game.

He'd met Molly's sister, Katie DeMaio, in the Prosecutor's office and had been immediately attracted to the dedicated young attorney. She was a throwback to the days when the Spanish invaded Ireland and left a legacy of descendants with olive skin and dark hair to contrast with the intense blue of Celtic eyes. But Katie had subtly discouraged him when he'd suggested getting together, and he'd philosophically dismissed her from his thoughts. There were plenty of mighty attractive ladies who enjoyed his company well enough.

But hearing Molly and Bill and their kids talk about Katie, what fun she could be, how chopped up she was over her husband's death, had rekindled his interest. Then in the past few months he'd been at a couple of parties at Bill and Molly's and found to his chagrin that he was far more intrigued by Katie DeMaio than he wanted to be.

Richard shrugged. He was here on police business. A thirty-year-old woman had committed suicide. It was his job to look for any medical signs which might indicate that Vangie Lewis had not taken her own life. Later today he'd perform an autopsy. His jaw tightened as he thought of the fetus she was carrying. Never had a chance. How was that for motherly love? Cordially, objectively, he already disliked the late Vangie Lewis.

A young cop from Chapin River let him in. The living room was to the left of the foyer. A guy in an airline captain's uniform was sitting on the couch, hunched forward, clasping and unclasping his hands. He was a lot paler than many of the deceased Richard dealt with and was trembling violently. Richard felt a brief twinge of sympathy. The husband. Some brutal kick to come home and find your wife a suicide. He decided to talk with him later. "Which way?" he asked the cop.

"Back here." He nodded his head to the rear of the house. "Kitchen straight ahead, bedrooms to the right. She's in the master bedroom."

Richard walked quickly, absorbing as he did the feel of the house. Expensive, but carelessly furnished, without flair or even interest. The glimpse of the living room had shown him the typical no-imagination interior-designer look you see in so many Main Street decorator shops in small towns. Richard had an acute sense of color. Privately he thought it helped him considerably in his work. But clashing shades registered on his consciousness like the sound of discordant notes.

Charley Nugent, the detective in charge of the Homicide Squad, was in the kitchen. The two men exchanged brief nods. "How does it look?" Richard asked.

"Let's talk after you see her."

In death Vangie Lewis was not a pretty sight. The long blond hair seemed a muddy brown now; her face was contorted; her legs and arms, stiff with the onslaught of rigor mortis, had the appearance of being stretched on wires. Her coat was buttoned and, because of her pregnancy, hiked over her knees. The soles of her shoes were barely showing under a long flowered caftan.

Richard pulled the caftan up past her ankles. Her legs, obviously swollen, had stretched the panty hose. The sides of her right shoe bit into the flesh.

Expertly he picked up one arm, held it for an instant, let it drop. He studied the mottled discoloration around her mouth where the poison had burned it.

Charley was beside him. "How long you figure?"

"Anywhere from twelve to fifteen hours, I'd guess. She's pretty rigid." Richard's voice was noncommittal, but his sense of harmony was disturbed. The coat on. Shoes on. Had she just come home, or had she been planning to go out? What had suddenly made her take her own life? The tumbler was beside her on the bed. Bending down, he sniffed it. The unmistakable bitter-almond scent of cyanide entered his nostrils. Incredible how many suicides took cyanide ever since that Jones-cult mess in Guyana. He straightened up. "Did she leave a note?"

Charley shook his head. Richard thought that Charley was in the right job. He always looked mournful; his lids drooped sadly over his eyes. He seemed to have a perpetual dandruff problem. "No letters; no nothing. Been married ten years to the pilot; he's the guy in the living room. Seems pretty broken up. They're from Minneapolis; just moved east less than a year ago. She always wanted to have a baby. Finally got pregnant and was in heaven. Started decorating a nursery; talks baby morning, noon and night."

"Then she kills it and herself?"

"According to her husband, she'd been nervous lately. Some days she had some sort of fixation that she was going to lose the baby. Other times she'd act scared about giving birth. Apparently knew she was showing some signs of a toxic pregnancy."

"And rather than give birth or face losing the baby, she kills herself?" Richard's tone was skeptical. He could tell Charley wasn't buying it either. "Is Phil with you?" he asked. Phil was the other senior member of the Homicide team from the Prosecutor's office.

"He's out around the neighborhood talking to people."

"Who found her?"

"The husband. He just got in from a flight. Called for an ambulance. Called the local cops."

Richard stared at the burn marks around Vangie Lewis' mouth. "She must have really splashed that in," he said meditatively, "or maybe tried to spit it out but it was too late. Can we talk to the husband, bring him in here?"

"Sure." Charley nodded to the young cop, who turned and scampered down the long hallway.

When Christopher Lewis came into the bedroom, he looked as though he were on the verge of getting sick. His complexion was now a sickly green. Perspiration, cold and clammy, beaded on his forehead. He had pulled open his shirt and tie. His hands were shoved into his pockets.

Richard studied him appraisingly. Lewis looked distraught, sick, nervous. But there was something missing. He did not look like a man whose life has been shattered.

Richard had seen death countless times. He'd witnessed some next of kin grieving in dumbstruck silence. Others shrieked hysterically, screamed, wept, threw themselves on the deceased. Some touched the dead hand, trying to understand. He thought of the young husband whose wife had been caught in a shoot-out while they were getting out of their car to do the grocery shopping. When Richard got there, he was holding the body, bewildered, talking to her, trying to get through to her.

That was grief.

Whatever emotion Christopher Lewis was experiencing now, Richard would stake his life on the fact that he was not a heartbroken husband.

Charley was questioning him. "Captain Lewis, this is tough for you, but it will make it easier all around if we can ask you some questions."

"Here?" It was a protest.

"You'll see why. We won't be long. When was the last time you saw your wife?"

"Two nights ago. I was on a run to the Coast."

"And you arrived home at what time?"

"About an hour ago."

"Did you speak with your wife in those two days?"

"No."

"What was your wife's mental state when you left?"

"I told you."

"If you'd just tell Dr. Carroll."

"Vangie was worried. She'd become quite apprehensive that she might miscarry."

"Were you alarmed about that possibility?"

"She'd become quite heavy, looked like she was retaining fluid, but she had pills for that and I understand it's quite a common condition."

"Did you call her obstetrician to discuss this with him, to reassure yourself?"

"No."

"All right. Captain Lewis, will you look around this room and see if you notice anything amiss. It isn't easy, but will you study your wife's body carefully and see if there's anything that in some way is different. For example, that glass. Are you sure it's the one from your bathroom?"

Chris obeyed. His face going progressively whiter, he carefully looked at every detail of his dead wife's appearance.

Through narrowed eyes, Charley and Richard watched him.

"No," he whispered finally. "Nothing."

Charley's manner became brisk. "Okay, sir. As soon as we take some pictures, we'll remove your wife's body for an autopsy. Can we help you get in touch with anyone?"

"I have some calls to make. Vangie's father and

mother. They'll be heartbroken. I'll go into the study and phone them now."

After he'd left, Richard and Charley exchanged glances.

"He saw something we missed," Charley said flatly.

Richard nodded. "I know." Grimly the two men stared at the crumpled body.

◆ 7 ◆

Before she'd hung up, Katie had told Molly about the accident and suggested lunch. But Molly's twelve-year-old Jennifer and her six-year-old twin boys were home from school recovering from flu. "Jennifer's okay, but I don't like to leave those boys alone long enough to empty the garbage," Molly had said, and they'd arranged that she would pick Katie up and bring her back to her own house.

While she waited, Katie bathed quickly, managing to wash and blow-dry her hair using only her right hand. She put on a thick wool sweater and well-tailored tweed slacks. The red sweater gave some hint of color to her face, and her hair curled loosely just below her collar. As she bathed and dressed, she tried to rationalize last night's hallucination.

Had she even *been* at the window? Or was that part of the dream? Maybe the shade had snapped up by itself, pulling her out of a nightmare. She closed her eyes as once more the scene floated into her consciousness. It had seemed so real: the trunk light had shone directly into the trunk on the staring eyes, the long hair, the high-arched eyebrows. For one instant it had seemed so clear. That was what frightened her: the clarity of the image. The face had been familiar even in the dream.

Would she talk to Molly about that? Of course not. Molly had been worried about her lately. "Katie, you're too pale. You work too hard. You're getting too quiet." Molly had bullied her into the scheduled operation. "You can't let that condition go on indefinitely. That hemorrhaging can be dangerous if you let it go." And then she'd added, "Katie, you've got to realize you're a young woman. You should take a real vacation, relax, go away."

From outside, a horn blew loudly as Molly pulled up in her battered station wagon. Katie struggled into a warm beaver jacket, turning the collar up around her ears, and hurried out as fast as her swollen knees would allow. Molly pushed open the door for her and leaned over to kiss her. She eyed her critically. "You're not exactly blooming. How badly *were* you hurt?"

"It could have been a lot worse." The car smelled vaguely of peanut butter and bubble gum. It was a comforting, familiar smell, and Katie felt her spirits begin to lift. But the mood was broken instantly when Molly said, "Our block is some mess. Your people have the Lewis place blocked off, and some detective from your office is going around asking questions. He caught me just as I was leaving. I told him I was your sister and we did the number on how wonderful you are."

Katie said, "It was probably Phil Cunningham or Charley Nugent."

"Big guy. Beefy face. Nice."

"Phil Cunningham. He's a good man. What kind of questions were they asking?"

"Pretty routine. Had we noticed what time she left or got back—that kind of thing."

"And did you?"

"When the twins are sick and cranky, I wouldn't notice if Robert Redford moved in next door. Anyhow, we can barely see the Lewises' house on a sunny day, never mind at night in a storm."

They were driving over the wooden bridge just before the turn to Winding Brook Lane. Katie bit her lip. "Molly, drop me off at the Lewis house, won't you?"

Molly turned to her, astonished. "Why?"

Katie tried to smile. "Well, I'm an assistant prosecutor, and for what it's worth, I'm also adviser to the Chapin River Police Department. I wouldn't normally have to go, but as long as I'm right here, I think I should."

The hearse from the Medical Examiner's office was just backing into the driveway of the Lewis home. Richard was in the doorway watching. He came over to the car when Molly pulled up. Quickly Molly explained: "Katie's having lunch with me and thought she should stop by here. Why don't you come over with her, if you can?"

He agreed and helped Katie out of the car. "I'm glad you're here," he said. "There's something about this setup I don't like."

Now that she was about to see the dead woman, Katie felt her mouth go dry. She remembered the image of the face in her dream. "The husband is in the den," Richard said.

"I've met him. You must have too. At Molly's New Year's Day party. No. You came late. They'd left before you arrived."

Richard said, "All right. We'd better talk about it later. Here's the room."

She forced herself to look at the familiar face, and

recognized it instantly. She shuddered and closed her eyes. Was she going crazy?

"You all right, Katie?" Richard asked sharply.

What kind of fool was she? "I'm perfectly all right," she said, and to her own ears her voice sounded normal enough. "I'd like to talk to Captain Lewis."

When they got to the den, the door was closed. Without knocking, Richard opened it quietly. Chris Lewis was on the phone, his back to them. His voice was low but distinct. "I know it's incredible, but I swear to you, Joan, she didn't know about us."

Richard closed the door noiselessly. He and Katie stared at each other. Katie said, "I'll tell Charley to stay here. I'm going to recommend to Scott that we launch a full investigation." Scott Myerson was the Prosecutor.

"I'll do the autopsy myself as soon as they bring her in," Richard said. "The minute we're positive it was the cyanide that killed her, we'd better start finding out where she got it. Come on; let's make the stop at Molly's a quick one."

Molly's house, like her car, was a haven of normality. Katie often stopped there for a glass of wine or dinner on her way home from work. The smell of good food cooking; the kids' feet clattering on the stairs; the blare of the television set; the noisy young voices, shouting and battling. For her it was re-entry into the real world after a day of dealing with murderers, kidnappers, muggers, vandals, deviates, arsonists and penny-ante crooks. And dearly as she loved the Kennedys, the visit made her appreciate the serene peace of her own home. Except, of course, for the times that she would feel the emptiness of her house and try to imagine what it would be like if John were still alive and their children had started to arrive.

"Katie! Dr. Carroll!" The twins came whooping up

to greet them. "Did you see all the cop cars, Katie? Something happened next door!" Peter, older than his twin by ten minutes, was always the spokesman.

"Right next door!" John chimed in. Molly called them "Pete and Repeat." "Get lost, you two," she ordered now. "And leave us alone while we eat."

"Where are the other kids?" Katie asked.

"Billy, Dina and Moira went back to school this morning, thank God," Molly said. "Jennifer's in bed. I just looked in and she's dozed off again. Poor kid still feels lousy."

They settled at the kitchen table. The kitchen was large and cheerfully warm. Molly produced Reubens from the oven, offered drinks, which they refused, and poured coffee. Molly had a way with food, Katie thought. Everything she fixed tasted good. But when Katie tried to eat, she found her throat was closed. She glanced at Richard. He had piled hot mustard onto the corned beef and was eating with obvious pleasure. She envied him his detachment. On one level he could enjoy a good sandwich. On the other, she was sure that he was concentrating on the Lewis case. His forehead was knitted; his thatch of brown hair looked ruffled; his blue-gray eyes were thoughtful; his rangy shoulders hunched forward as with two fingers he lightly drummed the table. She'd have bet that they were both pondering the same question: Who had been on the phone with Chris Lewis?

She remembered the only conversation she'd had with Chris. It had been at the New Year's party, and they'd discussed hijacking. He'd been interesting, intelligent, pleasant. With his rugged good looks, he was a very appealing man. And she remembered that he and Vangie had been at opposite ends of the crowded room and he'd been unenthused when she, Katie, congratulated him on the coming baby.

"Molly, what was your impression of the

Lewises—I mean their relationship to each other?" she asked.

Molly looked troubled. "Candidly, I think it was on the rocks. She was so hung up with being pregnant that whenever they were here she kept yanking the conversation back to babies, and he obviously was upset about it. And since I had a hand in the pregnancy, it was a real worry for me."

Richard stopped drumming his fingers and straightened up. "You had *what?*"

"I mean, well, you know me, Katie. The day they moved in, last summer, I went rushing over and invited them to dinner. They came, and right away Vangie told me how much she hoped to have a baby and how upset she was about her best childbearing years being over because she'd turned thirty."

Molly took a gulp of her Bloody Mary and eyed the empty glass regretfully. "I told her about Liz Berkeley. She never was able to conceive until she went to a gynecologist who's something of a fertility expert. Liz had just given birth to a little girl and of course was ecstatic. Anyhow, I told Vangie about Dr. Highley. She went to him and a few months later conceived. But since then I've been sorry I didn't keep out of it."

"Dr. Highley?" Katie looked startled.

Molly nodded. "Yes, the one who's going to . . ."

Katie shook her head, and Molly's voice trailed off.

◆ 8 ◆

Edna Burns liked her job. She was bookkeeper-receptionist for the two doctors who staffed and ran the Westlake Maternity Concept team. "Dr. Highley's the big shot," she confided to her friends. "You know, he was married to Winifred Westlake and she left him everything. He runs the whole show."

Dr. Highley was a gynecologist/obstetrician, and as Edna explained, "It's a riot to see the way his patients act when they finally get pregnant; so happy you'd think they invented kids. He charges them an arm and a leg, but he's practically a miracle worker.

"On the other hand," she'd explain, "Highley is also the right person to see if you've got an internal problem that you *don't* want to grow. If you know what I mean," she'd add with a wink.

Dr. Fukhito was a psychiatrist. The Westlake Maternity Concept was one of holistic medicine: that mind and body must be in harmony to achieve a successful pregnancy and that many women could not conceive because they were emotionally charged with fear and anxiety. All gynecology patients consulted Dr. Fukhito at least once, but pregnant patients were required to schedule regular visits.

Edna enjoyed telling her friends that the Westlake Concept had been dreamed up by old Dr. Westlake, who had died before he acted on it. Then, eight years ago, his daughter Winifred had married Dr. Highley, bought the River Falls Clinic when it went into bankruptcy, renamed it for her father and set up her husband there. "She and the doctor were crazy about each other," Edna would sigh. "I mean she was ten years older than he and nothing to look at, but they were real lovers. He'd have me send her flowers a couple of times a week, and busy as he is, he'd go shopping with her for her clothes. Let me tell you, it was some shock when she died. No one ever knew her heart was that bad.

"But," she'd add philosophically, "he keeps busy. I've seen women who never were able to conceive become pregnant two and three times. Of course, a lot of them don't carry the babies to term, but at least they know there's a chance. And you should see the kind of care they get. I've seen Dr. Highley bring women in and put them to bed in the hospital for two months before a birth. Costs a fortune, of course, but buh-lieve me, when you want a baby and can afford it, you'll pay anything to get one. But you can read about it yourself, pretty soon," she'd add. *"Newsmaker* magazine just did an article about him and about the Westlake Maternity Concept. It's coming out Thursday. They came last week and photographed him in his office standing next to the pictures of all those babies he's delivered. Real nice. And if you think we're busy now, wait till that comes out. The phone'll never be on the hook."

Edna was a born bookkeeper. Her records were marvels of accuracy. She loved receipts and took a sensual pride in making frequent and healthy bank deposits in her employer's account. A neat but prominent sign on her desk let it be known that all payments must be made in cash; no monthly bills would be rendered; retainer fees and payment schedules would be explained by Miss Burns.

Edna had been told by Dr. Highley that unless specifically instructed otherwise, she was to be sure to make follow-up appointments with people as they left;

41

that if for any reason a patient did not keep the next appointment, Edna should phone that patient at home and firmly make a new one. It was a sound arrangement and, as Edna gleefully noted, a financial bonanza.

Dr. Highley always complimented Edna on the excellent records she maintained and her ability to keep the appointments book full. The only time Dr. Highley really gave her the rough side of his tongue was when she was overheard talking to one patient about another's problems. She had to admit that had been foolish, but she'd allowed herself a couple of Manhattans for lunch that day and that had lowered her guard.

The doctor had finished up his lecture by saying, "Any more talking and you're through."

She knew he meant it.

Edna sighed. She was tired. Last night both doctors had had evening hours, and it had been hectic. Then she'd worked on the books for a while. She couldn't wait to go home this evening, and wild horses wouldn't drag her out again. She'd put on a robe and mix herself a nice batch of Manhattans. She had a canned ham in the refrigerator, so she'd make that do for supper and watch television.

It was nearly two o'clock. Three more hours and she could clear out. While it was quiet she had to check yesterday's calendar to make sure she'd made all the necessary future appointments. Frowning nearsightedly, she leaned her broad, freckled face on a thick hand. Her hair felt messy today. She hadn't had time to set it last night. She'd been kind of tired after she had a few drinks.

She was an overweight woman of forty-four who looked ten years older. Her unleavened youth had been spent taking care of aging parents. When Edna saw pictures of herself from Drake Secretarial School she was vaguely surprised at the pretty girl she'd been a quarter of a century ago. Always a mite too heavy, but pretty nevertheless.

Her mind was only half on the page she was reading, but then something triggered her full attention. She paused. The eight-o'clock appointment last night for Vangie Lewis.

Last night Vangie had come in early and sat talking with Edna. She was sure upset. Well, Vangie was kind of a complainer, but so pretty Edna enjoyed just looking at her. Vangie had put on a lot of weight during the pregnancy and, to Edna's practiced eye, was retaining a lot of fluid. Edna prayed that Vangie would deliver that baby safely. She wanted it so much.

So she didn't blame Vangie for being moody. She really wasn't well. Last month Vangie had started wearing those moccasins because her other shoes didn't fit anymore. She'd shown them to Edna. "Look at this. My right foot is so bad, I can only wear these clodhoppers my cleaning woman left behind. The other one is always falling off."

Edna had tried to kid her. "Well, with those glass slippers I'll just have to start calling you Cinderella. And we'll call your husband Prince Charming." She knew Vangie was nuts about her husband.

But Vangie had just pouted and said impatiently, "Oh, Edna, Prince Charming was Sleeping Beauty's boyfriend, not Cinderella's. Everybody knows that."

Edna had just laughed. "Mama must have been mixed up. When she told me about Cinderella she said Prince Charming came around with the glass slipper. But never mind—before you know it, you'll have your baby and be back in pretty shoes again."

Last night Vangie had pulled up that long caftan she'd started wearing to hide her swollen leg. "Edna," she'd said, "I can hardly even get this clodhopper on. And for what? God Almighty, for what?" She'd been almost crying.

"Oh, you're just getting down in the dumps, honey," Edna had said. "It's a good thing you came in to talk to Dr. Fukhito. He'll relax you."

Just then Dr. Fukhito had buzzed and said to send Mrs. Lewis in. Vangie started down the corridor to his office. Just as she left the reception area, she stumbled. She'd walked right out of that loose left shoe.

"Oh, to hell with it!" she cried, and just kept going. Edna had picked up the moccasin, figuring Vangie would come back for it when she finished with Dr. Fukhito.

Edna always stayed late Monday nights to work on the books. But when she was ready to go home around nine o'clock, Vangie still hadn't come back. Edna decided to take a chance and ring Dr. Fukhito and just tell him that she'd leave the shoe outside the office door in the corridor.

But there was no answer in Dr. Fukhito's office. That meant that Vangie must have walked out the door that led directly to the parking lot. That was crazy. She'd catch her death of cold getting her foot wet.

Irresolutely Edna had held the shoe in her hand and locked up. She went out to the parking lot toward her own car just in time to see Vangie's big red Lincoln Continental with Dr. Highley at the wheel pull out. She'd tried to run a few steps to wave to him, but it was no use. So she'd just gone home.

Maybe Dr. Highley had already made a new appointment with Vangie, but Edna would phone her just to be sure. Quickly she dialed the Lewis number. The phone rang once, twice.

A man's voice answered: "Lewises' residence."

"Mrs. Lewis, please." Edna assumed her Drake

Secretarial School business voice, crisp but friendly. She wondered if she was talking to Captain Lewis.

"Who's calling?"

"Dr. Highley's office. We want to set up Mrs. Lewis' next appointment."

"Hold on."

She could tell the transmitter was being covered. Muffled voices were talking. What could be going on? Maybe Vangie had been taken sick. If so, Dr. Highley should be told at once.

The voice at the other end began to speak. "This is Detective Cunningham of the Valley County Prosecutor's office. I'm sorry, but Mrs. Lewis has died suddenly. You can tell her doctor that he'll be contacted tomorrow morning by someone on our staff."

"Mrs. Lewis died!" Edna's voice was a howl of dismay. "Oh, what happened?"

There was a pause. "It seems she took her own life." The connection was broken.

Slowly Edna lowered the receiver. It wasn't possible. It just wasn't possible.

The two-o'clock appointments arrived together: Mrs. Volmer for Dr. Highley, Mrs. Lashley for Dr. Fukhito. Mechanically Edna greeted them.

"Are you all right, Edna?" Mrs. Volmer asked curiously. "You look upset or something."

She knew that Mrs. Volmer had talked to Vangie in the waiting room sometimes. It was on the tip of her tongue to tell her that Vangie was dead. But some instinct warned her to tell Dr. Highley first.

His one-thirty appointment came out. He was on the intercom. "Send Mrs. Volmer in, Edna." Edna glanced at the women. There was no way she could talk on the intercom without their hearing her.

"Doctor, may I step in for a moment, please? I'd like to have a word with you." That sounded so efficient. She was pleased at her own control.

"Certainly." He didn't sound very happy about it. Highley was a bit scary; still, he could be nice. She'd seen that last night.

She moved down the hall as fast as her overweight body would allow. She was panting when she knocked at his office door. He said, "Come in, Edna." His voice was edged with irritation.

Timidly she opened the door and stepped inside his office.

"Doctor," she began hurriedly, "you'll want to know. I just phoned Mrs. Lewis, Vangie Lewis, to make an appointment. You told me you want to see her every week now."

"Yes, yes. And for heaven's sake, Edna, close that door. Your voice can be heard through the hospital."

Quickly she obeyed. Trying to keep her voice low, she said, "Doctor, when I phoned her house, a detective answered. He said she killed herself and that they're coming to see you tomorrow."

"Mrs. Lewis what?" He sounded shocked.

Now that she could talk about it, Edna's words crowded in her mouth, tumbling out in a torrent. "She was so upset last night, wasn't she, Doctor? I mean we both could see it. The way she talked to me and the way she acted like she didn't care about anything. But you must know that; I thought it was the nicest thing when I saw you drive her home last night. I tried to wave to you, but you didn't see me. So I guess of all people you know how bad she was."

"Edna, how many people have you discussed this with?"

There was something in his tone that made her very nervous. Flustered, she avoided his eyes. "Why, nobody, sir. I just heard this minute."

"You did not discuss Mrs. Lewis' death with Mrs. Volmer or anyone else in the reception area?"

"No . . . no, sir."

"And not with the detective on the phone?"

"No, sir."

"Edna, tomorrow when the police come, you and I will tell them everything we know about Mrs. Lewis' frame of mind. But listen to me now." He pointed his finger at her and leaned forward. Unconsciously, she stepped back. "I don't want Mrs. Lewis' name mentioned by you to anyone—*anyone*, do you hear? Mrs. Lewis was an extremely neurotic and unstable woman. But the fact is that her suicide reflects very badly on our hospital. How do you think it's going to look in the papers if it comes out that she was a patient of mine? And I certainly won't have you gossiping in the reception room with the other patients, some of whom have very tenuous holds on the fetuses they are carrying. Do you understand me?"

"Yes, sir," Edna quavered. She should have known he'd think she'd gossip about this.

"Edna, you like your job?"

"Yes, sir."

"Edna, do not discuss with anyone—*anyone*, mind you—*one word* about the Lewis case. If I hear you have so much as mentioned it, you're finished here. Tomorrow we'll talk with the police, but no one else. Mrs. Lewis' state of mind is confidential. Is that clear?"

"Yes, sir."

"Are you going out with friends tonight? You know how you get when you drink."

Edna was close to tears. "I'm going home. I'm not feeling well, Doctor. I want to have my wits about me tomorrow when the police talk to me. Poor little Cinderella." She gulped as easy tears came to her eyes. But then she saw the expression on his face. Angry. Disgusted.

Edna straightened up, dabbed at her eyes. "I'll send Mrs. Volmer in, Doctor. And you don't have to worry," she added with dignity. "I value our hospital. I know how much your work means to you and to our patients. I'm not going to say one single word."

The rest of the afternoon was busy. She managed to push the thought of Vangie to the back of her mind as she talked with patients, made future appointments, collected money, reminded patients if they were falling behind in their payments.

Finally, at five o'clock she could leave. Warmly wrapped in a leopard-spotted fake-fur coat and matching hat, she drove home to her garden apartment in Edgeriver, six miles away.

◆ 9 ◆

In the clinically impersonal autopsy room of the Valley County Morgue, Richard Carroll gently removed the fetus from the corpse of Vangie Lewis. His long, sensitive fingers lifted the small body, noting that the amniotic fluid had begun to leak. Vangie Lewis could not have carried this baby much longer. He judged that it weighed about two and a half pounds. It was a boy.

The firstborn son. He shook his head at the waste as he laid it on an adjacent slab. Vangie had been in an advanced state of toxemia. It was incredible that any doctor had allowed her to progress so far in this condition. He'd be interested to know what her white-cell count had been. Probably terrifically high.

He'd already sent fluid samples to the laboratory. He had no doubt that the cyanide killed the woman.

Her throat and mouth were badly burned. She'd swallowed a huge gulp of it, God help her.

The burns on the outside of her mouth? Carefully Richard examined them. He tried to visualize the moment she'd drunk the poison. She'd started to swallow, felt the burning, changed her mind, tried to spit it out. It had run over her lips and chin.

To him it didn't wash.

There were fine white fibers clinging to her coat. They looked as though they'd come from a blanket. He was having them analyzed. It seemed to him that she had been lying on a chenille spread. He wanted to compare the fiber from the spread with those taken from the coat. Of course, the coat was pretty tired-looking, and they might have been picked up at any time.

Her body had become so bloated that it looked as though Vangie had just put on whatever clothes she could find that would cover her.

Except for the shoes. That was another incongruous note. The shoes were well cut and expensive. More than that, they looked quite new. It was unlikely Vangie could have been outdoors on Monday in those shoes and have them in such mint condition. There were no water spots or snow marks on them, even though the ankles of her panty hose had spatters of dirty snow. Didn't that suggest that she must have been out, come in, decided to leave again, changed her shoes and then committed suicide?

That didn't wash either.

Another thing. Those shoes were awfully tight. Particularly the right foot. She could barely lace the shoe, and the vamp was narrow. It would have been like putting on a vise. Considering the rest of the way she was dressed, why bother to put on shoes that will kill you?

Shoes that will kill you . . .

The phrase stuck in Richard's mind. He straightened up. He was just about finished here. As soon as they had a lab report he could tell Scott Myerson what he had found.

Once more he turned to study the fetus. The cyanide had entered its bloodstream. Like its mother, it must have died in agony. Carefully Richard examined it. The miracle of life never ceased to awe him; if anything, it grew with every experience he had with death. He marveled at the exquisite balance of the body: the harmony of its parts, muscles and fibers, bones and sinews, veins and arteries; the profound complexity of the nervous system, the ability of the body to heal its own wounds, its elaborate attempt to protect its unborn.

Suddenly he bent over the fetus. Swiftly he freed it from the placenta and studied it under the strong light. Was it possible?

It was a hunch, a hunch he had to check out. Dave Broad was the man for him. Dave was in charge of prenatal research at Mt. Sinai. He'd send this fetus to him and ask for an opinion.

If what he believed was true, there was a damn good reason why Captain Chris Lewis would have been upset about his wife's pregnancy.

Maybe even upset enough to kill her!

Scott Myerson, the Valley County Prosecutor, scheduled a five o'clock meeting in his office for Katie, Richard and the two Homicide Squad detectives assigned to the Lewis suicide. Scott's office did not fit the television world's image of a prosecutor's private chambers. It was small. The walls were painted a sickly yellow. The furniture was battered; the ancient files were battleship gray. The windows looked out on the county jail.

Katie arrived first. Gingerly she eased into the one reasonably comfortable extra chair. Scott looked at her with a hint of a smile. He was a small man with a surprisingly deep voice. Large rimmed glasses, a dark, neat mustache and meticulously tailored conservative suit made him look more like a banker than a law enforcer. He had been in court all day on a case he was personally trying and had spoken to Katie only by phone. Now he observed her bandaged arm and the bruise under her eye and the wince of pain that came over her face as she moved her body.

"Thanks for coming in, Katie," he said. "I know how overloaded you are and do appreciate it. But you'd better take tomorrow off."

Katie shook her head. "No. I'm okay, and this soreness will probably be a lot better in the morning."

"All right, but remember, if you start feeling rotten, just go home." He became businesslike. "The Lewis case. What have we got on it?"

Richard and the detectives came in while she was

talking. Silently they settled in the three folding chairs remaining.

Scott tapped a pencil on his desk as he listened. He turned to the detectives. "What did you come up with?"

Phil Cunningham pulled out his notebook. "That place was no honeymoon cottage. The Lewises went to some neighborhood gatherings." He looked at Katie. "Guess your sister tried to have them included. Everyone liked Chris Lewis. They thought Vangie was a pain in the neck—obviously jealous of him; not interested in getting involved with any activities in the community; not interested in *anything*. At the parties she was always hanging on him; got real upset if he talked more than five minutes to another woman. He was very patient with her. One of the neighbors said her husband told her after one of those parties that if he were married to Vangie, he'd kill her with his bare hands. Then when she got pregnant she was really insufferable. Talked baby all the time."

Charley had opened his notebook. "Her obstetrician's office called to set up an appointment. I said we'd be in to talk to her doctor tomorrow."

Richard spoke quietly. "There are a few questions I'd like to ask that doctor about Vangie Lewis' condition."

Scott looked at Richard. "You've finished the autopsy?"

"Yes. It was definitely cyanide. She died instantly. The mouth and throat were badly burned. Which leads to the crucial point."

There were a water pitcher and paper cups on top of the file. Walking over to the file, Richard poured a generous amount of water into a paper cup. "Okay," he said, "this is filled with dissolved cyanide. I am about to kill myself. I take a large gulp." Quickly he swallowed. The paper cup was still nearly half full. The others watched him intently.

He held up the paper cup. "In my judgment, Vangie Lewis must have drunk at least the approximately three ounces I just swallowed in order to have the amount of cyanide we found in her system. So far it checks out. But here's the problem. The outside of her lips and chin and even neck were burned. The only way that could have happened would have been if she spat some of the stuff out . . . quite a lot of it out. But if she swallowed as much as she did in one gulp, it means her mouth was empty. Did she then take another mouthful and spit it out? No way. The reaction is instantaneous."

"She couldn't have swallowed half of the mouthful and spat out the rest?" Scott asked.

Richard shrugged. "There was too much both in her system and on her face to suggest a split dose. Yet the amount spilled on the spread was negligible, and there were just a few drops at the bottom of the glass. So if she was holding a full tumbler, she'd have had to splash some of it all over her lips and chin, then drink the rest of it to justify the amount expended. It *could* have happened that way, but I don't believe it. The other problem is the shoes she had on."

Quickly he explained his belief that Vangie Lewis could not have walked comfortably in the shoes that had been laced to her feet. While she listened, Katie visualized Vangie's face. The dead face she had seen in the dream and the dead face she'd seen on the bed slid back and forth in her mind. She forced her attention back to the room and realized Charley was talking to Scott. ". . . Richard and I both feel the husband noticed something about the body that he didn't tell us."

"I think it was the shoes," Richard said.

Katie turned to him. "The phone call Chris Lewis made. I told you about that before, Scott."

"You did." Scott leaned back in his chair. "All right. You two"—he pointed to Charley and Phil—"find out everything you can about Captain Lewis. See who this Joan is. Find out what time his plane came in this morning. Check on phone calls Vangie Lewis made the last few days. Have Rita see Mrs. Lewis' doctor and get his opinion of her mental and physical condition."

"I can tell you about her physical condition," Richard said. "If she hadn't delivered that baby soon, she could have saved her cyanide."

"There's another thing," Scott said. "Where did she get the cyanide?"

"No trace of it in the house," Charley reported. "Not a drop. But she was something of a gardener. Maybe she had some stashed away from last summer."

"Just in case she decided to kill herself?" Scott's voice was humorless. "Is there anything else?"

Richard hesitated. "There may be," he said slowly. "But it's so far out . . . and in light of what I've just heard, I think I'm barking up the wrong tree. So give me another twenty-four hours. Then I may have something else to throw on the table."

Scott nodded. "Get back to me." He stood up. "I believe we all agree. We're not closing this as a suicide." He looked at Richard. "One more question. Is there any chance that she died somewhere else and was put back in her bed?"

Richard frowned. "Possible . . . but the way the blood congealed in her body tells me she was lying in the position in which we found her from the minute she drank that cyanide."

"All right," Scott said. "Just a thought. Let's wrap it up for tonight."

Katie started to get up. "I know it's insane, but . . ." She felt Richard's arm steadying her.

"You sure look stiff," he interrupted.

For an instant she'd been about to tell them about the crazy dream she'd had in the hospital. His voice snapped her back to reality. What a fool she'd have appeared to them. Gratefully she smiled at Richard. "Stiff in the head mostly, I think," she commented.

♦ 11 ♦

He could not let Edna destroy everything he'd worked for. His hands gripped the wheel. He could feel the trembling in them. He had to calm down.

The exquisite irony that she of all people had seen him drive the Lincoln out of the parking lot. Obviously she'd assumed that Vangie was with him in the car. But the minute she told her story to the police, everything would be over. He could hear the questions: "You drove Mrs. Lewis home, Doctor. What did you do when you left her? Did you call a cab? What time was that, Doctor? Miss Burns tells us that you left the parking lot shortly after nine P.M."

The autopsy would certainly prove that Vangie had died around that time. What would they think if he told them he'd walked back to the hospital in that storm?

Edna had to be silenced. His medical bag was on the seat next to him. The only thing in it was the paperweight from his office desk. He didn't usually bother to carry a bag with him anymore, but he'd taken it out this morning planning to put the moccasins in it. He'd intended to drive into New York for dinner and leave the shoes in separate litter cans to be collected in the morning.

But this morning Hilda had come in early. She'd stood in the foyer talking to him while he put on his gray tweed overcoat. She'd handed him his hat and the bag. It was impossible to transfer the moccasins from the Burberry to the bag in front of her. What would she have thought? But no matter. The Burberry was to the back of the closet. She had no reason to go near it, and tonight when he finished with Edna he would go home. He'd get rid of the shoes tomorrow night.

It was a stroke of luck that Edna lived so near the hospital. That was why he knew her apartment. Several times he'd dropped off work for her when she was laid up with sciatica. He'd just had to check the apartment number to be sure. He'd have to make it look like a murder committed during a felony. Katie DeMaio's office would be involved, but would certainly never connect the homicide of an obscure bookkeeper with either her employer or Vangie Lewis.

He'd take her wallet, grab any bits of jewelry she had. Racking his brain, he remembered that she owned a butterfly-shaped pin with a minuscule ruby and an engagement ring with a dot of a diamond in it. She'd shown them to him when he'd left some work at her place a few months ago.

"This was my mother's ring, Doctor," she'd said proudly. "Dad and she fell in love on their first date and he brought it to her on their second date. Would you believe they were both in their early forties then? Dad gave it to me when Mom died. That was three years ago, and you know he didn't live but two months without her. Of course, Mom had smaller fingers; that's why I wear it on my pinkie. And he gave her the pin on their tenth anniversary."

He'd chafed through the tiresome recital, but now realized that like everything else, it was potentially useful. He'd been sitting by her bed. She kept her cheap plastic jewelry box in the night-table drawer. That ring, the pin and the wallet from her handbag would be easy to carry and would clearly establish a robber-connected murder.

Then he'd get rid of them and the shoes and that would be the end.

Except for Katie DeMaio.

He rubbed the underside of his lower lip over his upper lip. His mouth was dry.

He had to think about Edna's apartment. How would he get in? Did he dare ring the bell, let her admit him? Suppose she wasn't alone?

But she would be alone. He was sure of it. She was going home to drink. He could tell from the nervous, eager movements she made while he watched her from the corridor. She'd been excited, agitated, obviously filled with the stories she wanted to tell to the police tomorrow.

Freezing perspiration drenched him at the thought that she might have decided to talk to the patients in the reception room before she talked to him about Vangie. The Ednas of this world want an audience. Listen to me. Notice me. I exist!

Not for long, Edna, not for long.

He was driving into her apartment area. Last time he'd left the car behind her apartment in one of the visitor stalls. Did he dare drive right there now? It was cold, windy, dark. Few people would be standing around. Anyone who was coming in would be hurrying, not noticing a perfectly ordinary dark, medium-priced car. Last time he'd walked around the end of her apartment-building unit. She lived on the ground floor of the last apartment. Thick bushes tried to hide a rusting chain-link fence that separated the complex from a steep ravine which dropped down a dozen feet and terminated in railroad tracks, a spur of the main line.

Edna's bedroom window backed onto the parking lot. There were high untrimmed bushes under her window. The window was ground level—quite low, if he remembered correctly. Suppose that window was unlocked? By now, if he had any judgment, Edna would be very drunk. He could go in and out by the window. That would lend credence to the burglary. Otherwise, he'd ring the bell, go in, kill her and then leave. Even if he were found out, were seen, he'd simply say that he'd stopped by to drop off papers, then decided not to leave them because she was drinking. Some intruder must have come in later. No one in his right mind would accuse a wealthy doctor of robbing a penniless bookkeeper.

Satisfied, he slowed down as he approached the apartment complex. The double units, all exactly the same, looked stark and forlorn in the cold February night.

The parking area had a half-dozen cars in it. He drove between a camper and a station wagon. His car disappeared into the cavelike space the larger vehicles provided. He pulled on his surgical gloves and put the paperweight in his coat pocket. Sliding cautiously out, he closed the door noiselessly and disappeared into the deep shadows cast by the building. Silently he thanked the gods that Edna lived in the very last apartment. Absolutely no chance of his mistaking where to go.

Her bedroom shade was pulled down most of the way, but she had a plant in the window. The shade rested on the top of the plant, and he could see in clearly. The room was lighted by a foyer fixture. The window was open a crack. She must be in the living room or dining area. He could hear the faint sound of a television program. He would go in through the window.

Glancing rapidly about, he once again assured himself that the area was deserted. With steely-strong gloved fingers he raised the window, noiselessly pulled up the shade, quietly lifted the plant out onto the ground. Later it would be clear proof of the method of entry. He hoisted himself onto the windowsill. For a big man he was surprisingly agile.

He was in the bedroom. In the dim light he absorbed the virginal tidiness, the candlewick bedspread, the crucifix over the bed, the framed photos of an elderly couple, the lace runner on the scarred top of the mahogany-veneer dresser.

Now for the necessary part, the part he detested. He felt for the paperweight in his pocket. He had decided to bludgeon her. Once he had read that a doctor had been proved guilty of murder because of the flawlessly accurate stabbing. He could not risk having his medical knowledge reveal him. It was his medical knowledge that had brought him to this place.

He began to tiptoe down the short foyer. Bathroom to the right. Living room six feet ahead to the left. Cautiously he peered into it. The television set was on, but the room was empty. He could hear the sound of a chair creaking. She must be at the dinette table. With infinite care he moved into the living room. This was the moment. If she saw him and screamed . . .

But her back was to him. Wrapped in a woolly blue robe, she was slumped in a chair at the head of the table. One hand was next to an outsized cocktail glass, the other folded in her lap. A tall pitcher in front of her was almost empty. Her head was on her chest. Faint, even breathing told him she was asleep. She smelled heavily of alcohol.

Quickly he appraised the situation. His eye fell on the hissing radiator to the right of the table. It was the old-fashioned kind with sharp, exposed pipes. Was it possible he didn't need the paperweight after all? Maybe . . .

"Edna," he whispered softly.

"Wha . . . oh . . ." She looked up at him with bleary eyes. Confused, she began to rise, twisting awkwardly in her chair. "Doctor . . ."

A mighty shove sent her smashing backward. Her head cracked against the radiator. Blinding lights exploded in her brain. Oh, the pain! Oh, God, the pain! Edna sighed. The soothing warmth of her gushing blood floated her into darkness. The pain spread, intensified, peaked, receded, ended.

He jumped back, careful to stay clear of the spattered blood, then bent over her carefully. As he watched, the pulse in her throat flickered and stopped. He held his face close to hers. She had stopped breathing. He slipped the paperweight into his pocket. He wouldn't need it now. He wouldn't have to bother robbing her. It would look as though she'd fallen. He was lucky. He was meant to be safe.

Quickly retracing his steps, he went back into the bedroom. Scanning to assure himself that the parking area was still empty, he stepped out the window, remembered to replace the plant, pulled down the shade and closed the window to the exact place where Edna had had it.

As he did, he heard the persistent chiming of a doorbell—*her doorbell!* Frantically he looked around. The ground, hard and dry, offered no evidence of his footprints. The windowsill was meticulously clean. No disturbed dust there. He'd stepped over it, so no sign of his shoes marred the white surface.

He ran back to his car. Quietly the engine started. Without turning on his headlights he drove out of the apartment complex. As he approached Route 4, he turned on the lights.

Who was standing on Edna's doorstep? Would that person try to get in? Edna was dead. She couldn't gossip about him now. But it had been so close, so terribly close.

Adrenaline pounded through his veins. Now there was only one possible threat left: Katie DeMaio.

He would begin to remove that threat now. Her accident had given him the excuse he needed to start medication.

It was a matter of hospital record that her blood count was low. She had received a transfusion in the emergency room.

He would order another transfusion for her on the pretense of building her up for the operation.

He would give cumadin pills to her. They would short-circuit her clotting apparatus and negate the benefits of the transfusion. By Friday when she came into the hospital she'd be on the verge of hemorrhaging.

It might be possible to perform emergency surgery without administering further anticoagulants. But if necessary he would inject her with heparin. There would be a total depletion of the coagulation precursors. She would not survive that surgery.

The initial low blood count, the cumadin and the heparin would be as effective on Katie DeMaio as the cyanide had been on Vangie Lewis.

◆ 12 ◆

Richard and Katie left Scott's office together. She had known he'd be annoyed if she suggested calling a cab to take her home. But when they got into his car, he said, "Dinner first. A steak and a bottle of wine will set your juices running."

"What juices?" she asked cautiously.

"Saliva. Stomach. Whatever."

He chose a cabin-type restaurant that perched precariously on the Palisades. The small dining room was warmed by a blazing fire and lit by candles.

"Oh, this is nice," she said.

The proprietor obviously knew Richard well. "Dr. Carroll, a pleasure," he said as he guided them to the table in front of the fireplace and pulled out a chair for Katie.

She grinned as she sat down, thinking that either Richard rated or she must look as chilled and woebegone as she felt.

Richard ordered a bottle of St. Emilion; a waiter produced hot garlic bread. They sat in companionable silence, sipping and nibbling. Katie realized it was the first time she had been with him like this, across a small table, separated from everyone else in the room, looking at each other.

Richard was a big man with a wholesome, thoroughly healthy look that was manifested in his thick crop of dark brown hair, his strong, even features and broad, rangy shoulders. When he's old, he'll have a leonine quality, she thought.

"You just smiled," Richard said. "The usual penny for your thoughts."

She told him.

"Leonine." He considered the word thoughtfully. "A lion in winter. I'd settle for that. Are you interested in what I'm thinking?"

"Sure."

"When your face is in repose, your eyes are very sad, Katie."

"Sorry. I don't mean them to be. I don't think of myself as being sad."

"Do you know I've been wanting to ask you out for the last six months but it took an accident that might have killed you to make it happen?"

"You never asked me out," she said evasively.

"You never *wanted* to be asked out. There's a definite signal you release. 'Do Not Disturb.' Why?"

"I don't believe in going out with anyone I work with," she said, "just on general principles."

"I can understand that. But that's not what we're talking about. We enjoy each other's company. We both know it. But you're having none of it. Here's the menu."

His manner changed, became brisk. *"L'entrecôte* and the steak *au poivre* are the specialties here," he told her. When she hesitated, he suggested, "Try the *poivre.* It's fantastic. Rare," he added hopefully.

"Well done," Katie said.

At his look of horror she laughed out loud. "Of course rare."

His face cleared. He ordered salads with house dressing and baked potatoes, then leaned back and studied her.

"Are you having none of it, Katie?"

"The salad? The steak?"

"No. Don't keep weaving and dancing. All right, I'm not being fair. I'm trying to pin you down and you're a captive audience. But tell me what you do when you're not at the office or the Kennedys'. I know you ski."

"Yes. I have a college friend who's divorced. The winter after John died, she dragged me up to Vermont with her. Now she and I and two couples rent a condominium in Stowe during the ski season. I go weekends as often as I can. I'm not a great skier, but I enjoy it."

"I used to ski," Richard said. "Had to give it up because of a twisted knee. I should try it again. Maybe you'll invite me up sometime with you." He did not wait for an answer. "Sailing is my sport. I took my boat to the Caribbean last spring and went from island to island . . . 'brilliance of cloudless days with broad bellying sails, they glide to the wind tossing green water . . .' Here's your steak," he finished lightly.

"And you also quote William Carlos Williams," she murmured.

She had secretly expected him to be impressed that she knew the quotation, but he didn't seem surprised. "Yes, I do," he said. "The house dressing is good, isn't it?"

They lingered over coffee. By then Richard had told her about himself. "I was engaged during med school to the girl next door. I think you know I grew up in San Francisco."

"What happened?" Katie asked.

"We kept postponing the wedding. Eventually she married my best friend, whoever he is." Richard smiled. "I'm joking, of course. Jean was a very nice girl. But there was something missing. One night when for the fourth or fifth time we were discussing getting married, she said, 'Richard, we love each other, but we both know there's something more.' She was right."

"No regrets; no second thoughts?" Katie asked.

"Not really. That was seven years ago. I'm a little surprised that the 'something more' didn't happen along before now."

He did not seem to expect her to comment. Instead he began to talk about the Lewis case. "It makes me so angry; any waste of life affects me like that. Vangie Lewis was a young woman. She should have had a lot of years ahead of her."

"You're convinced it wasn't a suicide?"

"I'm not *convinced* of anything. I'll need to have much more information before I pass judgment."

"I don't see Chris Lewis as a murderer. It's too easy to get a divorce today if you want to be free."

"There's another angle to that." Richard pressed his lips together. "Let's hold off talking about it."

It was nearly ten-thirty when they turned into Katie's driveway. Richard looked quizzically at the handsome fieldstone house. "How big is this place?" he asked. "I mean how many rooms have you got?"

"Twelve," Katie said reluctantly. "It was John's house."

"I didn't think you bought it on an assistant prosecutor's salary," Richard commented.

She started to open the car door. "Hold it," he said. "I'll come around. It may still be slippery."

She had not planned to invite him in, but he did not give her the chance to say good night at the door. Taking the key from her hand, he put it in the lock, turned it, opened the door and followed her in. "I'm not going to stay," he said, "but I do admit to an overwhelming curiosity as to where you keep yourself."

She turned on the light and watched somewhat resentfully as he looked over the foyer and then the living room. He whistled. "Very, very nice." He walked over to John's portrait and studied it. "From what I heard, he was quite a guy."

"Yes, he was." Uncomfortably, Katie realized that on nearly every table there was a picture of herself and John. Richard went from one to the next. "A trip abroad?"

"Our honeymoon." Her lips were stiff.

"How long were you married, Katie?"

"One year."

He watched as a look of pain flickered over her face; it was more than that: an expression of surprise too, as though she were still puzzled about what had happened. "When did you find out that he was sick? It was cancer, I understand."

"Shortly after we got back from our honeymoon."

"So you never really had more than that trip, did you? After that it was a deathwatch. Sorry, Katie; my job makes me blunt—too blunt for my own good, I guess. I'll take off now." He hesitated. "Don't you believe in drawing these drapes when you're alone here?"

She shrugged. "Why? No one's going to come barging in on me."

"You, of all people, should be aware of the number of home burglaries. And in this location you'd be a prime target, especially if anyone knew you're alone here. Do you mind?"

Without waiting for an answer he went over to the window and pulled the draperies shut. "I'll be on my way. See you tomorrow. How are you going to get to work? Will your car be ready?"

"No, but the service people are going to lend me one. They'll drop it off in the morning."

"Okay." For a moment he stood with his hand on the knob, then in a highly credible brogue said, "I'll be leavin' ye, Katie Scarlett. Lock your door, now. I wouldn't want anyone tryin' to break into Tara." He bent down, kissed her cheek and was gone.

Smiling, Katie closed the door. A memory raced

through her mind. She was five years old, joyously playing in the muddy backyard in her Easter dress. Her mother's outraged cry. Her father's amused voice doing his Gerald O'Hara imitation: "It's the land, Katie Scarlett"—then, in a wheedling voice, to her mother: "Don't get mad at her. All good Micks love the land."

The clock chimed musically. After Richard's bear-warm presence, the room seemed hollow. Quickly she turned out the light and went upstairs.

The phone rang just as she got into bed. Molly has probably been trying to get me, she thought as she lifted the receiver. But it was a man's voice who responded when she said hello.

"Mrs. DeMaio?"

"Yes."

"This is Dr. Highley. I hope I'm not calling too late, but I've tried several times to reach you this evening. The fact that you were in an accident and were in our hospital overnight has come to my attention. How are you feeling?"

"Quite well, Doctor. How nice of you to call."

"How is the bleeding problem? According to your records you had a transfusion here last night."

"I'm afraid it's about the same. I thought I was over my period, but it started again yesterday. I honestly think I may have been a bit light-headed when I lost control of the car."

"Well, as you know, you should have taken care of this condition at least a year ago. Never mind. It will all be behind you by this time next week. But I do want you to have another transfusion to build you up for the surgery, and I also want you to start in on some pills. Can you come to the hospital tomorrow afternoon?"

"Yes. As a matter of fact, there was a chance I was coming anyhow. You've heard about Mrs. Lewis?"

"I have. A terrible and sad situation. Well, then, I'll see you tomorrow. Call in the morning and we'll arrange a definite time."

"Yes, Doctor. Thank you, Doctor."

Katie hung up. As she turned out the light, she reflected that Dr. Highley hadn't really appealed to her on her first visit. Was it because of his reserved, even aloof attitude?

It shows how you can misjudge people, she decided. It's very nice of him to personally keep trying to get in touch with me tonight.

♦ 13 ♦

Bill Kennedy rang the bell of the Lewis house. An orthopedic surgeon at Lenox Hill Hospital, he had been operating all day and did not hear about Vangie Lewis' death until he returned home. Tall, prematurely white, scholarly and somewhat shy in his professional life, Bill became a different person when he entered the warm haven of the home Molly created for him.

Her bustling presence made it possible for him to leave behind the problems of his patients and relax. But tonight the atmosphere had been different. Molly had already fed the children and given them strict orders to stay out of the way. Briefly she told him about Vangie. "I called and asked Chris to come to dinner and to sleep in the den tonight rather than be alone over there. He doesn't want to, but you go drag him here. I'm sure he'll at least come to dinner."

As he walked between the houses, Bill considered the shock it would be to come home and find he had lost Molly. But it wouldn't be the same for Chris Lewis. No one in his right mind could think that that marriage had been anything like his and Molly's. Bill had never told Molly that one morning when he was having coffee at a drugstore near the hospital he'd seen Chris in a booth with a very pretty girl in her early twenties. It was written all over the two of them that they were involved with each other.

Had Vangie known about the girl? Was that why she'd committed suicide? But so violently! His mind flashed back to the summer. Vangie and Chris had been over for a barbecue. Vangie had started to roast a marshmallow and gotten her hand too near the heat. Her finger had blistered and she'd carried on as though she'd been covered with third-degree burns. She'd gone shrieking to Chris, who had tried to calm her down. Embarrassed for her, Chris had explained, "Vangie has a low pain tolerance." By the time Bill got salve and applied it, the blister was practically nonexistent.

Where would a person of Vangie's emotional makeup get the courage to take cyanide? Anyone who'd read anything about that poison would know that even though death was almost instantaneous, one died in agony.

No. Bill would have sworn that Vangie Lewis committing suicide would have swallowed sleeping pills and fallen asleep. Showed how little anyone knew about the human mind . . . even someone like himself who was supposed to be a pretty good judge of people.

Chris Lewis opened the door. Ever since he'd spotted him with the girl, Bill had been somewhat reserved with Chris. He just didn't cotton to men who ran around when their wives were pregnant. But now the sight of Chris's drawn face and the genuine sadness in his eyes called up Bill's compassion. He gripped the younger man's arms. "I'm terribly sorry."

Chris nodded woodenly. It seemed to him that like an onion peeling layer by layer, the meaning of the day was sinking in on him. Vangie was dead. Had their quarrel driven her to kill herself? He couldn't believe it, and yet he felt lonely, frightened and guilty. He allowed Bill to persuade him to come to dinner. He had to get out of the house—he couldn't think clearly there. Molly and Bill were good people. Could he trust them with what he knew? Could he trust *anyone?* Numbly reaching for a jacket, he followed Bill down the street.

Bill poured a double Scotch for him. Chris gulped it. When the glass was half-empty he forced himself to slow down. The whiskey burned his throat and chest, making a passage through the tension. Calm down, he thought, calm down. Be careful.

The Kennedy kids came into the den to say good night. Well-behaved kids, all of them. Good-looking too. The oldest boy, Billy, resembled his father. Jennifer was a dark-haired beauty. The younger girls, Dina and Moira, were fair like Molly. The twins. Chris almost smiled. The twins looked like each other. Chris had always wanted children. Now his unborn child had died with Vangie. Another guilt. He had resented her pregnancy. His child, and he hadn't wanted it, not for one single second. And Vangie had known it. What had, *who* had driven her to kill herself? Who? That was the question. Because Vangie hadn't been alone last night.

He hadn't told the police. It would be opening up a can of worms, *begging* them to start an investigation. And where would that lead? To Joan. The other woman. To him.

The clerk had seen him leave the motel last night.

He'd started to come home, to have it out with Vangie. He'd even jotted down figures to discuss with her. She could have the house. He'd give her twenty thousand a year, at least until the baby was eighteen. He'd carry a large insurance policy on his life for her. He'd educate the baby. She could keep on going to that Japanese psychiatrist she was so crazy about. Only let me go, Vangie. Please let me go. I can't spend any more of my life with you. It's destroying both of us. . . .

He'd gotten as far as the house. Somewhere around midnight he'd arrived. He'd driven in and the minute the garage door opened, knew something was up. Because he'd almost rammed the Lincoln. She'd parked in his space. No, someone else parked her car in *his* space. Because no way would Vangie ever try to drive that wide car into the area between the posts and the right wall. The garage was an oversized one. One side could hold two cars. That was the side Vangie always used. And she needed every inch. She was a lousy driver, and her peripheral vision probably wasn't that great either. She simply couldn't judge space well. Chris always parked his Corvette in the narrower side. But last night the Lincoln had been expertly parked there.

He'd gone in and found the house empty. Vangie's handbag was on the chaise in their room. He'd been puzzled but not alarmed. Obviously she'd gone off with someone to stay overnight. He'd even been pleased that maybe she had a girlfriend to confide in. He'd always tried to make her develop friends. And Vangie could be secretive. He wondered if she'd forgotten her handbag. Vangie was forgetful, or maybe she'd packed an overnight bag and didn't want to bother with the heavy purse.

The house depressed Chris. He decided to go back to the motel. He hadn't told Joan about coming home. He was careful to say as little as possible to Joan about

Vangie. To Joan, any mention of Vangie was a continuing reminder of what she saw to be her own position as an interloper. If he'd told Joan this morning that he and Vangie had quarreled and Vangie had obviously been so upset she'd gone to stay with someone rather than be alone, Joan would have been heartsick.

But then this morning he'd found Vangie dead. Somebody had parked the car for her before midnight. Somebody had driven her home after midnight. And those shoes. The one day she'd worn them she'd complained endlessly about them. That was around Christmas when he'd taken her to New York, trying to give her some fun. Fun! God, what a miserable day. She hadn't liked the play. The restaurant didn't serve veal piccata and she'd set her heart on it. And she'd talked incessantly about how the shoe dug into her right ankle.

For weeks now she'd worn nothing but those dirty moccasins. He'd asked her to please get some decent shoes, but she'd said these were the only comfortable ones. Where were they? Chris had searched the house thoroughly. Whoever drove her home might know.

He hadn't told the police any of this. He hadn't wanted to involve Joan. "I checked into a motel because my wife and I had quarreled. I wanted a divorce. I decided to come home and try to reason with her. She wasn't here and I left." It hadn't seemed necessary to drag all this in. Even the shoes really weren't that important. Vangie might have wanted to be fully dressed when she was found. That swollen leg embarrassed her. She was vain.

But he should have told the cops about his being here, about the way the car was parked.

"Chris, come into the dining room. You'll feel better if you eat something." Molly's voice was gentle.

Wearily, Chris looked up. The soft hallway light silhouetted Molly's face, and for the first time he could see a family resemblance between her and Katie DeMaio.

Katie DeMaio. Her *sister*. He couldn't discuss this with Bill and Molly. It would put Molly in the middle. How could she honestly advise him whether or not to keep quiet about his coming home last night when her own sister was in the Prosecutor's office? No. He'd have to decide this on his own.

He brushed a hand over burning eyes. "I would like to have something, Molly," he said. "Whatever it is, sure smells good. But I'll have to leave pretty quickly. The funeral director is coming to the house for Vangie's clothes. Her mother and father want to be able to see her before the interment."

"Where will it be?" Bill asked.

"The coffin will be flown to Minneapolis tomorrow afternoon. I'll be on that plane too. The service will be the next day. The Medical Examiner released her body late this afternoon." The words hammered in his ears . . . Coffin . . . Body . . . Funeral . . . Oh, God, he thought, this had to be a nightmare. I wanted to be free of you, Vangie, but I didn't want you to die. I drove you to suicide. Joan's right. I should have stood by you.

At eight he went back to his house. At eight thirty, when the funeral director came, he had a suitcase with underwear and the flowing caftan Vangie's parents had sent her for Christmas.

The funeral director, Paul Halsey, was quietly sympathetic. He requested the necessary information quickly. Born April 15. He jotted down the year. Died February 15—just two months short of her thirty-first birthday, he commented.

Chris rubbed the ache between his eyes. Something was wrong. Even in this unreal situation where *everything* was wrong, there was something specific. "No," he said, "today's the *sixteenth,* not the *fifteenth.*"

"The death certificate clearly states that Mrs. Lewis died between eight and ten P.M. last night, February fifteenth," Halsey said. "You're thinking the sixteenth because you *found* her this morning. But the medical examiner who performed the autopsy can pinpoint the time of death accurately."

Chris stared at him. Waves of shock dissolved his sense of exhaustion and unreality. He had been home at midnight and the car and Vangie's purse had been here. He'd waited around for about half an hour before he drove back to the motel in New York. When he'd come home this morning, he'd assumed that Vangie had come in sometime after he left and killed herself.

But at midnight she'd already been dead three or four hours. That meant that sometime after midnight, after he left, someone had brought her body here, put it on her bed and laid the empty glass beside her.

Someone had wanted to make it seem that Vangie had committed suicide.

Had she killed herself somewhere else? Had someone brought her back who simply didn't want to be involved? Of course not. Vangie had never inflicted the pain of cyanide poisoning on herself. Her murderer had staged the suicide.

"Oh, Christ," Chris whispered. "Oh, Christ." Vangie's face filled his vision. The wide, thickly lashed, petulant eyes; the short, straight nose; the honey-colored hair that fell over her forehead; the small, perfectly formed lips. At the last moment she must have known. Someone had held her, forced that poison into her, viciously killed her and the baby she was carrying. She must have been so frightened. A tearing wrench of pity brought tears to his eyes. No one, no *husband,* could be silent and let those deaths go unpunished.

But if he told the police; if he started an investigation, there was one person they would inevitably accuse. As the funeral director stared at him, Chris said aloud, "I have to tell them, and they're going to blame it on me."

♦ 14 ♦

He hung up the phone slowly. Katie DeMaio suspected nothing. Even when she mentioned Vangie Lewis' name there hadn't been any hint that her office wanted anything more than to discuss Vangie's emotional state with him.

But Katie's accident had happened barely twenty-four hours ago. She was probably still experiencing a certain amount of shock reaction.

Her blood count was already low. Tomorrow when the cumadin was introduced into her system, the clotting mechanism would begin to collapse, and with the further hemorrhaging she'd begin to feel disoriented, light-headed. Certainly she would not be analytical enough to separate a supposed nightmare from an actual event.

Unless, of course, there were too many questions about the suicide. Unless the possibility of Vangie's body's having been moved was introduced and discussed in her office.

The danger was still so great.

He was in the library of the Westlake home—his home now. The house was a manorlike Tudor. It had archways and built-in bookcases and marble fireplaces and hand-blocked antique wallpaper and Tiffany stained-glass windows: the kind of home impossible to duplicate today at any price. The craftsmanship wasn't available.

The Westlake House. The Westlake Hospital. The Westlake Maternity Concept. The name had served him well, given him immediate entrée, socially and professionally. He was the distinguished obstetrician who had met Winifred Westlake on a transatlantic sailing, married her and relocated in America to carry on her father's work.

The perfect excuse for having left England. No one, including Winifred, knew about the years before Liverpool at Christ Hospital in Devon.

Toward the end she had started to ask questions.

It was nearly eleven o'clock and he hadn't had dinner yet. Knowing what he was going to do to Edna had robbed him of the desire to eat.

But now that it was over, the release had come. Now the need for food had become a craving. He went into the kitchen. Hilda had left dinner for him in the microwave oven: a small Cornish hen with wild rice. He just needed to heat it up for a few minutes. When he had time he preferred to cook his own meals. Hilda's food was without imagination, even though it was well enough prepared.

She was a good housekeeper, too. He liked coming home to the elegant orderliness of this place, to sip a drink, to eat when he chose, to spend hours working on his notes in the library, unthreatened by the possibility of someone's dropping in, as occasionally happened at his hospital laboratory.

He needed the freedom of the house. He'd gotten rid of the live-in housekeeper Winifred and her father had had. Hostile bitch, looking at him with sour, sullen eyes, swollen with weeping. "Miss Winifred was almost never sick until . . ."

He'd stared at her and she hadn't finished. What she was going to say was "until she married you."

Winifred's cousin resented him bitterly, had tried to make trouble after Winifred's death. But he couldn't prove anything. There hadn't been one shred of tangible evidence. They'd dismissed the cousin as a disgruntled ex-heir.

Of course, there hadn't been that much money at all. Winifred had sunk so much into purchasing the hospital. Now his research was taking staggering amounts, and most of it had to come directly from the practice. He couldn't apply for a grant, of course. But even so, he could manage. Women were willing to pay anything to conceive.

Hilda had set the table for him in the small dining room off the pantry—the morning room it used to be called. He would not eat any meal in the kitchen, but the twenty-by-thirty-foot dining room was ostentatious and ridiculous for a solitary diner. This room with its round pedestal table, Queen Anne cabinet and view of the tree-filled side lawn was far more appealing.

Selecting a chilled bottle of Pouilly-Fuissé from the refrigerator, he sat down to eat.

He finished dinner thoughtfully, his mind running over the exact dosage he would give Katie DeMaio. The cumadin would not be suspected in her bloodstream after death. Failure of coagulation would be attributed to the transfusions. If he had to administer the heparin, traces of it and the cumadin might show if there was a thorough autopsy. But he had an idea of what he could do to circumvent that.

Before going to bed, he went out to the foyer closet. He'd get those moccasins safely in his bag now, not risk a recurrence of this morning's annoyance. Reaching back into the closet, he put his hand in one pocket of the Burberry and pulled out a misshapen shoe. Expectantly he put his free hand in the other pocket— first matter-of-factly, then urgently. Finally he grabbed the coat and rummaged frantically all over it. Then he sank to his knees and pawed through the overshoes neatly stacked on the closet floor.

Finally he stood up, staring at the battered moccasin he was holding. Again he saw himself tugging the shoe off Vangie's right foot.

The *right* shoe.

The shoe he was holding.

Hysterically he began to laugh—noisy, rattling sounds wrenched from the frustrated fury of his being. After all the danger, after the ignominious crawling around the parking lot like a dog sniffing to pick up a scent, he had botched it.

Somehow in the dark, probably that time he'd shrunk against the shrubbery when the car roared into the parking lot, the shoe had fallen out of his pocket. The shoe he'd *found* was the one he'd already *had*.

And somewhere, the battered, shabby, ugly left moccasin that Vangie Lewis had been wearing was waiting to be found; waiting to trace her footsteps back to him.

◆ 15 ◆

Katie had set the clock radio for six A.M., but was wide awake long before the determinedly cheery voice of the CBS anchorman wished her a bright morning. Her sleep had been troubled; several times she'd almost started to jump up, frightened by a vague, troubling dream.

She always turned the thermostat low at night.

Shivering, she ran to adjust it, then quickly made coffee and brought a cup back upstairs to bed.

Propped against the pillows, the thick comforter wrapped around her, she eagerly sipped as the heat of the cup began to warm her fingers. "That's better," she murmured. "And now, what's the matter with me?"

The antique Williamsburg dresser with its oval center mirror was directly opposite the bed. She glanced into it. Her hair was tousled, a dark brown smudge against the ivory eyelet-edged pillowcases. The bruise under her eye was now purple tinged with yellow. Her eyes were swollen with sleep. Deep crescents accentuated the thinness of her face. As Mama would say, I look like something the cat dragged in, she reflected.

But it was more than the way she looked. It was even more than the overall achiness from the accident. It was a heavy feeling of apprehension. Had she started to dream that queer, frightening nightmare again last night? She couldn't be sure.

Vangie Lewis. A line from John's funeral service came to her: "We who are saddened at the certainty of death . . ." Death was certain, of course. But not like that. It was bad enough to think of Vangie taking her own life, but it seemed impossible that anyone would choose to kill her by forcing cyanide down her throat. She simply didn't believe Chris Lewis was capable of that kind of violence.

She thought of Dr. Highley's call. That damn operation. Oh, there were thousands of D-and-C's performed every year on women of every age. It wasn't the operation itself. It was the reason for it. Suppose the D-and-C didn't clear up the hemorrhaging? Dr. Highley had hinted that eventually it might be necessary to consider a hysterectomy.

If only she had become pregnant during the year with John. But she hadn't.

Suppose she did remarry someday. Wouldn't it be a bitter, miserable trick if by then she couldn't have children? Knock it off, she warned herself. Remember that line from *Faust?* We weep for what we may never lose.

Well, at least she was getting the operation over with. Check in Friday night. Operation Saturday, home Sunday. At work Monday. No big deal.

Molly had called her after she got to the office yesterday. She'd said, "Katie, I could tell you didn't want me to talk in front of Richard, but don't you think it would be better to postpone going to the hospital till next month? You got a pretty good shaking up."

She'd been vehement. "No way. I want to be through with this; and besides, Molly, I wouldn't be surprised if this darn business contributed to the accident. I felt light-headed a couple of times Monday."

Molly had been distressed. "Why didn't you tell me?"

"Oh, come on," Katie had said. "You and I both hate complainers. When it's really bad, I swear I'll yell for you."

"I hope so," Molly said. "I guess you might as well get it over with." Then she'd asked, "Are you going to tell Richard?"

Katie had tried not to sound exasperated. "No, and I'm not going to tell the elevator operator or the street-crossing guard or Dial-a-Friend. Just you and Bill. And that's where we leave it. Okay?"

"Okay. And don't be a smart-ass." Molly had hung up decisively, her tone a combination of affection and authoritativeness, the warning-signal voice she used when one of the kids was getting out of line.

I'm not your child, Molly, girl, Katie thought now. I love you, but I'm not your child. But as she sipped the coffee she wondered if she was leaning too much on Molly and Bill, drawing emotional support from them. Was she indeed coasting on their coattails out of the mainstream of life?

Oh, John. She glanced instinctively at his picture. This morning it was just that, a picture. A handsome, grave-looking man with gentle, penetrating eyes. Once during that first year after his death she'd picked up that picture, stared at it, then slammed it face down on the dresser crying, "How could you have left me?"

The next morning she'd been back on balance, ashamed of herself, and had made a resolution never to have three glasses of wine when she was feeling low. When she'd straightened the picture, she'd found a gouge in the lovely old dresser top which had been caused by the embossed silver frame. She'd tried to explain to the picture. "It isn't just self-pity, Judge. I'm angry for *you*. I wanted you to have another forty years. You knew how to enjoy life; how to do something worthwhile with life."

For who hath known the mind of the Lord? or who hath been His counsellor? That phrase from the Bible had flitted across her mind that day.

Remembering, Katie thought, I'd better think along those lines now.

Stripping off her pale green nightgown, she went into the bathroom and turned on the shower. The nightgown trailed over the bench at her dressing table. In college she'd favored striped drop-seat p.j.'s. But John had bought her exquisite gowns and peignoirs in Italy. It still seemed appropriate to wear them here in this house, in his bedroom.

Maybe Richard was right. Maybe she was keeping a deathwatch. John would be the first one to blast her for that.

The hot shower helped to pick up her spirits. She had a plea-bargaining session scheduled for nine, a sentencing at ten and two new cases to begin preparing for trial for next week. And she had plenty of work to do on this Friday's trial. It's Wednesday already, she thought with dismay. I'd better get a move on.

She dressed quickly, selecting a soft brown wool skirt and a new turquoise silk shirt with full sleeves that covered the bandage on her arm.

The loan car from the service station arrived as she finished a second coffee. She dropped the driver back at the station, whistled as she saw the extensive damage to the front of her car, counted her blessings that she hadn't been seriously injured and drove to the office.

It had been a busy night in the county. A fourteen-year-old girl had been raped. People were talking about a drunken-driving accident that had resulted in four deaths. A local police chief had called requesting that the Prosecutor help set up a lineup for the victim to view suspects who had been picked up after an armed robbery.

Scott was just coming out of his office. "Lovely night," Katie observed.

He nodded. "Son of a bitch—that jerk who rammed into the car with all those kids was so blotto he couldn't stand up straight. All four kids were killed. They were seniors at Pascal Hills on the way to a prom-committee meeting. Incidentally, I was planning to send Rita over to talk to the doctors at Westlake Hospital, but she's covering the rape case. I'm especially interested in the psychiatrist Vangie Lewis was going to. I'd like his opinion as to her mental state. I can send Charley or Phil, but I think a woman would be less noticeable over there, might be able to drift around a bit and see if Mrs. Lewis talked to the nurses or became friendly with other patients. But it'll have to wait until tomorrow. Rita's been up all night, and now she's driving around with that kid who was raped to see if she can spot her attacker. We're pretty sure he lives near her."

Katie hesitated. She had not planned to tell Scott that she was Dr. Highley's patient or that she'd be checking into Westlake Friday night. But it would be unthinkable to have someone from the office report that to him. She temporized. "Maybe I can help out. Dr. Highley is my gynecologist. I actually have an appointment with him today." She pressed her lips together, deciding there was no need to go into a tiresome recital about her scheduled operation.

Scott's eyebrows shot up. As always when he was surprised, his voice became deeper. "What are your impressions of him? Richard made some crack yesterday about Vangie's condition; seemed to think that Highley was taking chances with her."

Katie shook her head. "I don't agree with Richard. Dr. Highley's specialty is difficult pregnancies. He's practically considered a miracle man. That's the very point. He tries to bring to viable term the babies other doctors lose." She thought of his phone call to her. "I can vouch for the fact that he's a very concerned doctor."

Scott's frown made deep crease lines in his forehead and around his eyes. "That's your gut-level reaction to him? How long have you known him?"

Trying to be objective, Katie thought about the doctor. "I don't know him long or well. The gynecologist I used to go to retired and moved a couple of years ago, and I'd just not bothered about another one. Then when I started having trouble—well, anyhow, my sister Molly knew about Dr. Highley because her friend raves about him. Molly goes to someone in New York, and I didn't want to bother with that. So I

made an appointment last month. He's very knowledgeable." She remembered her examination. He had
been gentle but thorough. "You're quite right to have
come," he'd said. "In fact, I must suggest, that you
should not have ignored this condition for over a year.
I think of the womb as a cradle that must always be
kept in good repair."

The one thing that had surprised her was that he did
not have a nurse in attendance. Her other gynecologist
had always called the nurse in before he began an
examination; but then, he'd been from another generation. She judged Dr. Highley to be in his mid-
forties.

"What's your schedule today?" Scott asked.

"Busy morning, but this afternoon is adjustable."

"All right. You go see Highley, and talk to the shrink
too. Get a feeling of whether or not they think she was
capable of suicide. Find out when she was over there
last. See if she talked about the husband. Charley and
Phil are checking on Chris Lewis now. I was awake
half the night and kept thinking that Richard is right.
Something about that suicide stinks. Talk to the
nurses too."

"Not the nurses," Katie smiled. "The receptionist,
Edna. She knows everybody's business. I wasn't in the
waiting room two minutes last month before I found
myself giving her my life history. In fact, maybe you
ought to hire her to interrogate witnesses."

"I ought to hire a lot of people," Scott commented
dryly. "Talk to the Board of Freeholders. All right, I'll
see you later."

Katie went into her own office, grabbed her files and
rushed to her appointment with a defense attorney
about an indicted defendant. She agreed to drop a
heroin charge from "possession with intent to distrib-
ute" to simple "possession." From there she hurried
to a second-floor courtroom where she reflectively

listened as a twenty-year-old youth she had prosecuted was sentenced to seven years in prison. He could have received twenty years for the armed robbery and atrocious assault. Of the seven years, he'd probably serve one-third the term and be back on the streets. She knew his record by heart. Forget rehabilitation with this bird, she thought.

In the sheaf of messages waiting for her, there were two phone calls from Dr. Carroll. One had come in at nine fifteen, the other at nine forty. She called back, but Richard was out on a case. Her feeling of slight pressure at the two calls was replaced by a sensation of disappointment when she couldn't reach him.

She phoned Dr. Highley's office fully expecting to hear the nasal warmth of Edna's voice. But whoever answered was a stranger, a crisp, low-spoken woman. "Doctors' offices."

"Oh!" Katie thought swiftly and decided to ask for Edna. "Is Miss Burns there?"

There was a fraction of a minute's pause before the answer came. "Miss Burns won't be in today. She called in sick. I'm Mrs. Fitzgerald."

Katie realized how much she was counting on talking to Edna. "I'm sorry Miss Burns is not well." Briefly she explained that Dr. Highley expected her call and that she'd also like to see Dr. Fukhito. Mrs. Fitzgerald put her on hold and a few minutes later came back on the line.

"They'll both see you, of course. Dr. Fukhito is free fifteen minutes before the hour anytime between two and five, and Dr. Highley would prefer three o'clock if it is also convenient for you."

"Three o'clock with Dr. Highley is fine," Katie said, "and then please confirm three forty-five with Dr. Fukhito." Lowering the phone, she turned to the work on her desk.

At lunchtime, Maureen Crowley, one of the office

secretaries, popped her head in and offered to bring a sandwich to Katie. Deep in preparation for Friday's trial, Katie nodded affirmatively.

"Ham on rye with mustard and lettuce and dark coffee," Maureen said.

Katie looked up, surprised. "Am I really that predictable?"

The girl was about nineteen, with a mane of red-gold hair, emerald-green eyes and the lovely pale complexion of the true redhead. "Katie, I have to tell you, about food you're in a rut." The door closed behind her.

"You look peaked." "You're on a deathwatch." "You're in a rut."

Katie swallowed over a hard lump in her throat and was astonished to realize she was close to tears. I *must* be sick if I'm getting this thin-skinned, she thought.

When the sandwich and coffee arrived, she ate and sipped, only vaguely aware of what she was having. The case on which she was trying to concentrate was a total blur. Vangie Lewis' face was constantly before her. But why had she seen it in a nightmare?

♦ 16 ♦

Richard Carroll had had a rough night. The phone rang at eleven o'clock, a few minutes after he got home from Katie's house, to inform him that four kids were in the morgue.

He replaced the receiver slowly. He lived on the seventeenth floor of a high-rise north of the George

86

Washington Bridge. For moments he stared out the wall-length picture window at the New York skyline, at the cars darting swiftly down the Henry Hudson Parkway, at the blue-green lights that revealed and silhouetted the graceful lines of the George Washington Bridge.

Right now phones were ringing to tell the parents of those youngsters that their children wouldn't be coming home.

Richard looked around his living room. It was comfortably furnished with an oversized sofa, roomy armchairs, an Oriental rug in tones of blue and brown, a wall bookcase and sturdy oak tables that had once graced the parlor of a New England ancestor's farmhouse. Original watercolors with sailing themes were scattered tastefully on the walls. Richard sighed. His deep leather reclining chair was next to the bookcase. He'd planned to fix a nightcap, read for an hour and turn in. Instead he decided to go to the morgue to be there when the parents came to identify those youngsters. God knew there was precious little anyone could do for those people, but he knew he'd feel better for trying.

It was four A.M. before he got back to the apartment. As he undressed he wondered if he was getting too saddened by this job. Those kids were so messed up; the crash impact had been terrific. Yet you could see how attractive they'd all been in life. One girl particularly got under his skin. She had dark hair, a slim, straight nose, and even in death she was graceful.

She reminded him of Katie.

The thought that Katie had been in an automobile accident Monday night jolted Richard anew. It seemed to him that they'd progressed light-years in their relationship in the couple of hours they'd spent together at dinner.

What was she afraid of, poor kid? Why couldn't she let go of John DeMaio? Why couldn't she say "Thanks for the memory" and move on?

As he got into bed he felt bleakly grateful that he'd been able to help the parents a little. He'd been able to assure them that the youngsters had died instantly, that they probably never knew or felt anything.

He slept restlessly for two hours and was in the office by seven. A few minutes later a summons came that an old lady had hanged herself in a deteriorating section of Chester, a small town at the north end of the county. He went to the death scene. The dead woman was eighty-one years old, frail and birdlike. A note was pinned to her dress: *There's nobody left. I'm so sick and tired. I want to be with Sam. Please forgive me for causing trouble.*

The note brought into focus something that had been nagging Richard. From everything he'd heard about Vangie Lewis, it seemed in character that if she'd taken her life, she'd have left a note to explain or to blame her action on her husband.

Most women left notes.

When he got back to the office Richard tried phoning Katie twice, hoping to catch her between court sessions. He wanted to hear the sound of her voice. For some reason he'd felt edgy about leaving her alone in that big house last night. But he was unable to reach her.

Why did he have a hunch that she had something on her mind that was troubling her?

He went back to the lab and worked straight through until four thirty. Returning to his office, he picked up his messages and was absurdly pleased to see that Katie had returned his calls. Why wouldn't she? he asked himself cynically. An assistant prosecutor wouldn't ignore calls from the Medical Examiner. Quickly he phoned her. The switchboard operator in the Prosecutor's section said that Katie had left and wouldn't be back today. The operator didn't know where she was going.

Damn.

That meant he wouldn't get to talk to her today. He was having dinner in New York with Clovis Simmons, an actress on one of the soaps. Clovis was fun; he always enjoyed himself with her, but the signs were that she was getting serious.

Richard made a resolve. This was the last time he'd take Clovis out. It wasn't fair to her. Refusing to consider the reason for that sudden decision, he leaned back in his chair and scowled. A mental alarm was sending out a beeping signal. It reminded him of traveling in the Midwest when the radio station would suddenly announce a tornado watch in effect. A *warning* was the sure thing. A *watch* suggested potential trouble.

He had not been exaggerating when he'd told Scott that if Vangie Lewis had not delivered that baby soon she wouldn't have needed the cyanide. How many women got into that same kind of condition under the Westlake Maternity Concept? Molly raved about the obstetrician because one of her friends had had a successful pregnancy. But what about the failures over there? How many of *them* had there been? Had there been anything unusual about the ratio of deaths among Westlake's patients? Richard switched on the intercom and asked his secretary to come in.

Marge was in her mid-fifties. Her graying hair was carefully bubbled in the style made popular by Jacqueline Kennedy in the early sixties. Her skirt was an inch over her plump knees. She looked like a suburban housewife on a television game show. She was in fact an excellent secretary who thoroughly enjoyed the constant drama of the department.

"Marge," he said, "I'm playing a hunch. I want to do some unofficial investigating of Westlake Hospital —just the maternity section. That maternity concept has been in operation for about eight years. I'd like to know how many patients died either in childbirth or from complications of pregnancy and what the ratio is between deaths and the number of patients treated there. I don't want to let it out that I'm interested. That's why I don't want to ask Scott to have the records subpoenaed. Do you know anybody over there who might look at the hospital records for you on the quiet?"

Marge frowned. Her nose, not unlike a small, sharp canary's beak, wrinkled. "Let me work on it."

"Good. And something else. Check into any malpractice suits that have been filed against either of the doctors over at Westlake Maternity. I don't care whether the suits were dropped or not. I want to know the reason for them, if any exist at all."

Satisfied at getting the investigation under way, Richard dashed home to shower and change. Seconds after he left his office, a call came for him from Dr. David Broad of the prenatal laboratory at Mt. Sinai Hospital. The message Marge took asked that Richard contact Dr. Broad in the morning. The matter was urgent.

Katie left for the hospital at quarter to three. The weather had settled into a tenacious, somber, cloudy cold spell. But at least the warmth of the cars had melted most of the sleet from the roads. She deliberately slowed down as she rounded the curve that had been the starting point of her accident.

She was a few minutes early for her appointment, but could have saved her time. The receptionist, Mrs. Fitzgerald, was coolly pleasant, but when Katie asked if she filled in for Edna very often, Mrs. Fitzgerald replied stiffly, "Miss Burns is almost never absent, so there's very little need to substitute for her."

It seemed to Katie that the answer was unduly defensive. Intrigued, she decided to pursue the issue. "I was so sorry to hear that Miss Burns is ill today," she added. "Nothing serious, I hope?"

"No." The woman was distinctly nervous. "Just a virus sort of thing. She'll be in tomorrow, I'm sure."

There were several expectant mothers sitting in the reception area, but they were deep in magazines. There was no way Katie could feasibly strike up a conversation with them. A pregnant woman, her face puffy, her movements slow and deliberate, came from the corridor that led to the doctors' offices. A buzzer sounded at the desk. The receptionist picked up the phone.

"Mrs. DeMaio, Dr. Highley will see you now," she said. She sounded relieved.

Katie walked quickly down the corridor. Dr.

Highley's office was the first one, she remembered. Following the printed instructions to knock and enter, she opened the door and stepped into the medium-sized office. It had the air of a comfortable study. Bookshelves lined one wall. Pictures of mothers with babies nearly covered a second wall. A club chair was placed near the doctor's elaborately carved desk. Katie remembered that the examining room, a lavatory and a combination kitchen/instrument-sterilizing area completed the suite. The doctor was behind his desk. He stood up to greet her. "Mrs. DeMaio." His tone was courteous; the faint British accent, barely perceptible. He was a medium-tall man, about five feet eleven inches. His face, smooth-skinned with rounded cheeks, terminated in a plump oval chin. His body gave the impression of solid strength, carefully controlled. He looked as though he could easily put on weight. Thinning sandy hair, streaked with gray, was carefully combed in a side part. Eyebrows and lashes, the same sandy shade, accentuated protruding steel-gray eyes. Feature by feature he was not an attractive man, but his overall appearance was imposing and authoritative.

Katie flushed, realizing that he was aware of her scrutiny and not pleased by it. She sat down quickly and to establish rapport thanked him for the phone call.

He dismissed her gratitude. "I wish you had something to thank me for. If you had told the emergency-room doctor that you were my patient, he would have given you a room in the west wing. Far more comfortable, I assure you. But just about the same view," he added.

Katie had started to fish in her shoulder bag for a pad and paper. She looked up quickly. "View. Anything would be better than the one I thought I had the other night. Why . . ." She stopped. The pad in her hand reminded her that she was here on official business. What would he think of her talking about nightmares? Unconsciously she tried to straighten up in the too-low, too-soft chair.

"Doctor, if you don't mind, let's talk about Vangie Lewis first." She smiled. "I guess our roles are reversed at least for a few minutes. I get to ask the questions."

His expression became somber. "I only wish there were a happier reason for our roles to be reversed. That poor girl. I've thought of little else since I heard the news."

Katie nodded. "I knew Vangie slightly, and I must say I've had the same reaction. Now, it's purely routine, of course, but in the absence of a note, my office does like to have some understanding of the mental state of a suicide victim." She paused, then asked, "When was the last time you saw Vangie Lewis?"

He leaned back in the chair. His fingers interlocked under his chin, revealing immaculately clean nails. He spoke slowly. "It was last Thursday evening. I've been having Mrs. Lewis come in at least weekly since she completed the halfway point of her pregnancy. I have her chart here."

He indicated the manila file on his desk. It was tabbed LEWIS, VANGIE. It was an impersonal item, Katie decided, a reminder that exactly one week ago Vangie Lewis had lain in the examining room adjoining this office having her blood pressure checked, the heartbeat of her fetus confirmed.

"How was Mrs. Lewis," she asked, "physically and emotionally?"

"Let me answer as to her physical condition first. It was a worry, of course. There was danger of toxic pregnancy, which I was watching very closely. But you see, every additional day she carried increased the baby's chance of survival."

"Could she have carried the baby to full term?"

"Impossible. In fact, last Thursday I warned Mrs. Lewis that it was highly likely that we would have to bring her in within the next two weeks and induce labor."

"How did she respond to that news?"

He frowned. "I expected Mrs. Lewis to have a very valid concern for the baby's life. But the fact is that the closer she came to the potential birth, the more it seemed to me that she feared the birth process. The thought even crossed my mind that she was not unlike a little girl who wanted to play house, but would have been terrified if her doll turned into a real baby."

"I see." Katie doodled reflectively on the pad she was holding. "But did Vangie show any specific depression?"

Dr. Highley shook his head. "I did not see it. However, I think that answer should come from Dr. Fukhito. He saw her on Monday night, and he's better trained than I to recognize that symptom if it's being masked. My overall impression was that she was getting morbidly fearful of giving birth."

"A last question," Katie asked. "Your office is right next to Dr. Fukhito's. Did you at any time Monday night see Mrs. Lewis?"

"I did not."

"Thank you, Doctor. You've been very helpful." She slipped her pad back into her shoulder bag. "Now it's your turn to ask questions."

"I don't have too many. You answered them last night. When you've finished talking with Dr. Fukhito, please go to room 101 on the other side of the hospital. You'll be given a transfusion. Wait about a half hour before driving after you've received it."

"I thought that was for people who gave blood," Katie said.

"Just to make sure there's no reaction. Also . . ." He reached into the deep side drawer of his desk. Katie caught a glimpse of small bottles in exquisite order in the drawer. He selected one containing about nine or ten pills. "Take the first one of these tonight," he said. "Then one every four hours tomorrow; the same on Friday. Take four pills in all tomorrow and Friday. You have just enough here. I must stress that it's very important you don't neglect this. As you know, if this operation does not cure your problem, we must consider more radical surgery."

"I'll take the pills," Katie said.

"Good. You'll be checking in around six o'clock Friday evening."

Katie nodded.

"Fine. I'll be making my late rounds and will look in on you. You're not worried, I trust?"

She had admitted her fear of hospitals to him on the first appointment. "No," she said, "not really."

He opened the door for her. "Till Friday, then, Mrs. DeMaio," he said softly.

◆ 18 ◆

The investigative team of Phil Cunningham and Charley Nugent returned to the Prosecutor's office at four P.M. exuding the strained excitement of hounds who have treed their quarry. Rushing into Scott Myerson's office, they proceeded to lay their findings before him.

"The husband's a liar," Phil said crisply. "He wasn't due back till yesterday morning, but his plane developed engine trouble. The passengers were off-loaded in Chicago, and he and the crew deadheaded back to New York. He got in Monday evening."

"Monday evening!" Scott exploded.

"Yeah. And checked into the Holiday Inn on West Fifty-seventh Street."

"How did you get that?"

"We got a list of his crew on the Monday flight and talked to all of them. The purser lives in New York. Lewis gave him a ride into Manhattan and then ended up having dinner with him. Lewis told some cock-and-bull story about his wife being away and he was going to stay in the city overnight and take in a show."

"He told the purser that?"

"Yeah. He parked the car at the Holiday Inn, checked in; then they went to dinner. The purser left him at seven twenty. After that Lewis got his car, and the garage records show he had it for over two hours. Brought it back at ten. And get this. He took off again at midnight and came back at two."

Scott whistled. "He lied to us about his flight. He lied to the purser about his wife. He was somewhere in his car between eight and ten and between midnight and two A.M. What time did Richard say Vangie Lewis died?"

"Between eight and ten P.M.," Ed said.

Charley Nugent had been silent. "There's more," he said. "Lewis has a girlfriend, a Pan Am stewardess. Name's Joan Moore. Lives at 201 East Eighty-seventh Street in New York. The doorman there told us Captain Lewis drove her home from the airport yesterday morning. She left her bag with him and they went for coffee in the drugstore across the street."

Scott tapped his pencil on the desk, a sure sign that

he was about to issue orders. His assistants waited, notebooks in hand.

"It's four o'clock," Scott said crisply. "The judges will be leaving soon. Get one of them on the phone and ask him to wait around for fifteen minutes. Tell him we're having a search warrant sworn out."

Phil sprinted from his chair and reached for the telephone.

"You"—Scott pointed to Charley—"find out what funeral director picked up Vangie Lewis' body in Minneapolis. Get to him. The body is not to be interred, and make damn sure Chris Lewis doesn't decide to cremate it. We may want to do more work on it. Did Lewis say when he was coming back?"

Charley nodded. "He told us he'd return tomorrow immediately after the services and interment."

Scott grunted. "Find out what plane he's coming in on and be waiting for him. Invite him here for questioning."

"You don't think he'll try to skip?" Charley asked.

"No, I don't. He'll try to brazen it through. If he has any brains he'll know that we have nothing specific on him. And I want to talk to the girlfriend. What do you know about her?"

"She shares an apartment with two other stewardesses. She's planning to switch to Pan Am's Latin American Division and fly out of Miami. She's down in Fort Lauderdale right now signing a lease on an apartment. She'll be back late Friday afternoon."

"Meet her plane too," Scott said. "Invite her here for a few questions. Where was she Monday night?"

"In flight on her way to New York. We're absolutely certain."

"All right." He paused. "Something else. I want the phone records from the Lewis house, particularly from the last week, and when you do the search see if there isn't some kind of answering machine on one of the phones. He's an airline captain. It would make sense to have one."

Phil Cunningham was hanging up the phone. "Judge Haywood will wait."

Scott reached for the phone, swiftly dialed Richard's office, asked for him and softly muttered, "Damn. The one day he leaves early has to be today!"

"Do you need him right now?" Charley's tone was curious.

"I want to know what he meant by saying there was something else that didn't jibe. Remember that remark? It might be important to know what it is. All right, let's get busy. And when you search that house, search it with a fine-tooth comb. And look for cyanide. We've got to find out fast where Vangie Lewis got the cyanide that killed her.

"Or where Captain Lewis got it," he added quietly.

♦ 19 ♦

By contrast with Dr. Highley's office, Dr. Fukhito's seemed more spacious and brighter. The writing table with long, slender lines occupied less space than Dr. Highley's massive English desk. Graceful cane-backed chairs with upholstered seats and arms and a matching chaise substituted for the clubby leather chairs in the other office. Instead of the wall with framed pictures of mothers and babies, Dr. Fukhito had a series of exquisite reproductions of Ukiyo-e woodcuts.

Dr. Fukhito was tall for a Japanese. Unless, Katie

thought, his posture was so upright that he seemed even taller than he probably was. No, she judged him to be about five feet ten.

Like his associate, Dr. Fukhito was expensively and conservatively dressed. His pin-striped suit was accentuated by a light blue shirt and silk tie in muted tones of blue. His jet-black hair and small, neat mustache complemented pale gold skin and brown eyes more oval than almond-shaped. By either Oriental or Occidental standards he was a strikingly handsome man.

And probably a very good psychiatrist, Katie thought as she reached for her notebook, deliberately giving herself time to absorb impressions.

Last month her visit with Dr. Fukhito had been brief and informal. Smiling, he'd explained, "The womb is a fascinating part of the anatomy. Sometimes, irregular or inordinate flowing may indicate an emotional problem."

"I doubt it," Katie had told him. "My mother had the same problem for years, and I do understand it's hereditary, or can be."

He'd queried her about her personal life. "And suppose a hysterectomy becomes necessary someday? What would you feel about that?"

"I would feel terrible," Katie had replied. "I've always wanted a family."

"Then have you any plans to be married? Have you a relationship with someone?"

"No."

"Why not?"

"Because right now I'm more interested in my job." She had terminated the interview abruptly. "Doctor, you're very kind, but I don't have any big emotional hang-ups, I can assure you. I'm looking forward very much to being relieved of this problem, but I assure you it's a purely physical one."

He had acceded gracefully, standing up at once and holding out his hand. "Well, if you're to become Dr. Highley's patient, please remember I'm right here. And if a time comes when you'd like to talk things out with someone, you might want to try me."

Several times in the past month it had fleetingly crossed Katie's mind that it might not be a bad idea to talk with him to get a professional and objective view of where she was at emotionally. Or, she wondered, had that thought sprung into being much more recently—for instance, since last night's dinner with Richard?

Pushing that thought away, she straightened in the chair and held up her pen. Her sleeve fell back, revealing her bandaged arm. To her relief, he did not question her about it.

"Doctor, as you know, a patient of yours and Dr. Highley's, Vangie Lewis, died sometime Monday evening."

She noticed that his eyebrows rose slightly. Was it because he was expecting her to positively state that Vangie committed suicide?

She continued, "Doctor, you saw Vangie at about eight o'clock that night. Isn't that true?"

He nodded. "I saw her at precisely eight o'clock."

"How long did she stay?"

"About forty minutes. She phoned Monday afternoon and asked for an appointment. I usually work until eight on Monday night and was completely booked. I told her so and suggested she come in Tuesday morning."

"How did she respond?"

"She began to cry over the phone. She acted quite distressed, and of course, I told her to come in, that I could see her at eight."

"Why was she so distressed, Doctor?"

He spoke slowly, choosing his words carefully. "She had quarreled with her husband. She was convinced he did not love her or want the baby. Physically, the strain of the pregnancy was beginning to tell on her. She was quite immature, really—an only child who had been inordinately spoiled and fussed over. The physical discomfort was appalling to her, and the prospect of the birth had suddenly become frightening."

Unconsciously, his eyes shifted to the chair at the right of his desk. She had sat in it Monday evening, that long caftan folding around her. Much as she had claimed to want a baby, Vangie had hated maternity clothes, hated losing her figure. In the last month she'd tried to conceal her outsized body and swollen leg by wearing floor-length dresses. It was a miracle she hadn't tripped and fallen the way they flapped around her feet.

Katie stared at him curiously. This man was nervous. What advice had he given Vangie that had sent her rushing home to kill herself? Or had sent her to a killer if Richard's hunch was right? The quarrel Chris Lewis had not admitted that he and Vangie had quarreled.

Leaning forward quickly, Katie asked, "Doctor, I realize that you want to protect the confidentiality of Mrs. Lewis' discussions with you, but this is an official matter. We do need to know whatever you can tell us about the quarrel Vangie Lewis had with her husband."

It seemed to him that Katie's voice came from far off. He was seeing Vangie's eyes terrified and staring at him. With a fierce effort he cleared his thoughts and looked directly at Katie. "Mrs. Lewis told me that she believed her husband was in love with someone else; that she'd accused him of that. She told me she had warned him that when she found out who the woman was she'd make her life hell. She was angry, agitated, bitter and frightened."

"What did you tell her?"

"I promised her that before and during the birth she would be given everything necessary to make her comfortable. I told her that we hoped she would have the baby she'd always wanted and that it might be the instrument to give her marriage more time."

"How did she react to that?"

"She began to calm down. But then I felt it necessary to warn her that after the baby was born, if her marriage relationship did not improve, she should consider the possibility of terminating it."

"And then?"

"She became furious. She swore that she would never let her husband leave her, that I was like everyone else, on his side. She got up and grabbed her coat."

"What did you do, Doctor?"

"It was clearly time for me to do nothing. I told her to go home, get a good night's sleep and to call me in the morning. I realized it was far too early for her to deal with the seemingly irrevocable fact that Captain Lewis wanted a divorce."

"And she left?"

"Yes. Her car was parked in the rear parking area. Occasionally she'd ask if she could use my private entrance in order to go out the back way. Monday night she didn't ask. She simply walked out through that door."

"And you never heard from her again?"

"No."

"I see." Katie got up and walked over to the paneled wall with the pictures. She wanted to keep Dr. Fukhito talking. He was holding something back. He was nervous.

"I was a patient here myself Monday night, Doctor," she said. "I had a minor automobile accident and was brought here."

"I'm glad it was minor."

"Yes." Katie stood in front of one of the pictures. *A Small Road at Yabu Koji Atagoshita.* "That's lovely," she said. "It's from the *Hundred Views of Yedo* series, isn't it?"

"Yes. You're very knowledgeable about Japanese art."

"Not really. My husband was the expert and taught me a little about it, and I have other reproductions from the series, but this one is beautiful. Interesting, isn't it, the concept of one hundred views of the same place?"

He became watchful. Katie's back was to him and she did not see that he pressed his lips into a rigid line.

Katie turned around. "Doctor, I was brought in here around ten o'clock Monday night. Can you tell me, is there any chance that Vangie Lewis did not leave at eight o'clock; that she was still around the hospital; that at ten o'clock, when I was brought in, semiconscious, I might have seen her?"

Dr. Fukhito stared at Katie, feeling clammy wet fear crawl across his skin. He forced himself to smile. "I don't see how," he said. But Katie noticed that his knuckles were clenched and white, as if he were forcing himself to sit in his chair, not to run away, and something—was it fury or fear?—flashed in his eyes.

◆ 20 ◆

At five o'clock Gertrude Fitzgerald turned the phone over to the answering service and locked the reception desk. Nervously she phoned Edna's number. Again there was no answer. There was no doubt. Edna had been drinking more and more lately. But she was such a cheerful, good person. Really loved everybody. Gertrude and Edna often had lunch together, usually in the hospital cafeteria. Sometimes Edna would say, "Let's go out and get something decent." That meant she wanted to go to the pub near the hospital where she could get a Manhattan. Those days Gertrude always tried to make her keep it down to one drink. She'd kid her along. "You can have a couple tonight, honey," she'd say.

Gertrude understood Edna's need to drink. She didn't drink herself, but she understood that hollow, burning feeling when all you do is go to work every day and then go home and stare at four walls. She and Edna laughed sometimes about all the articles that told you to take up yoga or tennis or join a bird-watching club or take a course. And Edna would say, "I couldn't get these fat legs in the cross-leg position; there's no way I'll ever touch the ground without bending my knees; I'm allergic to birds and at the end of the day I'm too tired to worry about the history of ancient Greece. I just wish that somewhere along the way I'd meet a nice guy who wanted to come home to me at night, and buh-lieve me, I wouldn't care if he snored."

Gertrude was a widow of seven years, but at least she had the children and grandchildren; people who cared about her, called her up, sometimes borrowed a few hundred bucks; people who needed her. She had her own lonely times, God knew, but it wasn't the same as it was for Edna. She'd *lived*. She was sixty-two years old, in good health, and she had something to look back on. .

She could swear Dr. Highley had known she was lying when she said Edna had called in sick. But Edna had admitted that Dr. Highley had warned her about the drinking. And Edna needed the job. Those old parents of hers had cost her a mint before they died. Not that Edna ever complained. Sad thing was, she wished they were still around; she missed them.

Suppose Edna *hadn't* been drinking? Suppose she was sick or something? The thought made Gertrude catch her breath sharply. No two ways about it. She'd have to check up on Edna. She'd drive over to her house right now. If she was drinking, she'd make her stop and sober her up. If she was sick, she'd take care of her.

Her mind settled, Gertrude got up from the desk briskly. Something else. That Mrs. DeMaio from the Prosecutor's office. She'd been very nice, but you could tell she'd been anxious to talk to Edna. She'd probably phone Edna tomorrow. What could she want of her? Whatever would Edna be able to tell her about Mrs. Lewis?

It was an intriguing problem, one that kept Gertrude occupied as she drove the six miles to Edna's apartment. But she was still unable to come up with an answer by the time she drove into the visitors' parking area behind Edna's apartment and walked around to the front door.

The lights were on. Even though the shiny, self-lined drapery was drawn, Gertrude could tell that there were lights coming from the living room and dinette. As she neared the door, she heard the faint sound of voices. The television set, of course.

A momentary irritation flashed through her. She might just get really annoyed if Edna was sitting all nice and comfortable in her recliner and hadn't even bothered to answer the phone. She, Gertrude, had covered her work for her, covered her absence and now driven miles out of her way to make sure she wasn't in need.

Gertrude rang the bell. It pealed in a clanging double chime. She waited. Even though she listened hard, there was no sound of hurrying feet approaching the door, or a familiar voice calling, "Right with you." Maybe Edna was rinsing her mouth with Scope. She was always afraid that one of the doctors might drop in with emergency work to do. That had happened a few times on days Edna was out. That was how Dr. Highley had first noticed Edna's problem.

But there was no reassuring sound of voice or footsteps. Gertrude shivered as she firmly pushed the bell again. Maybe Edna was sleeping it off. It was so terribly cold. She wanted to get home herself.

By the time she'd rung the bell four times, the annoyance had passed and Gertrude was thoroughly alarmed. There was no use fooling around; something was wrong and she had to get into the apartment. The superintendent, Mr. Krupshak, lived directly across the court. Hurrying over, Gertrude told her story. The super was eating dinner and looked annoyed, but his wife, Gana, reached for the wide key ring on a nail over the sink. "I'll go with you," she said.

The two women hurried across the courtyard together. "Edna's a real friend," Gana Krupshak volunteered. "Sometimes in the evening I pop in on her and we visit and have a drink together. My husband doesn't approve of liquor, even wine. Just last night I stopped over at about eight. I had a Manhattan with her, and she told me that one of her favorite patients had killed herself. Well, here we are."

The women were on the small porch leading to Edna's apartment. The superintendent's wife fumbled with the keys. "It's this one," she murmured. She inserted the key into the lock, twisted it. "This lock has a funny little thing—you have to kind of jiggle it."

The lock turned and she pushed open the door as she spoke.

The two women saw Edna at exactly the same moment: lying on the floor, her legs crumpled under her, her blue robe open, revealing a flannel nightgown, her graying hair plastered around her face, her eyes staring, crusted blood making a crimson crown on the top of her head.

"No. No." Gertrude felt her voice rise, high, shrill, an entity she could not control. She pressed her knuckles to her mouth.

In a dazed voice Gana Krupshak said, "It's just last night I was sitting here with her. And"—the woman's voice broke—"she was pretty under the weather—you know what I mean, the way Edna could get—and she was talking about a patient who killed herself. And then she phoned that patient's husband." Gana began to sob—noisy, racking sounds. "And now poor Edna is dead too!"

Chris Lewis stood next to Vangie's parents to the right of the coffin, numbly acknowledging the sympathetic utterances of friends. When he'd phoned them about her death, they had agreed that they would view her body privately, have a memorial service tomorrow morning followed by a private interment.

Instead, when he'd arrived in Minneapolis this afternoon, he found that they had arranged for public viewing tonight and that after the chapel service tomorrow morning a cortege would follow Vangie's body to the cemetery.

"So many friends will want to say good-bye to our little girl. To think that two days ago she was alive, and now she's gone," her mother sobbed.

Was it only Wednesday? It seemed to Chris that weeks had passed since he'd walked into that nightmare scene in the bedroom yesterday morning. *Yesterday morning.*

"Doesn't our baby look lovely?" her mother was asking the visitor who had just approached the coffin.

Our little girl. Our baby. If only you had let her grow up, Chris thought, it might all have been so different. Their hostility to him was controlled, but lurked below the surface ready to spring out. "A happy girl does not take her own life," her mother had said accusingly.

They looked old and tired and shattered with grief—plain, hardworking people who had denied themselves everything to surround their unexpectedly beautiful child with luxury, who had brought her up to believe her wish was law.

Would it be easier for them when the truth was revealed that someone had taken Vangie's life? Or did he owe it to them to say nothing, to keep that final horror from them? Her mother was already trying to find comfort, to frame a version she could live with: "Chris was on a trip and we're so far away, and my baby was feeling so sick and she took a sip of something and went to sleep."

Oh, God, Chris thought, how people twist truth, twist life. He wanted to talk to Joan. She'd been so upset when she heard about Vangie that she'd hardly been able to talk. "Did she know about us?" He'd finally had to admit to her that Vangie suspected that he was interested in someone else.

Joan would be back from Florida Friday evening. He was going to return to New Jersey tomorrow afternoon right after the funeral. He would say nothing to the police until he'd had a chance to talk to Joan, to warn her that she might be dragged into this. The police would be looking for a motive for him to kill Vangie. In their eyes, Joan would be the motive.

Should he leave well enough alone? *Did* he have the right to drag Joan into this, to unearth something that would hurt Vangie's parents even more?

Had there been someone else in Vangie's life? Chris glanced over at the coffin, at Vangie's now-peaceful face, the quietly folded hands. He and Vangie had scarcely lived as man and wife in the past few years. They'd lain side by side like two strangers; he emotionally drained from the endless quarreling, she wanting to be cajoled, babied. He'd even suggested separate rooms, but she'd become hysterical.

She became pregnant two months after they moved to New Jersey. When he'd agreed to one more final try at the marriage, he had made a genuine effort to make it work. But the summer had been miserable. By August he and Vangie had barely been speaking. Only once, around the middle of the month, had they slept together. He had thought it an irony of fate that after ten years she had become pregnant just as he met someone else.

A suspicion that Chris realized had been sitting somewhere in his subconscious sprang full-blown to life. Was it possible that Vangie had become involved with another man, a man who did not want to take responsibility for her and a baby? Had she confronted that other man? Vangie had threatened that if she knew whom Chris was seeing, she'd make her wish she were dead. Suppose she had been having some kind of affair with a married man. Suppose she'd hurled hysterical threats at *him?*

Chris realized that he had been shaking hands, murmuring thanks, looking into familiar faces and not really seeing them: neighbors from the condominium where he and Vangie had lived before the move to New Jersey; airline friends; friends of Vangie's parents. His own parents were retired in North Carolina. Neither was well. He had told them not to make the trip to Minneapolis in the bitterly cold weather.

"I'm very sorry." The man who was clasping his hand was in his mid-sixties. He was a slightly built man, but sturdily attractive, with winter-gray hair and bushy brows over keen, penetrating eyes. "I'm Dr. Salem," he said, "Emmet Salem. I delivered Vangie and was her first gynecologist. She was one of the prettiest things I ever brought into this world, and she never changed. I only wish I hadn't been away when she phoned my office Monday."

Chris stared at him. "Vangie phoned you Monday?"

"Yes. My nurse said she was quite upset. Wanted to see me immediately. I was teaching a seminar in

Detroit, but the nurse made an appointment with me for her for today. She was planning to fly out yesterday, from what I understand. Maybe I could have helped her."

Why had Vangie called this man? Why? It seemed to Chris that it was impossible to think. What would make her go back to a doctor she hadn't seen in years? She wasn't well, but if she wanted a consultation, why a doctor thirteen hundred miles away?

"Had Vangie been ill?" Dr. Salem was looking at him curiously, waiting for an answer.

"No, not ill," Chris said. "As you probably know, she was expecting a baby. It was a difficult pregnancy from the beginning."

"Vangie was what?" The doctor's voice rose. He stared at Chris in astonishment.

"I know. She had just about given up hope. But in New Jersey she started the Westlake Maternity Concept. You may have heard of it, or of Dr. Highley— Dr. Edgar Highley."

"Captain Lewis, may I speak with you?" The funeral director had a hand under his arm, was propelling him toward the private office across the foyer from the viewing room.

"Excuse me," Chris said to the doctor. Nonplussed by the director's agitation, he allowed himself to be guided into the office.

The funeral director closed the door and looked at Chris. "I've just received a call from the Prosecutor's office in Valley County, New Jersey," he said. "Written confirmation is on the way. We are forbidden to inter your wife's body. Your wife's body is to be flown back to the Medical Examiner's office in Valley County immediately after the service tomorrow."

They know it wasn't a suicide, Chris thought. They already know that. There was nothing he could do to hide it. Once he had a chance to talk to Joan Friday night, he'd tell the Prosecutor's office everything he knew or suspected.

Without answering the funeral director, he turned and left the office. He wanted to speak to Dr. Salem, find out what Vangie had said to the nurse on the phone.

But when he went back to the other room, Dr. Salem was already gone. He had left without speaking to Vangie's parents. Vangie's mother rubbed swollen eyes with a damp crumpled handkerchief. "What did you say to Dr. Salem that made him leave like that?" she asked. "Why did you upset him so terribly?"

♦ 22 ♦

Wednesday evening he arrived home at six o'clock. Hilda was just leaving. Her plain, stolid face was guarded. He was always aloof with her. He knew she liked and wanted this job. Why not? A house that stayed neat; no mistress to constantly give orders; no children to clutter it.

No children. He went into the library, poured a Scotch and broodingly watched from the window as Hilda's broad body disappeared down the street toward the bus line two blocks away.

He had gone into medicine because his own mother had died in childbirth. His birth. The accumulated stories of the years, listened to from the time he could understand, told by the timid, self-effacing man who had been his father. "Your mother wanted you so much. She knew she was risking her life, but she didn't care."

Sitting in the chemist's shop in Brighton, watching his father prepare prescriptions, asking questions: "What is that?" "What will that pill do?" "Why do you put caution labels on those bottles?" He'd been fascinated, drinking in the information his father so willingly shared with him—the one topic his father could talk about; the only world his father knew.

He'd gone to medical school, finished in the top ten percent of his class; internships were offered in leading hospitals in London and Glasgow. Instead he chose Christ Hospital in Devon, with its magnificently equipped research laboratory—the opportunity it gave for both research and practice. He'd become staff; his reputation as an obstetrician had grown rapidly.

And his project had been held back, retarded, cursed by his inability to test it.

At twenty-seven he'd married Claire, a distant cousin of the Earl of Sussex—infinitely superior to him in social background, but his reputation, the expectation of future prominence had been the leveler.

And the incredible ignominy. He who dealt in birth and fertility had married a barren woman. He whose walls were covered with pictures of babies who never should have been carried to term had no hope of becoming a father himself.

When had he started to hate Claire? It took a long time—seven years.

It was when he finally realized that she didn't care; had never cared; that her disappointment was faked; that she'd *known* before she married him that she could not conceive.

Impatiently he turned from the window. It would

be another cold, wind-filled night. Why did February, the shortest month of the year, always seem to be the longest one? When all this was over he'd take a vacation. He was getting edgy, losing grip on his nerves.

He had nearly given himself away this morning when Gertrude told him that Edna had phoned in sick. He'd grasped the desk, watched his knuckles whiten. Then he'd remembered. The fluttering pulse that had stopped beating, the unfocused eyes, the muscles relaxing in extremis. Gertrude was covering for her friend. *Gertrude was lying.*

He'd frowned at Gertrude. When he spoke he'd made his voice icy. "It is most inconvenient that Edna is absent today. I hope and expect that she will be here tomorrow."

It had worked. He could tell from the nervous licking of the lips, from Gertrude's averted eyes. She believed that he was furious at Edna's absence. She probably knew that he'd spoken sharply to Edna about her drinking.

Gertrude might prove to be an ally.

POLICE: And how did the doctor respond when you told him Miss Burns was absent?
GERTRUDE: He was quite angry. He's very methodical. He doesn't like anything that upsets the routine.

The missing shoe. This morning he'd gone to the hospital soon after dawn and once again searched the parking lot and the office. Had Vangie been wearing it when she came into his office Monday night? He realized that he couldn't be sure. She'd been wearing that long caftan, her winter coat buttoned awkwardly over it. The caftan was too large; the coat strained at the abdomen. She lifted the caftan to show him her swollen right leg. He'd seen the moccasin on that foot, but he'd never noticed the other shoe. Had she been wearing it? He simply didn't know.

If it had fallen off in the parking lot when he carried her body to the car, someone had picked it up. Maybe a maintenance man had seen it; discarded it. Often patients who were checking out had overflowing shopping bags, stuffed with cards or plants and last-minute personal items that didn't fit in the suitcase, and lost things between the hospital room and the parking lot. He'd inquired at the lost-and-found desk, but they had no footwear. It might simply have been thrown into the rubbish bag.

He thought about lifting Vangie out of the trunk of the car, carrying her past the shelves in her garage. They had been filled with garden tools. Was it possible that the looser shoe had perhaps brushed against something protruding? If it was found on a shelf in the garage, questions would be asked.

If Vangie did *not* have the shoe on when she left Fukhito's office, her stocking sole would have become soiled. But the portico between the offices was sheltered. If her left foot was badly soiled, he'd have noticed it when he laid her out on the bed.

The horror of finding that he was carrying the *right* shoe, the shoe that he had struggled to pull off Vangie's foot, had unnerved him. The more fool he. After the terrible, terrible risk.

The right shoe was in his bag in the trunk of the car. He wasn't sure whether to dispose of it—not until he was positive the other one wouldn't still show up.

Even if the police started an intensive investigation into the suicide, there was nothing that constituted evidence against him. Her file in the office could bear intensive professional scrutiny. Her true records, all the true records of the special cases, were in the wall safe here. He defied anyone to locate that safe. It wasn't even in the original plans of the house. Dr. Westlake had installed it personally. Only Winifred had known about it.

No one had any reason to suspect him—no one except Katie DeMaio. She'd been on the verge of telling him something when he'd mentioned the view from the hospital room, but she had changed her mind abruptly.

Fukhito had come in to him just as he was locking up tonight. Fukhito was nervous. He'd said, "Mrs. DeMaio was asking a lot of questions. Is it possible that they don't believe Mrs. Lewis committed suicide?"

"I really don't know." He'd enjoyed Fukhito's nervousness; understood the reason for it.

"That interview you gave to *Newsmaker* magazine; that's going to come out tomorrow, isn't it?"

He'd looked at Fukhito disdainfully. "Yes. But I assure you I gave the distinct impression I use a number of psychiatric consultants. Your name will not appear in the article."

Fukhito was not relieved. "Still, it's going to put the spotlight on this hospital; on us," he complained.

"On *yourself*—isn't that what you're saying, Doctor?"

He'd almost laughed aloud at the troubled, guilty look on Fukhito's face.

Now, finishing his Scotch, he realized that he had been overlooking another avenue of escape. If the police came to the conclusion that Vangie had been murdered; if they *did* investigate Westlake; it would be an easy matter to reluctantly suggest that they interrogate Dr. Fukhito. Especially in view of his past.

After all, Dr. Fukhito was the last person known to have seen Vangie Lewis alive.

♦ 23 ♦

After leaving Dr. Fukhito, Katie went to the east wing of the hospital for the transfusion. It was given to her in a curtained-off area near the emergency room. As she lay on top of a bed, her sleeve rolled back, the needle strapped in her arm, she tried to reconstruct her arrival at the hospital Monday night.

She thought she remembered being in this room, but she wasn't sure. The doctor who had sewed the cut in her arm looked in. "Hi, I thought I saw you at the desk. I see Dr. Highley ordered another transfusion. I hope you're looking into that low blood count."

"Yes. I'm under Dr. Highley's care."

"Fine. Let's take a look at that arm." He rebandaged it as she lay there. "Good job. Have to admit it myself. You won't have a scar to show your grandchildren."

"If I have any," Katie said. "Doctor, tell me, was I on this bed Monday night?"

"Yes, we had you in here after the X-rays. You don't remember?"

"It's all such a blur."

"You lost a lot of blood. You were in a pretty good state of shock."

"I see."

When the transfusion was finished, she remembered that Dr. Highley had told her not to drive for twenty minutes. She decided to go to the admitting office and fill out the necessary forms for an inpatient

117

stay. Then she wouldn't have to bother with them Friday evening.

When she left the hospital it was nearly six o'clock. She found herself automatically turning the car in the direction of Chapin River. Nonsense, she thought. You're having dinner with Molly and Bill tomorrow night. Forget about dropping in tonight.

The decision settled, she made a U-turn and drove to Palisades Parkway. She was getting hungry, and the thought of going home did not appeal to her. Who was the poet who had written on the joys of solitude and then had finished the poem with the lines "But do not go home alone after five. / Let someone be waiting there"?

Well, she had learned to cope with loneliness, had taught herself to genuinely enjoy a quiet evening of reading with the stereo playing.

The feeling of emptiness that came over her lately was something new.

She passed the restaurant where she and Richard had eaten the night before, and on impulse swung into the parking area. Tonight she'd try the other specialty, the *entrecôte*. Maybe in the warm, intimate, quiet restaurant she'd be able to think.

The proprietor recognized her and beamed with pleasure. "Good evening, madam. Dr. Carroll did not make a reservation, but I have a table near the fireplace. He is parking the car?"

She shook her head. "Just me tonight, I'm afraid."

For an instant the man looked embarrassed, but recovered quickly. "Then I suspect we have made a new and beautiful friend." He led her to a table near the one she had shared with Richard.

Nodding at the suggestion of a glass of Burgundy, Katie leaned back and felt the same sense of unwinding she'd experienced the night before. Now if she could just collect her thoughts, sort out the impressions that she'd received talking to Dr. Highley and Dr. Fukhito about Vangie Lewis.

Taking out her pad, she began to scan what she had jotted down during the interviews. Dr. Highley. She'd expected him to explain or defend the fact that Vangie Lewis was obviously in serious trouble with her pregnancy. He had done exactly that, and what he told her was completely reasonable. He was going day by day to buy the baby time. The remarks he'd made about Vangie's reaction to the impending birth rang true. She'd heard from Molly the story of Vangie's hysterical reaction to a blister on the finger.

What then? What more did she want of Dr. Highley? She thought of Dr. Wainwright, the cancer specialist in New York, who had taken care of John. After John died, he'd spoken to her, his face and voice filled with pain. "I want you to know, Mrs. DeMaio, we tried everything possible to save him. Nothing was left undone. But sometimes God takes it out of our hands."

Dr. Highley had expressed regret over Vangie's death, but certainly not sorrow. But of course, he had to stay objective. She'd heard Bill and Richard discussing the need to stay objective when you practice medicine. Otherwise you'd constantly be torn in two and end up useless.

Richard. Inadvertently her eyes slid over to the table where she'd been with him. He'd said, "We both know we could enjoy each other." He was right. She did know it. Maybe that was why she usually felt unsettled with him, as though things could be taken out of her hands. Is it possible that it could happen twice in a lifetime? From the very beginning you *know* something is right, someone is right.

When she and Richard were leaving Molly's after that quick lunch yesterday, Molly had asked them both to dinner Thursday night—tomorrow. Molly said, "Liz and Jim Berkeley are coming over. She's the one who thinks Dr. Highley is God. You two might be interested in talking with her."

Katie realized how much she was looking forward to that dinner.

Again she looked down at her notes. Dr. Fukhito. Something was wrong there. It seemed to her that he'd deliberately weighed every word he said when he'd discussed Vangie's Monday-night visit. It had been like watching someone step by step through a mined field. What was he afraid of? Even allowing for the reasonable concern of protecting the doctor-patient relationship, he'd been afraid he would say something that she would pounce on.

Then he'd been openly hostile when she asked if by any chance Vangie might still have been in the hospital at ten o'clock when she, Katie, was brought in.

Suppose she *had* glimpsed Vangie? Suppose Vangie had been just leaving Dr. Fukhito's office; had been walking somewhere in the parking lot? That would explain seeing her face in that crazy nightmare.

Dr. Fukhito had said that Vangie left by his private entrance.

No one had seen her go.

Suppose she *hadn't* left? Suppose she'd stayed with the doctor. Suppose he'd left with her or followed her home. Suppose he'd realized that she was suicidal, that he was responsible in some way . . .

Enough to make him nervous.

The waiter arrived to take her order. Before she put away the pad, Katie made one final note: *Investigate Dr. Fukhito's background.*

◆ 24 ◆

Even before he crossed the George Washington Bridge and drove down the Harlem River and FDR Drive Wednesday evening, Richard knew that he should have cancelled the date with Clovis. He was preoccupied about Vangie Lewis' death; his subconscious was suggesting that he had missed something in the autopsy. There had been something he'd intended to examine more closely. What was it?

And he was worried about Katie. She had looked so thin last night. She'd been extremely pale. It wasn't until she'd had a couple of glasses of wine that some color had come into her face.

Katie wasn't well. That was it. He was a doctor and should have spotted it sooner.

That accident. How carefully had she been examined? Was it possible that she'd been hurt more than anyone realized? The thought haunted Richard as he turned onto the Fifty-third Street exit from the FDR Drive and headed for Clovis' apartment one block away.

Clovis had a pitcher of very dry martinis waiting to be poured and a plate of hot crabmeat-filled puffs fresh from the oven. With her flawless skin, tall, slender body and Viking coloring, she reminded Richard of a young Ingrid Bergman. Until recently he'd toyed with the idea that they might end up together. Clovis was intelligent, interesting and good-tempered.

But as he returned her kiss with honest affection, he

121

was acutely aware that he'd never worry about Clovis the way he now found himself worrying about Katie DeMaio.

He realized Clovis was talking to him. ". . . and I'm not home ten minutes. The rehearsal ran over. There was a lot of rewriting. So I fixed the drinks and nibbles and figured you could relax while I get dressed. Hey, are you listening to me?"

Richard accepted the drink and smiled apologetically. "I'm sorry. I'm on a case that won't let go. Do you mind if I make a couple of calls while you're getting ready?"

"Of course I don't mind," Clovis said. "Go ahead and dial away." She picked up her glass and started toward the foyer that led into the bedroom and bath.

Richard took his credit card from his wallet and dialed the operator. There was no way he was going to put a call to one woman on another woman's phone bill. Quickly he gave his account number to the operator. When the connection went through, he allowed the phone to ring a dozen times before he finally gave up. Katie wasn't home.

Next he tried Molly's house. Probably Katie had stopped there. But Molly had not spoken to her at all today.

"I don't really expect her," Molly said. "You're both coming tomorrow night. Don't forget that. She'll probably call me later. But I wish she'd gone home by now. She could stand taking it easy."

It was the opening he needed. "Molly, what's the matter with Katie?" he asked. "There is something wrong physically, isn't there? Besides the accident, I mean?"

Molly hesitated. "I think you'd better talk to Katie about that."

Certainty. Cold fear washed over him.

"Molly, I want to know. *What's the matter with her?*"

"Oh, not much," Molly said hastily. "I promise you that. But it's nothing she wanted to discuss. And now I've probably said more than I should. See you tomorrow."

The connection broke. Richard frowned into the dead receiver. He started to replace it on the cradle, then on impulse put through a call to his office. He spoke to the assistant on the evening shift. "Anything unusual going on?" he asked.

"We just got a call for the wagon. A body was found in an apartment in Edgeriver. Probably an accident, but the local police thought we'd better take a look. Scott's people are heading over there."

"Switch me to Scott's office," Richard said.

Scott did not waste time on preliminaries. "Where are you?" he demanded.

"In New York. Do you need me?"

"Yes. This woman who was found in Edgeriver is the receptionist Katie wanted to talk to today at Westlake. Name's Edna Burns. Supposedly she phoned in sick today, but there's no question she's been dead a good twenty-four hours. Body was found by a co-worker from Westlake. I'm trying to get Katie. I'd like her to go over there."

"Give me the address," Richard said.

He wrote it quickly and hung up the phone. Katie had wanted to question this Edna Burns about Vangie Lewis, and now Edna Burns was dead. He knocked on Clovis' bedroom door. She opened it, wrapped in a terry-cloth robe. "Hey, what's the hurry?" she asked, smiling. "I just got out of the shower."

"Clo, I'm sorry." Quickly he explained. Now he was frantic to get away.

She was clearly disappointed. "Oh, of course I

understand, but I was counting on seeing you. It's been a couple of weeks—you do know that. All right. Go, but let's have dinner tomorrow night. Promise?"

Richard temporized. "Well, very soon." He started to leave, but she caught him by the arm and pulled his face down for a kiss.

"Tomorrow night," she told him firmly.

◆ 25 ◆

On the way home from the restaurant, Katie turned over in her mind the conversation she'd had with Edna Burns on her first visit to Dr. Highley. Edna was a born listener. Katie was not given to discussing her personal affairs, but when Edna took the preliminary information, she had clucked sympathetically. Not quite believing her own ears, Katie had heard herself telling Edna all about John.

How much had *Vangie* told Edna? She'd been going to Westlake since last summer. How much did Edna know about Dr. Fukhito? There was something oddly intimidating about his nervousness. Why should he be nervous?

Katie pulled up in front of her house and decided not to put the car away yet. It was Wednesday and Mrs. Hodges had been here. The house smelled faintly of lemon wax. The mirror over the antique marble table in the hall was shining. Katie knew her bed had been made with fresh linen; the ceramic kitchen tile would be gleaming; the furniture and rugs had been vacuumed; her laundry would be back in the drawers or closet.

Mrs. Hodges had worked full time when John was alive. Now pensioned off, she'd begged for the chance to come in one day a week and take care of "my house."

It wouldn't last much longer. It couldn't. Mrs. Hodges was past seventy now.

Whom would she get when Mrs. Hodges no longer came in? Who would exercise the same care with the valuable bric-a-brac, the antiques, the English furniture, the lovely old Orientals?

"It's time to sell," Katie thought. "I know it."

Taking off her coat, she tossed it on a chair. It was only a quarter of eight. The night loomed long ahead of her. Edna had told her that she lived in Edgeriver. That was less than twenty minutes' drive away. Suppose she phoned Edna now? Suppose she suggested driving down to see her? Mrs. Fitzgerald had said that Edna was expected at work tomorrow, so she couldn't be too sick. If Katie was any judge, Edna would love a chance to gossip about Vangie Lewis.

Mrs. Hodges always left a freshly baked cake or pie or muffins in the bread box for Katie. She'd take whatever was there now down to Edna and have a cup of tea with her. A lot of gossip could be exchanged over a teapot.

Edna was listed in the telephone book. Quickly Katie dialed her number. It rang once and the receiver was picked up. She formed the words "Hello, Miss Burns," but never got to speak them.

A man's voice said, "Yes." The short word was delivered in a clipped, not-unfamiliar voice.

"Is Miss Burns there?" Katie asked. "This is Mrs. DeMaio from the Prosecutor's office."

"Katie!"

Now she recognized the voice. It was Charley Nugent, and he was saying, "Glad Scott got in touch with you. Can you come right down?"

"Come down?" Afraid of what she'd hear, Katie asked the question: "What are you doing at Edna Burns's apartment?"

"Don't you know? She's dead, Katie. Fell—or was pushed—into the radiator. Split her head open." His voice lowered. "Get this, Katie. She was last seen alive around eight o'clock last night. A neighbor was with her." His voice became a whisper. "The neighbor heard her on the phone with Vangie Lewis' husband. Edna Burns told Chris Lewis that she was going to talk to the police about Vangie's death."

◆ 26 ◆

After he finished the second Scotch he went into the kitchen and opened the refrigerator. He had told Hilda not to prepare anything for him tonight, but had given her a long shopping list. He nodded in approval at the new items in the meat drawer: the boneless breasts of chicken, the filet mignon, the double loin lamb chops. Fresh asparagus, tomatoes and watercress were in the vegetable bin. Brie and Jarlsberg were in the cheesebox. Tonight he'd have the lamb chops, asparagus and a watercress salad.

Emotional exhaustion always compelled him to eat. The night Claire died, he'd left the hospital, to all outward appearances a husband benumbed with grief, and had gone to a quiet restaurant a dozen blocks away and eaten heavily. Then he'd trudged home masking an acute sense of well-being with the weary posture of the grief-stricken. The friends who were gathered waiting to greet him, to commiserate with him had been deceived.

"Where were you, Edgar? We were worried about you."

"I don't know. I don't remember. I've just been walking."

It had been the same after Winifred's death. He'd left her relatives and friends at the grave site, refused invitations to join them for dinner. "No. No. I need to be alone." He'd come back to the house, waited long enough to answer a few phone calls, then contacted the answering service. "If anyone phones, please explain that I'm resting and that I'll return all calls later."

Then he'd gotten into the car and driven to the Carlyle in New York. There he had requested a quiet table and ordered dinner. Halfway through the meal he looked up and saw Winifred's cousin, Glenn Nickerson, across the room—Glenn, the high school athletic coach who had been Winifred's heir until he came along. Glenn was dressed in the dark blue suit and black tie he'd worn to the funeral, a bargain-priced, ill-fitting suit obviously bought specially for the occasion. His normal garb was a sports jacket, slacks and loafers.

Nickerson was obviously watching him. He'd lifted his glass in a toast, a mocking smile on his face. He might as well have shouted his thoughts: "To the grieving widower."

He'd done what was necessary: walked over to him without the slightest sign of distress and spoken pleasantly. "Glenn, why didn't you join me when you saw I was here? I didn't realize you came to the Carlyle. This was a favorite dining spot of ours. We became engaged here—or did Winifred ever tell you that? I'm not Jewish, but I think that one of the most beautiful customs in this bewildering world is that of the Jewish faith, where after a death the family eats eggs to symbolize the continuity of life. I am here to quietly celebrate the continuity of love."

Glenn had stared at him, his expression stony. Then he'd stood up and signaled for his check. "I admire your ability to philosophize, Edgar," he said. "No. I don't consider the Carlyle one of my regular eating spots. I simply followed you here because I had decided to visit you and reached your block just as your car pulled out. I had the feeling it might be interesting to keep an eye on you. How right I was."

He'd turned his back on Glenn, walked with dignity back to his own table and not glanced in his direction again. A few minutes later he'd seen Glenn at the door of the dining room on his way out.

The next week, Alan Levine, the doctor who'd treated Winifred, indignantly told him that Glenn had asked to see Winifred's medical records.

"I threw him out of my office," Alan said heatedly. "I told him that Winifred had developed classic angina symptoms and that he would do himself a favor if he studied the current statistics on women in their early fifties' having heart attacks. Even so, he had the gall to speak to the police. I had a call from the Prosecutor's office asking in so many words if a heart ailment could be induced. I told them that being alive today was enough to induce heart trouble. They backed off immediately, said it was obviously a disinherited relative trying to cause trouble."

But you *can* induce heart trouble, Dr. Levine. You can prepare intimate little dinners for your dear wife. You can use her susceptibility to gastroenteritis to bring on attacks so strong that they register as heart seizures on her cardiogram. After enough of these the lady apparently has a fatal seizure. She dies in the presence of her own physician, who arrives to find the physician husband applying mouth-to-mouth resuscitation. No one suggests an autopsy. And even if someone had, there would have been little risk.

The only risk would have occurred if they had thought to delve into Claire's death.

The chops were nearly cooked. He expertly seasoned the watercress, removed the asparagus from the steamer and took a half-bottle of Beaujolais from the wine rack in the pantry.

He had just begun to eat when the phone rang. He debated ignoring it, then decided that at this time it was dangerous to miss any calls. Slapping his napkin on the table, he hurried to the extension in the kitchen. "Dr. Highley," he said curtly.

A sob sounded over the phone. "Doctor—oh, Dr. Highley. It's Gertrude, Gertrude Fitzgerald. Doctor, I decided to go see Edna on my way home."

He tightened his grip on the receiver.

"Doctor, Edna is dead. The police are here. She fell. Doctor, could you come here right away? They're talking about performing an autopsy. She always hated autopsies. She used to say how terrible it was to cut up dead people. Doctor, you know how Edna was when she drank. I told them that you've been here in her apartment; that you've caught her drinking. Doctor, come here and tell them how you would find her sometimes. Oh, please come here and convince them that she fell and that they don't have to cut her up."

Before she left the house, Katie made a cup of tea and carried it to the car. Driving with one hand, she held the bubbling liquid to her lips with the other. She'd planned to bring cake down to Edna and have tea with her. And now Edna was dead.

How could a person she'd met only once have made such an impression on her? Was it simply that Edna was such a good person, so truly concerned with the patients? So many people were so indifferent, so non-caring. In that one conversation with Edna last month, it had been so easy to talk about John.

And Edna had understood. She'd said, "I know what it is to watch someone die. On the one hand, you want the misery to be over for them. On the other hand you don't want to let them go." She'd shared the aftermath of loss. "When both Mom and Dad died, all my friends said, 'Now you're free, Edna.' And I said, 'Free for what?' And I bet you felt that way too."

Edna reassured her about Dr. Highley. "You couldn't find a better doctor for any GYN problem. That's why it makes me so mad when I hear him criticized. And all those people who file malpractice suits! Let me tell you, I could shoot them myself. That's the trouble when people think you're God. They think you can do the impossible. I tell you when a doctor loses a patient today, he has to worry. And I don't just mean obstetricians. I mean geriatric doctors too. I guess nobody's supposed to die anymore."

What had Charley meant by telling her that Edna

had phoned Chris Lewis last night? In practically the same breath Charley had suggested the possibility of foul play.

"I don't believe it," Katie said aloud as she turned off Route 4 onto Edgeriver. It would be like Edna to call Chris Lewis to express her sympathy. Was Charley suggesting Edna might have in some way *threatened* Chris Lewis?

She had a vague idea of where the apartment development was and was able to find it easily. She mused that as garden apartments went, this one was getting somewhat rundown. When she sold the house she'd probably move into a high-rise for a while. There were some buildings overlooking the Hudson that had lovely apartments with terraces. And it would be interesting to be near New York. She'd be more likely to go to the theater and museums. *When* I sell the house, she thought. At what point did *if* become *when?*

Charley had told her that Edna's apartment was the last one in units 41 through 60. He'd said to drive behind that row and park. She slowed down, realizing that a car had entered the development from another road and was pulling into that same area ahead of her. It was a black medium-sized car. For a moment the driver hesitated, then chose the first parking spot available on the right. Katie pulled around him. If Edna's apartment was the end one on the left, she'd try to get closer to it. She found a spot directly behind that building and parked. She got out of the car, realizing that she must be looking at the back window of Edna's apartment. The window was raised an inch. The shade was pulled down to the top of a plant. A faint light could be seen from inside the apartment.

Katie thought of the view from her bedroom windows. They looked over the little pond in the woods behind the house. Edna had gazed out at a parking area and a rusting chain-link fence. Yet she had told Katie how much she enjoyed her apartment, how cozy it was.

Katie heard footsteps behind her and turned quickly. In the lonely parking area, any sound seemed menacing. A figure loomed near her, a silhouette accentuated by the dim light from the solitary lamppost. A sense of familiarity struck her.

"Excuse me. I hope I didn't startle you." The cultured voice had a faint English accent.

"Dr. Highley!"

"Mrs. DeMaio. We didn't expect to see each other so soon and under such tragic circumstances."

"Then you've heard. Did my office call you, Doctor?"

"It's chilly. Here. Let's take this footpath around the building." Barely touching her elbow with his hand, he followed her on the path. "Mrs. Fitzgerald called me. She substituted for Miss Burns today and evidently she was the one to find her. She sounded terribly upset and begged me to come. I don't have any details of what happened as yet."

"Neither do I," Katie replied. They were turning the corner to the front of the building when she heard rapid footsteps behind them.

"Katie."

She felt the pressure of the doctor's fingers on her elbow tighten and then release as she looked back. Richard was there. She turned, absurdly glad to see him. He grasped both her shoulders. In a gesture that ended even as it began, he pulled her to him. Then his hands dropped. "Scott reached you?"

"No. I happened to call Edna myself. Oh, Richard, this is Dr. Edgar Highley." Quickly she introduced the two men, and they shook hands.

Katie thought, How absurd this is. I am making

introductions and a few feet inside that door a woman is lying dead.

Charley let them in. He looked relieved to see them. "Your people should be here in a couple of minutes," he told Richard. "We've got pictures, but I'd like you to have a look too."

Katie was used to death. In the course of her job, she constantly held up vivid and gory pictures of crime victims. She was usually able to separate herself from the emotional aspect and concentrate on the legal ramifications of wrongful death.

But it was a different matter to see Edna crumpled against the radiator in the kind of flannel nightgown her own mother considered indispensable; to see the blue terry-cloth robe so like the ones her mother used to pick up on sale at Macy's; to see the solid evidence of loneliness—the slices of canned ham, the empty cocktail glass.

Edna had been such a cheery person, who found some small measure of happiness in this shabbily furnished apartment, and even the apartment had betrayed her. It had become the scene of her violent death.

Gertrude Fitzgerald was sitting on the old-fashioned velour couch at the opposite end of the L-shaped room, out of sight of the body. She was sobbing softly. Richard went directly into the dinette to examine the dead woman. Katie walked over to Mrs. Fitzgerald and sat beside her on the couch. Dr. Highley followed her and pulled up a straightbacked chair.

Gertrude tried to talk to them. "Oh, Dr. Highley, Mrs. DeMaio, isn't this terrible, just terrible?" The words brought a fresh burst of sobs. Katie gently put a hand on the trembling shoulders. "I'm so sorry, Mrs. Fitzgerald. I know you were fond of Miss Burns."

"She was always so nice. Such fun. She always made me laugh. And maybe she had that little weakness. Everybody has a little weakness, and she never bothered anyone with it. Oh, Dr. Highley, you'll miss her too."

Katie watched as the doctor bent over Gertrude, his face grave. "I surely will, Mrs. Fitzgerald. Edna was a marvelously efficient person. She took so much pride in her work. Dr. Fukhito and I used to joke that she had our patients so relaxed by the time we saw them that she could have put Dr. Fukhito out of his job."

"Doctor," Gertrude blurted out, "I told them you've been here. I told them that. You knew Edna's little problem. It's just silly to say she didn't fall. Why would anyone want to hurt her?"

Dr. Highley looked at Katie. "Edna suffered from sciatica, and when she was laid up I occasionally dropped off work for her to do at home. Certainly not more than three or four times. On one occasion when she was supposed to be ill, I came here unexpectedly and it was then I realized that she had a serious drinking problem."

Katie looked past him and realized that Richard had completed examining the body. She got up, walked over to him and looked at Edna. Silently she prayed:

Eternal rest grant unto her, Oh Lord. May legions of angels greet her. May she be conducted to a place of refreshment, light and peace.

Swallowing over the sudden lump in her throat, she quietly asked Richard what he had found.

He shrugged. "Until I have had a chance to see how bad the fracture is, I'd say it could go either way. Certainly it was a hell of a smash, but if she was drunk—and it's obvious she was—she might have stumbled when she tried to get up. She was a pretty heavy woman. On the other hand, there's a big difference between being run over by a car and by a train. And that's the kind of difference we have to evaluate."

"Any sign of forced entry?" Katie asked Charley.

"None. But these locks are the kind you could spring with a credit card. And if she was as drunk as we think she was, anyone could have walked in on her."

"Why would anyone walk in on her? What were you telling me about Captain Lewis?"

"The superintendent's wife—name's Gana Krupshak—was a buddy of Edna Burns. Fact is, she was with Mrs. Fitzgerald when the body was found. We let her go to her own apartment just before you came. She's shook up bad. Anyhow, last night she came over here around eight o'clock. She said Edna already had a bag on. She stayed till eight thirty, then decided to put out the ham, hoping Edna would eat something and start to sober up. Edna told her about Vangie's suicide."

"Exactly *what* did she tell her?" Katie asked.

"Nothing much. Just mentioned Vangie's name and how pretty she'd been. Then Mrs. Krupshak went into the kitchen and she heard Edna dialing the phone. Mrs. Krupshak could hear most of the conversation. She swears Edna called whoever she was talking to 'Captain Lewis' and told him she had to talk to the police tomorrow. And get this. Krupshak swears she heard Edna give Lewis directions for driving here and then Edna said something about Prince Charming."

"Prince Charming!"

Charley shrugged. "Your guess is as good as mine. But the witness is positive."

Richard said, "Obviously we'll treat this as a potential homicide. I'm beginning to agree with Scott's hunch about Chris Lewis." He glanced into the living room. "Mrs. Fitzgerald looks pretty washed out. Are you through talking to her, Katie?"

"Yes. She's in no condition to question now."

"I'll get one of the squad cars to drive her home," Charley volunteered. "One of the other guys can follow in her car."

Katie thought, I do not believe Chris Lewis could have done this to Edna; I don't believe he killed his wife. She looked around. "Are you *sure* there's nothing valuable missing?"

Charley shrugged. "This whole place would go for about forty bucks in a garage sale. Her wallet's in her pocketbook; eighteen dollars there. Credit cards. The usual. No sign of anything being disturbed, let alone ransacked."

"All right." Katie returned to Dr. Highley and Gertrude. "We're going to have you driven home, Mrs. Fitzgerald," she said gently.

"What are they going to do to Edna?"

"They must investigate the extent of her head injuries. I don't think they'll probe beyond that. But if there is even the faintest chance that someone did this to Edna, we have to know it. Think of it as a way of showing we valued her life."

The woman sniffled. "I guess you're right." She looked at the doctor. "Dr. Highley, I had an awful nerve asking you to come here. I'm sorry."

"Not at all." He was reaching into his pocket. "I brought these sedatives along in case you needed them. As long as you're being driven home, take one right now."

"I'll get a glass of water," Katie said. She went to the sink in the bathroom. The bathroom and bedroom were off a rear foyer. As she let the water run cold, she realized that she hated the idea that Chris Lewis was emerging as a prime suspect in two deaths.

Taking the water glass back to Gertrude, she again sat beside her. "Mrs. Fitzgerald, just to satisfy ourselves, we want to be positive there's no possibility of Edna's having been robbed. Do you know if she kept any valuables—any jewelry, perhaps?"

"Oh, she had a ring and a pin she was so proud of. She only wore them on special occasions. I wouldn't know where she kept them. This is the first time I've been here, you see. Oh, wait a minute. Doctor, I remember that Edna said she showed you her ring and pin. In fact, she told me she showed you her hiding place for them when you were here. Perhaps you can help Mrs. DeMaio."

Katie looked into the cold gray eyes. He hates this, she thought. He's really angry to be here. He doesn't want to be part of this.

Had Edna had a crush on the doctor? she wondered suddenly. Had she exaggerated the number of times he might have dropped off work, maybe even hinted to Gertrude that he was a little interested in her? Maybe without even meaning to shade the truth, she'd invented a little romance, fantasized a possible relationship with him. If so, it was no wonder Mrs. Fitzgerald had rushed to summon him, no wonder he looked acutely embarrassed and uncomfortable now.

"I really don't know of hiding places," he said, his voice stiff with an undercurrent of sarcasm. "One time Edna did show me a pin and ring that were in a box in her night-table drawer. I hardly consider that a hiding place."

"Would you show me, Doctor?" Katie asked.

Together they walked down the short foyer into the bedroom. Katie switched on the lamp, a cheap ginger-jar base with a pleated paper shade.

"It was in there," Dr. Highley told her, pointing to the drawer in the night table on the right side of the bed.

137

Using only the very tips of her fingers, Katie opened the drawer. She knew that there'd probably be a complete search for evidence and the fingerprint experts would be called in.

The drawer was unexpectedly deep. Reaching into it, Katie pulled out a blue plastic jewelry case. When she raised the lid, the bell-like tinkle of a music box intruded on the somber silence. A small brooch and a thin old diamond ring were nestled against cotton velvet.

"Those are the treasures, I guess," Katie said, "and that, I would imagine, eliminates the robbery theory. We'll keep this in the office until we know who the next of kin is." She started to close the drawer, then stopped and looked down into it.

"Oh, Doctor, look." Hastily she set the jewelry box on the bed and reached into the drawer.

"My mother used to keep her mother's old battered black hat for sentimental reasons," she said. "Edna must have done the same thing."

She was tugging at an object, pulling it out, holding it up for him to see.

It was a brown moccasin, heavily scuffed, badly worn, battered and shabby. It was shaped for the left foot.

As Dr. Edgar Highley stared at the shoe, Katie said, "This was probably her mother's and she considered it such a treasure she kept it with that pathetic jewelry. Oh, Doctor, if memorabilia could talk, we'd have a lot of stories to hear, wouldn't we?"

♦ 28 ♦

At precisely eight A.M. Thursday morning, the Investigative Squad of the Homicide Division of Valley County pulled up to the Lewis home. The six-man team was headed by Phil Cunningham and Charley Nugent. The detectives in charge of fingerprinting were told to concentrate on the bedroom, master bath and kitchen.

It was admittedly a slim possibility that they would find significant fingerprints that did not belong to either Chris or Vangie Lewis. But the lab report had raised another question. Vangie's fingerprints were on the tumbler that had been lying next to her, but there was some question about the positioning of those prints. Vangie had been right-handed. When she poured the cyanide crystals into the glass, it would have been natural for her to hold the glass with her left hand and pour with her right. But only her right prints were on the tumbler. It was an inconclusive, troublesome fact that further discredited the apparent suicide.

The medicine chests in both bathrooms and the guest powder room had already been searched after the body was found. Once again they were examined in minute detail. Every bottle was opened, sniffed. But the bitter-almond scent they were looking for was not to be found.

Charley said, "She must have kept the cyanide in *something.*"

"Unless she was carrying just the amount she used

139

in the glass and then flushed the envelopes or capsule she had it in down the john?" Phil suggested.

The bedroom was carefully vacuumed in the hope of finding human hair that did not come from the head of either Vangie or Chris. As Phil put it: "Any house can have hairs from delivery people, neighbors, anybody. We're all shedding hair all the time. But most people don't bring even good friends into the bedroom. So if you find human hair that doesn't belong to the people who sleep in the bedroom, you just might have something."

Particular attention was given to the shelves in the garage. The usual half-empty cans of paint, turpentine, some garden tools, hoses, insecticides, rose powder and weed killer were there in abundance. Phil grunted in annoyance as the prong of a hand spade pulled at his jacket. That prong had been protruding over the edge of the shelf, its handle wedged into place between the end of the shelf and a heavy paint can. Bending to free his sleeve, he noticed a sliver of printed cotton hooked on the prong.

That print. He'd seen it recently. It was that faded Indian stuff; madras. The dress Vangie Lewis was wearing when she died.

He called the police photographer out to the garage. "Get a picture of that," he said, pointing to the tool. "I want a close-up of that material." When the picture was taken, he carefully removed the piece of material from the prong and sealed it in an envelope.

In the house, Charley was going through the desk in the living room. Funny, he thought. You can get a real slant on people from the way they keep their records. Chris Lewis obviously had taken care of all the bookkeeping in the family. The checkbook stubs were precisely written, the balances accurate to the penny. Bills were apparently paid in full as they came in. The large bottom drawer held upright files. They were alphabetically arranged: AMERICAN EXPRESS; BANK AMERICARD; FEDERATED ANSWERING SERVICE; INSURANCE; PERSONAL LETTERS.

Charley reached for the personal-letter file. Quickly he leafed through it. Chris Lewis maintained a regular correspondence with his mother. *Many thanks for the check, Chris. You shouldn't be so generous.* That was written only two weeks ago. A January letter began: *Got Dad the TV for the bedroom and he's enjoying it so much.* One from last July: *The new air conditioner is such a blessing.*

If Charley was disappointed at not finding more significant personal data, he did admit grudgingly that Christopher Lewis was a concerned and generous son to aging parents. He reread the mother's letters, hoping for clues to Vangie and Chris's relationship. The recent letters all ended the same way: *Sorry Vangie isn't feeling well* or *Women do sometimes have difficult pregnancies* or *Tell Vangie we're rooting for her.*

At noon, Charley and Phil decided to leave the rest of the team to complete the search and return to the office themselves. They were scheduled to meet Chris Lewis' plane at six o'clock. They had ruled out forced entry. There was no trace of cyanide in the house or garage. The contents of Vangie's stomach revealed that she'd eaten lightly on Monday; that she had probably had toast and tea about five hours before she died. A new loaf of bread in the bread box had two slices missing. The soiled dishes in the dishwasher told their own story: a single dinner plate, cup and saucer, salad dish, probably from Sunday night; a juice glass and cup, Monday's breakfast; a cup, saucer and plate with toast crumbs from the Monday supper.

Vangie had apparently dined alone Sunday night;

no one had eaten with her Monday night. The coffee mug in the sink had not been there Tuesday morning. Undoubtedly Chris Lewis had made himself instant coffee sometime after the body was found.

The driveway and grounds were being searched with minute care and so far revealed nothing unusual.

"They'll be at this all day, but we haven't missed anything," Charley said flatly. "And other than the fact that she tore her dress on that prong on the garage shelf, we've come up with a big zero. Wait a minute. We still haven't checked the answering service for messages."

He got the Federated Answering Service number from the file in the desk, dialed and identified himself. "Give me any messages left for either Captain or Mrs. Lewis starting with Monday," he ordered.

Taking out his pen, he began to write. Phil looked over his shoulder: *Monday, February 15, 4:00 P.M. Northwest Orient Reservations phoned. Mrs. Lewis is confirmed on Flight 235 at 4:10 P.M. from LaGuardia Airport to the Twin Cities of Minneapolis/St. Paul on Tuesday, February 16.*

Phil whistled silently. Charley asked, "Did Mrs. Lewis receive that message?"

He held the phone slightly away from his ear so that Phil could hear. "Oh, yes," the operator said. "I was on the board myself Monday evening and gave it to her at about seven thirty." The operator's voice was emphatic. "She sounded very relieved. In fact, she said, 'Oh, thank God.'"

"All right," Charley said. "What else have you got?"

"Monday, February fifteenth, nine thirty P.M. Dr. Fukhito left word for Mrs. Lewis to call him at home as soon as she got in. He said she had his home number."

Charley raised one eyebrow. "Is that it?"

"Just one more," the operator replied. "A Miss

Edna Burns called Mrs. Lewis at ten P.M. Monday. She wanted Mrs. Lewis to be sure and phone her no matter how late it was."

Charley doodled triangles on the pad as the operator told him that there were no further messages on the service for either Tuesday or Wednesday, but that she knew a call had come through Tuesday evening and had been picked up by Captain Lewis. "I was just starting to answer when he came on," she explained. "I got right off." In reply to Charley's question, she affirmed that Mrs. Lewis had not learned about either Dr. Fukhito's or Miss Burns's call. Mrs. Lewis had not contacted the service after seven thirty on Monday night.

"Thank you," Charley said. "You've been very helpful. We'll probably want a complete file of messages you've taken for the Lewises going back some time, but we'll be in touch about that later on."

He hung up the receiver and looked at Phil. "Let's go. Scott's going to want to hear all about this."

"How do you read it?" Phil asked.

Charley snorted. "How else can I read it? As of seven thirty Monday evening Vangie Lewis was planning to go to Minneapolis. A couple of hours later she's dead. As of ten o'clock Monday night, Edna Burns had an important message for Vangie. The next night Edna's dead and the last person who saw her alive heard her talking to Chris Lewis telling him she had information for the police."

"What about that Japanese shrink who called Vangie Monday night?" Phil asked.

Charley shrugged. "Katie talked to him yesterday. She may have some answers for us."

29

For Katie, Wednesday night seemed endless. She'd gone to bed as soon as she returned from Edna's apartment, remembering first to take one of the pills Dr. Highley had given her.

She'd slept fitfully, her subconscious restless with images of Vangie's face floating through a dream. Before she woke up, that dream dissolved into a new one: Edna's face as it had looked in death; Dr. Highley and Richard bending over her.

She'd awakened with vague, troubling questions that eluded her, refusing to come into focus. Her grandmother's battered old black hat. Why was she thinking about that hat? Of course. Because of that shabby old shoe Edna obviously prized; the one she had kept with her jewelry. That was it. But why just *one* shoe?

Grimacing as she got out of bed, she decided that the soreness throughout her body had intensified during the night. Her knees, bruised from slamming into the dashboard, felt stiffer now than they had right after the accident. I'm glad the Boston Marathon isn't being run today, she thought wryly. I'd never win.

Hoping that a hot bath might soak some of the achiness away, she went into the bathroom, leaned down and turned on the taps in the tub. A wave of dizziness made her sway, and she grabbed the side of the tub to keep from falling. After a few moments the sensation receded, and she turned slowly, afraid that she might still faint. The bathroom mirror revealed the deathly pallor of her skin, the faint beads of perspiration on her forehead. It's this damn bleeding, she thought. If I weren't going into the hospital tomorrow night, I'd probably end up being carried in.

The bath did reduce some of the stiffness. Beige foundation makeup minimized the paleness. A new outfit—a shirred skirt and matching jacket in heather tweed and a crew-neck sweater—completed the attempt at camouflage. At least now I don't look as though I'm about to fall on my face, she decided, even if I am.

With her orange juice she swallowed another of Dr. Highley's pills and thought about the still-incredible fact of Edna's death. After they left Edna's apartment, she and Richard had gone to a diner for coffee. Richard ordered a hamburger, explaining that he'd planned to have dinner in New York. He'd been taking someone out. She was sure of it. And why not? Richard was an attractive man. He certainly didn't spend all his evenings sitting in his own apartment or in family situations at Molly and Bill's. Richard had been surprised and pleased when she told him that she'd gone back to the Palisades restaurant. Then he'd become preoccupied, almost absentminded. Several times he'd seemed to be on the verge of asking her a question, then apparently changed his mind. Even though she protested, he'd insisted on following her home, going into the house with her, checking that doors and windows were locked.

"I don't know why I feel uncomfortable about you alone in this place," he'd told her.

She'd shrugged. "Edna was in a garden apartment with thin walls. No one realized she was hurt and needed help."

"She didn't," Richard said shortly. "She died almost instantly. Katie, that Dr. Highley. You know him?"

145

"I questioned him about Vangie this afternoon," she'd hedged.

Richard's frown had lightened. "Of course. All right. See you tomorrow. I imagine Scott will call a meeting about Edna Burns."

"I'm sure he will."

Richard had looked at her, his expression troubled. "Bolt the door," he'd said. There had been no light-hearted good-bye kiss on the cheek.

Katie put her orange-juice glass in the dishwasher. Hurriedly she grabbed a coat and her handbag and went out to the car.

Charley and Phil were beginning the search of the Lewis house this morning. Scott was consciously drawing a web around Chris Lewis—a circumstantial web, but a strong one. If only she could prove that there was another avenue to explore before Chris was indicted. The trouble with being arrested on a homicide charge is that even if you prove your innocence, you never lose the notoriety. In years to come people would be saying, "Oh, that's Captain Lewis. He was involved in his wife's death. Some smart lawyer got him off, but he's guilty as sin."

She arrived at the office just before seven thirty and wasn't surprised to find Maureen Crowley already there. Maureen was the most conscientious secretary they had. Beyond that, she had a naturally keen mind and could handle assignments without constantly asking for direction. Katie stopped at her desk. "Maureen, I've got a job. Could you come in when you have a minute?"

The girl got up quickly. She had a narrow-waisted, graceful young body. The green sweater she was wearing accentuated the vivid green of her eyes. "How about now, Katie? Want coffee?"

"Great," Katie replied, then added, "but no ham on rye—at least, not yet."

Maureen looked embarrassed. "I'm sorry I said that yesterday. You, of all people, are not in a rut."

"I'm not sure about that." Katie went into her office, hung up her coat and settled down with the pad she'd used at Westlake Hospital.

Maureen brought in the coffee, pulled up a chair and waited silently, her steno book on her lap.

"Here's the problem," Katie said slowly. "We're not satisfied that the Vangie Lewis death is a suicide. Yesterday I talked with her doctors, Dr. Highley and Dr. Fukhito, at Westlake Hospital."

She heard a sharp intake of breath and looked up quickly. The girl's face had gone dead white. As Katie watched, two bright spots darkened her cheekbones.

"Maureen, is anything the matter?"

"No. No. I'm sorry."

"Did I say anything to startle you?"

"No. Really."

"All right." Unconvinced, Katie looked back at her pad. "As far as we know, Dr. Fukhito, the psychiatrist at Westlake, was the last person to see Vangie Lewis alive. I want to find out as much as I can about him as fast as possible. Check the Valley County Medical Society and the AMA. I've heard he does volunteer work at Valley Pines Hospital. Maybe you can learn something there. Emphasize the confidentiality, but find out where he came from, where he went to school, other hospitals he's been connected with, his personal background: whatever you can get."

"You don't want me to talk to anyone at Westlake Hospital?"

"Good heavens, no. I don't want anyone there to have any idea we're checking on Dr. Fukhito."

For some reason the younger woman seemed relieved. "I'll get right on it, Katie."

"It's not really fair to have you come in early to do other work and then throw a job at you. Good old

Valley County isn't into overtime. We both know that."

Maureen shrugged. "That doesn't matter. The more I do in this office, the more I like it. Who knows? I may go for a law degree myself, but that means four years of college and three years of law school."

"You'd be a good lawyer," Katie said, meaning it. "I'm surprised you didn't go to college."

"I was insane enough to get engaged the summer I finished high school. My folks persuaded me to take the secretarial course before I got married so at least I'd have some kind of skill. How right they were. The engagement didn't stand the wait."

"Why didn't you start college last September instead of coming to work?" Katie asked.

The girl's face became brooding. Katie thought how unhappy she looked and decided that Maureen must have been pretty hurt about the breakup.

Not quite looking at Katie, Maureen said, "I was feeling restless and didn't want to settle down to being a schoolgirl. It was a good decision."

She went out of the room. The telephone rang. It was Richard. His voice was guarded. "Katie, I've just been talking to Dave Broad, the head of prenatal research at Mt. Sinai. On a hunch, I sent the fetus Vangie Lewis was carrying over to him. Katie, my hunch was right. Vangie *was not pregnant with Chris Lewis' child. The baby I took from her womb has distinctly Oriental characteristics!*"

30

Edgar Highley stared at Katie DeMaio as she stood with that shoe in her hand, holding it out to him. Was she mocking him? No. She believed what she was saying, that the shoe had had some sentimental memory for Edna.

He *had* to have that shoe. If only she didn't talk about it to the Medical Examiner or the detectives. Suppose she decided to show it to them? Gertrude Fitzgerald might recognize it. She'd been at the desk many times when Vangie came in. He'd heard Edna joke with her about Vangie's glass slippers.

Katie put the shoe back, closed the drawer and walked out of the bedroom, the jewelry box tucked under her arm. He followed her, desperate to hear what she would say. But she simply handed the jewelry box to the detective. "The ring and pin are here, Charley," she said. "I guess that shoots any possibility of burglary. I didn't go through the bureau or closet."

"It doesn't matter. If Richard suspects wrongful death, we'll search this place with a fine-tooth comb in the morning."

There was a staccato rap at the door, and Katie opened it to admit two men carrying a stretcher.

Edgar Highley walked back to Gertrude. She had drunk the water in the glass Katie had given her. "I'll get you more water, Mrs. Fitzgerald," he said quietly. He glanced over his shoulder. The others all had their backs to him, as they watched the attendants prepare

149

to lift the body. It was his chance. He had to risk taking the shoe. As long as Katie hadn't mentioned it immediately, it was unlikely she'd bring it up now.

He walked rapidly to the bathroom, turned on the tap and slipped across the hall to the bedroom. Using his handkerchief to avoid fingerprints, he opened the night-table drawer. He was just reaching for the shoe when he heard footsteps coming down the hall. Quickly he pushed the drawer shut, stuffed his handkerchief into his pocket and was standing at the door of the bedroom when the footsteps stopped.

Willing himself to appear calm, he turned. Richard Carroll, the Medical Examiner, was standing in the foyer between the bedroom and the bathroom. His eyes were questioning. "Doctor," he said, "I'd like to ask you a few questions about Edna Burns." His voice was cold.

"Certainly." Then, in what he hoped was a casual tone, he added, "I have just been standing here thinking of Miss Burns. What a shame her life was so wasted."

"Wasted?" Richard's voice was sharply questioning.

"Yes. She actually had a good mathematical mind. In this computer age Edna might have used that talent to make something of herself. Instead, she became an overweight, gossiping alcoholic. If that seems harsh, I say it with real regret. I was fond of Edna, and quite frankly I shall miss her. Excuse me. I'm letting the water run. I want to give Mrs. Fitzgerald a glass of cold water. Poor woman, she's terribly distressed."

Dr. Carroll stood aside to let him pass. Had his criticism of Edna distracted the Medical Examiner from wondering what he was doing in Edna's room?

He rinsed the glass, filled it and brought it to Gertrude. The attendants had left with the body, and Katie DeMaio was not in the room.

"Has Mrs. DeMaio left?" he asked the detective.

"No. She's talking to the super's wife. She'll be right back."

He did not want to leave himself until he was sure that Katie did not talk about the shoe in front of Gertrude. But when she came back a few minutes later, she did not mention it.

They left the apartment together. The local police would keep it under surveillance until the official search was completed.

Deliberately he walked with Katie to her car, but then the Medical Examiner joined them. "Let's have coffee, Katie," he said. "You know where the Golden Valley diner is, don't you?"

The Medical Examiner waited until she was in the car and had started to pull out before he said, "Good night, Dr. Highley" and abruptly left.

As he drove home, Edgar Highley decided there was a personal relationship of some sort between Katie DeMaio and Richard Carroll. When Katie bled to death, Richard Carroll would be both professionally and emotionally interested in the cause of death. He would have to be very, very careful.

There was hostility in Carroll's attitude toward him. But Carroll had no reason to be hostile to him. Should he have gone over to Edna's body? But what would have been the point? He should not have pushed her so hard. Should he have robbed her? That had been his original intention. If he had, he would have found the shoe last night.

But Edna had talked. Edna had told Gertrude that he'd been at her apartment. Edna might even have made it sound more frequent, more important. Gertrude had told Katie that he knew where the pitiful jewelry was kept. If they decided Edna had been murdered, would they tie the murder to Edna's job at the hospital? What else had Edna told people?

The thought haunted him as he drove home.

Katie was the key. Katie DeMaio. With her safely out of the way there was no evidence to tie him to Vangie's death—or Edna's. The office files were in perfect order. The current patients could bear the most minute scrutiny.

He turned into his driveway, drove into the garage, entered the house. The lamb chops were on the plate, cold and edged with grease; the asparagus had wilted, the salad was limp and warm. He would reheat the food in the microwave oven, prepare a fresh salad. In a few minutes the table would look as it had before the phone call.

As he once again prepared the food, he found himself becoming calm. He was so near to being safe. And soon it would be possible to share his genius with the world. He already had his success. He could prove it beyond doubt. Someday he would be able to proclaim it. Not yet, but someday. And he wouldn't be like that braggart who claimed to have successfully cloned but refused to offer even a shred of proof. He had accurate records, scientific documentation, pictures, X-rays, the step-by-step, day-by-day accounts of all the problems that had arisen and how he had dealt with them. All in the files in his secret safe.

When the proper time came he would burn the files about the failures and claim the recognition that was due him. By then there would surely be more triumphs.

Nothing must stand in his way. Vangie had nearly spoiled everything. Suppose he had not met her just as she came out of Fukhito's office? Suppose she hadn't told him about her decision to consult Emmet Salem?

Happenstance. Luck. Call it what you will.

But it had also been happenstance that sent Katie DeMaio to the window just as he left with Vangie's body. And exquisite irony that Katie had come to him in the first place.

Once again he sat down at the table. With intense satisfaction he saw that the dinner looked as appetizing, as delicious as when he'd first prepared it. The watercress was crisp and fresh; the chops bubbling; the asparagus piping hot under a delicate hollandaise. He poured wine into a thin goblet, admiring the delicate satiny feel of the crystal as he picked it up. The wine had the hearty Burgundy flavor he'd been anticipating.

He ate slowly. As always, food restored his sense of well-being. He would do what he must, and then he'd be safe.

Tomorrow was Thursday. The *Newsmaker* article would be on the stands. It would enhance his social as well as his medical prestige.

The fact that he was a widower lent him a specific appeal. He knew how his patients talked. "Dr. Highley is so brilliant. He's so distinguished. He has a beautiful home in Parkwood."

After Winifred's death, he had allowed his connections with her friends to lapse. There was too much hostility there. That cousin of hers kept making insinuations. He knew it. That was why these three years he hadn't bothered with another woman. Not that he found solitude a sacrifice. His work was all-absorbing, all-satisfying. The time dedicated to it had been rewarded. His worst professional critics admitted that he was a good doctor, that the hospital was magnificently equipped, that the Westlake Maternity Concept was being copied by other physicians.

"My patients are not allowed to drink or smoke during their pregnancies," he had told the *Newsmaker* interviewer. "They are required to follow a specific diet. Many so-called barren women would have the babies they want if they would show the same dedication as athletes in training. Many of the long-range health problems suffered today would have been prevented entirely if mothers had not been eating the wrong food, taking the wrong medication. We have had the visible example of what Thalidomide did to scores of unfortunate victims. We recognize that a mother on drugs may produce an infant addict; an alcoholic mother will often be delivered of a retarded, undersized, emotionally disturbed child. But what of the many problems that we consider simply the lot of man . . . Bronchitis, dyslexia, hyperactivity, asthma, hearing and sight impairment? I believe that the place to eliminate these is not in the laboratory, but in the womb. I will not accept a patient who will not cooperate with my methods. I can show you dozens of women I have treated with a history of several miscarriages who now have children. Many more could experience that same joy, *if* they were willing to change their habits, particularly their eating and drinking habits. Many others would conceive and bear a child if their emotions were not so disturbed that in effect they are wearing mental contraceptives far more efficient than any device for sale in the drugstore. This is the reason, the basis of the Westlake Maternity Concept."

The *Newsmaker* reporter had been impressed. But her next question was a loaded one. "Doctor, isn't it a fact that you have been criticized for the exorbitant fees you charge?"

"Exorbitant is *your* word. My fees, aside from rather spartan living expenses, are spent to develop the hospital and to pursue prenatal study."

"Doctor, isn't it a fact that a large percentage of your cases have been women who miscarried several times under your care, even *after* following your schedule rigidly—and paying you ten thousand dollars, plus all hospital and lab expenses?"

"It would be insanity for me to claim that I could bring every difficult pregnancy to term. Yes. There have been cases where the desired pregnancy was begun, but spontaneously aborted. After several of these occurrences, I suggest that my patient adopt a child and help to arrange a suitable adoption."

"For a fee."

"Young woman, I assume you are being paid to interview me. Why don't *you* use your time for volunteer work?"

It had been foolish to attack the reporter like that. Foolish to risk animosity, foolish to give her any reason to discredit him, to delve too deeply into his background. He'd told her that he'd been obstetrical chief in Liverpool before his marriage to Winifred. But of course he hadn't discussed Christ Hospital in Devon.

The interviewer's next question had been meant to entrap him.

"Doctor, you perform abortions, do you not?"

"Yes, I do."

"Isn't that incongruous for an obstetrician? To try to save one fetus and to eliminate another?"

"I refer to the womb as a cradle. I despise abortion. And I deplore the grief I witness when women come to me who have no hope of conceiving because they have had abortions and their wombs have been pierced by stupid, blundering, careless doctors. I think everyone—and I include my colleagues—would be astounded to learn how many women have denied themselves any hope of motherhood because they decided to defer that motherhood by abortion. It is my wish that all women carry their babies to healthy term. For those who do not want to, at least I can make sure that when they eventually want a child, they will still be able to have one."

That point had been well received. The reporter's attitude had changed.

He finished eating. Now he leaned back in the chair and poured more wine into his glass. He was feeling expansive, comfortable. The laws were changing. In a few years he'd be able to announce his genius without fear of prosecution. Vangie Lewis, Edna Burns, Winifred, Claire . . . they'd be unrelated statistics. The trail would be cold.

He studied the wine as he drank, refilled his glass and drank again. He was tired. Tomorrow morning he had a cesarean section scheduled—another difficult case that would add to his reputation. It had been a difficult pregnancy, but the fetus had a strong heartbeat; it should be delivered safely. The mother was a member of the socially prominent Payne family. The father, Delano Aldrich, was an officer of the Rockefeller Foundation. This was the sort of family whose championship would make the difference if the Devon scandal were ever to surface again.

Only one obstacle left. He had brought Katie DeMaio's file home from the office. He would begin now to prepare the substitute file that he would show to the police after her death.

Instead of the history she'd given him of prolonged periods of bleeding over the past year, he would write, "Patient complains of frequent and spontaneous hemorrhaging, unrelated to monthly cycles." Instead of sponginess of uterine walls, probably familial, a condition that would be remedied indefinitely by a simple D-and-C, he would note findings of vascular breakdown. Instead of a slightly low hemoglobin he would indicate that the hemoglobin was chronically in the danger zone.

He went into the library. The file marked KATHLEEN

DeMaio which he had taken from the office was on top of his desk. From the drawer he extracted a new file and put Katie's name on it. For half an hour he worked steadily, consulting the office file for information on her previous medical history. Finally he was finished. He would bring the revised file with him to the hospital. He added several paragraphs to the file he had taken from the office, the one he would put in the wall safe when completed.

Patient was in minor automobile accident on Monday night, February 15. At 2:00 A.M. patient, in sedated condition, observed from the window of her room the transferral of the remains of Vangie Lewis by this physician. Patient still does not understand that what she observed was a true event rather than an hallucination. Patient is slightly traumatized by accident, and persistent hemorrhaging. Inevitably she will be able to achieve clear recollection of what she observed and for this reason cannot be permitted to remain as a threat to this physician.

Patient received blood transfusion on Monday night in emergency room of hospital. This physician prescribed second transfusion on pretense of preparation for Saturday surgery. This physician also administered anticoagulant medication, cumadin pills to be taken on regular basis until Friday night.

Pursing his lips, he laid down the pen. It was easy to imagine how he would complete this report.

Patient entered the hospital at 6:00 P.M. Friday, February 19, complaining of dizziness and general weakness. At 9:00 P.M. this physician, accompanied by Nurse Renge, found the patient hemor-

*rhaging. Blood pressure was falling rapidly. With
whole blood hanging, emergency surgery was performed at 9:45 P.M.*

*The patient, Kathleen Noel DeMaio, expired at
10:00 P.M.*

He smiled in anticipation of completing this troublesome case. Every detail was perfectly planned,
even to assigning Nurse Renge to floor duty Friday
night. She was young, inexperienced and terrified of
him.

After putting the file in the temporary hiding place
in the top desk drawer, he went upstairs to bed and
slept soundly until six in the morning.

Three hours later he delivered a healthy baby boy by
cesarean section to Mrs. Delano Aldrich and accepted
as his due the tearful gratitude of the patient and her
husband.

◆ **31** ◆

The funeral service for Vangie was held on Thursday
morning at ten o'clock in the chapel of a Minneapolis
funeral home. His heart aching with pity for Vangie's
parents, Chris stood beside them, their muffled sobs
assaulting him like hammer blows. Could he have
done things differently? If he had not at first tried to
placate Vangie, would she be lying here now? If he'd
insisted that she go with him to a marriage counselor
years ago, would it have helped their marriage? He
had suggested that to her. But she had refused. "I
don't need any counseling," she'd said. "And don't

you suggest anytime I get upset about anything that there's something the matter with me. It's the other way around. You never get upset about anything; you don't care about anything or anybody. You're the problem, not me."

Oh, Vangie. Vangie. Was truth somewhere in the middle? He had stopped caring very early in their marriage.

Her parents had been outraged to hear that Vangie could not be buried, that her body was to be shipped back east. "Why?"

"I simply don't know." There was no use in answering beyond that—not now.

"Amazing grace, how sweet the sound." The soloist's soprano voice filled the chapel. "I once was lost but now am found."

Months ago, last summer, he'd felt life was bleak and hopeless. Then he'd gone to that party in Hawaii. And Joan had been there. He could remember the precise moment he'd seen her. She was on the terrace in a group of people. Whatever she'd said made them all laugh, and she'd laughed too, her eyes crinkling, her lips parting, her head tilting back. He'd gotten a drink and joined that group. And he hadn't left Joan's side again that evening.

". . . was blind and now I see." The Medical Examiner would not have released Vangie's body Tuesday night if he'd suspected foul play. What had happened to change his mind?

He thought of Edna's call. How much talking had she done to other people? Could she throw some light on Vangie's death? Before he left Minneapolis, he had to call Dr. Salem. He had to find out what he knew about Vangie that had made him react with such shock last night. Why had Vangie made an appointment to see him?

There had been someone else in Vangie's life. He

was sure of it now. Suppose Vangie had killed herself in front of someone and that person brought her home? God knew she'd have had plenty of opportunity to be involved with another man. He was away from home at least half the month. Maybe she had met someone after they moved to New Jersey.

But would Vangie have caused herself pain?

Never!

The minister was saying the final prayer. ". . . when every tear shall be dried . . ." Chris led Vangie's parents into the anteroom and accepted the expressions of sympathy from the friends who had attended the service. Vangie's parents were going to stay with relatives. They had agreed that the body should be cremated in New Jersey and the urn returned to be buried in the family plot.

Finally Chris was able to get away. It was just after eleven o'clock when he arrived at the Athletic Club in downtown Minneapolis and took the elevator to the fourteenth floor. There in the solarium he ordered a Bloody Mary and took it to a phone.

When he reached Dr. Salem's office, he said, "This is Vangie Lewis' husband. It's urgent I speak with the doctor immediately."

"I'm sorry," the nurse told him. "Dr. Salem left a short time ago for the American Medical Association convention in New York. He will not be back until next week."

"New York." Chris digested the information. "Can you tell me where he's staying, please? It may be necessary for me to contact him there."

The nurse hesitated. "I suppose it's all right to tell you that. I'm sure Dr. Salem intends to get in touch with you. He asked me to look up your New Jersey phone number, and I know he took your wife's medical records with him. But just in case he misses you, you can reach him at the Essex House on Central

Park South in New York City. His extension there is 3219."

Chris had pulled out the small notebook that he kept in a compartment of his wallet. Repeating the information, he wrote it down quickly.

The top of the page was already filled. On it were Edna Burns's address and the directions to her apartment in Edgeriver.

♦ 32 ♦

Scott called a noon meeting in his office with the same four people who had been present at the meeting a day and a half earlier to discuss Vangie Lewis' death.

This meeting was different. Katie could feel the heightened atmosphere as she went into the office. Scott had Maureen waiting with a pen and paper.

"We're bringing sandwiches in here," he said. "I'm due in court again at one thirty and we've got to move fast on Captain Lewis."

It was as she'd expected, Katie thought. Scott is zeroing in on Chris. She looked at Maureen. The girl had an aura of nervousness around her that was almost visible. It started when I gave her that assignment this morning, Katie thought.

Maureen caught her glance and half-smiled. Katie nodded, "Uh-huh. The usual." Then added, "Did you have any luck with the phoning?"

Maureen looked at Scott, but he was scanning a file and ignoring them. "So far not much. Dr. Fukhito's not a member of the AMA or the Valley Medical Society. He donates a lot of his time to disturbed children at Valley Pines Psychiatric Clinic. I have a call in to the University of Massachusetts. He attended medical school there."

"Who told you that?" Katie asked.

Maureen hesitated. "I remember hearing it somewhere."

Katie had a feeling of evasiveness in the answer, but before she could probe further, Richard, Charley and Phil came into the office together. Quickly they gave their lunch choices to Maureen, and Richard pulled a chair next to Katie's. He tossed his arm over her chair and touched the back of her head. His fingers were warm and strong as for an instant he massaged her neck muscle. "Boy, are you tense," he said.

Scott looked up, grunted, and began to speak. "All right, by now you all know that the baby Vangie Lewis was carrying had Oriental characteristics. So that opens two possibilities. One: with the birth imminent it's possible she panicked and killed herself. She must have been frantic knowing she could never pass the baby off as her husband's. The second possibility is that Christopher Lewis found out that his wife had been having an affair and killed her. Let's try this. Suppose he went home unexpectedly Monday evening. They quarreled. Why was she rushing home to Minneapolis? Was it because she was afraid of him? Don't forget, he never admitted she was going home and she expected to be gone before he returned from his trip. From what Katie tells us, the psychiatrist claims she ran out of his office nearly hysterical."

"The *Japanese* psychiatrist," Katie said. "I have Maureen checking on him right now."

Scott looked at her. "Are you suggesting that you think there was something between him and Vangie?"

"I'm not suggesting anything yet," Katie replied. "The fact that he's Oriental certainly doesn't say that Vangie didn't know another Oriental man. But I can tell you this. He was nervous when I spoke with him yesterday, and he was carefully choosing every word he said to me. I certainly did not get the whole truth from him."

"Which brings us to Edna Burns," Scott said. "What about it, Richard? Did she fall or was she pushed?"

Richard shrugged. "It is not impossible that she fell. The alcohol level in her blood was point two five. She was blotto. She was heavy."

"What about that business of drunks and babies' being able to fall without getting hurt?" Katie asked.

Richard shook his head. "That may be true about breaking bones, but not when your skull cracks into a sharp metal object. I would say that unless someone admits killing Edna, we'll never be able to prove it."

"But it is possible she was murdered?" Scott persisted.

He shrugged. "Absolutely."

"And Edna was heard talking to Chris Lewis about Prince Charming." Katie spoke slowly. She thought of the handsome psychiatrist. Would someone like Edna refer to *him* as Prince Charming? Would she have called Chris after Vangie's death to tell him she suspected an affair? "I don't believe that," she said.

The men looked at her curiously. "What don't you believe?" Scott asked.

"I don't believe that Edna was vicious. I know she wasn't. I don't think she ever would have called Chris Lewis after Vangie died to hurt him by telling him about an affair Vangie was having."

"She may have felt sorry enough for him that she didn't want him to consider himself a bereaved husband," Richard said.

"Or she may have been looking for a few bucks," Charley suggested. "Maybe Vangie told her something Monday night. Maybe she knew Chris and Vangie had quarreled and why they'd quarreled. She had nothing. Apparently she was still paying off medical bills for her parents, and they've been dead a couple of years. Maybe she didn't think there was any harm in putting the arm on Lewis. She did threaten to go to the police."

"She said she had something to tell the police," Katie objected. "That's the way the super's wife put it."

"All right," Scott said. "What about the Lewis house? What did you turn up?"

Charley shrugged. "So far, not much. There's a phone number with a 621 area code scribbled on the pad beside the kitchen phone. It's not Vangie's parents' number, we know that. We thought we'd call it from here. Maybe Vangie was talking to a friend, gave some of her plans. The other thing is that she tore that dress she was wearing on a prong sticking out from the shelf in the garage."

"What do you mean the dress she was wearing?" Scott demanded.

"The dress she was found in. You couldn't miss it. It was a long job with one of those madras print designs."

"Where are the clothes she was wearing?" Scott asked Richard.

"The lab probably still has them," Richard said. "We were going over them on a routine check."

Scott picked up the message pad Charley had handed him and tossed it to Katie. "Why don't you dial this now? If it's a woman, you might get more out of her."

Katie dialed the number. There was a pause and then a phone began ringing. "Dr. Salem's office."

"It's a doctor's office," she whispered, her hand over the phone. To the person on the other end she said, "Perhaps you can help me. I'm Kathleen

DeMaio from the Valley County, New Jersey, Prosecutor's office. We're conducting a routine inquiry into the death of Mrs. Vangie Lewis last Monday, and she had the doctor's phone number on her pad."

She was interrupted: "Oh, that is a coincidence. I just hung up with Captain Lewis. He's trying to reach the doctor too. As I explained to him, Dr. Salem is on his way to New York right now to the AMA convention. You can reach him later in the day at the Essex House Hotel on Central Park South."

"Fine. We'll do that." On a chance, Katie added, "Do you know anything about Mrs. Lewis' call? Did she speak with the doctor?"

"No. She did not. She spoke to me. She called Monday and was so disappointed that he wasn't going to be back in his office till Wednesday. I made an emergency appointment for her on Wednesday because he was going right out again. She said she had to see him."

"One last question," Katie said: "What kind of doctor is Dr. Salem?"

The woman's tone became proud. "Oh, he's a prominent obstetrician and gynecologist."

"I see. Thank you. You've been very helpful." Katie hung up the phone and reported the conversation to the others.

"And Chris Lewis knew about the appointment," Scott said, "and he wants to talk to the doctor now. I can't wait to get at him tonight. We'll have a lot of questions for him."

There was a knock at the door and Maureen came in without waiting for a response. She was carrying a cardboard tray with inserts for coffee cups and a bag of sandwiches. "Katie," she said, "that call from Boston about Dr. Fukhito is just coming in. Do you want to take it?"

Katie nodded. Richard reached over and picked up

the phone, holding it out to her. As she waited for the call to be switched, Katie became aware of a slow, persistent headache. That rap against the steering wheel hadn't been hard enough for a concussion, but she realized that her head had been bothering her the last few days. I just am not operating on all cylinders, she thought. So many things were teasing her mind. What was she trying to recall? Something. Some impression.

When she explained her credentials, she was quickly switched to the head of personnel at the University of Massachusetts Medical School. The man's voice was guarded. "Yes, Dr. Fukhito graduated from U Mass in the first third of his class. He interned at Massachusetts General and later became affiliated with the hospital and also had a private practice. He left the hospital seven years ago."

"Why did he leave?" Katie asked. "You must understand this is a police investigation. All information will be kept confidential, but we must know if there are any factors in Dr. Fukhito's past that we should be aware of."

There was a pause; then the informant said, "Dr. Fukhito was asked to resign seven years ago, and his Massachusetts license was suspended for a period of one year. He was found guilty of unethical behavior after he unsuccessfully defended a malpractice suit."

"What was the cause of the suit?" Katie asked.

"A former patient sued Dr. Fukhito for inducing her to have a personal relationship with him when she was under psychiatric treatment. She had recently been divorced and was in great emotional difficulty. As a result of that relationship she bore Dr. Fukhito's child."

Molly bustled around her kitchen rejoicing in the fact that all the children were back in school. Even twelve-year-old Jennifer had been well enough to go this morning; in fact, had pleaded to go. "You're just like Katie," Molly had scolded, "when you set your head to anything. Well, all right, but you can't walk. It's too cold. I'll drive you."

Bill was not going into New York until the afternoon. He was planning to attend one of the seminars at the AMA convention. They were enjoying a rare chance to chat in peace as Bill sat at the table sipping coffee and Molly sliced vegetables. "I'm sure Katie and Richard and the Berkeleys will enjoy each other," Molly was saying. "Jim Berkeley is bright and he's a lot of fun. Why is it that most people in advertising really *are* so interesting?"

"Because their stock in trade is words," Bill suggested. "Although I must say I've met some that I wouldn't spend time looking up again."

"Oh, sure," Molly agreed absently. "Now, if Liz just doesn't spend the whole evening talking about the baby . . . Although I must say she's getting better about that. When I phoned to invite her the other day she only spent the first twenty minutes on Maryanne's latest trick . . . which,- incidentally, is to blow her oatmeal all over the place as she's being fed. Isn't that cute?"

"It is if it's your first baby and you waited fifteen years to have one," Bill commented. "I seem to remember every time Jennifer blinked you recorded it in her baby book."

Molly began slicing celery. "Remember your aunt gave me a baby book to keep for the twins. I don't think I ever got the wrapping paper off it . . . Anyhow, it should be fun. And even if Liz does rave about the baby, maybe a little of it will sink in on Katie and Richard."

Bill's eyebrows rose. "Molly, you're about as subtle as a sledgehammer. You'd better watch out or they'll start avoiding each other completely."

"Nonsense. Don't you see the way they look at each other? There's something smoldering—better than smoldering—there. My God, Richard called me last night to see if Katie was here and then wanted to know if there was something the matter with her. You should have heard how worried he sounded. I tell you he's crazy about her, but just is smart enough not to show it and scare her off."

"Did you tell him about the operation?"

"No. Katie gave me hell the other morning when I asked if she had told him. Honest to God, the way most people let everything hang out these days . . . Look, why can't she just say to Richard, 'I've got this problem, it's a nuisance, Mother had it and had to have a D-and-C every couple of years, and it looks like I'm built like her'? Instead, the poor guy is obviously worried that it's something serious. I don't think it's fair to him."

Bill got up, walked over to the sink, rinsed out his cup and saucer and put them in the dishwasher. "I don't think you have ever realized that Katie has been desperately hurt by losing the two men she loved and counted on . . . your father when she was eight, and then John when she was twenty-four. She reminds me of the last scene in *Gone With the Wind* when Rhett says to Scarlett, 'I gave my heart to you and you broke it. Then I gave it to Bonnie and she broke it. I'll not risk it a third time.' That's something of Katie's problem. But frankly, I think she's got to work it out herself. Your hovering over her like a mother hawk isn't helping her. I'd like nothing better than to see her get together with Richard Carroll. He'd be good for her."

"And he plays golf with you," Molly interjected.

Bill nodded. "That too." He picked up a stalk of celery and nibbled on it. "A word of advice. If Katie doesn't want to tell Richard about this operation, don't fill him in. That's not fair to her. If he's persistent in being concerned about her, it has to make some sort of statement to her. You've gotten them together. Now—"

"Now bug off," Molly sighed.

"Something like that. And tomorrow night when Katie goes into the hospital, you and I are going to the Met. I got tickets for *Otello* months ago and I don't plan to change them. You be there when she comes out of the recovery room Saturday morning, but it won't hurt her any to wish she had someone with her. Friday evening maybe she'll do a little thinking."

"Go into the hospital by herself?" Molly protested.

"By herself," Bill said firmly. "She's a big girl."

The telephone rang. "Pray it isn't the school nurse saying one of the kids started with the virus again," Molly muttered. Her "Hello" was guarded. Then her tone became concerned. "Liz, hi. Now, don't tell me you're going to cancel on me tonight."

She listened. "Oh, for heaven's sake, bring her along. You have the folding carriage. . . . Sure, we'll put her up in our room and she'll be fine. . . . Of course I don't mind. So if she wakes up we'll bring her down and let her join the party. It'll be like old times around here. . . . Great. See you at seven. Bye."

She hung up. "Liz Berkeley's regular baby-sitter had

to cancel and she's afraid to leave her with someone she doesn't know, so she's bringing the baby along."

"Fine." Bill looked at the kitchen clock. "I'd better get out of here. It's getting late." He kissed Molly's cheek. "Will you quit worrying about your little sister?"

Molly bit her lip. "I can't. I've got this creepy feeling about Katie, like something might happen to her."

♦ 34 ♦

When Richard returned to his office, he stood for a long time staring out the window. His view was somewhat more appealing than the one from Scott's office. Besides the northeast corner of the county jail, a distinct section of the pocket-sized park in front of the courthouse was visible to him. Only half aware of what he was seeing, he watched as a flurry of sleet-weighted snow pelted the already-slick frozen grass.

Wonderful weather, he thought. He glanced up at the sky. Heavy snow clouds were forming. Vangie Lewis' body was being flown into Newark from Minneapolis on a two-thirty flight. It would be picked up at seven and brought to the morgue. Tomorrow morning he'd re-examine it. Not that he expected to find anything more than he already knew. There were absolutely no bruise marks on it. He was sure of that. But there was something about her left foot or leg that he had noticed and dismissed as irrelevant.

He pushed that thought aside. It was useless to speculate until he could re-examine the body. Vangie had obviously been highly emotional. Could she have been induced to suicide by Fukhito? If Vangie was carrying Fukhito's child, he must have been panicked. He'd be finished as a doctor if he were found to be involved with a patient again.

But Chris Lewis had a girlfriend—a good reason for wanting his wife out of the way. Suppose he had learned of the affair? Apparently even Vangie's parents hadn't known she was planning to come home to Minneapolis. Was it possible Vangie hoped to be delivered of the baby by the Minnesota obstetrician and keep quiet about it? Maybe she'd say she'd lost it. If she wanted to preserve her marriage, she might have been driven to that. Or if she realized a divorce was inevitable, the absolute proof of her infidelity might have weighed in the settlement.

None of it rang true.

Sighing, Richard reached over, snapped on the intercom and asked Marge to come in. She had been at lunch when he returned from Scott's office and he had not collected his messages.

She hurried in with a sheaf of slips in her hand. "None of these are too important," she informed him. "Oh, yes, there was one right after you went to Mr. Myerson's office. A Dr. Salem. He didn't ask for you by name; he wanted the Medical Examiner. Then he asked if we had performed the autopsy on Vangie Lewis. I said you were the M.E. and that you'd performed it personally. He was catching a plane from Minneapolis, but asked if you'd call him at the Essex House in New York around five o'clock. He sounded anxious to talk to you."

Richard pursed his lips in a soundless whistle. "I'm anxious to talk to *him*," he said.

"Oh, and I got the statistics on the Westlake obstetrical patients," Marge said. "In the eight years of the Westlake Maternity Concept, sixteen patients have died either in childbirth or of toxic pregnancies."

"Sixteen?"

"Sixteen," Marge repeated with emphasis. "However, the practice is huge. Dr. Highley is considered an excellent doctor. Some of the babies he's brought to term are near miracles, and the women who died had all been warned by other doctors that they were high pregnancy risks."

"I'll want to study all the fatalities," Richard said. "But if we ask Scott to subpoena the files from the hospital, we'll alert them, and I don't want to do that yet. Have you got anything else?"

"Maybe. In these eight years two people filed malpractice suits against Dr. Highley. Both suits were dismissed. And a cousin of his wife's came in and claimed that he didn't believe she'd died of a heart attack. The Prosecutor's office contacted her personal physician and he said the cousin was crazy. The cousin had been the sole heir before Winifred Westlake married Dr. Highley, so that may be why he wanted to start trouble."

"Who was Winifred Westlake's personal physician?"

"Dr. Alan Levine."

"He's a top internist," Richard said. "I'll have a talk with him."

"How about the people who filed the malpractice suits? Do you want to know who they are?"

"Yes, I do."

"I figured that. Here."

Richard looked down at the two names on the sheet of paper Marge handed him. *Anthony Caldwell, Old Country Lane, Peapack, N.J.,* and *Anna Horan, 415 Walnut Street, Ridgefield Park, N.J.*

"You do nice work, Marge," he said.

She nodded. "I know." Her tone was satisfied.

"Scott is in court by now. Will you leave word for him to call me when he gets back to his office? Oh, and tell the lab I want Vangie Lewis' clothes available to put on her first thing tomorrow morning. All tests have to be finished on the clothing by this afternoon."

Marge left, and Richard turned to the work on his desk.

It was after four before Scott returned the call. He listened to Richard's decision to interview the complainants against Dr. Highley and was clearly not impressed. "Look, today there isn't any doctor, no matter who he is, who isn't hit by malpractice suits. If Dr. Schweitzer were still alive, so help me, he'd be defending himself against them in the jungle. But go ahead on your own if you want to. We'll subpoena the hospital records when you're ready for them. I am concerned about the high number of obstetrical deaths of mothers, but even that may be explainable. He does deal in high-risk pregnancies."

Scott's voice deepened. "What I'm most interested in is what this Dr. Salem has to say. You talk with him and get back to me and then I'll get in on the act. Between you and me, Richard, I think we're going to pull a tight-enough circumstantial case around Captain Chris Lewis that we may force him to come clean. We know that his movements are unaccounted for on Monday night, when his wife died. We know Edna Burns called him Tuesday night. We now know that the funeral director left him before nine on Tuesday night. After that he was alone and could easily have gone out. Suppose he did go down and see her? He's handy. Charley tells me he's got sophisticated tools in his garage. Edna was almost blind drunk when she called him. The neighbor told us that. Suppose he drove there, slipped the lock, got into the apartment and shoved that poor dame before she knew what hit her? Frankly, that's the way my gut sees it, and we'll have him here tonight to tell us all about it."

"You may be right," Richard said. "But I'm still going to check these people out."

He caught Dr. Alan Levine just as he was leaving his office. "Buy you a drink," Richard suggested. "I'll only take fifteen minutes."

They agreed to meet at the Parkwood Country Club. A midway point for both of them, it had the virtue of being quiet on weekdays. They'd be able to talk in the bar without worry about being overheard or having people drop over to say hello.

Alan Levine was a Jimmy Stewart-at-fifty-five look-alike—a fact that endeared him to his older patients. They enjoyed the easy cordiality of professionals who respected each other, enjoyed a drink together if their paths crossed, waved to each other on the golf links.

Richard came directly to the point. "For various reasons we're interested in Westlake Hospital. Winifred Westlake was your patient. Her cousin tried to insinuate that she did not die of a heart attack. What can you tell me about it?"

Alan Levine looked directly at Richard, sipped his martini, glanced out the picture window at the snow-covered fairway and pursed his lips. "I have to answer that question on a couple of levels," he said slowly. "First: Yes, Winifred was my patient. For years she'd had a near-ulcer. Specifically, she had all the classic symptoms of a duodenal ulcer, but it never showed up on X-ray. When she'd periodically experience pain, I'd have the usual X-rays done, get negative results, prescribe an ulcer diet, and she experienced relief almost immediately. No great problem.

"Then the year before she met and married Highley she had a severe attack of gastroenteritis which actually altered her cardiogram. I put her in the hospital for a suspected heart attack. But after two days in the hospital the cardiogram was well within the normal range."

"So there might or might not have been a problem with her heart?" Richard asked.

"I didn't think there was. It never showed up in the standard tests. But her mother died of a heart attack at fifty-eight. And Winifred was nearly fifty-two when she died. She was older than Highley by some ten years, you know. Several years after her marriage she began to come to me more frequently, constantly complaining of chest pains. The tests produced nothing significant. I told her to watch her diet."

"And then she had a fatal attack?" Richard asked.

The other doctor nodded. "One evening, during dinner, she had a seizure. Edgar Highley phoned his service immediately. Gave them my number, the hospital's number, told them to call the police. From what I was told, Winifred keeled over at the dining-room table."

"You were there when she died?" Richard queried.

"Yes. Highley was still trying to revive her. But it was hopeless. She died a few minutes after I arrived."

"And you're satisfied it was heart failure?" Richard asked.

Again there was the hint of hesitation. "She'd been having chest pains over a period of years. Not all heart trouble shows up on cardiograms. In the couple of years before she died she was suffering periodically from high blood pressure. There's no question that heart trouble tends to run in families. Yes. I was satisfied at the time."

"At the time." Richard underscored the words.

"I suppose the cousin's absolute conviction that something was wrong about her death has troubled me these three years. I practically threw him out of my office when he came in and as much as accused me of falsifying records. Figured he was a disgruntled relative who hated the guy who took his place in the will. But Glenn Nickerson is a good man. He's coach at Parkwood High, and my kids go there now. They're all crazy about him. He's a family man, active in his church, on the town council; certainly not the kind of man who would go off half-cocked at being disinherited. And certainly he must have known that Winifred would leave her estate to her husband. She was crazy about Highley. Why, I never could see. He's a cold fish if ever I met one."

"I gather you don't like him."

Alan Levine finished his drink. "I don't like him at all. And have you caught the article about him in *Newsmaker?* Just came out today. Makes a little tin god of him. He'll be even more insufferable, I suppose. But I've got to hand it to him. He's an excellent doctor."

"Excellent enough to have chemically induced a heart attack in his wife?"

Dr. Levine looked directly at Richard. "Frankly, I've often wished I'd insisted on an autopsy."

Richard signaled for the check. "You've been a great help, Alan."

The other man shrugged. "I don't see how. What possible use is any of this to you?"

"For the present, it gives me insight when I talk to some people. After that, who knows?"

They parted at the entrance to the bar. Richard fished in his pocket for change, went over to the public telephone and phoned the Essex House Hotel in New York. "Dr. Emmet Salem, please."

There was the jabbing sound of a hotel phone ringing. Three, four, five, six times. The operator broke in. "I'm sorry, but there's no answer there."

"Are you sure Dr. Salem has checked in?" Richard asked.

"Yes, sir, I am. He called specifically to say that he was expecting an important phone call and he wanted to be sure to get it. That was only twenty minutes ago. But I guess he changed his mind or something. Because we are definitely ringing his room and there's no answer."

♦ 35 ♦

When she left Scott's office, Katie called in Rita Castile and together they went over the material Katie would need for upcoming trials. "That armed robbery on the twenty-eighth," Katie said, "where the defendant had his hair cut the morning after the crime. We'll need the barber to testify. It's no wonder the witnesses couldn't make a positive identification. Even though we made him wear a wig in the lineup, he didn't look the same."

"Got it." Rita jotted down the barber's address. "It's too bad you can't let the jury know that Benton has a long juvenile record."

"That's the law," Katie sighed. "I sure hope that someday it stops bending backward to protect criminals. That's about all I have for you now, but I won't be coming in over the weekend, so next week will really be a mess. Be prepared."

"You won't be coming in?" Rita raised her eyebrows. "Well, it's about time. You haven't given yourself a full weekend off in a couple of months. I hope you're planning to go someplace and have fun."

Katie grinned. "I don't know how much fun it will

be. Oh, Rita, I have a hunch that Maureen is upset about something today. Without being nosy, is there anything wrong that you know about? Is she still down about the breakup with her fiancé?"

Rita shook her head. "No, not at all. That was just kid stuff, and she knew it. The usual going-steady-from-the-time-they-were-fifteen, an engagement ring the night of the prom. They both realized by last summer that they weren't ready to get married. He's in college now, so that's no problem."

"Then why is she so unhappy?" Katie asked.

"Regret," Rita said simply. "Just about the time they broke up she realized she was pregnant and had an abortion. She's weighted down with guilt about it. She told me that she keeps dreaming about the baby, that she hears a baby crying and is trying to find it. Said she'd do anything to have had the baby, even though she would have given it out for adoption."

Katie remembered how much she had hoped to conceive John's child, how furious she'd been when after his death someone commented that she was lucky not to be stuck with a baby. "Life is so crazy," she said. "The wrong people get pregnant, and then it's so easy to make a mistake you have to live with for the rest of your life. But that does explain it. Thanks for telling me. I was afraid I'd said something to hurt her."

"You didn't," Rita said. She gathered up the files Katie had assigned her. "All right. I'll serve these subpoenas and hunt for the barber."

After Rita left, Katie leaned back in her chair. She wanted to talk again with Gertrude Fitzgerald and Gana Krupshak. Mrs. Fitzgerald and Edna had been good friends; they'd often lunched together. Mrs. Krupshak had frequently dropped into Edna's apartment at night. Maybe Edna had said something to one of them about Dr. Fukhito and Vangie Lewis. It was worth a try.

She called Westlake Hospital and was told that Mrs. Fitzgerald was home ill; requested and got her home phone number. When the woman answered she was obviously still distraught. Her voice was weak and shaking. "I have one of my migraines, Mrs. DeMaio," she said, "and no wonder. Every time I think of how Edna looked, poor dear . . ."

"I was going to suggest that we get together either here or at your home," Katie said. "But I'll be in court all day tomorrow, so I guess it will have to wait until Monday. There's just one thing I would like to ask you, Mrs. Fitzgerald. Did Edna ever call either of the doctors she worked for 'Prince Charming'?"

"Prince Charming?" Gertrude Fitzgerald's voice was astonished. "Prince Charming? My goodness. Dr. Highley or Dr. Fukhito? Why would anyone call either of them Prince Charming? My heavens, no."

"All right. It was just a thought." Katie said good-bye and dialed Mrs. Krupshak. The superintendent answered. His wife was out, he explained. She'd be back around five.

Katie glanced at the clock. It was four thirty. "Do you think she'd mind if on my way home I stopped to talk to her for a few minutes? I promise I won't be long."

"Suit yourself," the man answered shortly, then added, "What's going on with the Burns apartment? How long before it gets cleared out?"

"That apartment is not to be entered or touched until this office releases it," Katie said sharply. She hung up, packed some files in her briefcase and got her coat. She'd have just enough time to talk to Mrs. Krupshak, then go home and change. She wouldn't stay late at Molly's tonight. She wanted one decent night's sleep before the operation. She knew she wouldn't sleep well in the hospital.

She was just ahead of the evening traffic, and Mrs. Krupshak was home when she rang her bell. "Now, isn't that timing?" she exclaimed to Katie. The shock of discovering Edna's body had begun to wear off for this woman, and clearly she was beginning to enjoy the excitement of the police investigation.

"This is my bingo afternoon," she explained. "When I told my friends what happened they could hardly keep their cards straight."

Poor Edna, Katie thought, then realized that Edna would have been delighted to be the center of an active discussion.

Mrs. Krupshak ushered her into an L-shaped living room, a mirror image of the unit Edna had lived in. Edna's living room had been furnished with an old-fashioned velour couch, matching straight-backed fireside chairs, a fading Oriental rug. Like Edna, the apartment had had its own innate dignity.

The superintendent's wife had an imitation-leather couch and club chair, an oversized cocktail table topped by an exactly centered plastic flower arrangement and an orange-toned autumnal print over the couch that picked up the wildly vivid shade of the carpeting. Katie sat down. This place is ordinary, she reflected. It's unimaginative, yet it's clean and comfortable and you get the feeling that even if her husband is brusque and unsociable, Gana Krupshak is a happy woman. Then Katie wondered why she was suddenly so concerned with defining happiness.

With a mental shrug she turned to the questions she wanted to ask. "Mrs. Krupshak," she said, "we talked last night, but of course, you were so shocked. Now I wonder if you would go over with me very carefully what happened last night: how long were you with

Edna; what did you talk about; did you get the impression that when she spoke to Captain Lewis she made an appointment with him."

Gana Krupshak leaned back in her chair, looked past Katie, half-closed her eyes and bit her lip.

"Now, let's see. I went over to Edna's right at eight o'clock, because Gus started to watch the basketball game and I thought, To hell with the basketball game, I'll pop over to Edna's and have a beer with her."

"And you went over there," Katie encouraged.

"I did. The only thing is, Edna had made a pitcher of Manhattans and they were about half gone and she was feeling pretty rocky. You know, like, sometimes she'd get in moods, kind of *down*, if you know what I mean, and I thought she was in one of those. Like, last Thursday was her mother's birthday and I stopped in then and she was crying about how much she missed her mother. Now, I don't mean she'd take it out on you, no way, but when I popped over there Thursday she was sitting with her folks' picture in her hands and the jewelry box on her lap and tears rolling down her cheeks. I gave her a big hug and said, 'Edna, I'm going to pour you a nice Manhattan and we'll toast your maw and if she was here she'd be joining us.' So if you know what I mean, I kind of kidded her out of the blues and she was fine, but when I went over Tuesday night and saw her under the weather I figured she really wasn't over the lonesome spell."

"Did she tell you she was still depressed Tuesday night?" Katie asked.

"No. No. That's it. She was kind of excited. She talked in a sort of rambly way about this patient who had died, how beautiful she'd been, like a doll, and how sick she'd been getting and how she—Edna, I mean—could tell the cops a lot about her."

"Then what happened?" Katie asked.

"Well, I had a Manhattan, or two, with her and then

figured I'd better get home because Gus gets in a snit if I'm still out when he goes to bed. But I hated to see Edna drink much more, because I knew she'd be feeling real bad in the morning, so I got out that nice canned ham and opened it and cut off a few slices for her."

"And that was when she made the call?"

"Just like I told you last night."

"And she talked to Captain Lewis about Prince Charming?"

"As God is my witness."

"All right, but one last thing, Mrs. Krupshak: do you know if Edna kept any articles of clothing of her mother's as a sentimental keepsake?"

"Clothing? No. She did have a lovely diamond pin and ring."

"Yes, yes, we found those last night. But—well, for example, my mother used to keep her mother's old black felt hat in her closet for sentimental reasons. I noticed an old moccasin in Edna's jewelry drawer. It was quite shabby. Did she ever show it to you or mention it?"

Gana Krupshak looked directly at Katie. "Absolutely not," she said flatly.

♦ 36 ♦

The *Newsmaker* article was on the stands Thursday morning. The phone calls began as soon as he went to his office after delivering the Aldrich baby. He instructed the switchboard to ring through directly to him. He wanted to hear the comments. They were beyond his expectations. "Doctor, when can I have an appointment? My husband and I have longed for a baby. I can fly to New Jersey at your convenience. God bless you for your work." The Dartmouth Medical School phoned. Would he consider a guest lecture? An article writer for *Ladies' Home Journal* wanted to interview him. Would Dr. Highley and Dr. Fukhito appear together on *Eyewitness News?*

That request troubled him. He'd been careful to give the *Newsmaker* reporter the impression that he worked with a number of psychiatrists, in the same sense a family lawyer might have his clients consult with any one of a dozen counselors. He had clearly suggested that the program was entirely under his control, not a joint effort. But the reporter had picked up Fukhito's name from a number of the safe patients he'd given her to interview. Now the reporter credited Fukhito as the psychiatrist who seemed to be primarily involved with Dr. Edgar Highley in the Westlake Maternity Concept.

Fukhito would be desperately troubled by the publicity. That was why he'd been chosen. Fukhito had to keep his mouth shut even if he ever started to get suspicious. He was in no position to allow a breath of scandal to hit Westlake. He'd be permanently ruined if that happened.

Fukhito was becoming a distinct liability. It would be easy enough to get rid of him now. He was giving a lot of time on a voluntary basis to the clinic at Valley Pines. He could undoubtedly become staff there now. Probably Fukhito would be glad to scramble for cover. Then he could start to rotate psychiatrists; he knew enough of them by now who weren't competent to counsel anyone. They'd be easy enough to dupe.

Fukhito would have to go.

The decision made, he signaled for his first patient to come in. She was new, as were the two scheduled after her. The third patient was an interesting case: a womb so tipped that she'd never be able to conceive without intervention.

She would be his next Vangie.

The phone call came at noon just as he was leaving for lunch. The nurse covering the reception desk was apologetic. "Doctor, it's a long-distance call from a Dr. Emmet Salem in Minneapolis. He's in a phone booth at the airport now and insists on speaking with you at once."

Emmet Salem! He picked up the phone. "Edgar Highley here."

"Dr. Highley." The voice was icy cold. "Dr. Highley from Christ Hospital in Devon?"

"Yes." A chill, sickening fear made his tongue heavy, his lips rubbery.

"Dr. Highley, I learned last night that you treated my former patient, Mrs. Vangie Lewis. I'm leaving for New York immediately. I'll be at the Essex House Hotel in New York. I must tell you that I am planning to consult with the Medical Examiner in New Jersey about Mrs. Lewis' death. I have her medical records with me. In fairness to you I suggest we discuss her case before I level accusations."

"Doctor, I'm troubled by your tone and insinuations." Now he could talk. Now his own voice hardened into chips of granite.

"My plane is boarding. I'll be checking into room 3219 of the Essex House Hotel shortly before five o'clock. You can call me there." The connection was broken.

He was waiting in the Essex House when Emmet Salem emerged from the cab. Swiftly he disappeared into an elevator to the thirty-second floor, walked past room 3219 until the corridor turned in a right angle.

Another elevator stopped at the floor. He listened as a key clicked, a bellman said, "Here we are, Doctor." A minute later the bellman emerged again. "Thank you, sir."

He waited until he heard the elevator stop at the floor for the bellman. The corridors were silent. But that wouldn't last long. Many of the delegates to the AMA convention were probably staying here. There was always the danger of running into someone he knew. But he had to take the chance. He had to silence Salem.

Swiftly he opened his leather bag and brought out the paperweight that only forty-eight hours ago he had intended to use to silence Edna. Incongruous, impossible—that he, the healer, the doctor, was repeatedly forced to kill.

He slipped the paperweight into his coat pocket, put on his gloves, grasped the bag firmly in his left hand and knocked on the door.

Emmet Salem pulled the door open. He'd just removed his suit jacket. "Forgot something?" His voice trailed off. Obviously he'd expected the bellman had come back.

"Dr. Salem!" He reached for Salem's hand, walking forward, backing the older man into the room, slipping the door closed behind him. "I'm Edgar Highley. It's good to see you again. You got off the phone so abruptly that I couldn't tell you I was having dinner with several colleagues who are attending the convention. I have only a very few minutes, but I'm sure we can clear up any questions."

He was still walking forward, forcing the other man to retreat. The window behind Salem was wide open. He'd probably had the bellman open it. The room was very hot. The window was low. His eyes narrowed. "I tried to phone you, but your extension is out of order."

"Impossible. I just spoke to the operator." Dr. Salem stiffened, his face suddenly cautious.

"Then I do apologize. But no problem. I'm so anxious to go over the Lewis file with you. I have it in my case here." He reached for the paperweight in his pocket, then cried, "Doctor, behind you, watch out!"

The other man spun around. Holding the paperweight in his fist, he crashed it on Salem's skull. The blow sent Emmet Salem staggering. He slumped against the windowsill.

Jamming the paperweight back into his pocket, Edgar Highley cupped his palms around Emmet Salem's foot and shoved up and out.

"No. No. Christ, please!" The half-conscious man slid out the window.

He watched dispassionately as Salem landed on the roof of the extension some fifteen floors below.

The body made a muffled thud.

Had it been seen? He had to hurry. From Salem's suit coat on the bed, he pulled out a key ring. The smallest key fitted the attaché case on the luggage rack.

The Vangie Lewis file was on top. Grabbing it, he shoved it into his own briefcase, relocked Salem's bag, returned the keys to the suit-coat pocket. He took the paperweight from his pocket and placed it in his own bag with the file. The wound had not spurted blood, but the paperweight was sticky.

He closed his own bag and glanced around. The room was in perfect order. There was no trace of blood on the windowsill. It had taken less than two minutes.

He opened the door cautiously and looked out. The corridor was empty. He stepped out. As he closed the door, the phone in Salem's room began to ring.

He did not dare be seen getting on the elevator on this floor. His picture was in the *Newsmaker* article.

Later people might be questioned. He might be recognized.

The fire-exit stairway was at the end of the corridor. He descended four levels to the twenty-eighth floor. There he reentered the carpeted corridor. An elevator was just stopping. He got on it, his eyes scanning the faces of the passengers. Several women, a couple of teen-agers, an elderly couple. No doctors. He was sure of that.

At the lobby he walked rapidly to the Fifty-eighth Street exit of the hotel, turned west and then south. Ten minutes later he reclaimed his car from the park-and-lock garage on West Fifty-fourth Street, tossed his bag into the trunk and drove away.

◆ 37 ◆

Chris arrived at the Twin Cities airport at ten minutes of one. He had an hour to wait before his plane left for Newark. Vangie's body would be on that plane. Yesterday, coming out here, he'd thought of nothing except that coffin in the hold of the plane. He'd held on to some semblance of normality by reassuring himself that soon it would be over.

He had to see Dr. Salem. Why had Dr. Salem been so upset? Tonight when he got off the plane at Newark, the Medical Examiner's office would be waiting for Vangie's body.

And the Prosecutor's office would be waiting for him. The certainty haunted Chris. Of course. If they were suspicious in any way about Vangie's death, they were going to look to him for answers. They'd be waiting to bring him in for questioning. They might even arrest him. If they'd investigated at all, they knew by now that he'd returned to the New Jersey area Monday night. He had to see Dr. Salem. If he was detained for questioning he might not be able to talk to him. He did not want to talk to the Prosecutor's office *about* Dr. Salem.

Once again he thought of Molly and Bill Kennedy. So what if Molly was Katie DeMaio's sister? They were good people, honest people. He should have trusted them, talked to them. He had to talk to someone.

He had to talk to Joan.

His need for her was a hunger. The minute he started to tell the truth, Joan became involved.

Joan, who in this sleazy world still held such inviolate principles, was about to be dragged through the mud.

He had the phone number of the stewardess with whom she was staying in Florida. Not knowing what he would say, he went to the phone, automatically gave his credit-card number, heard the ring.

Kay Corrigan answered. "Kay, is Joan there? It's Chris."

Kay knew about him and Joan. Kay's voice was concerned. "Chris, Joan has been trying to phone you. Tina called from the New York apartment. The Valley County Prosecutor's office has been around asking all kinds of questions about you two. Joan is frantic!"

"When will she be back?"

"She's over at the new apartment now. It doesn't have a phone. From there she has to go to the company personnel office in Miami. She won't be here till about eight tonight."

"Tell her to stay in and wait till I call her," Chris said. "Tell her I've got to talk to her. Tell her . . ." He broke the connection, leaned against the phone and pushed back a dry sob. Oh, God, it was too much, it was all too much. He couldn't think. He didn't know what to do. And in a few hours he'd be in custody, suspected of killing Vangie . . . maybe *charged* with killing Vangie.

No. There was another way. He'd get the flight into LaGuardia. He could still make it. Then he'd be in Manhattan and able to see Dr. Salem at almost the same time he reached the hotel. The Prosecutor's office wouldn't realize he wasn't on the Newark flight until six o'clock. Maybe Dr. Salem could help him somehow.

He barely made the LaGuardia flight. The coach section was full, but he bought a first-class ticket and was able to get on the plane. He didn't worry about his luggage, which was checked through to Newark.

On the plane he accepted a drink from the stewardess, waved away the food and listlessly thumbed through *Newsmaker* magazine. The page opened to SCIENCE AND MEDICINE. His eye caught the headline: "Westlake Maternity Concept Offers New Hope to Childless Couples." *Westlake.* He read the first paragraph. "For the past eight years, a small privately owned clinic in New Jersey has been operating a program called the Westlake Maternity Concept which has made it possible for childless women to become pregnant. Named after a prominent New Jersey obstetrician, the program is carried on by Dr. Edgar Highley, obstetrician-gynecologist, who was the son-in-law of Dr. Franklin Westlake . . ."

Dr. Edgar Highley. Vangie's doctor. Funny she never talked very much about him. It was always the psychiatrist. "Dr. Fukhito and I talked about Mama and Daddy today . . . he said it was obvious I was an only child . . . Dr. Fukhito asked me to draw a picture of Mama and Daddy as I visualized them; it was fascinating. I mean it really was interesting to see how I visualized them. Dr. Fukhito was asking about you, Chris."

"And what did you say, Vangie?"

"That you worshiped me. You do, don't you, Chris? I mean underneath that put-downy way you have with me, aren't I your little girl?"

"I'd rather you thought of yourself as my wife, Vangie."

"See, I can't talk with you about anything. You always get nasty. . . ."

He wondered if the police had talked to either of Vangie's doctors.

This last month she had looked so ill. He had suggested that she have a consultation. The company doctor would have recommended someone. Or Bill Kennedy would surely have been able to suggest someone from Lenox Hill. But of course, Vangie had refused to have a consultation.

Then on her own she'd made an appointment with Dr. Salem.

The plane landed at four thirty. Chris hurried through the terminal and hailed a cab. One of the few breaks of this rotten day was that he'd be ahead of the five-o'clock rush.

"The Essex House, please," he told the driver.

It was just two minutes of five when he reached the hotel. He headed for a lobby telephone. "Dr. Emmet Salem, please."

"Thank you, sir."

There was a pause. "That line is busy, sir."

He hung up. At least Dr. Salem was here. At least he'd have a chance to talk to him. He remembered he'd written Dr. Salem's extension in his notebook, opened it and dialed "3219." The phone rang . . .

again . . . again. After six rings he broke the connection and dialed the operator. Explaining that the line had been busy only a few minutes before, he asked the operator to try it for him.

The operator hesitated, spoke to someone, then came back. "Sir, I just gave this message to another party. Dr. Salem checked in, contacted me to say that he expected an important call and be sure to reach him and then apparently stepped out. Why don't you try again in a few minutes?"

"I'll do that. Thank you." Irresolutely Chris hung up the phone, walked over to a lobby chair facing the south elevator bank and sat down. The elevators opened and dislodged passengers, filled again, disappeared in a streak of ascending panel lights.

One elevator caught his attention. There was something vaguely familiar about someone on it. Dr. Salem? Quickly he scanned the passengers. Three women, some teen-agers, an elderly couple, a middle-aged man with a turned-up coat collar. No. Not Dr. Salem.

At five thirty Chris tried again. And at quarter of six. At five past six he heard the whispers that ran through the lobby like a flash fire. "Someone jumped from a window. The body spotted on the roof of the extension." From somewhere along Central Park South the wail of an ambulance and the yip-yip of police cars were frantic explosions of increasing sound.

With the certainty of despair, Chris went to the bell captain's desk. "Who was it?" he asked. His tone was crisp, authoritative; suggested he had a right to know.

"Dr. Emmet Salem. He was a big shot in the AMA. Room 3219."

Walking with the measured gait of an automaton, Chris pushed through the revolving door at the Fifty-eighth Street entrance. A cab was cruising from west to east. He hailed it, got in and leaned back in the seat closing his eyes. "LaGuardia, please," he said; "the National Airlines terminal."

There was a seven-o'clock flight to Miami. He could just make it.

In three hours he'd be with Joan.

He had to get to Joan, try to make her understand before he was arrested.

♦ 38 ♦

Twelve-year-old Jennifer threw open the door as Katie came up the walk. "Katie, hi." Her voice was joyous, her hug sturdy. The two smiled at each other. With her intense blue eyes, dark hair and olive skin, Jennifer was a younger version of Katie.

"Hi, Jennie. How do you feel?"

"Okay. But how about you? I was so worried when Mom told me about your accident. You sure you're okay now?"

"Let's put it this way: by next week I'll be in great shape." She changed the subject. "Anybody here yet?"

"Everybody. Dr. Richard is here too. . . . You know what his first question was?"

"No."

"'Is Katie here yet?' I swear he's got a case on you, Katie. Mom and Dad think so too. I heard them talking about it. How about you? Have you got a case on him?"

"Jennifer!" Half laughing, half irritated, Katie started up the short staircase toward the den in the back of the house, then looked back over her shoulder. "Where are the other kids?"

"Mom shipped them off with a baby-sitter to eat at McDonald's and then to a movie. She said the Berkeley baby would never sleep if the twins were around."

"Good thinking," Katie murmured. She started down the foyer to the den. After leaving Gana Krupshak, she'd gone home, showered and changed. She'd left the house at quarter of seven thinking, Very soon Chris Lewis will be in Scott's office being questioned. . . . What explanation could he give for not admitting that he was in the New Jersey area Monday night? Why hadn't he volunteered that immediately?

She wondered if Richard had spoken to the Minnesota doctor yet. He might have cleared up a lot of questions. She'd try to get Richard aside and ask him.

Driving over, she had resolved to put the case out of her mind for the rest of the evening. Maybe *not* thinking about it for a while would help her to follow up the elusive threads that kept escaping her—

She reached the den. Liz and Jim Berkeley were seated on the couch, their backs to her. Molly was passing hors d'oeuvres. Bill and Richard were standing by the window talking. Katie studied Richard. He was wearing a navy blue pin-striped suit that she'd never seen before. His dark brown hair had touches of gray she'd never noticed. His fingers on the stem of the glass he was holding were long and finely shaped. Funny how this past year she'd seen him as a composite, never noticing details. It seemed to her that she was like a camera that had been locked into one position and was just beginning to focus again. Richard looked serious. His forehead was creased. She wondered if he was telling Bill about the Lewis fetus. No, he wouldn't discuss that even with Bill.

At that moment Richard turned his head and saw

her. "Katie." His smile matched the pleased tone in his voice. He came hurrying over to her. "I've been listening for the doorbell."

So often in these three years she'd entered a room where she was the outsider, the loner, amidst couples. Now here tonight, Richard had been waiting for her, listening for her.

Before she had time to consider her feelings, Molly and Bill were saying hello, Jim Berkeley had stood up and the usual confusion of greetings was taking place.

On the way to the dining room she did manage to ask Richard if he'd reached Dr. Salem. "No. Apparently I just missed him at five," Richard explained. "Then I tried again from my place at six, but there was no answer. I left this number with the hotel operator and with my answering service. I'm very anxious to hear what that man has to say."

By tacit agreement, none of them brought up the Lewis suicide until dinner was almost over. And then it came about because Liz Berkeley said, "What luck. I have to admit I've been holding my breath that Maryanne wouldn't wake up and be fussy. Poor kid, her gums are so swollen she's in misery."

Jim Berkeley laughed. He was darkly handsome with high cheekbones, charcoal-brown eyes and thick black eyebrows. "When Maryanne was born, Liz used to wake her up every fifteen minutes to make sure she was still breathing. But since she's teething, Liz has become like every other mother." He imitated her voice. "Quiet, dummy, don't wake up the baby."

Liz, a Carol Burnett type, with sinewy slenderness, an open, pleasant face and flashing brown eyes, made a face at her husband. "You have to admit I'm calming down to being normal. But she *is* a miracle to us. I'd just about given up hope and then we tried to adopt, but now there just aren't babies. Especially with the two of us in our late thirties, they told us to forget it.

And then Dr. Highley. He's a miracle maker, that man."

Katie watched as Richard's eyes narrowed. "You genuinely think that?" Richard queried.

"Positively. I mean, Dr. Highley isn't the warmest person on earth—" Liz began.

"What you mean is that he's an egocentric son of a bitch and as cold a fish as ever I've met," her husband interrupted. "But who gives a damn about that? What matters is that he knows his business, and I have to say he took excellent care of Liz. Put her to bed in the hospital almost two months before the delivery and personally checked on her three or four times a day."

"He does that with all his difficult pregnancies," Liz said. "Not just me. Listen, I pray for that man every night. The difference that baby has made in our lives, I can't even begin to tell you! And don't let this one fool you"—she nodded in the direction of her husband— "he's up ten times a night to make sure that Maryanne is covered and that there's no draft on her. Tell the truth." She looked at him. "When you went up to the john before, didn't you look in on her?"

He laughed. "Sure I did."

Molly said what Katie was thinking. "That's the way Vangie Lewis would have felt about her child."

Richard looked at Katie questioningly and she shook her head. She knew he was wondering if she'd told Molly and Bill that the Lewis baby was Oriental. Deliberately Richard pulled the conversation from Vangie. "I understand that you used to live in San Francisco," he said to Jim. "I grew up there. In fact, my father still practices at San Francisco General. . . ."

"One of my favorite towns," Jim replied. "We'd go back there in a minute, wouldn't we, Liz?"

As the others chatted, Katie listened with half a mind, contributing enough to the conversation that her silence wasn't noticeable. She had so much thinking to do. These few days in the hospital would give her time for that too. She was feeling light-headed and fatigued, but did not want to make a move too soon for fear of breaking up the party.

Her chance came as they left the table to go into the living room for a nightcap. "I'm going to say good night," Katie said. "I have to admit I haven't slept well this week and I'm really bushed."

Molly looked at her knowingly and did not protest. Richard said, "I'll walk you to the car."

"Fine."

The night air was cold, and she shivered as they started down the walk. Richard noticed immediately and said, "Katie, I'm worried about you. I know you're not feeling up to par. You don't seem to want to talk about it, but at least let's have dinner tomorrow night. With the way the Lewis case is breaking, the office will be a zoo tomorrow."

"Richard, I'm sorry. I can't. I'm going away this weekend." Katie realized her tone was apologetic.

"You're *what?* With all that's happening at the office? Does Scott know that?"

"I . . . I'm committed." What a lame, stupid thing to say, Katie thought. This is ridiculous. I'm going to tell Richard that I'll be in the hospital. The driveway lights were on his face, and his expression of mingled disappointment and disapproval was unmistakable.

"Richard, it's not something I've talked up, but . . ."

The front door was thrown open. "Richard, Richard!" Jennifer's shout was rushed and excited. "Clovis Simmons is on the phone."

"Clovis Simmons!" Katie said. "Isn't she the actress on that soap opera?"

"Yes. Oh, hell, I was supposed to call her and forgot. Hold on, Katie. I'll be right back."

"No. I'll see you in the morning. You go ahead."
Katie got into the car and pulled the door closed. She
fished for the ignition key in her handbag, found it
and inserted it into the lock. Richard looked irreso-
lute for an instant, then hurried into the house,
listening as Katie's car drove away. Hell, he thought,
of all the times. His "Hello, Clovis" was brusque.

"Well, Doctor, it's a shame I have to track you
down, but we did discuss dinner, didn't we?"

"Clovis, I'm *sorry.*" No, Clovis, he thought, *you*
discussed dinner. *I* didn't.

"Well, obviously it's too late now." Her tone was
cool. "Actually, I just got in from the taping and
wanted to apologize in case you'd kept the evening. I
should have known better."

Richard glanced at Jennifer, who was standing at
his elbow.

"Clovis, look, let me call you tomorrow. I can't talk
very well now."

There was a sharp click in his ear. Richard hung up
the phone slowly. Clovis was angry, but more than
that, she was hurt. How much we take people for
granted, he thought. Just because I wasn't serious
about her, I didn't bother to think about her feelings.
Tomorrow he could only call and apologize and be
honest enough to tell her that there was someone else.

Katie. Where was she going this weekend? Was
there someone else for her? She'd looked so troubled,
so worried. Was it that he'd been misreading her all
along? He'd put her reticence, her lack of interest in
him to the probability that she was living in the past.
Maybe there was someone else in her life. Was he
being as much a fool about her feelings as in a
different way he'd been with Clovis?

The possibility sheared away the pleasure of the
evening. He'd make his excuses and go home. It still
wouldn't be too late to try Dr. Salem again.

He went into the living room. Molly, Bill and the Berkeleys were there. And swathed in blankets, sitting straight up on Liz's lap, was a baby girl.

"Maryanne decided to join the party," Liz said. "What do you think of her?" Her smile was proud as she turned the baby to face him.

Richard looked into solemn green eyes set in a heart-shaped face. Jim Berkeley was sitting next to his wife, and Maryanne reached over and grabbed his thumb.

Richard stared at the family. They might have posed for a magazine cover: the smiling parents, the beautiful offspring. The parents handsome, olive-skinned, brown-eyed, square-featured; the baby fair-complexioned, red-blond, with brilliant green eyes.

Who the hell do they think they're kidding? Richard thought. That child has to be adopted.

♦ 39 ♦

Phil Cunningham and Charley Nugent watched in disgust as the final stragglers filed through the waiting room at Newark Airport's Gate 11. Charley's perpetually mournful expression deepened.

"That's it." He shrugged. "Lewis must have figured we'd be waiting for him. Let's go."

He headed for the nearest pay phone and dialed Scott. "You can go home, boss," he said. "The Captain didn't feel like flying tonight."

"He wasn't on board? How about the coffin?"

"That came in. Richard's guys are picking it up.

Want us to hang around? There are a couple of indirect flights he might be on."

"Forget it. If he doesn't contact us tomorrow, I'm issuing a pickup order for him as a material witness. And first thing in the morning, I want you to go through Edna Burns's apartment with a fine-tooth comb."

Charley hung up the phone. He turned to Phil. "If I know the boss, I'd say that by tomorrow night at this time there'll be a warrant out for Lewis' arrest."

Phil nodded. "And after we get Lewis, I hope we can hang something on that shrink if he was the one who made that poor gal pregnant."

The two men wearily started down the stairs to the exit. They passed the baggage area, ignoring the people clustered around the carousels waiting for their luggage. A few minutes later the area was deserted. Only one unclaimed bag circled forlornly on the ramp: a large black carryall, properly tagged, in accordance with airline regulations, CAPT. CHRISTOPHER LEWIS, NO. 4, WINDING BROOK LANE, CHAPIN RIVER, N.J. Inside the bag, placed there at the last minute, was the picture Vangie's parents had pressed on Chris.

It was a nightclub photo of a youthful couple. The inscription read, *Remembrance of my first date with Vangie, the girl who will change my life. Love, Chris.*

♦ 40 ♦

Richard phoned the Essex House Hotel as soon as he reached his apartment after leaving the Kennedys'. But once again there was no answer on Dr. Salem's number. When the operator came back on the line, he said, "Operator, did Dr. Salem receive my message to phone me? I'm Dr. Carroll."

The woman's voice was oddly hesitant. "I'll check, sir."

While he was waiting, Richard reached over and flipped on the television set. *Eyewitness News* had just begun. The camera was focusing on Central Park South. Richard watched as the marquee of the Essex House Hotel was featured on the screen. Even as the telephone operator said, "I'm connecting you with our supervisor," Richard heard reporter Gloria Rojas say, "This evening in the prestigious Essex House Hotel, headquarters for the American Medical Association convention, a prominent obstetrician-gynecologist, Dr. Emmet Salem of Minneapolis, Minnesota, fell or jumped to his death."

◆ 41 ◆

Joan Moore sat distractedly by the telephone. "Kay, what time did he say he'd phone?" she asked. Her voice trembled, and she bit her lip.

The other young woman looked at her with concern. "I told you, Joan. He called about eleven thirty this morning. He said he'd be in touch with you tonight and that you should wait in for his call. He sounded upset."

The doorbell rang insistently, making them both jump from their chairs. Kay said, "I don't expect anybody." Some instinct made Joan run to the door and yank it open.

"Chris—oh, my God, Chris!" She threw her arms around him. He was ghastly white, his eyes were bloodshot, he swayed as she held him. "Chris, what is it?"

"Joan, Joan." His voice was nearly a sob. Hungrily he pulled her to him. "I don't know what's happening. There's something wrong about Vangie's death, and now the only man who might have told us about it is dead too."

He had planned to go directly home from the Essex House, but after he drove out of the parking lot and started up the West Side Highway in the heavy traffic, he changed his mind. He was so terribly hungry. His stomach had been empty all day. He never ate before operating, and this morning the call from Salem had come just before he would have left for lunch.

He didn't want to take the time to prepare food tonight. He'd go to the Carlyle. Then if the question ever arose as to his whereabouts tonight, he could truthfully admit he had been in New York. The maître d' would emphatically reassure the police that Dr. Edgar Highley was a valued and frequent patron.

He would have smoked salmon, vichyssoise, a rack of lamb . . . His mouth salivated in anticipation. The sudden, terrible depletion of energy now that it was over needed to be corrected. There was still tomorrow. Inevitably there'd be a thorough investigation when Kathleen DeMaio died. But her former gynecologist had retired and moved away. No one would loom from the past with old medical records to challenge him.

And then he'd be safe. Right now, all over the AMA convention, doctors were probably discussing the *Newsmaker* article and the Westlake Maternity Concept. Their remarks would be tinged with jealousy, of course. But even so, there would be offers for him to speak at future AMA seminars. He was now on the path to public fame. And Salem, who might have stopped him, was finished. He was anxious to go through Vangie's medical history in the file he'd taken from Salem. He'd incorporate it with his own records. That history would be invaluable in his future research.

The last new patient this morning. She would be next. He parked on the street in front of the Carlyle. It was nearly six thirty. Parking would be legal at seven. He'd just wait in the car until then. It would give him a chance to calm himself down.

His bag was locked in the trunk. Vangie's file, the paperweight and the shoe were in it. How should he dispose of the shoe and the paperweight? Where should he dispose of them? Any one of the overflowing trash baskets in this city would do. No one would fish them out. They'd be collected in the morning together with the tons of garbage that accumulated every twenty-four hours in this city of eight million, lost in the smell of decaying food and discarded newspapers. . . .

He'd do it on the way home, under cover of darkness, never noticed.

A sense of buoyancy at the anticipation of how well it was going made him suddenly straighten up in his seat. He leaned over and looked into the rearview mirror. His skin was glistening, as if with perspiration about to burst through the pores. His eyelids and the skin under his eyes were accumulating fatty tissue. His hairline still showed no sign of receding, but the dark sandy hair was shot with silver now . . . He was starting to age. The subtle change that began in the mid-forties was happening to him. He was forty-five now. Young enough, but also time to become aware of the swift passage of years. Did he want to remarry? Did he want to father children of his own? He'd wanted, expected them from Claire. When they hadn't come he'd checked his own sperm count, found it surprisingly low, secretly blamed himself all those years for Claire's inability to conceive. Until he learned that she'd made a fool of him.

He would not have minded having a child by Winifred. But she was virtually past childbearing years when they married. After she became suspicious of him, he didn't bother to touch her. When you are planning to eliminate someone, she is already dead to you, and sex is for the living.

But now. A younger woman, a woman unlike Claire and Winifred. Claire, haughtily demeaning him with her sneering comments about his father's apothecary; Winifred the do-gooder, with her causes and charities. Now he needed a wife who would not only be socially at ease, but also like to entertain, to travel, to mingle.

He hated those things. He knew his contempt showed. He needed someone who would take care of all that for him, soften his image.

One day he would be able to carry out his work publicly. One day he would have the fame he deserved. One day the fools who said his work was impossible would be forced to acknowledge his genius.

It was seven o'clock. He got out of the car and carefully locked it. He walked to the entrance of the Carlyle, his dark blue suit covered by a blue cashmere coat, his shoes shined to a soft luster, his silver-tipped hair unruffled by the biting night drafts.

The doorman held the door open for him. "Good evening, Dr. Highley. Pretty bad weather, isn't it, sir?"

He nodded without answering and went into the dining room. The corner table he preferred was reserved, but the maître d' quickly switched the expected diners to another table and led him to it.

Wine warmed and soothed him. The dinner gave him the strength he was anticipating. The demitasse and brandy restored him to total balance. His mind was clear and brittle. He reviewed each step of the procedure that would lead Katie DeMaio to death by hemorrhage.

There would be no mistakes.

He was just signing his check when the maître d' came to his table, his footsteps uncharacteristically hurried, his manner agitated. "Dr. Highley, I'm afraid there's a problem."

His finger gripped the pen. He looked up.

"It's just, sir, that a young man was observed prying the trunk of your car. The doorman saw him just as he got it open. Before he could be stopped, he had stolen a bag from the trunk. The police are outside. They believe it was a drug addict who chose your car because of the MD license plates."

His lips were rubbery. It was hard to form words. Like an X-ray machine he mentally examined the contents of the bag: the bloodstained paperweight; the medical file with both Vangie and Salem's names on it; Vangie's moccasin.

When he spoke, his voice was surprisingly steady. "Do the police believe that my bag will be recovered?"

"I asked that question, sir. I'm afraid they just don't know. It might be discarded a few blocks from here after he's taken what he wants from it, or it might never show up again. Only time will tell."

♦ 43 ♦

Before she went to bed, Katie packed an overnight bag for her stay in the hospital. The hospital was halfway between the house and the office, and it would have been an unnecessary waste of time to return home for the bag tomorrow.

She realized that she was packing with a sense of urgency. She'd be so glad to get this over with. The heavy sense of being physically out of tune was wearing her down mentally and emotionally. Tonight she'd felt almost buoyant setting out for Molly's. Now she felt depleted, exhausted, depressed. It was all physical, wasn't it?

Or was the nagging thought that maybe Richard was involved with someone contributing to the feeling of depression?

Maybe when this wasn't hanging over her, she'd be able to think more clearly. It felt as though her mind were being plagued by half-completed thoughts like swarms of mosquitoes, landing, biting, but gone before she could reach them. Why did she have the sensation of missing threads, of not asking the right questions, of misreading signals?

By Monday she'd be feeling better, thinking straight.

Wearily, she showered, brushed her teeth and hair and got into bed. A minute later she pulled herself up on one elbow, reached for her handbag and fished out the small bottle Dr. Highley had given her.

Almost forgot to take this, she thought as she swallowed the pill with a gulp from the water glass on her night table. Turning off the light, she closed her eyes.

◆ 44 ◆

Gertrude Fitzgerald wearily let the water run cold in the bathroom tap and opened the prescription bottle. The migraine was beginning to let up. If it didn't start in on the other side of her head, she'd be all right by the morning. This last pill should do it.

Something was bothering her . . . something over and beyond Edna's death. It had to do with Mrs. DeMaio's call. It was so silly, asking if Edna had ever called Dr. Fukhito or Dr. Highley Prince Charming. Perfect nonsense.

But *Prince Charming*.

Edna *had* talked about him. Not in relation to the doctors, but somehow in the last couple of weeks. If she could only remember. If Mrs. DeMaio had asked if Edna had ever mentioned him, it might have helped her remember right away. Now it was eluding her, the exact circumstance.

Or was she imagining it? Power of suggestion.

When this headache was finished, she'd be able to think. Really think. And maybe remember.

She swallowed the pill and got into bed. She closed her eyes. Edna's voice sounded in her ears. "And I said that Prince Charming won't . . ."

She couldn't remember the rest.

◆ 45 ◆

At four A.M. Richard gave up trying to sleep, got out of bed and made coffee. He had phoned Scott at home about Emmet Salem's death, and Scott had immediately alerted the New York police that his office wanted to cooperate in the investigation. More than that it had been impossible to accomplish. Mrs. Salem was not at home in Minneapolis. The doctor's answering service could only supply the emergency number of the doctor covering the practice and did not know how to reach his nurse.

Richard began writing notes. *1. Why did Dr. Salem phone our office? 2. Why did Vangie make an appointment with him? 3. The Berkeley baby.*

The Berkeley baby was the key. Was the Westlake Maternity Concept as successful as had been touted? Or was it a cover-up for private adoptions for women who either couldn't conceive or could not carry babies to term? Was the fact that they were being put to bed in the hospital two months before the supposed delivery nothing but a cover-up for what would become an obvious nonpregnant condition?

Babies were hard to adopt. Liz Berkeley had openly admitted that she and her husband had tried that route. Suppose Edgar Highley had said to them, "You'll never have your own child. I can get you a child. It will cost you money and it will have to be absolutely confidential."

They'd have gone along with it. He'd stake his life on that.

But Vangie Lewis had been pregnant. So she didn't fit into the adoptive pattern. Granted she was desperate to have a child . . . but how the hell did she expect to pass off an Oriental baby on her husband? Was there any chance that there was Oriental blood in either family? He'd never considered that.

The malpractice suits. He had to find out the reason those people sued Highley. And Emmet Salem had been Vangie's doctor. His office would have her medical records. That would be a place to start.

Vangie's body had come back on the plane that Chris Lewis did not take. It was in the lab now. First thing in the morning he'd review the autopsy findings. He'd go over the body again. There was something . . . It had seemed unimportant at the time. He'd brushed over it. He'd been too involved with the fetus and the cyanide burns.

Could Vangie have simply spilled the cyanide on herself? Maybe she'd been frantically nervous. But the glass would have had more prints. She'd have picked it up, refilled it; there'd be something—an envelope, a vial—that she'd have used to hold more cyanide.

It hadn't happened like that.

At five thirty Richard turned out the light. He set the alarm for seven. At last sleep came. And he dreamed of Katie. She was standing behind Edna Burns's apartment looking in the window, and Dr. Edgar Highley was watching her.

◆ 46 ◆

As befits a bookkeeper, Edna had kept meticulous records. When the search team headed by Phil Cunningham and Charley Nugent descended on her apartment on Friday morning, they found a simple statement in the old-fashioned breakfront:

Since my one blood relative never bothered to inquire about or send a card to my dear parents in their illness, I have decided to leave my worldly goods to my friends, Mrs. Gertrude Fitzgerald and Mrs. Gana Krupshak. Mrs. Fitzgerald is to receive my diamond ring and whatever household possessions she cares to have. Mrs. Krupshak is to receive my diamond pin, my imitation fur coat and whatever household possessions Mrs. Fitzgerald does not wish to have. I have discussed my funeral with the establishment that handled my parents' arrangements so beautifully. My $10,000 insurance policy less funeral expenses is assigned to the nursing home which took such fine care of my parents and to whom I am still financially indebted.

Methodically the team dusted for fingerprints, vacuumed for hair and fibers, searched for signs of forced entry. A smear of dirt on the bottom of the windowsill plant in the bedroom caused the crinkles around Phil's eyes and forehead to settle into a deep frown. He went around the back of the apartment building, thoughtfully scraped a sample of frozen dirt into an envelope and with his fingertips pushed up the bedroom window. For an average-sized person, it was low enough to step over.

"Possible," he said to Charley. "Someone could have come in here and sneaked up on her. But with the ground so frozen, you'd probably never be able to prove it."

As the final step, they rang the doorbells of all the neighbors in the courtyard. The question was simple: had anyone noticed any strangers in the vicinity on Tuesday night?

They had not really expected success. Tuesday night had been dark and cold. The untrimmed shrubbery would have made it possible for anyone who did not want to be seen to stay in the shadows of the building.

But at the last apartment they had unexpected success. An eleven-year-old boy had just come home from school for lunch. He heard the question asked of his mother.

"Oh, I told a man which apartment Miss Burns lived in," he reported. "You remember, Ma, when you made me walk Porgy just before I went to bed, after *Happy Days* . . ."

"That would be around nine thirty," the boy's mother said. "You didn't tell me you spoke to anyone," she said accusingly to her son.

The boy shrugged. "It was no big deal. A man parked at the curb just when I was coming back down the block. He asked me if I knew which apartment Miss Burns was in. I pointed it out. That's all."

"What did he look like?" Charley asked.

The boy frowned. "Oh, he was nice-looking. He had sort of dark hair and he was tall and *his car was neat*. It was a 'Vette."

Charley and Phil looked at each other. "Chris Lewis," Charley said flatly.

211

On Friday morning, Katie got into the office by seven o'clock and began a final review of the case she was trying. The defendants were eighteen- and seventeen-year-old brothers accused of vandalizing two schools by setting fires in twelve classrooms.

Maureen came in at eight thirty carrying a steaming coffeepot. Katie looked up. "Boy, I'm going all out to nail those two," she said. "They did it for kicks—*for kicks*. When you see the way people are struggling to pay taxes to keep up the schools their kids go to, it's sickening; it's more than a crime."

Maureen reached for Katie's coffee cup and filled it. "One of those schools is in my town, and the children next door go there. The ten-year-old had just finished a project for the science fair. It was fantastic—a solar heating unit. Poor little kid worked on it for months. It got burned in the fire. There was just nothing left of it."

Katie jotted a note on the side of her opening statement. "That gives me some extra ammunition. Thanks."

"Katie . . ." Maureen's voice was hesitant.

Katie looked up into troubled green eyes. "Yes?"

"Rita told me that she told you about . . . about the baby."

"Yes, she did. I'm terribly sorry, Maureen."

"The thing is I can't seem to get over it. And now this Vangie Lewis case . . . all the talk about that . . . only brings it back. I've been trying to forget. . . ."

Katie nodded. "Maureen, I'd have given anything to have had a baby when John died. That year I prayed I'd get pregnant so I'd have something of him. When I think of all the friends I have who elect never to have children or who have an abortion as casually as they have their hair set, I wonder about the way life works out. I just pray God that someday I will have children of my own. You will too, of course, and we'll both appreciate them because of not having the ones we wanted before."

Maureen's eyes were filled with tears. "I hope so. But the thing about the Vangie Lewis case is—"

The telephone rang. Katie reached for it. It was Scott. "Glad you're in, Katie. Can you run over here for a minute?"

"Of course." Katie got up. "Scott wants me now. We'll talk later, Maureen." Impulsively she hugged the girl.

Scott was standing by the window staring out. Katie was sure he was not seeing the barred windows of the county jail. He turned when she came in.

"You're on trial today—the Odendall brothers?"

"Yes. We have a good case."

"How long will it take?"

"Most of the day, I'm sure. They're bringing character witnesses from their kindergarten teacher on up, but we'll get them."

"You usually do, Katie. Have you heard about Dr. Salem yet?"

"You mean the doctor from Minneapolis who called Richard? No, I haven't spoken to anyone this morning. I went straight to my office."

"He fell—or was pushed—out a window in the Essex House last night a few minutes after he checked into the hotel. We're working with the New York police on it. And incidentally, Vangie Lewis' body arrived from Minneapolis last night, but Lewis wasn't on the flight."

Katie stared at Scott. "What are you saying?"

"I'm saying that he probably took the flight that went into LaGuardia. It would have gotten him into New York about the time Salem checked in. I'm saying that if we find he was anywhere in the vicinity of that hotel, we may be able to wrap this case up. I don't like the Lewis suicide, I don't like the Edna Burns accidental death and I don't like the idea that Salem fell from a window."

"I don't believe Chris Lewis is a murderer," Katie said flatly. "Where do you think he is now?"

Scott shrugged. "Hiding out in New York, probably. My guess is that when we talk to his girlfriend she'll lead us to him, and she's due in from Florida tonight. Can you hang around this evening?"

Katie hesitated. "This is the one weekend I have to be away. It's something I can't change. But I'll be honest, Scott. I feel so absolutely lousy that I'm not even thinking straight. I'll get through this trial . . . I'm well prepared; but then I will leave."

Scott studied her. "I've told you all week that you shouldn't have come in," he said, "and right now you look paler than you did Tuesday morning. All right, get the trial over with and clear out of here. There'll be plenty of work on this case next week. We'll go over everything Monday morning. You think you'll be in?"

"Positively."

"You should have a complete checkup."

"I'm going to see a doctor this weekend."

"Good."

Scott looked down at his desk, a signal that the meeting was over. Katie went back to her own office. It was nearly nine, and she was due in the courtroom. Mentally she reviewed the schedule of the pills Dr.

Highley had given her. She'd taken one last night, one at six o'clock this morning. She was supposed to take one every three hours today. She'd better swallow one now before going down to court. She washed it down with the last sip of coffee from the cup on her desk, then gathered her file. The sharp edge of the top page of the brief slit her finger. She gasped at the quick thrust of pain and popping a tissue from her top drawer wrapped it around the finger and hurried from the room.

Half an hour later as, with the rest of the people in the courtroom, she rose to acknowledge the entrance of the judge, the tissue was still wet with blood.

♦ 48 ♦

Edna Burns was buried on Friday morning after an eleven-o'clock Mass of the Resurrection at St. Francis Xavier Church. Gana Krupshak and Gertrude Fitzgerald followed the coffin to the nearby cemetery and, holding hands tightly, watched Edna placed in the grave with her parents. The priest, Father Durkin, conducted the final ceremony, sprinkled holy water over the coffin and escorted them back to Gertrude's car.

"Will you ladies join me for a cup of coffee?" he asked.

Gertrude dabbed at her eyes and shook her head. "I really have to get to work," she said. "I'm taking Edna's place until they find a new receptionist, and the doctors both have office hours this afternoon."

Mrs. Krupshak also declined. "But Father, if you're on your way back to the rectory, would you drop me off? Then I won't take Gertrude out of her way."

"Of course."

Gana turned to Gertrude. Impulsively she said, "Why don't you come by for dinner with us tonight? I have a nice pot roast I'm cooking."

The thought of going back to her own solitary apartment had been upsetting Gertrude, and she quickly accepted the offer. It would be good to talk about Edna tonight with the other person who'd been her friend. She wanted to express to Gana what a crying shame it was that neither of the doctors had come to the Mass, although at least Dr. Fukhito had sent flowers. Maybe talking it out with Gana would help her to think clearly and she'd be able to get a handle on that thought which kept buzzing around inside her head—about something that Edna had said to her.

She said good-bye to Gana and Father Durkin, got into her car, turned on the ignition and released the brake. Dr. Highley's face loomed in her mind: those big, fishlike, cold eyes. Oh, he'd been nice enough to her Tuesday night, giving her the pill to calm her down and what-have-you. But there was something funny about him that night. Like when he went to get her a drink of water, she'd started to follow him. She didn't want him waiting on her. He'd turned on the water tap, then gone into the bedroom. From the hall she'd seen him take out his handkerchief and start to open Edna's night-table drawer.

Then that nice Dr. Carroll had started to walk down the hall and Dr. Highley had closed the drawer, stuffed the handkerchief in his pocket and backed up so it looked like he was just standing in the bedroom doorway.

Gertrude had let Dr. Carroll pass her, then slipped

back into the living room. She didn't want them to think she was trying to overhear what they were saying. But if Dr. Highley wanted something from that drawer, why didn't he just say so and get it? And why on earth would he open the drawer holding a handkerchief over his fingers? Certainly he didn't think Edna's apartment was too dirty for him to touch. Why, it was immaculate!

Dr. Highley always was a strange man. Truth to tell, like Edna, she'd always been a little afraid of him. No way would she agree to take over Edna's job if it was offered to her. Her mind decided on that point, Gertrude steered the car off the cemetery road and onto Forest Avenue.

♦ 49 ♦

The lifeless body of Vangie Lewis was placed on the slab in the autopsy room of the Valley County Medical Examiner. His face impassive, Richard watched as his assistant removed the silk caftan that was to have been Vangie's burial robe. What had seemed soft and natural in the gentle light of the funeral parlor now resembled a department-store mannequin, features with a total absence of life.

Vangie's blond hair had been carefully coiffed to flow loose on her shoulders. Now the hair spray had begun to harden, separating the hairs into thin, straw-like groups. Fleetingly, Richard remembered that St. Francis Borgia had given up a life at court and entered a monastery after viewing the decaying body of a once-beautiful queen.

Sharply, he pulled his mind to the medical problem at hand. He had missed something about Vangie's body on Tuesday afternoon. He was sure of that. It had something to do with her legs or feet. He would concentrate his attention there.

Fifteen minutes later he found what he was seeking: a two-inch scratch on Vangie's left foot. He had dismissed it because he'd been so involved with the cyanide burns and the fetus.

That scratch was fresh. There was no sign of healing skin. That was what had bothered him. Vangie's foot had been scratched shortly before her death, and Charley had found a piece of the cloth from the dress she was wearing when she died protruding from a sharp implement in the garage.

Richard turned to his assistant. "The lab is supposed to be finished with the clothes Mrs. Lewis was wearing when we brought her in. Will you please get them and dress her in them again. Call me when she's ready."

Back in his office, he scribbled on a pad: *Shoes Vangie was wearing when found. Sensible walking shoes, cut fairly high on sides. Could not have been wearing them when foot was scratched.*

He began to examine the notes he'd made during the night. The Berkeley baby. He was going to talk to Jim Berkeley, get him to admit that the baby was adopted.

But what would that prove?

Nothing of itself, but it would begin the investigation. Once that admission was made, the whole Westlake Maternity Concept would be exposed as a gigantic fraud.

Would anyone kill to prevent that fraud from being exposed?

He needed to see Dr. Salem's medical records on

Vangie Lewis. By now, Scott must have reached Dr. Salem's office. Quickly, he dialed Scott. "Have you spoken to Salem's nurse?"

"Yes, and also to his wife. They're both terribly broken up. Both swear he had no history of high blood pressure or dizziness. No personal problems, no money problems, a full schedule of lecturing for the next six months. So I say, forget both the suicide and the accidental-fall angles."

"How about Vangie Lewis? What did the nurse know?"

"Dr. Salem asked her to get out Vangie's file yesterday morning in his office. Then, just before he left for his plane, he made a long-distance phone call."

"That might have been the one to me."

"Possibly. But the nurse said that he told her he had other long-distance calls to make, but he'd use his credit card from the airport after he checked in for his flight. Apparently he had a thing about getting to the airport with a lot of time to spare."

"Is she sending Vangie's file to us? I want to see it."

"No, she's not." Scott's voice hardened. "Dr. Salem took it with him. She saw him put it in his attaché case. That case was found in his room. But the Lewis file wasn't in it. And get this: After Dr. Salem left, Chris Lewis phoned his office. Said he had to talk to Salem. The nurse told him where Dr. Salem would be staying in New York, even to giving him the room number. I'll tell you something, Richard: by the end of the day I expect to be swearing out a warrant for Lewis' arrest."

"You mean you think there was something in that file that Chris Lewis would kill to get? I find that hard to believe."

"Someone wanted that file," Scott said. "That's pretty obvious, isn't it?"

Richard hung up the phone. *Someone* wanted the file. The medical file. Who would know what was in it that might be threatening?

A doctor.

Was Katie right in her suspicions about the psychiatrist? What about Edgar Highley? He'd come to Valley County with the imprimatur of the Westlake name, a name respected in New Jersey medical circles.

Impatiently, Richard searched on his desk for the slip of paper Marge had given him with the names of the two patients who had filed malpractice suits against Edgar Highley.

Anthony Caldwell, Old Country Lane, Peapack.

Anna Horan, 415 Walnut Street, Ridgefield Park.

Turning on the intercom, he asked Marge to try to phone both people.

Marge came in a few minutes later. "Anthony Caldwell is no longer at that address. He moved to Michigan last year. I got a neighbor on the phone. She told me that his wife died of a tubal pregnancy and that he filed suit against the doctor, but it was dismissed. She was anxious to talk about it. Said Mrs. Caldwell had been told by two other doctors that she'd never conceive, but that as soon as she started the Westlake Maternity Concept program she became pregnant. But she was terribly sick all the time and finally died in her fourth month."

"That gives me enough information for the moment," Richard said. "We're going to subpoena all the hospital records. What about Mrs. Horan?"

"I caught her husband home. He's a law student at Rutgers. Says she's working as a computer programmer. Gave me her phone number at the job. Shall I get her for you now?"

"Yes, please."

Marge picked up Richard's phone, dialed and asked

for Mrs. Anna Horan. A moment later, she said, "Mrs. Horan, one moment please. Dr. Carroll is calling."

Richard took the phone. "Mrs. Horan."

"Yes." There was a lilting inflection in her voice, an accent he could not place.

"Mrs. Horan, you filed a malpractice suit last year against Dr. Edgar Highley. I wonder if I might ask you some questions about that case. Are you free to talk?"

The voice on the other phone became agitated. "No . . . not here."

"I understand. But it's urgent. Would it be possible for you to stop by my office after work today and talk with me?"

"Yes . . . all right." Clearly, the woman wanted to get off the phone.

Richard gave the office address and offered directions, but was interrupted.

"I know how to get to you. . . . I'll be there by five thirty."

The connection was broken. Richard looked at Marge and shrugged. "She's not happy about it, but she's coming in."

It was nearly noon. Richard decided to go to the courtroom where Katie was trying the Odendall case and see if she'd have lunch with him. He wanted to ventilate his thoughts about Edgar Highley. Katie had interviewed him. What had her reaction been? Would she agree that maybe there was something wrong about the Westlake Maternity Concept—either a baby ring or a doctor who took criminal chances with his patients' lives?

When he got to the courtroom, it was deserted except for Katie, who was still at the prosecutor's table.

Preoccupied with her notes, she barely looked up when he came over to her. At his suggestion of lunch, she shook her head.

"Richard, I'm up to my eyes in this. Those skunks have retracted their confession. Now they're trying to say someone else set the fires, and they're such convincing liars I swear the jury is falling for it. I've got to work on the cross-examination." Her eyes went back to her notes.

Richard studied her. Her usually olive skin was deadly pale. Her eyes when she'd looked up at him had been heavy and clouded. He noticed the tissue wrapped around her finger. Gently, he reached over and unwound it.

Katie looked up. "What . . . oh, that darn thing. It must be deep. It's been bleeding off and on all morning. I needed that."

Richard studied the cut. Released from the tissue, it began to flow rapidly. Pressing the tissue over the cut, he reached for a rubber band and wound it above the cut. "Leave this on for about twenty minutes. That should stop it. Have you been having any clotting problems, Katie?"

"Yes, some. But oh, Richard, I can't talk about it now. This case is running away from me and I feel so lousy." Her voice broke.

The courtroom was empty except for the two of them. Richard reached down and put his arms around her. He hugged her head against his chest and put his lips on her hair. "Katie, I'm going to clear out now. But wherever you go this weekend, do some thinking. Because I'm throwing my hat in the ring. I want you. I want to take care of you. If there's someone you're seeing now, tell him he's got stiff competition, because whoever he is, he's not watching out for you. If it's the past that's holding you, I'm going to try to break that hold."

He straightened up. "Now go ahead and win your case. You can do it. And for God's sake, take it easy this weekend. Monday, I'm going to need your input on an angle I see developing in the Lewis case."

All morning she'd felt so cold—so desperately, icy cold. Even the long-sleeved wool dress hadn't helped. Now, so close to Richard, the warmth of his body communicated itself to her. As he turned to leave, she impulsively grasped his hand and held it against her face. "Monday," she said.

"Monday," he agreed, and left the courtroom.

♦ 50 ♦

Before they left the garden apartment complex where Edna had lived, Charley and Phil rang the Krupshaks' doorbell. Gana had just returned from the funeral.

"We're finished with our investigation in the apartment," Charley told her. "You're free to enter it." He showed her the note Edna had left. "I have to check on whether this constitutes a will, but all that stuff isn't worth a thousand dollars, so my guess is that we'll return that jewelry to you, and you and Mrs. Fitzgerald can divide it and the furniture. At least, you can look it over and decide it between yourselves; but don't remove anything yet."

The two investigators returned to the office and went directly to the lab, where they turned in the contents of the vacuum bag, the plant that had been on the windowsill and the traces of earth they had removed from the ground. "Run these through right away," Phil directed. "This stuff gets top priority."

Scott was waiting for them in his office. At the news

that Chris had been in the vicinity of Edna's apartment on Tuesday night, he grunted with satisfaction. "Lewis seems to have been all over the map this week," he said, "and wherever he's been someone has died. I sent Rita over to New York this morning with a picture of Chris Lewis. Two bellmen positively identify him as being in the lobby of the Essex House around five o'clock. I'm putting out an APB for him and swearing out a warrant for his arrest."

The phone rang. Impatiently, he reached for it and identified himself. Then his expression changed. "Put her on," he said quickly. Holding his hand over the speaker, he said, "Chris Lewis' girlfriend is calling from Florida . . . Hello, yes, this is the Prosecutor." He paused. "Yes, we are looking for Captain Lewis. Do you know where he is?"

Charley and Phil exchanged glances. Scott's forehead furrowed as he listened. "Very well. He'll be on the plane with you arriving in Newark at seven P.M. I'm very glad to know that he's surrendering voluntarily. If he wishes to consult with a lawyer, he may want to have one here. Thank you."

He hung up the phone. "Lewis is coming in," he said. "We'll crack this case open tonight."

♦ 51 ♦

Through the long, sleepless night, Edgar Highley rationalized the problem of the stolen bag. It might never show up. If it had been abandoned after the thief went through it, the odds were he'd never see it again. Few people would take the trouble to try to return it. More than likely they'd simply keep the bag and throw out the contents.

Suppose the bag were recovered intact by the New York police? His name and the address of the hospital were inside it. If the police phoned him, they'd probably ask for a list of the contents. He'd simply mention some standard drugs, a few instruments and several patients' files. A medical file with the name VANGIE LEWIS on the tab would mean nothing to them. They probably wouldn't bother to study it. They'd just assume it was his. If they asked about the shoe and the bloodstained paperweight, he would deny any knowledge of them; he'd point out that obviously, the thief must have put them there.

It would be all right. And tonight the last risk would be removed. At five A.M. he gave up trying to sleep; showered, standing under the hot needle spray nearly ten minutes until the bathroom was filled with steam; wrapped himself in a heavy ankle-length robe and went down to the kitchen. He was not going in to the office until noon, and he'd make his hospital rounds just before that. Until then, he'd go over his research notes. Yesterday's patient would be his new experiment. But he hadn't yet chosen the donor.

♦ 52 ♦

At four o'clock, Richard, Scott, Charley and Phil studied the body of Vangie Lewis, now dressed in the clothes in which she had died. The scrap of flowered material that had been found on the prong in the garage exactly fitted the tear near the hem of her dress. The panty hose on her left foot showed a two-inch slash directly over the fresh cut.

"No trace of blood on the hosiery," Richard said. "She was already dead when her foot caught on the prong."

"How high was the shelf that prong was on?" Scott asked.

Phil shrugged. "About two feet from the floor."

"Which means that someone carried Vangie Lewis in through the garage, laid her on her bed and tried to give the appearance of a suicide," Scott said.

"Without question," Richard agreed. But he was frowning. "How tall is Chris Lewis?" he asked.

Scott shrugged. "He's a big one. Maybe six feet four. Why?"

"Let's try something. Wait a minute." Richard left the room, returning with a ruler. Carefully, he marked the wall at heights of two, three and four feet from the floor. "If we assume Chris Lewis was the one who carried Vangie in, I suggest that she would not have been scratched by that prong." He turned to Phil. "You're sure the shelf was two feet off the ground?"

Phil shrugged. "Within an inch." Charley nodded in agreement.

"All right. I'm six feet two." Gently, Richard put one arm under the dead woman's neck, the other under her knees. Picking her up, he walked over to the wall. "Look where her foot touches. She was small. It wouldn't have been grazed by any object lower than three feet on the shelf *if* she was carried by a tall man. On the other hand . . ." He walked over to Phil. "How tall are you . . . About five feet ten?"

"Just about."

"All right. Chris Lewis has over six inches on you. Take her and see where her foot falls when you hold her."

Gingerly, Phil accepted the body and walked by the wall. Vangie's foot trailed against the first mark Richard had made. Quickly, Phil laid her back on the slab.

Scott shook his head. "Inconclusive. Impossible to figure. Maybe he was bending over, trying to hold her away from him." He turned to the attendant. "We'll want those clothes as evidence. Take good care of them. Get some photos of the cut, the stocking and the dress."

He walked with Richard back to his office. "You're still thinking about the psychiatrist, aren't you?" he asked. "He's about five ten."

Richard hesitated and decided not to say anything until he had spoken with Jim Berkeley and the woman patient who had pressed the malpractice suit. He changed the subject. "How's Katie doing?"

Scott shook his head. "Hard to say. Those bums are blaming the vandalism on one of their friends who was killed on his motorcycle last November. Their new story is they took the rap for him because they felt sorry for his folks, but now their minister has persuaded them for the sake of their own family they have to tell the truth."

Richard snorted. "The jury isn't falling for that, is it?"

Scott said, "It's out now. Listen, no matter how hard you try to pick your jury, there's always one bleeding-heart on it who will fall for a sob story. Katie's done a great job, but it could go either way. Okay. I'll see you later."

At four thirty, Jim Berkeley returned Richard's call. "I understand you've been trying to reach me." His voice was guarded.

"Yes." Richard matched the other man's impersonal tone. "It's important that I speak with you. Can you stop in my office on your way home?"

"Yes, I can." Now Jim's voice became resigned. "And I think I know what you want to talk about."

◆ 53 ◆

Edgar Highley turned from the girl on the examining table. "You may get dressed now."

She had claimed to be twenty, but he was sure she wasn't more than sixteen or seventeen. "Am I . . ."

"Yes, my dear. You are very definitely pregnant. About five weeks, I should think. I want you to return tomorrow morning and we will terminate the pregnancy."

"I was wondering: do you think I should maybe have the baby and have it adopted?"

"Have you told your parents about this?"

"No. They'd be so upset."

"Then I suggest you postpone motherhood for several years at least. Ten o'clock tomorrow."

He left the room, went into his office and looked up the phone number of the new patient he had chosen yesterday. "Mrs. Englehart, this is Dr. Highley. I want to begin your treatment. Kindly come to the hospital tomorrow morning at eight thirty and prepare to spend the night."

◆ 54 ◆

While the jury was deliberating, Katie went into the courthouse cafeteria. She carefully chose a small table at the end of the room and sat with her back to the other tables. She did not want anyone to either join or notice her. The light-headed feeling was persistent now; she felt fatigued and weak, but not hungry. Just a cup of tea, she thought. Mama always thought that a cup of tea would cure all the ills of the world. She remembered coming back to the house from John's funeral, her mother's voice concerned, gentle: "I'll make you a nice hot cup of tea, Katie."

Richard. Mama would love Richard. She always liked big men. "Your dad was a skinny little one, but oh, Katie, didn't he seem like a big man?"

Yes, he did.

Mama was coming up for Easter. That was just six weeks from now. Mama would be so delighted if she and Richard got together.

I do want that, don't I? Katie thought as she sipped the tea. It's not just because I'm so aware of loneliness this week.

It was more than that. Much more. But this weekend in the hospital, she'd be able to sort things through, to think quietly.

She sat for nearly an hour, absently sipping the tea,

reviewing every step of her summation. Had she convinced the jury that the Odendall boys were lying? The minister. She'd scored there. He'd agreed that neither boy was a churchgoer; that neither boy had ever consulted him for any reason before. Was it possible that he was being used by them to bolster their story? "Yes," he agreed. "It is possible." She had made that point. She was sure of it.

At five o'clock she returned to the courtroom. As she entered, the jury sent word to the judge that it had reached a verdict.

Five minutes later, the foreman announced the verdict: "Robert Odendall, not guilty on all counts. Jonathan Odendall, not guilty on all counts."

"I don't believe it." Katie wasn't sure if she had spoken aloud. The judge's face hardened into angry lines. He dismissed the jury curtly and told the defendants to stand up.

"You are very lucky," he snapped, "luckier than I hope you'll ever be again in either of your lives. Now clear out of my courtroom, and if you're smart you'll never appear before me again."

Katie stood up. No matter if the judge clearly felt the verdict was erroneous, she had lost the case. She should have done more. She felt rather than saw the victorious smile the defense attorney shot at her. A thick, hard lump burned in her throat, making it impossible to swallow. She was within inches of tears. Those two criminals were about to be released on the streets after flouting justice. A dead boy had been labeled a criminal.

She stuffed her notes into her briefcase. Maybe if she hadn't felt so lousy all week she'd have conducted a better case. Maybe if she'd had this hemorrhaging problem taken care of a year ago instead of delaying and putting it off with this crazy, childish fear of hospitals, she wouldn't have had the accident Monday night.

"Will the State please approach the bench?"

She looked up. The judge was beckoning to her. She walked over to him. The spectators were filing out. She could hear delighted squeals as the Odendalls embraced their gum-chewing, braless girlfriends.

"Your Honor." Katie managed to keep her voice steady.

The judge leaned over and whispered to her: "Don't let it get you down, Katie. You proved that case. Those little bastards will be back here in two months on other charges. We both know it, and next time you'll nail them."

Katie tried to smile. "That's just what I'm afraid of, that they will be back. God knows how much damage they'll be doing before we can nail them. But thanks, Judge."

She left the courtroom and went back to her office. Maureen looked up hopefully. Katie shook her head and watched the expression change to sympathy. She shrugged. "What can you do, huh?"

Maureen followed her into her office. "Mr. Myerson and Dr. Carroll are in a meeting. They don't want to be disturbed. But of course, you can go in."

"No. I'm sure it's the Lewis case, and I'd be of no use to them or anyone else right now. I'll catch up on Monday."

"All right. Katie, I'm sorry about the Odendall verdict, but try not to take it so hard. You really look sick. Are you all right to drive? You're not dizzy or anything?"

"No, really, and I'm not going far. I'll be driving just fifteen minutes and then I won't budge till Sunday."

As she walked to the car, Katie shuddered. The temperature had gotten up to about forty degrees in the afternoon, but was dropping rapidly again. The wet, damp air penetrated the loose sleeves of her red wool wraparound coat and pierced her nylon hose. She thought longingly of her own room, her own bed. How great it would be to be able to go there now, to just go to bed with a hot toddy and sleep the weekend away.

At the hospital, the admitting office had her completed forms waiting. The clerk was briskly bright.

"My goodness, Mrs. DeMaio, you certainly rate. Dr. Highley has given you the bedroom of Suite One on the third floor. That's like going on a vacation. You'll never dream you're in a hospital."

"He said something about that," Katie murmured. She was not about to confide her fear of hospitals to this woman.

"You may be a bit lonesome up there. There are just three suites on that floor, and the other two are empty. And Dr. Highley is having the living room of your suite redecorated. Why, I don't know. It was done less than a year ago. But anyhow, you won't need it. You'll only be here till Sunday. If you want anything, all you have to do is press the buzzer. The second-floor nursing station takes care of both the second- and third-floor patients. They're all Dr. Highley's patients anyhow. Now, here's your wheelchair. If you'll just get into it, we'll whisk you upstairs."

Katie stared in consternation. "You don't mean I have to use a wheelchair now?"

"Hospital regulations," the admitting clerk said firmly.

John in a wheelchair going up for chemotherapy. John's body shrinking as she watched him die. John's voice weakening, his wry, tired humor as the wheelchair was brought to his bed: "Swing low, sweet chariot, coming for to carry me home." The antiseptic hospital smell.

Katie sat down in the chair and closed her eyes. There was no turning back. The attendant, a middle-aged, solidly plump volunteer, pushed the chair down the corridor to the elevator.

"You're lucky to have Dr. Highley," she informed Katie. "His patients get the best care in the hospital. You push that buzzer for someone and you'll have a nurse at your beck and call in thirty seconds. Dr. Highley is strict. The whole staff trembles when he's around, but he's good."

They were at the elevator. The attendant pushed the button. "This place is so different from most hospitals. Most places don't want to see you until you're ready to deliver, and then they shove you out when the baby is a couple of days old. Not Dr. Highley. I've seen him put pregnant women to bed here for two months just as a precaution. That's why he has suites, so people can have a homelike atmosphere. Mrs. Aldrich is in the one on the second floor. She delivered by cesarean yesterday and hasn't stopped crying. She's that happy. Her husband's just as bad. He slept on the sofa in the living room of her suite last night. Dr. Highley encourages that. Well, here's the elevator."

Several other people got on the elevator with them. They glanced at Katie curiously. Observing the magazines and flowers they were carrying, she decided they were obviously visitors. She felt oddly removed from them. The minute you become a patient you lose your identity, she thought. You become a case.

They got off at the third floor. The corridor was carpeted in a soft green shade. Excellent reproductions of Monet and Matisse paintings enhanced by recessed framing were scattered along the walls.

In spite of herself, Katie was reassured. The volunteer wheeled her down the corridor and turned right. "You're in the end suite," she exclaimed. "It's kind of far off. I don't think there's even any other patients on this floor today."

"That's all right with me," Katie murmured. She thought of John's room. The two of them wanting to absorb each other, to stockpile against the separation. Ambulatory patients coming to the door, looking in. "How's it going today, Judge? He looks better, doesn't he, Mrs. DeMaio?"

And she, lying, "Indeed he does." Go away, go away. We have so little time.

"I don't mind being alone on the floor," she repeated.

She was wheeled into a bedroom. The walls were ivory; the carpet, the same soft green as the corridor. The furniture was antique white. Printed draperies in shades of ivory and green matched the bedspread. "Oh, this is nice," Katie exclaimed.

The attendant looked pleased. "I thought you'd like it. The nurse will be in in a few minutes. Why don't you just put your things away and make yourself comfortable?"

She was gone. Somewhat uncertainly, Katie undressed, put on a nightgown and warm robe. She put her clothes in the closet. What in God's name would she do for the long, dreary evening that stretched before her? Last night at this time she'd been dressing to go to Molly's dinner party. And when she'd arrived, Richard had been waiting for her.

She realized she was swaying. Instinctively, she reached for the dresser and held on to it. The light-headed feeling passed. It was probably just the rushing, and the aftermath of the trial and— Let's face it, she thought: apprehension.

She was in a hospital. No matter how she tried to

push away the thought, she was in a hospital. Incredible, childish, that she could not overcome her fear. Daddy. John. The two people she'd loved best in the world had gone into the hospital and died. No matter how she tried to intellectualize, rationalize, she could not lose that terrible feeling of panic. Well, maybe this stay would get her over it. Monday night hadn't been that bad.

There were four doors in the room. The closet door, the bathroom door, the one leading to the corridor. The other one must go into the living room. She opened it and glanced in. As the admitting clerk had told her, it was pulled apart. The furniture was in the middle of the room and covered with painter's drop cloths. She flicked on the light. Dr. Highley surely was a perfectionist. There was nothing the matter with the walls that she could see. No wonder hospital costs were so outrageous.

Shrugging, she turned off the light, closed the door and walked over to the window. The hospital was U-shaped, the two wings parallel to each other at right angles behind the main section.

She'd been on the other side Monday night, exactly opposite where she was now. Visitors' cars were beginning to fill the lot. Where was the parking stall she'd dreamed about? Oh, of course—that one, over to the side, directly under the last light post. There was a car parked there now, a black car. In her dream it had been a black car. Those wired spokes; the way they glinted in the light.

"How are you feeling, Mrs. DeMaio?"

She spun around. Dr. Highley was standing in the room. A young nurse was hovering at his elbow.

"Oh, you startled me. I'm fine, Doctor."

"I knocked, but you didn't hear me." His voice was gently reproving. He came over to the window and drew the drapery. "No matter what we do, these windows are drafty," he commented. "We don't want you catching cold. Suppose you sit on the bed and let me check your pressure. We'll want to take some blood samples too."

The nurse followed him. Katie noticed that the girl's hands were trembling. She was obviously in awe of Dr. Highley.

The doctor wrapped the pressure cuff around her arm. A wave of dizziness made Katie feel as though the walls of the room were receding. She clutched at the mattress.

"Is there anything wrong, Mrs. DeMaio?" The doctor's voice was gentle.

"No, not really. I'm just a touch faint."

He began to pump the bulb. "Nurse Renge, kindly get a cold cloth for Mrs. DeMaio's forehead," he instructed.

The nurse obediently rushed into the bathroom. The doctor was studying the pressure gauge. "You're a bit low. Any problems?"

"Yes." Her voice sounded as though it belonged to someone else, or maybe as though she were in an echo chamber. "My period started again. It's been dreadfully heavy since Wednesday."

"I'm not surprised. Frankly, if you hadn't scheduled this operation, I'm quite sure you'd have been forced to have it on an emergency basis."

The nurse came out of the bathroom with a neatly folded cloth. She was biting her lower lip to keep it from quivering. Katie felt a rush of sympathy for her. She neither wanted nor needed a cold compress on her forehead, but leaned back against the pillow. The nurse put it on her head. The cloth was soaking, and she felt freezing water run down her hairline. She resisted the impulse to brush it away. The doctor would notice, and she didn't want the nurse to be reprimanded.

A flash of humor raised her spirits. She could just see telling Richard, "And this poor, scared kid practically drowned me. I'll probably have bursitis of the eyebrows from now on."

Richard. She should have told him she was coming here. She wanted him with her now.

Dr. Highley was holding a needle. She closed her eyes as he drew blood from a vein in her right arm. She watched him put the blood-filled vacu-tubes on the tray the nurse held out to him.

"I want these run through immediately," he said brusquely.

"Yes, Doctor." The nurse scurried out, obviously delighted to get away.

Dr. Highley sighed. "I'm afraid that timid young woman is on desk duty tonight. But you won't require anything special, I'm sure. Did you complete taking the pills I gave you?"

Katie realized that she had not taken the three-o'clock pill and it was now after six.

"I'm afraid I skipped at three o'clock," she apologized. "I was in court and everything but the trial went out of my mind, and I guess I'm overdue for the last one."

"Do you have the pills with you?"

"Yes, in my handbag." She glanced at the dresser.

"Don't get up. I'll hand it to you."

When she took the bag from him, she unzipped it, fished inside and brought out the small bottle. There were just two pills in it. The night table held a tray with a carafe of ice water and a glass. Dr. Highley poured water into the glass and gave it to her. "Finish these," he said.

"Both of them?"

"Yes. Yes. They're very mild, and I did want you to have them by six." He handed her the glass and dropped the empty jar into his pocket.

Obediently, she swallowed the pills, feeling his eyes on her. His steel-rimmed glasses glinted under the overhead light. The glint. The spokes of the car glinting.

There was a blur of red on the glass as she laid it down. He noticed it, reached for her hand and examined her finger. The tissue had become damp again.

"What's this?" he asked.

"Oh, nothing. Just a paper cut, but it must be deep. It keeps bleeding."

"I see." He stood up. "I've ordered a sleeping pill for you. Please take it as soon as the nurse brings it."

"I really prefer not to take sleeping pills, Doctor. They seem to cause an overreaction in me." She wanted to sound vehement. Instead, her voice had a lazy, weak quality.

"I'm afraid I insist on the pill, Mrs. DeMaio, particularly for someone like yourself who is likely to spend the night in sleepless anxiety without it. I want you well rested in the morning. Oh, here's your dinner now."

Katie watched as a thin, sixtyish woman carrying a tray came into the room and glanced nervously at the doctor. They're all petrified of him, she thought. Unlike the usual plastic or metal hospital tray, this one was made of white wicker and had a side basket that held the evening newspaper. The china was delicate, the silverware gracefully carved. A single red rose stood in a slender vase. Double loin lamb chops were kept hot by a silver dome over the dinner plate. An arugula salad, julienne string beans, small hot biscuits, tea and sherbet completed the meal. The attendant turned to go.

"Wait," Dr. Highley commanded. He said to Katie,

"As you will see, all my patients are served fare that compares favorably with the food in a first-class restaurant. I think one of the abiding wastes in hospitals is the tons of institutional food that are thrown out daily while patients' families bring in CARE packages from home." He frowned. "However, I think I would prefer if you did not eat dinner tonight. I've come to believe that the longer a patient fasts before surgery, the less likelihood she will experience discomfort after it."

"I'm not at all hungry," Katie said.

"Fine." He nodded to the attendant. She picked up the tray and hurried out.

"I'll leave you now," Dr. Highley told Katie. "You *will* take the sleeping pill."

Her nod was noncommittal.

At the door he paused. "Oh, I regret, your phone apparently isn't working. The repairman will take care of it in the morning. Is there anyone you expect to call you here tonight? Or perhaps you'll be having a visitor?"

"No. No calls or visitors. My sister is the only one who knows I'm here, and she's at the opera tonight."

He smiled. "I see. Well, good night, Mrs. DeMaio, and please relax. You can trust me to take care of you."

"I'm sure I can."

He was gone. She leaned back on the pillow, closing her eyes. She was floating somewhere; her body was drifting, drifting like . . .

"Mrs. DeMaio." A young voice was apologetic. Katie opened her eyes. "What . . . oh, I must have dozed." It was Nurse Renge. She was carrying a tray with a pill in a small paper cup. "You're to take this now. It's the sleeping pill Dr. Highley ordered. He said I was to stay and be sure you took it." Even with Dr. Highley gone, the girl seemed nervous. "It always makes patients mad when we have to wake them up to give them a sleeping pill, but that's the way it works in the hospital."

"Oh." Katie reached for the pill, put it in her mouth, gulped down water from her carafe.

"Would you like to get settled in bed now? I'll turn down your covers for you."

Katie realized she'd been sleeping on top of the spread. She nodded, pulled herself up and went into the bathroom. There she removed the sleeping pill from under her tongue. Some of it had already dissolved, but she managed to spit out most of it. No way, she thought. I'd rather be awake than have nightmares. She splashed water on her face, brushed her teeth and returned to the bedroom. She felt so weak, so vague.

The nurse helped her into bed. "You really are tired, aren't you? Well, I'll tuck you in, and I'm sure you'll have a good night's sleep. Just push the buzzer if you need me for anything."

"Thank you." Her head was so heavy. Her eyes felt glued together.

Nurse Renge went over and pulled down the shade. "It's started to snow again, but it's going to change to rain. It's a wicked night, a good night to be in bed."

"Open the drapes and raise the window just about an inch, won't you?" Katie murmured. "I always like fresh air in my bedroom."

"Certainly. Shall I turn off the light now, Mrs. DeMaio?"

"Please." She didn't want to do anything except sleep.

"Good night, Mrs. DeMaio."

"Good night. Oh, what time is it, please?"

"Just eight o'clock."

"Thank you."

The nurse left. Katie closed her eyes. Minutes passed. Her breathing became even. At eight thirty, she was not aware of the faint sound that was caused when the handle on the door from the living room of the suite began to turn.

♦ 55 ♦

Gertrude and the Krupshaks lingered over Gana's potroast dinner. Gratefully, Gertrude acceded to Gana's urgings to have seconds, to have a generous slice of homemade chocolate cake.

"I don't usually eat this much," she apologized, "but I haven't swallowed a morsel since we found poor Edna."

Gana nodded soberly. Her husband picked up his coffee cup and dessert plate. "The Knicks are playing," he announced. "I'm gonna watch." His blunt tone was not ungracious. He settled himself in the living room and switched on the dial.

Gana sighed. "The Knicks . . . the Mets . . . the Giants . . . One season after the other. But on the other hand, he's *here*. I can look across the room and there he is. Or if I come home from bingo, I know I'm not going into an empty place, like poor Edna always had to."

"I know." Gertrude thought of her own solitary home, then reflected on her oldest granddaughter. "Gran, why not come to dinner?" or "Gran, are you going to be home Sunday? We thought we'd drop in to say hello." She could have it a lot worse.

"Maybe we should go in and take a look at Edna's place," Gana said. "I don't want to rush you . . . I mean, have more coffee, or another piece of cake . . ."

"No. Oh, no. We should go in. You kind of hate to do it, but it's something you can't avoid."

"I'll get the key."

They hurried across the courtyard. While they were at the table, the wet, cold combination of snow and rain had once again begun to fall. Gana dug her chin into her coat collar. She thought of Edna's lovely imitation-leopard coat. Maybe she could take it home tonight. It was hers.

Inside the apartment, they became quiet. The fingerprinting powder the detectives had used was still visible on the tabletops and door handles. Inadvertently, they both stared at the spot where Edna's crumpled body had lain.

"There's blood on the radiator," Gana muttered. "Gus'll probably repaint it."

"Yes." Gertrude shook herself. Get this over with. She knew her granddaughter's taste. Besides the velour couch, Nan would love those matching chairs, the tall-backed ones with mahogany arms and legs. One was a rocker, the other a straight chair. She remembered Edna's telling her that when she was a child, they'd been covered in blue velvet with a delicate leaf pattern. She'd had them redone inexpensively and always sighed, "They never looked the same."

If Nan had them re-covered in velvet again, they'd be beautiful. And that piecrust table. Altman's had copies of that in the reproduction gallery. Cost a fortune, too. Of course, this one was pretty nicked, but Nan's husband could refinish anything. Oh, Edna, Gertrude thought. You were smarter than most of us. You knew the value of things.

Gana was at the closet removing the leopard coat.

"Edna loaned me this last year," she said. "I was going to a social with Gus. I love it."

It did not take them long to finish sharing the contents of the apartment. Gana had little interest in the furniture; what Gertrude did not want she was giving to the Salvation Army; but she was delighted when Gertrude suggested she take the silver plate and good china. They agreed that Edna's wardrobe would also go to the Salvation Army. She had been shorter and heavier than either of them.

"I guess that's it," Gana sighed. "Except for the jewelry, and the police will give that back to us pretty soon. You get the ring, and she left the pin to me."

The jewelry. Edna had kept it in the night-table drawer. Gertrude thought of Tuesday night. That was the drawer Dr. Highley had started to open.

"That reminds me," she said: "we never did look there. Let's make sure we didn't forget anything." She pulled it open. She knew that the police had removed the jewelry box. But the deep drawer was not empty. A scuffed moccasin lay at the bottom of it.

"Well, as I live and breathe," Gana sighed. "Now, can you tell me why Edna would save that thing?" She picked it up and held it to the light. It was out of shape; the heel was run down; white stains on the sides suggested it had been exposed to salted snow.

"That's it!" Gertrude cried. "That's what had me mixed up."

At Gana's mystified expression, she tried to explain. "Mrs. DeMaio asked me if Edna called one of the doctors Prince Charming. And that's what confused me. Of course she didn't. But Edna did tell me how Mrs. Lewis wore terrible old moccasins for her appointments. Why, she pointed them out to me only a couple of weeks ago when Mrs. Lewis was leaving. Edna said that she always kidded Mrs. Lewis. The left shoe was too loose, and Mrs. Lewis was always walking out of it. Edna used to tease Mrs. Lewis that she must be expecting Prince Charming to pick up her glass slipper."

"But Prince Charming wasn't Cinderella's boyfriend," Gana protested. "He was in the 'Sleeping Beauty' fairy tale."

"That's what I mean. I told Edna that she had it mixed up. She just laughed and said that Mrs. Lewis told her the same thing, but that her mother told her the story that way and it was good enough for her."

Gertrude reflected. "Mrs. DeMaio was so anxious when she asked about that Prince Charming talk. And Wednesday night—I wonder: could Mrs. Lewis' shoe be what Dr. Highley wanted from this drawer? Is that possible? You know, I've half a mind to go to Mrs. DeMaio's office and talk to her, or at least leave a message for her. Somehow I just feel I shouldn't wait till Monday."

Gana thought of Gus, who wouldn't have his eyes off the set until nearly midnight. Her acquisitive desire for excitement surged. She'd never been in the Prosecutor's office. "Mrs. DeMaio asked me whether Edna kept her mother's old shoe for sentimental reasons," she said. "I'll bet she was talking about this moccasin. Tell you what: I'll drive over there with you. Gus'll never know I'm gone."

Jim Berkeley parked his car in the courthouse lot and went into the main lobby. The directory showed that the Medical Examiner's office was on the second floor in the old wing of the building. He had seen the expression on Richard Carroll's face last night when he'd looked at the baby. Anger and resentment had made him want to say, "So the baby doesn't look like us. So what?" But it would have been stupid to do that. Worse, it would have been useless.

After several wrong turns in the labyrinth of the building, he found Richard's office. The secretarial desk was empty, but Richard's door was open, and he came out immediately when he heard the reception-area door snap shut. "Jim, it's good of you to come." Obviously, he was trying to be friendly, Jim thought. He was trying to make this seem a casual meeting. His own greeting was reserved and cautious. They went inside. Richard eyed him. Jim stared back impassively. There was none of the easy humor of last night's dinner.

Obviously, Richard got the message. His manner became businesslike. Jim stiffened.

"Jim, we're investigating Vangie Lewis' death. She was a patient at Westlake Maternity Clinic. That's where your wife had the baby."

Jim nodded.

Richard was obviously picking his words carefully. "We are disturbed at some problems that we see coming out of our investigation. Now, I want to ask

245

you some questions—and I swear to you that your answers will remain in this room. But you can be of tremendous help to us, if—"

"*If* I tell you that Maryanne is adopted. Is that it?"

"Yes."

The anger drained from Jim. He thought of Maryanne. Whatever the cost, she was worth having. "No, she is not adopted. I was at her birth. I filmed it. She has a small birthmark on her left thumb. It shows in those pictures."

"It is quite unlikely for two brown-eyed parents to have a green-eyed child," Richard said flatly. Then he stopped. "Are you the baby's father?" he asked quietly.

Jim stared down at his hands. "If you mean would Liz have had an affair with another man? No. I'd stake my life and my soul on that."

"How about artificial insemination?" Richard asked. "Dr. Highley is a fertility expert."

"Liz and I discussed that possibility," Jim said. "We both rejected it years ago."

"Might Liz have changed her mind and not told you? It's not that unusual anymore. There are some fifteen thousand babies born every year in the United States by that means."

Jim reached into his pocket and pulled out his wallet. Flipping it open, he showed Richard two pictures of Liz, himself and the baby. In the first one, Maryanne was an infant; her eyes were almost shut. The second was a recent Kodachrome. The contrast between the skin tone and eye color of the parents and the baby was unmistakable.

Jim said, "The year before Liz became pregnant, we learned that it was almost impossible for us to adopt. Liz and I discussed artificial insemination. We both decided against it, but I was more emphatic than she.

Maryanne had light brown hair when she was born, and blue eyes. A lot of babies start out having blue eyes and then they turn the parents' color. So it's just the last few months that it's become obvious that something is wrong. Not that I care. That baby is everything to us." He looked at Richard. "My wife won't even tell a social lie. She's the most honest person I've ever known in my life. Last month I decided to make it easy for her. I said that I'd been wrong about artificial insemination, that I could see why people went ahead with it."

"What did she say?" Richard asked.

"She knew what I meant, of course. She said that if I thought she could make a decision like that and not tell me, I didn't understand our relationship.

"I apologized to her, swore I didn't mean that; went through hell trying to reassure her. Finally, she believed me." He stared at the picture. "But of course, I know she was lying," he blurted out.

"Or else she wasn't aware of what Highley did to her," Richard said flatly.

◆ 57 ◆

Dannyboy Duke zigzagged across Third Avenue, racing toward Fifty-fifth and Second, where he had the car parked. The woman had missed her wallet just as he got on the escalator. He'd heard her scream, "That man, the dark-haired one—he just robbed me."

He'd managed to slide through the wall of women on Alexander's main floor, but that bitch came rushing down the escalator after him, shouting and pointing as he went out the door. The security guard would probably chase him.

If he could just get to the car. He couldn't ditch the wallet. It was stuffed with hundred-dollar bills. He'd seen them, and he needed a fix.

It had been a good idea to go into Alexander's fur department. Women brought cash to Alexander's. It took too long to get a check or credit card cleared. He'd found that out when he worked as a stock boy there while he was still in high school.

Tonight he'd worn a coat that made him look like a stock boy. Nobody had paid any attention to him. The woman had one of those big, open pocketbooks; she'd held it by one strap as she rummaged through the coat rack. It had been easy to grab her wallet.

Was he being followed? He didn't dare look back. He'd call too much attention to himself. Better to stay against the sides of the buildings. Everyone was hurrying. It was so lousy cold. He could afford a fix; plenty of fixes now.

And in a minute he'd be in the car. He wouldn't be a man running in the street. He'd drive away, over the Fifty-ninth Street Bridge, and be home in Jackson Heights. He'd get his fix.

He looked back. No one running. No cops. Last night had been so lousy. The doorman had almost grabbed him when he broke into that doctor's car. And what did he get for his risk? No drugs in the bag. A medical file, a messy paperweight and an old shoe, for Christ sake.

The pocketbook he'd grabbed later from the old lady. Ten lousy bucks. He'd barely been able to get enough stuff to tide him over today. The pocketbook and bag were in the back seat of the car. He'd have to get rid of them.

He was at the car. He opened it, slipped in. Never,

never, no matter how bad off he was, would he get rid of the car. Cops don't expect you to drive away. If you're spotted, they check the subway stations.

He put the key into the ignition, turned on the engine. Even before he saw the flashing dome light, he heard the siren of the police car as it raced the wrong way up the block. He tried to pull out, but the squad car cut him off. A cop, his hand on the butt of his pistol, jumped out. The headlights were blinding Danny.

The cop yanked open his door, looked in and removed the ignition key. "Well, Dannyboy," he said. "You're still at it, right? Don't you never learn any new tricks? Now get the hell out, keep your god-damned hands where I can see them and brace so I can read you the goddamned *Miranda*. You're what—a three-time loser? I figure you got ten to fifteen coming, we get lucky with a judge."

♦ 58 ♦

The plane circled over Newark. The descent was bumpy. Chris glanced at Joan. She was holding his hand tightly, but he knew it had nothing to do with flying. Joan was absolutely fearless in a plane. He'd heard her argue the point with people who hated to fly. "Statistically, you're much safer in a plane than in a car, a train, a motorcycle or your bathtub," she'd say.

Her face was composed. She'd insisted they have a drink when cocktails were served. Neither one of them had wanted dinner, but they'd both had coffee.

Her expression was serious but composed. "Chris," she'd said, "I can bear anything except thinking that because of me Vangie committed suicide. Don't worry about dragging me into this. You tell the truth when you're questioned and don't hold anything back."

Joan. If they ever got through this, they'd have a good life together. She was a woman. He still had so much to learn about her. He hadn't even realized he could trust her with the simple truth. Maybe he'd gotten so used to shielding Vangie, from trying to avoid arguments. He had so much to learn about himself, let alone Joan.

The landing was rough. Several passengers exclaimed as the plane bounced down. Chris knew the pilot had done a good job. There was a hell of a downwind. If it kept up, they'd probably close the airport.

Joan grinned at him.

"The stewardess must have brought us in." It was an old airline gag.

"Or at least was doing a little lap time."

They were silent as the plane taxied over to the gate. People meeting passengers had to wait past the security gate. But Chris was not surprised to see the two detectives who had been at the house after he found Vangie waiting for him.

"Captain Lewis. Miss Moore."

"Yes."

"Please come with us." Ed's voice was formal. "It is my duty to inform you that you are a suspect in the death of your wife, Vangie Lewis, as well as in several other possible homicides. Anything you say may be used against you. You are not required to answer questions. It is your right to call a lawyer."

Joan answered for him. "He doesn't need a lawyer. And he'll tell you everything he knows."

Molly settled back as the orchestra began the few bars of music that signaled the beginning of *Otello*. Bill *loved* opera. She *liked* it. Maybe that was part of the reason she couldn't relax. Bill was already totally absorbed, his expression serene and thoughtful. She glanced around. The Met was packed as usual. Their seats were excellent. They should be. Bill had paid seventy dollars for the pair. Overhead the chandeliers twinkled, glistened and then began to fade into silvery darkness.

She should have insisted on going to see Katie in the hospital tonight. Bill didn't, *couldn't* understand Katie's dread of hospitals. No wonder. Katie was ashamed to talk about it. The awful part was that there was a basis for her fear. Daddy *hadn't* gotten help in time. The old man who was in the room with him had told them that. Even Bill admitted that a lot of mistakes were made in hospitals.

With a start she heard applause as Placido Domingo descended from the ship. She'd heard nothing of the opera so far. Bill glanced over at her, and she tried to look as though she were enjoying herself. After the first act, she'd phone Katie. That would help to reassure her. Just hearing Katie's voice that she was all right. And by God, she'd be at that hospital early in the morning before the operation and make sure Katie wasn't too nervous.

The first act seemed interminable. She had never

realized it was so long. Finally, intermission came. Impatiently refusing Bill's suggestion of a glass of champagne from the lobby bar, she hurried to a phone. Quickly, she dialed and jammed in the necessary coins.

A few minutes later, white-lipped, she rushed to Bill. Half sobbing, she grabbed his arm. "Something's wrong, something's wrong . . . I called the hospital. They wouldn't put the call through to Katie's room. They said the doctor forbade calls. I got the desk and insisted the nurse check on Katie. She just came back. She's a kid, she's hysterical. Katie's not in her room. Katie's missing."

◆ 60 ◆

He left Katie's room and a smile of satisfaction flitted across his face. It was going very well. The pills were working. She was beginning to hemorrhage. The finger proved that her blood was no longer clotting.

He went down to the second floor and stopped in to see Mrs. Aldrich. The baby was in a crib by her bed. Her husband was with her. He smiled aloofly at the parents, then bent over the child. "A handsome specimen indeed," he proclaimed. "I don't think we'll trade him in."

He knew his attempts at humor were heavy-handed, but sometimes it was necessary. These people were important, very important. Delano Aldrich could direct thousands of dollars of research funds to Westlake. More research. He could work in the laboratory with animals, report his successes. Then, when he publicly began to work with women, all the experimentation of these years would make immediate success inevitable. Fame deferred is not necessarily fame denied.

Delano Aldrich was staring at his son, his face a study in awe and admiration. "Doctor, we still can't believe it. Everyone else said we'd never have a child."

"Everyone else was obviously wrong." It was her anxiety that had been the main problem. Fukhito had spotted that. Muscular dystrophy in her father's family. She knew she might be a carrier. That and some fibroid cysts in her womb. He'd taken care of the cysts and she'd become pregnant. Then he'd done an early test of the amniotic fluid and had been able to reassure her on the dystrophy question.

Still, she was a highly emotional, almost hyperactive personality. She'd had two early miscarriages over ten years ago. He'd put her to bed two months before the birth. And it had worked.

"I'll stop in in the morning." These people would be fervent witnesses for him if there was any question that Katie DeMaio's death was suspicious.

But there shouldn't be any question. The dropping blood pressure was a matter of hospital record. The emergency operation would take place in the presence of the top nurses on the staff. He'd even send for the emergency-room surgeon to assist. Molloy was on tonight. He was a good man, the best. Molloy would be able to tell the family and Katie's office that it had been impossible to stop the hemorrhaging, that Dr. Highley had headed a team working frantically.

Leaving the Aldriches, he went to Nurse Renge's desk. He had carefully manipulated the schedule so that she was on. A more experienced nurse would check on Katie every ten minutes. Renge wasn't that bright.

"Nurse Renge."

"Doctor." She stood up quickly, her hands fluttering nervously.

"I am quite concerned about Mrs. DeMaio. Her blood pressure is in the low normal limit, but I suspect the vaginal bleeding has been heavier than she realizes. I'm going out for dinner, then will come back. I want the lab report on her blood count ready. I did not want to distress her—she has a lifelong fear of hospitals—but I should not be surprised if we have to operate tonight. I'll make that judgment when I come back in about an hour. I persuaded her not to eat dinner, and if she requests any solid food, do not give it to her."

"Yes, Doctor."

"Give Mrs. DeMaio the sleeping pill, and do not in any way intimate to her that emergency surgery may be necessary. Is that clear?"

"Yes, Doctor."

"Very well."

He made a point of speaking to several people in the main lobby. He'd decided to have dinner at the restaurant adjacent to the hospital grounds. It wasn't bad. One could get a quite decent steak, and he wanted to be able later to present the image of a conscientious doctor.

I was concerned about Mrs. DeMaio. Instead of going home, I had dinner next door and went directly back to the hospital to check on her. Thank God I did. At least we tried.

And another important point. Even on a dismal night like this, it would not be unusual to walk over to the restaurant. That way no one would be quite sure how long he'd been gone.

Because while he was waiting for coffee to be served, he'd take the last necessary step. He had left Katie at five past seven. At quarter of eight he was in the restaurant. Katie was going to be given the sleeping pill at eight o'clock. It was a strong one. Thanks to her weakened condition, it would knock her out immediately.

By eight thirty it would be safe for him to go up the back stairs to the third floor, go into the living room of the suite, make sure Katie was asleep and give her the shot of heparin, the powerful anticoagulant drug, which combined with the pills would send her blood pressure and blood count plummeting.

He'd come back here and finish coffee, pay his bill and then return to the hospital. He'd take Nurse Renge up with him to check on Katie. Ten minutes later Katie would be in surgery.

She had made it so easy by not having visitors tonight. Of course, he'd been prepared for that possibility. He'd have slipped the heparin into the transfusion she'd be receiving during the operation. That would have been just as effective, but riskier.

The steak was adequate. Odd how hungry he became at times like this. He would have preferred waiting until after it was over to eat, but that would be almost impossible. By the time Katie's sister was reached it would be well after midnight, since she was at the opera. He'd wait at the hospital for her, to console her. She'd remember how kind he'd been. He wouldn't get home until two or three. He couldn't fast that long.

He permitted himself one glass of wine. He'd have preferred his usual half-bottle, but that was impossible tonight. Nevertheless, the one glass warmed him, made him more alert, helped his mind to rove over the possibilities, to anticipate the unexpected.

This would be the end of the danger. His bag had not shown up. It probably never would. The Salem threat had been eliminated. The papers reported his death as "fell or jumped." Edna was buried this morning. Vangie Lewis had been interred yesterday.

The moccasin in Edna's drawer would mean nothing to the people who disposed of her shabby belongings.

A terrible week. And so unnecessary. He should be allowed to openly pursue his work. A generation ago artificial insemination was considered outrageous. Now thousands of babies were born that way every year.

Go back hundreds of years. The Arabs used to destroy their enemies by infiltrating their camps and impregnating their mares with cotton soaked with the semen of inferior stallions. Remarkable genius to have planned that.

The doctors who had performed the first successful in vitro fertilization were geniuses.

But his genius surpassed them all. And nothing would stand in the way of his reaping the rewards due him.

The Nobel Prize. Some day he would receive it. For contributions to medicine not imagined possible.

He had single-handedly solved the abortion problem, the sterility problem.

And the tragedy was that if it were known, like Copernicus he would be considered a criminal.

"Did you enjoy your dinner, Doctor?" The waitress was familiar. Oh, yes, he had delivered her some years ago. A boy.

"Very much indeed. And how is your son?"

"Fine, sir. Simply fine."

"Wonderful." Incredible this woman and her husband had met his fee, giving him the money saved for a down payment for a home. Well, she'd got what she wanted.

"I'd like cappuccino, please."

"Certainly, Doctor, but that will take about ten minutes."

"While you're getting it, I'll make some phone

calls." He'd be gone less than ten minutes. Now the waitress wouldn't miss him.

Through the window he noticed that the snow had stopped. He couldn't, of course, take his coat from the checkroom. Slipping out the side door near the hallway with the telephones and rest rooms, he hurried back across the path. The cold bit at his face, but he scarcely noticed it. He was planning every step.

It was easy to keep in the shadows. He had his key to the fire exit in the rear of the maternity wing. No one ever used those stairs. He let himself into the building.

The stairway was brightly lighted. He turned off the switch. He could find his way through this hospital blindfolded. At the third floor he opened the door cautiously, listened. There was no sound. Noiselessly he stepped into the hall. An instant later he was inside the living room of Katie's suite.

That had been another problem he'd considered. Suppose someone accompanied her to the hospital: her sister, a friend? Suppose that person asked to stay overnight on the sofa bed in the living room? The Westlake Clinic openly encouraged sleeping in if the patient desired it. By ordering this living room repainted, he'd effectively blocked that possibility.

Planning. Planning. It was everything, as useful and necessary in life as in the laboratory.

This afternoon he had left the needle with the heparin in a drawer of an end table under the painter's drop cloth. The light from the parking lot filtered the window, giving him enough visibility to find the table at once. He reached for the needle.

Now for the most important moment of all. If Katie woke up and saw him, he'd be exposed to danger. Granted, she would probably fall back asleep immediately. Certainly she'd never question the injection. But when he returned with Nurse Renge later, if she was by some chance still conscious, if she said anything about the shot, it would be easy enough to explain: she was confused; she meant when I took the blood samples. Even so. Better if she didn't wake up now.

He was in the room, bending over her. He reached for her arm. The drapery was partly open. Faint light was coming into the room. He could see her profile. Her face was turned from him. Her breathing was uneven. She was talking in her sleep. He could not catch the words. She must be dreaming.

He slipped the needle into her arm, squeezed. She winced and sighed. Her eyes, cloudy with sleep, opened as she turned her head. In the dim light he could see the enlarged pupils. She looked up at him puzzled. "Dr. Highley," she murmured, "why did you kill Vangie Lewis?"

◆ 61 ◆

Scott Myerson was more tired than angry. Since Vangie Lewis' body had been found Tuesday morning, two other people had died. Two very decent people—a hard-working receptionist who deserved a few years' freedom after supporting and caring for aged parents and a doctor who was making a real contribution to medicine.

They had died because he had not moved fast enough. Chris Lewis was a murderer. Scott was sure of that. The web drawing around Lewis was unbreakable. If only they had realized immediately that

Vangie Lewis' death was a homicide. He'd have brought Lewis in for questioning immediately. They might have cracked him. And if they had, Edna Burns and Emmet Salem would be alive now.

Scott couldn't wait for the chance to get to Lewis. Any man who could murder his pregnant wife was capable of any cold-blooded murder. Lewis proved that. He was the worst kind of criminal. The one who didn't look or sound the part. The one you trusted and turned your back on.

Lewis and his girlfriend were landing at seven. They should be here by eight. Lewis was cool, all right. Knew better than to run. Thought he could brazen it out. Knows it's all circumstantial. But circumstantial evidence can be a lot better than eyewitness testimony when properly presented in court. Scott would try the case himself. It would be his pleasure.

At seven fifty, Richard walked into Scott's office. He did not waste time on preliminaries. "I think we've uncovered a cesspool," he said, "and it's called the Westlake Maternity Concept."

"If you're saying that the shrink was probably playing around with Vangie Lewis, I agree," Scott said. "But I thought we decided that this afternoon. Anyhow, it's going to be easy enough to find out. Get blood samples from the fetus and we'll bring Fukhito in. He can't refuse to have his blood tested. If he does, it's an open admission of guilt, and he'd be finished with medicine if another paternity case was proved."

"That's not what I'm talking about," Richard broke in impatiently. "It's Highley I'm after. I think he's experimenting with his patients. I just spoke to the husband of one of them. There's no way he's the baby's father, but he was present at the birth. He's been thinking that his wife agreed to artificial insemination without his permission. I think it goes beyond that. I think Highley is performing artificial insemination without his patients' *knowledge*. That's why they're able to produce miracle babies under his care."

Scott snorted. "You mean to say you think Highley would inject Vangie Lewis with the semen of an Oriental father and expect to get away with it? Come on, Richard."

"Maybe he didn't know the donor was Oriental. Maybe he made a mistake."

"Doctors don't make mistakes like that. Even allowing your theory to be true . . . and frankly, I don't buy it . . . that doesn't make him Vangie's murderer."

"There's something wrong with Highley," Richard insisted. "I've felt it from the first minute I laid eyes on him."

"Look, we'll investigate Westlake Maternity. That's no problem. If there's any kind of violation there, we'll find it and prosecute it. If you're right and he's inseminating women without their consent, we'll get him. That's a direct violation of the Offense Against the Person Act. But let's worry about that later. Right now Chris Lewis is my first order of business."

"Do this," Richard persisted. "Go back further with the check on Highley. I'm already looking into the malpractice suits against him. Some woman, a Mrs. Horan, will be here shortly to tell why she pressed a suit. But the *Newsmaker* article says he was in Liverpool, in England, before he came here. Let's phone there and see if we can find any trace of impropriety. They'll give you that information."

Scott shrugged. "Sure, go ahead."

The buzzer on his desk sounded. He switched on the intercom. "Bring him in," he said. Leaning back on his chair, he looked at Richard.

"The bereaved widower, Captain Lewis, is here with his paramour," he said.

♦ 62 ♦

Dannyboy Duke sat in the precinct house hunched miserably forward in a chair. He was perspiring; his nerves were on edge. His arms were trembling. It was hard to see. In another thirty seconds he'd have been away. He'd be in his apartment now, the blissful release of the fix soaring through his body. Instead, this steamy, sweaty hell.

"Give me a break," he whispered.

The cops weren't impressed. "You give *us* a break, Danny. There's blood on this paperweight, Danny. Who'd you hit with it? Come on, Danny. We know it wasn't the old lady whose pocketbook you grabbed last night. You pushed her down. She's got a broken hip. That's pretty lousy when you're seventy-five, Danny. Odds are she'll end up with pneumonia. Maybe die. That makes it murder two, Dannyboy. You help us, we'll see what we can do for you, you know?"

"I don't know what you're talking about," Danny whispered.

"Sure you do. The doctor's bag was in your car. So was the pocketbook. The wallet you just grabbed in Alexander's was in your pocket. We know you stole the bag last night. We've got the call right here. The doorman saw you do it in front of the Carlyle Hotel. He can identify you. But who'd you hit with that paperweight, Danny? Tell us about it. And what about that shoe, Danny? Since when do you save beat-up shoes? Tell us about that."

"It was in the bag," Danny whispered.

The two detectives looked at each other. One of them shrugged and turned to the newspaper on the desk behind him. The other dropped the file he had been examining back into the bag. "All right, Danny. We're calling Dr. Salem to find out just what he had in this bag. That'll settle it. It could go easier if you'd cooperate. You've been around long enough to figure that out."

The other detective looked up from the paper. "Dr. Salem?" His voice was startled.

"Yeah. That's the name on the file. Oh, I see. The nameplate says Dr. Edgar Highley. Guess he had a patient's file from some other doctor."

The younger detective came over to the table carrying the morning *Daily News*. He opened the file and examined the sheaf of papers with the name EMMET SALEM, M.D. printed across the top. He pointed to page three of the *News*. "Salem's the doctor who was found on the roof of the Essex House extension last night. The Valley County Prosecutor is working with our people on that case."

The police officers looked at Dannyboy with renewed interest and narrowed, suspicious eyes.

◆ 63 ◆

He watched as Katie's eyes closed and her breathing became even. She'd fallen asleep again. The question about Vangie had come from somewhere in her subconscious, triggered perhaps by a duplication of her mental state of Monday night. She might not even remember asking the question, but he couldn't take the chance. Suppose she talked about it again in front of Nurse Renge or the other doctors in the operating room before they anesthetized her? His mind groped for a solution. Her presence at the window last Monday night could still destroy him.

He had to kill her before Nurse Renge made her check, in less than an hour. The heparin shot would act to anticoagulate her blood immediately, but it would take several hours to complete the procedure. That was what he had planned. Now he couldn't wait. He had to give her a second shot, immediately.

He had heparin in his office. He didn't dare go near the hospital dispensary. He'd have to go down the fire stairs to the parking lot, use the private door to his office, refill the hypodermic needle and come back up here. It would take at least five minutes. The waitress would start to question his absence from the table, but there was no help for that. Satisfied that Katie was asleep, he hurried from the room.

♦ 64 ♦

The technician in the Valley County Forensic Lab worked overtime on Friday evening. Dr. Carroll had asked him to compare all microscopic samples from the home of the presumed suicide Vangie Lewis with all microscopic samples from the home of the presumed accident victim Edna Burns. Carefully he had sifted the vacuum-bag contents of the Lewis home and the Burns apartment and painstakingly searched for substances that might be out of the ordinary.

The technician knew he had a superb instinct for microscopic evidence, a hunch factor that rarely failed him. He was always particularly interested in loose hair, and he was fond of saying, "We are like fur-bearing animals. It's astonishing how much hair we are constantly shedding, including people who are virtually bald."

In the exhibits from the Lewis home he found an abundance of strands of the ash-blond hair of the victim. He'd also found medium brown hair, a fair quantity of it, in the bedroom. Undoubtedly the husband's, since those same hairs were in the den and living room.

But there were also a number of silverish-sandy hairs in the victim's bedroom. That was unusual. In the kitchen or living room, strands of hair could easily come from a visitor or deliveryman, but the bedroom? Even in this day, there were few non-family members who were invited to enter the bedroom. Shafts found there assumed special significance. The hair had come from a man's head. The length suggested that automatically. Some of the same strands were on the coat the victim had been wearing.

And then the technician found the connection Richard Carroll had been seeking. Several sandy hairs with silver roots were clinging to the faded blue bathrobe of Edna Burns.

He placed the samples of hair under powerful microscopes and painstakingly went through the sixteen points of comparison check.

There was absolutely no doubt. One person had been close to both dead women; close enough to have held a head near to Edna Burns's chest and to have brushed a head on Vangie Lewis' shoulder.

The technician reached for the phone to call Dr. Carroll.

♦ 65 ♦

She tried to wake up. There was a click: a door had closed. Someone had just been here. Her arm hurt. Dr. Highley. She dropped off . . . What had she said to Dr. Highley? Katie woke up a few minutes later and remembered. Remembered the black car and the shiny spokes and the light on his glasses. She'd seen that Monday night. Dr. Highley had carried Vangie Lewis to his car Monday night. Dr. Highley had killed Vangie.

Richard had suspected something. Richard had tried to tell her. But she wouldn't listen.

Dr. Highley knew she knew about him. Why had she asked him that question? She had to get out of here. He was going to kill her too. She'd always had nightmares about hospitals. Because somehow she'd known that she would die in a hospital.

Where had Dr. Highley gone? He'd be back. She knew that. Back to kill her. Help. She needed help. Why was she so weak? Her finger was bleeding. The pills he had given her. Since she'd been taking them she'd been so sick. The pills. They were making her bleed.

Oh God, help me, please. The phone. The phone! Katie fumbled for it. Her hand, weak and unsteady, knocked it over. Shaking her head, forcing her eyes to stay open, she pulled it up by the cord. Finally she had the receiver at her ear. The line was dead. Frantically she jiggled the cradle, tried dialing the operator.

Dr. Highley had said the phone was being repaired.

She pushed the bell for the nurse. The nurse would help her. But the click that should have turned on the light outside her door did not happen. She was sure the signal wasn't lighting the nurse's panel either.

She had to get out of here before Dr. Highley came back. Waves of dizziness nauseated her as she stood up.

She had to. Vangie Lewis. The long blond hair, the petulant, little-girl eagerness for a child. Dr. Highley had killed Vangie, killed her baby. Had there been others?

She made her way from the bed, holding on to the footrail. The elevator. She'd go down in the elevator to the second floor. There were people there—other patients, nurses.

From nearby a door closed. He was coming back. *He was coming back.* Frantically Katie looked at the open door to the corridor. He'd see her if she went out there. The bathroom door had no lock. The closet. He'd find her there. Through sheer willpower she managed to stumble to the door leading to the living room, open it, go inside, close it before he came into the bedroom.

Where could she go? He'd look for her immediately. She couldn't stay here. If she tried to go out into the foyer, she'd pass the open door of the bedroom. He'd see her. She had to go down the foyer and turn left, then down the long hall to the elevator. She was no match for him. Where could she go? She heard a door open inside. He was in the bedroom looking for her. Should she try to hide under the drop cloth? No. No. She'd be trapped there. He'd find her, drag her out. She bit her lip as dizziness clawed at the space behind her eyes. Her legs were rubbery, her mouth and skin spongy.

She stumbled to the door of the living room, the one that led to the hall. There was another door there, the fire exit. She'd seen it when she was wheeled in. She'd go down that to the second floor. She'd get help. She was in the hall. In a minute he'd be behind her.

The door to the fire stairs was heavy. She tugged at it . . . tugged again. Reluctantly it gave way. She opened it, stepped inside. It closed so slowly. Would he see it closing? The stairs. It was so dark here, terribly dark. But she couldn't turn on a light. He'd see it. Maybe he was running down the corridor toward the elevator. If he did that, she'd have an extra minute. She needed that minute. Help me. Help me. She grabbed onto the banister. The stairs were steep. Her bare feet were silent. How many stairs in a flight? Thirteen. No, that was a house. There was a landing here after eight steps. Then another flight. Eight more steps, then she'd be safe. Seven . . . five . . . one. She was at the door, tried to turn the handle. It was locked. It opened only from the other side.

From upstairs she heard the third-floor door open and heavy footsteps coming down the stairs.

♦ 66 ♦

Chris refused to call a lawyer. He sat opposite the Prosecutor. He had been so worried about this encounter, so afraid they wouldn't believe him. But Joan believed him; Joan had said, "It just makes sense that they'll be suspicious of you, Chris. Tell every single thing you know. Remember that quote from the Bible, 'The truth shall make you free.' " Chris looked from the Prosecutor to the two detectives who had met him at the airport. "I have nothing to hide," he said.

Scott was unimpressed. A bookish-looking young man carrying a stenographer's pad came into the room, sat down, opened the pad and took out a pen. Scott looked directly at Chris. "Captain Lewis, it is my duty to inform you that you are a suspect in the deaths of Vangie Lewis, Edna Burns and Dr. Emmet Salem. You may remain silent. You are not required to answer any questions. At any point you may refuse to continue answering questions. You are entitled to the services of a lawyer. Any statement that you make can be used against you. Is that perfectly clear?"

"Yes."

"Can you read?"

Chris stared at Scott. Was he being sarcastic? No, the man was deadly serious.

"Yes."

Scott shoved a paper across the desk. "This is a copy of the *Miranda* warning you have just heard. Please read it carefully. Be sure you understand it and then, if you are so disposed, sign it."

Chris read the statement swiftly, signed it and handed it back.

"Very well." Scott pushed the paper to one side. His manner changed, became somehow more intense. Chris realized the formal questioning was about to begin.

Funny, he thought, every night of your life, if you wanted to, you could watch some form of cops-and-robbers or courtroom drama show and you never expect to get involved in one yourself. The Prosecutor obviously believed that he had killed Vangie. Was he crazy not to have legal counsel? No.

The Prosecutor was talking. "Captain Lewis, have you been in any way ill-treated or abused?"

"I have not."

"Would you care for coffee or food?"

Chris rubbed his hand over his forehead. "I would

like coffee, please. But I am ready to answer your questions fully."

Even so, he was not prepared for Scott's question. "Did you murder your wife, Vangie Lewis?"

Chris looked directly at him. "I did not murder my wife. I do not know if she was murdered. But I do know this. If she died before midnight Monday night, she did not kill herself in our home."

Scott, Charley, Phil and the stenographer were startled into unprofessional astonishment as Chris calmly said, "I was there just before midnight Monday. Vangie was not home. I returned to New York. At eleven the next morning I found her in bed. It wasn't until the funeral director came to the house for clothes to dress my wife for burial and told me the time of death that I realized that her dead body must have been returned to our house. But even before that I knew something was wrong. My wife would never have worn or even tried to put on the shoes she was wearing when she was found. For six weeks before her death the only shoes she could wear were a pair of battered moccasins a cleaning woman had left. Her right leg and foot were badly swollen. She even used those moccasins as bedroom slippers . . ."

It was easier than he had expected. He heard the questions coming at him: "You left the hotel at eight P.M. Monday night and returned at ten. Where did you go?"

"To a movie in Greenwich Village. After I got back to the motel I couldn't sleep. I decided to drive home and talk to Vangie. That was shortly after midnight."

"Why didn't you stay and wait for your wife?" And then the one that was a hammerblow to his stomach: "Did you know your wife was carrying a Japanese fetus?"

"Oh, my God!" Horror somehow mingled with a sense of release flooded Chris's being. *It hadn't been his baby.* A Japanese fetus. That psychiatrist. Was he louse enough to do that to her? She'd trusted him so. Oh, God, the poor kid. No wonder she was getting so frightened to give birth. That must have been why she called Dr. Salem. She wanted to hide. Oh, God, she was such a child.

The questions came: "You were not aware your wife was involved with another man?"

"No. No."

"Why did you go to Edna Burns's apartment Tuesday night?"

The coffee came. He tried to answer. "Wait, please —can we take this just the way it happened?" He began to sip the coffee. It helped. "It was Tuesday night, just after I realized that Vangie had died before — she was brought home, that that woman, Edna Burns, called. She was almost incoherent. She rambled on about Cinderella and Prince Charming, said she had something for me, something I'd want to have, and she had a story for the police. I thought she might know who Vangie had been with. I thought if she told me, I might not have to admit that I'd been home Monday night. I wanted to keep Joan out of this."

He set down the coffee cup, remembering Tuesday night. It seemed so long ago. Everything was so out of proportion. "I drove to Miss Burns's housing development. Some kid was walking his dog and pointed out her apartment to me. I rang the bell and knocked on the door. The television was on, the light was on, but she didn't answer. I figured she'd passed out and there was no use trying to talk to her, that maybe she was just a crank. I went home."

"You never went in?"

"No."

"What time was that?"

"About nine thirty."

"All right. What did you do then?"

The questions, one after another; he drank more coffee. Truth. The simple truth. It was so much easier than evasion. Keep the future in mind. If they believed him, he and Joan would have a life together. He thought of the way she'd looked at him, thrown her arms around him last night in her apartment. For the first time in his entire life, he'd known there was someone he could go to in trouble; someone who would want to share it with him. Everyone else— Vangie, even his parents—had always leaned on him.

For better, for worse.

It would be *better* for them. Joan, my darling, he thought. He took a deep breath. They were asking about Dr. Salem.

◆ 67 ◆

Richard sat at Katie's desk as he waited for the staff director of Christ Hospital, Devon, to answer his phone. Only by emphasizing the urgency of his need to talk to someone in authority who had been at the hospital more than ten years had he been given the man's private number.

While he waited, he looked around. The table behind Katie's desk was filled with files she was working on. It was no wonder she hadn't taken any time off after her accident. But no matter how busy, she should have stayed home. This afternoon she'd looked lousy. And losing that case today must have upset her terribly. He wished he'd seen her before she left.

The phone continued to jab. The guy must be out or

asleep. Maybe it could wait till morning. No. He wanted to find out *now*.

There were snapshots in a frame on Katie's desk. Katie with an older woman, probably her mother. He knew the mother lived in Florida somewhere. Katie with Jennifer, Molly's oldest. Katie looked like Jen's big sister. Katie with a group of people in ski outfits. These must be the friends she stayed with in Vermont.

No picture of John DeMaio. But Katie wasn't the kind to subtly remind people at work that she was the widow of a prominent judge. And there certainly were plenty of pictures of him around that house.

The phone continued to ring. He'd give it another minute.

Richard realized he was pleased to note that there were no pictures of any other guy either. He'd been analyzing his reaction to Katie's announcement that she'd be away for the weekend. He'd tried to make it look as though he were surprised that she wouldn't be available with a big case breaking. Hell. That had nothing to do with it. He was worried that she was with some other guy.

"Yes." An angry, sleepy voice had answered the phone.

Richard straightened up, tightened his grip on the receiver. "Mr. Reeves? Mr. Alexander Reeves?"

"Yes."

Richard went directly to the point. "Sir, I apologize profusely for calling you at this hour, but the matter is vital. This is a transatlantic call. I'm Dr. Richard Carroll, the Medical Examiner of Valley County, New Jersey. I must have information about Dr. Edgar Highley."

The sleepiness vanished from the other man's voice. It became intense and wary. "What do you want to know?"

"I have just spoken with Queen Mary Clinic in

Liverpool and was surprised to learn that Dr. Highley had been on staff there a relatively short time. We had been led to believe otherwise. However, I was told that Dr. Highley was a member of the Christ Hospital staff for at least nine years. Is that accurate?"

"Edgar Highley interned with us after his graduation from Cambridge. He is a brilliant doctor and was invited to become staff, specializing in obstetrics and gynecology."

"Why did he leave?"

"After his wife's death he relocated in Liverpool. Then we heard he had emigrated to the United States. That's not uncommon, of course. Many of our physicians and surgeons will not tolerate the relatively low pay structure of our socialized medicine system."

"There was no other reason for Dr. Highley's resignation?"

"I don't understand your question."

Richard took a chance. "I think you do, Mr. Reeves. This is, of course, totally confidential, but I can't waste time being discreet. I believe that Dr. Highley may be experimenting with his pregnant patients, perhaps even with their lives. Is there any justification that you can offer to support that possibility?"

There was a long pause. The words that came next were slow and deliberately enunciated. "While he was with us, Dr. Highley was not only a practicing physician, but was deeply involved in prenatal research. He did quite brilliant experiments on embryos of frogs and mammals. Then a fellow doctor began to suspect that he was experimenting with aborted human fetuses—which is, of course, illegal."

"What was done about it?"

"It was kept very quiet, of course, but he was being watched very carefully. Then a tragedy occurred. Dr. Highley's wife died suddenly. There was no way we could prove anything, but the suspicion existed that

273

he had implanted her with an aborted fetus. Dr. Highley was asked to resign. This is, of course, absolutely confidential. In no way is there a shred of proof, and I must expect that you treat this conversation as inviolable."

Richard absorbed what he had heard. His hunch had been right. How many women had Highley killed experimenting on them? A question came into his mind—a wild, long-shot possibility.

"Mr. Reeves," he asked, "do you by any chance know a Dr. Emmet Salem?"

The voice warmed immediately. "Of course I do. A good friend. Why, Dr. Salem was visiting staff here at the time of the Highley scandal."

◆ 68 ◆

Silently Katie ran down the stairs to the main floor. Desperately she grasped the knob, tried to open the door. But it would not give. It was locked. Upstairs, the footsteps had paused. He was trying the second-floor knob, making sure that she had not escaped him. The footsteps started again. He was coming down. No one would hear her if she screamed. These heavy doors were fireproof. No hospital sounds could be heard here. On the other side of the door, there were people: visitors, patients, nurses. Less than six inches away. But they could not hear her.

He was coming. He would reach her, kill her. She felt heavy, dull pain in her pelvic area. She was flowing heavily. Whatever he had given her had started the hemorrhaging. She was dizzy. But she had

THE CRADLE WILL FALL

to get away. He had made Vangie's death look like suicide. He still might get away with that. Wildly she began rushing down the staircase. There was one more flight. It probably led to the basement of the hospital. He'd have to explain how and why she'd gotten there. The farther she got, the more questions would be asked. She stumbled on the last stair. Don't fall. Don't make it look like an accident. Edna had fallen. Or had she?

Had he killed Edna too?

But she'd be trapped here. Another door. This one would be locked too. Helplessly she turned the knob. He was on the mid landing. Dark as it was, she could see movement, a presence rushing down at her.

The door opened. The corridor was dimly lit. She was in the basement. She saw rooms ahead. Quiet. It was so quiet. The door snapped closed behind her. Could she hide somewhere? Help me. Help me. There was a switch on the wall. She pressed her hand on it. Her finger smeared it with blood. The corridor disappeared into blackness as a few feet behind her the door from the stairwell burst open.

♦ 69 ♦

Highley was suspected of causing his first wife's death. Winifred Westlake's cousin believed he had caused Winifred's death. Highley was a brilliant researcher. Highley may have been experimenting on some of the women who were his patients. Highley may have injected Vangie Lewis with the semen of an Oriental male. But why? Did he hope to get away with it?

Undoubtedly he knew Fukhito's background. Would he try to accuse him? Why? Had it been an accident? Had he used the wrong semen? Or had Vangie been involved with Fukhito? Was Dr. Highley's possible experimentation only incidental to Vangie's pregnancy?

Richard could not find the answer. He sat at Katie's desk twirling her Mark Cross pen. She always carried this. She must have rushed out of here this evening and forgotten to pick it up. But of course, she'd been upset. Losing that case must have rattled her badly. Katie would take that hard. Katie took a lot of things hard. He wished he knew where she was. He wanted to talk to her. The way her finger bled. He'd have to ask Molly if she knew whether or not Katie had a low platelet count. That could be a real problem.

A chill made Richard's fingers stiffen. That could be a sign of leukemia. Oh, God. Monday, he'd drag Katie to a doctor if he had to tie her up to do it.

There was a soft knock on the door and Maureen looked in. Her eyes were emerald green, large and oval. Beautiful eyes. Beautiful kid.

"Dr. Carroll."

"Maureen, I'm sorry I asked you to stay. I thought Mrs. Horan would be here long ago."

"It's all right. She did phone. She's on her way. Something came up at work and they needed her. But there are two women here. They're friends of the Miss Burns who died. They wanted to see Katie. I told them she was gone, and one of them mentioned your name. She met you the other night when you were at the Burns apartment; a Mrs. Fitzgerald."

"Fitzgerald? . . . Sure. Mrs. Fitzgerald is a part-time receptionist at Westlake Hospital." As Richard said "Westlake," he stood up. "Tell them to come on in. Maybe you'd better call Scott."

"Mr. Myerson is absolutely not to be disturbed. He

and Charley and Phil are still questioning Captain Lewis."

"All right. I'll talk to them. Then if it's anything much, we'll make them wait."

They came in together, Gana's eyes snapping with excitement. She had regretfully decided not to wear Edna's leopard coat. It just seemed too soon. But she had her story ready to tell.

Gertrude was carrying the moccasin in a paper bag. Her neat gray hair was every inch in place. Her scarf was knotted at her throat. The good dinner had faded into memory, and now more than anything she wanted to get home and to bed. But she was glad to talk to Dr. Carroll. She was going to tell him that the other night in poor Edna's apartment, Dr. Highley had been pulling open the night-table drawer. There was nothing in that drawer except the shoe. Did Dr. Carroll think that Dr. Highley wanted to get that shoe for any reason?

Mrs. DeMaio had been so interested in that Prince Charming business. Dr. Carroll might want to know about that too. He could tell Mrs. DeMaio when she came in Monday. Dr. Carroll was looking at them expectantly.

Gertrude leaned forward, shook the bag, and the shabby moccasin fell onto Katie's desk. Primly she began to explain, "That shoe is the reason we are here."

♦ 70 ♦

She zigzagged down the corridor. Would he know where the light switch was? Would he dare to turn it on? Suppose there was someone down here? Should she try to scream?

He knew this hospital. Where would she go? There had been a door at the end of the hall. The farthest door. Maybe he'd try the others first. Maybe she could lock herself in somewhere. She might miss the doors on the side. But if she ran straight, she'd have to touch that far wall. The door was in the middle. Her finger was bleeding. She'd try to smear blood on the door. When the nurse made her rounds, they'd start to search for her. Maybe they'd notice the bloodstains.

He was standing still. He was listening for her. Would he see a shadow when the door opened? Her outstretched hand touched a cold wall. Oh, God, let me find the door. Her hand ran down the wall. She touched a doorframe. Behind her she heard a faint squeaking sound. He had opened that first door. But now he wouldn't bother to look in that room. He'd realize he hadn't heard that squeak, that she hadn't tried that door. Her hand found a knob. She turned it deliberately, grinding her cut finger against it. A heavy formaldehyde smell filled her nostrils. From behind her she heard rushing feet. Too late. Too late. She tried to push the door closed, but it was shoved open. She stumbled and fell. She was so dizzy, so dizzy. She reached out. Her hand touched a pants leg.

"It's all over, Katie," Dr. Highley said.

♦ 71 ♦

"Are you sure this is your wife's shoe?" Scott demanded. Wearily Chris nodded. "I am absolutely certain. This is the one that was so loose on her . . . the left one."

"When Edna Burns phoned you, did she tell you she had this shoe?"

"No. She said she had something to tell the police and that she wanted to talk to me."

"Did you get an impression of blackmail . . . of threat?"

"No, drunken garrulousness. I knew she was from Westlake Hospital. I didn't realize then that she was the receptionist Vangie used to talk about. She said Edna was always kidding her about her glass slippers."

"All right. Your statement will be typed immediately. Read it carefully, sign it if you find it accurate and then you can go home. We'll want to talk with you again tomorrow morning."

For the first time Chris felt as though the Prosecutor had begun to believe him. He got up to go. "Where is Joan?"

"She's completed a statement. She can go with you. Oh, one thing: what impression do you have of Dr. Highley?"

"I never met him."

"Did you read this article about him?" Scott held up *Newsmaker* magazine.

Chris looked at the article, at the picture of Dr.

Highley. "I saw this yesterday on the plane into New York."

Memory jogged.

"That's it," he said. "That's what I couldn't place."

"What are you talking about?" Scott asked.

"That was the man who came down in the elevator at the Essex House last night when I was trying to reach Dr. Salem."

♦ 72 ♦

He switched on a light. Through the haze she could see his full-cheeked face, his eyes protruding as he stared down at her, his skin glistening with perspiration, his sandy hair falling untidily on his forehead.

She managed to stumble to her feet. She was in a small area like a waiting room. It was so cold. A thick steel door was behind her. She shrank back against the door.

"You've made it so easy for me, Mrs. DeMaio." Now he was smiling at her. "Everyone close to you knows about your fear of hospitals. When Nurse Renge and I make rounds in a few minutes, we'll assume you left the hospital. We'll call your sister, but she won't be home for several hours, will she? We won't start looking for you *in* the hospital until much later. Certainly no one will dream of looking for you here.

"An old man died in the emergency room tonight. He's in one of those vaults. Tomorrow morning when the undertaker comes for his body, you'll be found. It will be obvious what happened to you. You were hemorrhaging; you became disoriented, almost comatose. Tragically, you wandered down here and bled to death."

"No." His face was blurring. She was so dizzy. She was swaying.

He reached past her and opened the steel door. He pushed her through it, held her as she slid down. She had fainted. Kneeling beside her, he injected the last shot of heparin. She probably wouldn't recover consciousness again. Even if she did, she couldn't get out. From this side the door was locked. He looked at her thoughtfully, then got to his feet and brushed the smudge of dust from his trousers. At last he was finished with Katie DeMaio.

He closed the steel door that separated the vaults from the receiving area of the morgue and turned out the light. Cautiously he opened the door into the corridor and hurried down it, letting himself out into the parking lot of the hospital by the same door through which he'd come in fifteen minutes before.

A few minutes later, he was drinking lukewarm cappuccino, waving away the offer of the waitress to bring him a hot cup. "My calls took a bit longer than I expected," he explained. "And now I must hurry back to the hospital. There's a patient there about whom I'm quite concerned."

73

"Good night, Dr. Fukhito. I feel much better. Thank you." The boyish face managed a smile.

"I'm glad. Sleep well tonight, Tom." Jiro Fukhito got up slowly. This young man would make it. He'd been in deep depression for weeks, nearly suicidal. He'd been doing eighty miles an hour in a car that crashed. His younger brother was killed in the accident. Regret. Guilt. Overwhelming, more than the boy could handle.

Jiro Fukhito knew he had helped him through the worst of it. His work could be so satisfying, he reflected as he walked slowly down the corridor of Valley Pines Hospital. The work he did here, the volunteer work—this was where he wanted to practice.

Oh, he'd done enough for many of the patients at Westlake. But there were others he hadn't helped, hadn't been *allowed* to help.

"Good night, Doctor." A number of the patients in the psychiatric ward greeted him as he walked toward the elevator. He'd been asked to come full time on staff here. He wanted to accept that offer.

Should he start the investigation that would inevitably destroy him?

Edgar Highley wouldn't hesitate to reveal the Massachusetts case if he suspected that his associate had discussed his patient with the police.

But Mrs. DeMaio already suspected something.

She'd recognized his nervousness when she questioned him the other day.

He got into his car, sat in it irresolutely. Vangie Lewis did not commit suicide. She absolutely did not commit suicide by drinking cyanide. She had gotten on the subject of the Jones cult during one of their sessions when she was talking about religion.

He could see her sitting in his office, her earnest, shallow explanation of her religious beliefs. "I'm not one for going to church, Doctor. I mean I believe in God. But in my own way. I think about God sometimes. That's better than rushing off to a service you don't pay attention to anyhow, don't you think? And as for those cults. They're all crazy. I don't see how people get involved in them. Why, remember all those people who killed themselves because they were told to? Did you hear the tape of them screaming after they drank that stuff? I had nightmares about it. And they looked so *ugly*."

Pain. Ugliness. Vangie Lewis? Never!

Jiro Fukhito sighed. He knew what he had to do. Once again his professional life would pay for the terrible mistake of ten years ago.

But he had to tell the police what he knew. Vangie had run out of his office into the parking lot. But when he left, fifteen minutes later, her Lincoln Continental was still in the lot.

There was no longer any doubt in Jiro Fukhito's mind that Vangie had gone into Edgar Highley's office.

He drove out of the hospital parking lot and turned in the direction of the Valley County Prosecutor's office.

74

Scott held the moccasin. Richard, Charley and Phil sat around his desk.

"Let's try to put this together," Scott said. "Vangie Lewis did not die at home. She was taken there sometime between midnight and eleven A.M. The last known place she visited was Dr. Fukhito's office at the hospital. Vangie was wearing the moccasins Monday night. Somewhere in the hospital she lost one of them, and Edna Burns found it. Whoever brought her home put other shoes on her to try to cover up for the missing ones. Edna Burns found the shoe and was talking about it. And Edna Burns died.

"Emmet Salem wanted to reach you, Richard. He wanted to talk to you about Vangie's death. He came to New York and fell or was pushed to his death a few minutes later, and the file he was carrying on Vangie Lewis disappeared."

"And Chris Lewis swears that he saw Edgar Highley in the Essex House," Richard interjected.

"Which may or may not be true," Scott reminded him.

"But Dr. Salem knew about the scandal in Christ Hospital," Richard said. "Highley wouldn't want that to come out just when he's getting national publicity."

"That's no motive to kill," Scott said.

"How about Highley trying to get that shoe out of Edna's drawer?" Charley asked.

"We don't *know* that. That woman from the hospital claimed he was opening the drawer. He didn't

284

touch anything." Scott frowned. "Nothing hangs together. We're dealing with a prominent doctor. We can't go off half-cocked because he was involved ten years ago in a hushed-up scandal. The big problem is motive. Highley had no motive to kill Vangie Lewis."

The intercom buzzed. Scott switched it on. "Mrs. Horan is here," Maureen said.

"All right, bring her in, and I want you to take down her statement," Scott directed.

Richard leaned forward. This was the woman who had filed the malpractice suit against Edgar Highley.

The door opened and a young woman preceded Maureen into the room. She was a Japanese girl in her early twenties. Her hair fell loosely on her shoulders. Bright red lipstick was an incongruous note against her tawny skin. Her delicate, graceful carriage gave a floating effect even to the inexpensive pantsuit she was wearing.

Scott stood up. "Mrs. Horan, we appreciate your coming. We'll try not to keep you too long. Won't you sit down?"

She nodded. Clearly nervous, she wet her lips and deliberately folded her hands in her lap. Maureen unobtrusively sat behind her and opened her steno book.

"Will you state your name and address?" Scott asked.

"I am Anna Horan. I live at 415 Walnut Street in Ridgefield Park."

"You are or were Dr. Edgar Highley's patient?"

Richard turned quickly as he heard Maureen gasp. But the girl quickly recovered herself and, bending her head, resumed taking notes.

Anna Horan's face hardened. "Yes, I was that murderer's patient."

"That murderer?" Scott said.

Now her words came in a torrent. "I went to him

five months ago. I was pregnant. My husband is a second-year law student. We live on my salary. I decided I had to have an abortion. I didn't want to, but I thought I had to."

Scott sighed. "And Dr. Highley performed the procedure at your request and now you're blaming him?"

"No. That's not true. He told me to come back the next day. And I did. He took me to an operating room in the hospital. He left me, and I knew—I *knew*—that no matter how we managed, I wanted my baby. Dr. Highley came back; I was sitting up. I told him I'd changed my mind."

"And he probably told you that one out of two women say the same thing at that moment."

"He said, 'Lie down.' He pushed me down on the table."

"Was anyone else in the room? The nurse?"

"No. Just the doctor and me. And I said, 'I know what I'm saying.' And—"

"And you allowed him to persuade you?"

"No. No. I don't know what happened. He jabbed me with a needle while I was trying to get up. When I woke up, I was lying on a stretcher. The nurse said it was all over. She said I should rest for a while."

"You don't remember the procedure?"

"Nothing. Nothing. The last I remember is trying to get away." Her mouth worked convulsively. "Trying to save my baby. I wanted my baby. Dr. Highley took my baby from me."

A harsh, pained cry echoed Anna Horan's heartbroken sobs. Maureen's face was contorted, her voice a wail. "That's exactly what he did to me."

Richard stared at the weeping young women: the Japanese girl; Maureen with her red-gold hair and emerald-green eyes. And with absolute certainty he knew where he had seen those eyes before.

♦ 75 ♦

He got off at the second floor of the hospital and instantly felt the tension in the air. Frightened-looking nurses were scurrying in the hall. A man and woman in evening dress were standing by Nurse Renge's desk.

Quickly he walked over to the desk. His voice was disapproving and brittle as he asked, "Nurse Renge, is there something wrong?"

"Doctor, it's Mrs. DeMaio. *She's missing.*"

The woman was in her mid-thirties and looked familiar. Of course! She was Katie DeMaio's sister. What had made her come to the hospital?

"I'm Dr. Highley," he said to her. "What does this mean?"

Molly found it hard to talk. Something had happened to Katie. She knew it. She'd never forgive herself. "Katie . . ." Her voice broke.

The man with her interrupted. "I'm Dr. Kennedy," he said. "My wife is Mrs. DeMaio's sister. When did you see her, Doctor, and what was her condition?"

This was not a man to be easily deceived. "I saw Mrs. DeMaio a little more than an hour ago. Her condition is not good. As you probably know, she's had two units of whole blood this week. The laboratory is analyzing her blood now. I expect it to be low. As Nurse Renge will tell you, I expect to perform a D-and-C tonight rather than wait for the morning. I think Mrs. DeMaio has been concealing the extent of her hemorrhaging from everyone."

"Oh, God, then where is she?" Molly cried.

He looked at her. She'd be easier to convince. "Your sister has an almost pathological fear of hospitals. Is it possible that she would simply leave?"

"Her clothes are in the closet, Doctor," Nurse Renge said.

"Some clothes may be in the closet," he corrected. "Did you unpack Mrs. DeMaio's bag?"

"No."

"Then you don't know what other articles of apparel she had with her?"

"It's possible," Bill said slowly. He turned to Molly. "Honey, you know it's possible."

"We should have been here," Molly told him. "How bad is she, Doctor?"

"We must find her and get her back here. Would she be likely to go to her own home or to yours?"

"Doctor"—Nurse Renge's timid voice had a tremor—"that sleeping pill should have made Mrs. DeMaio fall asleep. It was the strongest one you ever ordered."

He glowered at her. "I ordered it for the very reason that I understood Mrs. DeMaio's anxiety. You were told to see that she swallowed it. She did not want the pill. Did you watch her take it?"

"I saw her put it in her mouth."

"Did you watch her swallow it?"

"No . . . not really."

He turned his back on the nurse in a gesture of contempt. He spoke to Molly and Bill, his voice reflective, concerned. "I hardly think Mrs. DeMaio is wandering around the hospital. Do you agree that she might have left of her own volition? She could simply have gotten on the elevator, gone to the lobby and walked out with the visitors who are coming and going all evening. Do you agree that's possible?"

"Yes. Yes. I do." Molly prayed, Please let it be that way.

"Then let's hope and expect that Mrs. DeMaio will be home very shortly."

"I want to see if her car is in the parking lot," Bill said.

The car. He hadn't thought about her car. If they started looking for her in the hospital now . . .

Bill frowned. "Oh, hell, she's still got that loan car. Molly, what make is it? I don't think I've even seen it."

"I . . . I don't know," Molly said.

Edgar Highley sighed. "I think even if you could identify her car, you'd be wasting your time looking in the parking lot. I would suggest that you phone her home. If she's not there, go and wait to see if she comes in. She's scarcely been gone an hour now. When you do contact her, please insist she return to the hospital. You can stay with her, Mrs. Kennedy. Doctor, if you feel it will comfort Mrs. DeMaio, I would be glad to have you with me in the operating room. But we must not allow that hemorrhaging to continue. Mrs. DeMaio is a very sick girl."

Molly bit her lip. "I see. Thank you, Doctor. You're very kind. Bill, let's just go to Katie's house. Maybe she's there now and not answering the phone."

They turned from him. They believed him. They would not suggest searching the hospital for several hours at least. And that was all he needed.

He turned to the nurse. In her own stupid, blundering way she had been an asset. Of course Katie had never swallowed that sleeping pill. Of course he was justified in having ordered it.

"I am sure that we'll be hearing from Mrs. DeMaio shortly," he said. "Call me immediately when you do. I'll be at my home." He smiled. "I have some records to complete."

"We must seize Dr. Highley's records before he has a chance to destroy them. To the best of your knowledge, does he keep all his records in his office?"

Jiro Fukhito stared at Richard. He had gone to the Prosecutor's office prepared to make a statement. They had listened to him almost impatiently, and then Dr. Carroll had outlined his incredible theory.

Was it possible? Jiro Fukhito reviewed the times when suspicions had formed in his mind, then were calmed by Highley's obstetrical genius. *It was possible.*

Records. They had asked him about records. "Edgar Highley would never keep records that suggest malfeasance in his office at the hospital," he said slowly. "There is always the danger of a malpractice subpoena. However, he frequently takes files to his home. I never could understand why he did that."

"Have search warrants sworn out immediately," Scott told Charley. "We'll hit the office and his home simultaneously. I'll take the squad to the house. Richard, you come with me. Charley, you and Phil take the office. We'll pick up Highley as a material witness. If he's not there, I want a stakeout on the house and we'll nab him as soon as he gets home."

"What worries me is that there may be someone he's experimenting on now," Richard said. "I'll lay odds that the hair shafts the lab found on Edna and Vangie's bodies came from Highley." He looked at his watch. It was nine thirty. "We'll wrap this up tonight," he predicted.

He wished Katie were here. She'd be relieved to know that Chris Lewis was about to be eliminated as a suspect. Her hunch about Lewis had been right. But his own hunch about Highley had been right too.

Dr. Fukhito stood up. "Do you need me any longer?"

"Not right now, Doctor," Scott said. "We'll be in touch with you. If by any chance you happen to hear from Dr. Highley before we arrest him, please do not discuss this investigation with him. You understand that?"

Jiro Fukhito smiled wearily. "Edgar Highley and I are not friends. He would have no reason to call me at home. He hired me because he knew he would have a hold over me. How right he was. Tonight I shall analyze my own conduct and determine how many times I have forced back suspicions that should have been explored. I dread the conclusion I shall reach."

He left the room. As he walked down the corridor, he saw a nameplate on a door: MRS. K. DeMAIO. Katie DeMaio. Wasn't she supposed to have gone into the hospital tonight? But of course, she never would go through with her operation while Edgar Highley was under investigation.

Jiro Fukhito went home.

◆ 77 ◆

She was drifting down a dark corridor. Way at the very end there was a light. It would be warm when she got there. Warm and safe. But something was holding her back. There was something she had to do before she died. She had to make them know what Dr. Highley was. Her finger was dripping blood now. She could feel it. She was lying on the floor. It was so cold. All these years she'd had nightmares that she'd die in the hospital. But it wasn't so bad after all. She'd been so afraid of being alone. Alone without Daddy, then alone without John. So afraid of risking pain. We are all alone. We're born alone and die alone. There's really nothing to be afraid of. Couldn't she possibly smear Dr. Highley's name on the floor with her finger? He was insane. He had to be stopped. Slowly, painfully, Katie moved her finger. Down, across, down again. H . . .

♦ 78 ♦

He got home at quarter past nine. The gratifying sense of having at last eliminated the final threat gave him a sense of total buoyancy. He had finished eating less than an hour ago, but somehow could not even remember the meal. Perhaps Hilda had left something for a snack.

It was better than he had hoped. Fondue. Hilda made remarkably good fondue. It was perhaps her best culinary accomplishment. He lit the Sterno can under the pot, adjusted it to a low flame. A crisp loaf of French bread was in a basket, covered by a damask napkin. He'd make a salad; there was sure to be arugula. He'd instructed Hilda to buy some today.

While the fondue heated, he would complete Katie DeMaio's file. He was anxious to be finished with it. He wanted to think about the two patients tomorrow:

the donor and the recipient. He was confident that he could duplicate his success.

But was that enough? Wouldn't it be more interesting if the recipient were given twins to carry? Two alien fetuses from separate donors?

The immuno-reactive theory he'd perfected might break down. Almost certainly it would. But how long would it take? What specific problems would develop?

He went into the library, opened the desk drawer and withdrew Katie DeMaio's file from the hidden compartment. On the last page he made a final entry:

> *Patient entered hospital at approximately 6:00 P.M. with blood pressure 100/60, hemoglobin no more than 10 grams. This physician administered the final two cumadin pills at 7:00 P.M. At 8:30 this physician returned to Mrs. DeMaio's room and administered 5 ml. heparin by injection. Mrs. DeMaio awakened briefly. In a near-comatose state she asked this physician, "Why did you kill Vangie Lewis?"*
>
> *This physician left Mrs. DeMaio to obtain more heparin. Obviously it was impossible to allow Mrs. DeMaio to repeat that question before witnesses. When this physician returned, patient had left room. Probably realizing what she had said, she tried to escape. Patient was apprehended and another 5 ml. of heparin was administered. Patient will hemorrhage to death tonight in Westlake Hospital.*
>
> *This file is now closed.*

He put down his pen, stretched, walked over to the wall safe and opened it. Bathed in light from the crystal sconces, the buff-colored files took on an almost golden sheen.

They *were* golden: the records of his genius at his

fingertips. Expansively he lifted them all out, laid them on his desk. Like a Midas savoring his treasure, he ran his fingers over the name tabs. His great successes. Berkeley and Lewis. His fingers stopped and his face darkened. Appleton, Carey, Drake, Elliot . . . failures. Over eighty of them. But not really failures. He had learned so much. They had all contributed. Those who had died, those who had aborted. They were part of the history.

Lewis. An addendum was necessary. To Vangie's file he added an account of his meeting with Emmet Salem.

The fondue must be ready. Irresolutely he looked at the files. Should he put them away now or give himself the pleasure of reading some of them? Perhaps he should study them. This week had been so difficult. He needed to refresh himself concerning some of the drug combinations he would want to use in the new case.

From somewhere in the distance a sound was beginning to penetrate the library: the wailing shriek of police sirens carried by the bone-chilling wind. The sound crescendoed into the room, then abruptly ceased. He hurried to the window, snatched back the drapery and glanced out. The police were here!

Had Katie been found? Had she been able to talk? With lightning movements he ran to the desk, stacked the files, replaced them in the still-open safe, closed it and slid back the panel.

Calm. He must be calm. His skin felt clammy. His lips and knees were rubbery. He must control himself. There was one last desperate card in the deck that he could always play.

If Katie had talked, it was all over.

But if the police were here for another reason, he might still be able to outwit them. Maybe Katie was already dead and her body had been found. Remember the questions and accusations when Claire died. They'd come to nothing. There had been absolutely no proof.

All the possibilities and consequences were exploding in his mind at once. It was exactly the same as during an operation or a delivery when something abruptly went wrong and he had to make an irrevocable decision.

And then it came. The icy, deliberate calm, the sense of power, the godlike omniscience that never failed him during difficult surgery. He felt it flowing through his body and brain.

There was a sharp, authoritative rap at the door. Slowly, deliberately, he smoothed his hair. His fingers, now miraculously dry and warm, tightened the knot in his tie. He walked to the front door and opened it.

◆ 79 ◆

As the squad car raced toward Edgar Highley's home, Scott methodically reviewed the statements he'd heard in the past few hours from Chris Lewis, Gertrude Fitzgerald, Gana Krupshak, Jiro Fukhito, Anna Horan and Maureen Crowley.

Seemingly they pointed in one direction: to Dr. Edgar Highley, placing him under grave suspicion of malpractice, malfeasance and murder.

Not three hours ago, most of this same circumstantial evidence had pointed to Chris Lewis.

Scott thought of Pick Up Sticks, the game he'd played as a kid. You had to remove the sticks from the pile, one by one, without disturbing the rest of them. If you so much as jiggled another stick, you lost. It was a game Scott had played skillfully. But the trouble was that almost always, no matter how much care he took, the pile would collapse.

Circumstantial evidence was like that. Piled up, it looks impressive. Take it apart piece by piece and it caves in.

Richard was sitting beside him on the back seat of the squad car. It was because of Richard's insistence on slanting all the evidence against Edgar Highley that they were here now rushing through Parkwood with sirens screeching. Richard had heated this investigation to fever pitch by arguing that Highley might destroy evidence if he knew he was under suspicion.

Edgar Highley was a prominent physician, an excellent obstetrician. A lot of important people were fervently indebted to him because of the babies he had delivered in their families. If this turned out to be a witch-hunt, the Prosecutor's office would be under attack from the press and the public.

"This stinks." Scott did not realize he'd spoken aloud.

Richard, deep in thought, turned to him frowning. "What stinks?"

"This whole business: this search, this assumption that Highley is a combination of genius and murderer. Richard, what proof have we got? Gertrude Fitzgerald *thinks* Highley was going into the night-table drawer for the shoe. Chris Lewis *thinks* he caught a glimpse of Highley in the Essex House. You *think* Highley has performed medical miracles.

"Look, even if the grand jury returns an indictment, which I doubt it will, a good lawyer could have this whole mess dismissed maybe without a trial. I've half a mind to turn around right now."

"Don't!" Richard grasped Scott's arm. "For God's sake, we've got to seize his records."

Scott hunched back in the seat, pulling his arm free.

"Scott," Richard urged, "forget everything except the number of maternity deaths at Westlake. That alone is sufficient reason for an investigation."

The squad car swerved around a corner. They were in the elegant west section of Parkwood. "All right," Scott snapped. "But remember, Richard, by tomorrow morning the two of us may be regretting this excursion."

"I doubt it," Richard said shortly. He wished he could overcome the growing worry that was grinding the pit of his stomach. It had nothing to do with this moment, this case.

It was Katie. He was desperately, irrationally worried about Katie. Why?

The car pulled into a driveway. "Well, this is it," Scott said sourly. The two detectives who were in the front seat jumped out of the car. As Richard started to get out, he noticed the movement of a drapery in a window at the far right of the house.

They had parked behind a black car with MD plates. Scott touched the hood. "It's still warm. He can't have been here long."

The younger detective who had driven the car rapped sharply on the front door. They waited. Scott stamped his feet impatiently, trying to warm them. "Why don't you ring the doorbell?" he asked irritably. "That's what it's there for."

"We were seen," Richard said. "He knows we're here."

The young investigator had just raised his finger to the bell when the door opened. Edgar Highley was standing in the foyer. Scott spoke first. "Dr. Highley?"

"Yes?" The tone was cold and questioning.

"Dr. Highley, I'm Scott Myerson, the Valley County Prosecutor. We have a search warrant for these premises, and it is my duty to inform you that you have become a suspect in the wrongful deaths of Vangie Lewis, Edna Burns and Dr. Emmet Salem. You have the right to consult a lawyer. You can refuse to answer questions. Anything you say may be used against you."

Suspect. They weren't sure. They hadn't found Katie. Every shred of evidence had to be circumstantial. He stepped aside, opening the door wider to allow them to enter. His voice was brittle with controlled fury as he said, "I cannot understand the reason for this intrusion, but come in, gentlemen. I will answer any questions you have; you are welcome to search my home. However, I must warn you, when I consult a lawyer it will be to bring suit against Valley County and against each one of you personally."

When he'd left Christ Hospital in Devon, he'd threatened to sue if any word of the investigation was leaked. And for the most part it had been kept quiet. He'd managed to see his file in the Queen Mary Clinic in Liverpool and there was no reference to it.

Deliberately he led them into the library. He knew he made an imposing figure sitting behind the massive Jacobean desk. It was vital that he unnerve them, make them afraid to question too closely.

With a gesture that barely escaped being contemptuous, he waved them to the leather couch and chairs. The Prosecutor and Dr. Carroll sat down; the other two men did not. Scott handed him the printed *Miranda* warning. Scornfully he signed it.

"We'll proceed with the search," the older detective said politely. "Where do you keep your medical records, Dr. Highley?"

"At my office, of course," he snapped. "However, please satisfy yourselves. I'm sure you will. There is a file drawer in this desk with personal papers." He stood up, walked over to the bar and poured Chivas Regal into a crystal tumbler. Deliberately he added ice and a splash of water. He did not go through the ritual of offering a drink to the others. If they'd come even minutes sooner he would still have had Katie's file in the desk drawer. They were trained investigators. They might notice the false bottom in that drawer. But they would never discover the safe—not unless they tore the house apart.

He sat down in the high-backed striped velvet chair near the fireplace, sipped the Scotch and eyed them coldly. When he'd come into the library he'd been so preoccupied that he hadn't noticed the fire Hilda had laid for him. It was burning splendidly. Later he'd have the fondue and wine here.

The questions began. When had he last seen Vangie Lewis?

"As I told Mrs. DeMaio . . ."

"You are sure, Doctor, that Mrs. Lewis did not enter your office Monday night after leaving Dr. Fukhito?"

"As I told Mrs. DeMaio . . ." They had no proof. Absolutely no proof.

"Where were you Monday night, Doctor?"

"Home. Right where you see me now. I came home directly after my office hours."

"Did you receive any phone calls?"

"None I recall." The answering service had taken no message Monday night. He'd checked.

"Were you in Edna Burns's apartment on Tuesday night?"

His smile, contemptuous. "Hardly."

"We'll want some hair samples from you."

Hair samples. Had some been found on Edna or in that apartment? How about Vangie? But he'd been in Edna's apartment with the police on Wednesday night. Vangie always wore that black coat to the office. Even if strands of his hair had been found near the dead women, they could be explained.

"Were you in the Essex House Hotel last night after five P.M.?"

"Absolutely not."

"We have a witness who is prepared to swear that he saw you get off the elevator there at approximately five thirty."

Who had seen him? He had glanced around the lobby as he got off the elevator. He was certain that no one he knew well was there. Maybe they were bluffing. Anyhow, eyewitness identification was notoriously unreliable.

"I was *not* in the Essex House last night. I was in New York at the Carlyle! I dine there frequently; in fact to my dismay my medical bag was stolen while I was dining there."

He'd give gratuitous information; make it seem as though he were becoming cooperative. It had been a mistake to mention Katie DeMaio's name. Would it be natural to tell these people that she was missing from the hospital? Obviously they didn't know she was a patient there. The sister had not yet contacted them. No. Say nothing about it. Doctor–patient confidentiality. Later he'd explain, "I would have told you, but of course assumed that Mrs. DeMaio had fled the hospital in nervous anxiety. I thought she would be troubled to have that fact a matter of record on her job."

But it was foolish to have mentioned the theft.

"What was in your bag?" The Prosecutor's interest seemed perfunctory.

"A basic emergency kit, a few drugs. Hardly worth the thief's effort." Should he mention that it contained files? No.

The Prosecutor was hardly listening. He beckoned

to the younger investigator. "Get that package out of the car."

What package? Edgar Highley's fingers gripped the glass. Was this a trick?

They sat in silence, waiting. The detective returned and handed a small parcel fastened with a rubber band to Scott. Scott yanked the rubber band and pulled off the wrapping paper, revealing a battered shoe. "Do you recognize this moccasin, Doctor?"

He licked his lips. Careful. Careful. Which foot would it fit? Everything depended on that. He leaned over, examined it. The *left* shoe, the one that had been in Edna's apartment. *They had not found his bag.*

"Certainly not. Should I recognize this shoe?"

"Vangie Lewis, your patient, wore it continually for several months. She saw you several times a week. And you didn't ever notice?"

"Mrs. Lewis wore a pair of rather shabby shoes. I certainly do not address my attention to specifically recognizing one particular shoe when it's placed before me."

"Did you ever hear of a Dr. Emmet Salem?"

He pursed his lips. "Possibly. The name seems familiar. I'd have to go through my records."

"Wasn't he on staff with you at Christ Hospital in Devon?"

"Of course. Yes. He was visiting staff. Indeed, I do remember him." How much did they know about Christ Hospital?

"Did you visit Dr. Salem last night at the Essex House?"

"I believe that question has already been answered."

"Were you aware that Vangie Lewis was carrying an Oriental baby?"

So that was it. Smoothly he explained: "Mrs. Lewis was becoming terrified at the prospect of giving birth.

301

That explains it, does it not? She knew that she could never make anyone believe her husband was the father."

Now they were asking about Anna Horan and Maureen Crowley. They were coming close; too close; like dogs baying as they closed in on their quarry.

"Those two young women are typical of many who demand abortions and then blame the physician when they experience emotional reactions. It's not uncommon, you know. Check with any of my colleagues."

Richard listened as Scott persisted in his questioning. Scott was right, he thought bleakly. Together everything added up. Separately everything was refutable, explainable. Unless they could prove wrongful death in the maternity cases, it would be impossible to charge Edgar Highley with anything and make it stick.

Highley was so composed, so sure. Richard tried to think how his father, a neurologist, would react if he were questioned about the wrongful death of one of his patients. How would Bill Kennedy react? How would he, Richard, react both as a person and as a doctor? Not like this man—not with this sarcasm, this scorn.

It was an act. Richard was sure of it. Edgar Highley was acting. But how could they prove it? With sickening certainty he knew they'd never find anything incriminating in Highley's records. He was far too clever for that.

Scott was asking about the Berkeley baby. "Doctor, you are aware that Mrs. Elizabeth Berkeley gave birth to a baby who has green eyes. Isn't that a medical impossibility when both parents and all four grandparents have brown eyes?"

"I would say so, but clearly Mr. Berkeley is not the father of that baby."

Neither Scott nor Richard had expected the admission. "That doesn't mean I know who the father is,"

Edgar Highley said smoothly, "but I seriously doubt that it is the obstetrician's business to delve into matters such as that. If my patient wishes to tell me that her husband is her baby's father, then so be it."

A shame, he thought. He would have to defer fame a little longer. He'd never be able to admit the success of the Berkeley baby now. But there would be others.

Scott looked at Richard, sighed and stood up. "Dr. Highley, when you go to your office tomorrow you will learn that we have seized all your hospital and office records. We are deeply concerned at the number of maternity deaths at Westlake Hospital, and that matter is under intensive investigation."

He was on safe ground. "I invite the most minute scrutiny of all my patients' records. I can assure you that the Westlake Maternity death ratio is remarkably low in consideration of the cases we handle."

The smell of the fondue was filling the house. He wanted to eat it. He was so hungry. Unless it was stirred, it would surely burn. Just a few minutes more.

The phone rang. "I'll let my service take it," he said, then knew he could not. Undoubtedly it would be the hospital saying that Mrs. DeMaio had not yet returned home and her sister was frantic. It might be the perfect opportunity to let the Prosecutor and Dr. Carroll know about Katie's disappearance. He picked up the phone. "Dr. Highley here."

"Doctor, this is Lieutenant Weingarden of the Seventeenth Precinct in New York. We've just arrested a man who answers the description of the person who stole a bag from the trunk of your car last night."

The bag.

"Has it been recovered?" Something in his voice was giving him away. The Prosecutor and Dr. Carroll were watching him curiously. The Prosecutor stalked over to the desk and openly reached for the other extension.

"Yes, we have recovered your bag, Doctor. That's exactly the point. Several of the items in it may lead to far more serious charges than theft. Doctor, will you describe the contents of your bag?"

"Some medicine—a few basic drugs; an emergency kit."

"What about a patient's file from the office of a Dr. Emmet Salem, a bloodstained paperweight and an old shoe?"

He could feel the hard, suspicious stare of the Prosecutor. He closed his eyes. When he spoke, his voice was remarkably controlled. "Are you joking?"

"I thought you'd say that, sir. We're cooperating with the Valley County Prosecutor's office concerning the suspicious death of Dr. Emmet Salem last night. I'll call the Prosecutor now. It looks as though the suspect might have killed Dr. Salem in the process of a theft. Thank you, sir."

He heard Scott Myerson's order to the New York policeman. "Don't hang up!"

Slowly he replaced the receiver he was holding on the cradle. It was all over. Now that they had the bag, it was all over. Whatever chance he had had of bluffing his way through the investigation was finished.

The paperweight sticky with Emmet Salem's blood. The medical file on Vangie Lewis that contradicted the information in his office records. The shoe, that miserable filthy object.

If the shoe fits . . .

He stared down at his feet, objectively contemplating the patina of his handsome English cordovans.

They'd never stop searching now until they found the true files.

If the shoe fits wear it.

The moccasins had never fit Vangie Lewis. The supreme irony was that they fit *him*. As clearly as though he had walked in them, they tied him to the deaths of Vangie Lewis, Edna Burns, Emmet Salem.

Hysterical laughter rumbled inside him, shaking his stolid frame. The Prosecutor had completed the call. "Dr. Highley," Scott Myerson's voice was formal, "you are under arrest for the murder of Dr. Emmet Salem."

Edgar Highley watched as the detective sitting at the desk stood up quickly. He hadn't realized the man had been taking notes. He watched as the detective pulled handcuffs from his pocket.

Handcuffs. Jail. A trial. Blobs of humanity passing judgment on *him*. He who had conquered the primary act of life, the birth process, a common prisoner.

He drew himself up. The indomitable strength was returning. He had performed an operation. Despite his brilliance the operation had failed. The patient was clinically dead. There was nothing left to do except turn off the life-sustaining apparatus.

Dr. Carroll was looking at him curiously. From the moment of their Wednesday night meeting, Carroll had been hostile. Somehow Edgar Highley was sure that Richard Carroll was the man who had become suspicious of him. But he had his revenge. Katie DeMaio's death was his revenge on Richard Carroll.

The detective was approaching him. The handcuffs caught the glint of the fire.

He smiled politely at him. "I have just remembered that I do have some medical records that might interest you," he said. He walked over to the wall, released the spring that held the panel in place. The panel slid back. Mechanically he opened the wall safe.

He could gather up the records, make a dash for the fireplace. The fire Hilda had laid was fairly brisk now. Before they could stop him, he could get rid of the most important files.

No. Let them know his genius. Let them mourn it.

He lifted the files out of the safe, stacked them on the desk. They were all staring at him now. Carroll walked over to the desk. The Prosecutor still had his hand on the phone. One detective was waiting with the handcuffs. The other detective had just come back into the room. Probably he'd been going through the house snooping into his possessions. Dogs hounding their quarry.

"Oh, there is another case you'll want to have."

He walked over to the table by the fireplace chair and reached for his Scotch. Carrying it to the safe, he sipped it casually. The vial was there, right in the back of the safe. He'd put it away Monday night for possible future use. The future was now. He'd never expected it to end this way. But he was still in control of life and death. The supreme decision was his alone to make. A burning smell was permeating the room. Regretfully he realized it was the fondue.

At the safe he moved quickly. He slipped the vial open and dumped the crystals of cyanide into his glass. As understanding swept over Richard's face, he held up the glass in a mocking toast.

"Don't!" Richard shouted, throwing himself across the room as Edgar Highley raised the glass to his lips and gulped down the contents. Richard knocked the glass away as Highley fell, but knew it was too late. The four men watched futilely, helplessly, as Highley's screams and groans died into writhing silence.

"Oh, God!" the younger detective said. He bolted from the room, his face green.

"Why'd he do it?" the other detective asked. "What a lousy way to die."

Richard bent over the body. Edgar Highley's face was convulsed; foaming bubbles were blistering his lips. The protruding gray eyes were open and staring.

He could have done so much good, Richard thought. Instead, he was an egocentric genius who used his God-given skill to experiment with lives.

"Once I got on the line with the New York police, he knew he couldn't lie or murder his way out anymore," Scott said. "You were right about him, Richard."

Straightening up, Richard went over to the desk and scanned the names on the files. BERKELEY, LEWIS. "These are the records we're looking for." He opened the Berkeley file. The first page began:

Elizabeth Berkeley, age 39, became my patient today. She will never conceive her own child. I have decided that she will be the next extraordinary patient.

"There's medical history here," he said quietly.

Scott was standing over the body. "And when you think that this nut was Katie's doctor," he muttered.

Richard looked up from reading Liz Berkeley's file. "What did you say?" he demanded. "Are you suggesting that Highley was treating Katie?"

"She had an appointment with him Wednesday," Scott replied.

"She had a *what?*"

"She happened to mention it when—" The phone interrupted him. Scott picked it up. "Yes," then said, "I'm sorry, this is not Dr. Highley. Who is calling, please?" His expression changed. Molly Kennedy. "Molly."

Richard stared. Apprehension strangled his neck muscles. "No," Scott said. "I can't put Dr. Highley on. What's the matter?"

He listened, then covered the mouthpiece with his hand. "Oh, Jesus," he said, "Highley admitted Katie to Westlake tonight and she's missing."

Richard yanked the phone from him. "Molly,

what's happened? Why was Katie there? What do you mean she's missing?"

He listened. "Come on, Molly. Katie would never walk out of a hospital. You should know that. Wait."

Dropping the phone, he frantically scattered the files on the desk. Near the bottom of the pile he found the one he dreaded to see. DeMaio, Kathleen. Opening it, he raced through it, his face paling as he read. He came to the last paragraph.

With the calm of desperation, he picked up the phone. "Molly, put Bill on," he ordered. As Scott and the detectives listened, he said, "Bill, Katie is hemorrhaging somewhere in Westlake Hospital. Call the lab at Westlake. We'll need to hang a bottle of O negative the minute we find her. Have them ready to take a blood sample and analyze for hemoglobin, hematocrit and type and cross-match for four units of whole blood. Tell them to have an operating room ready. I'll meet you there." He broke the connection.

Incredible, he thought. You can still function knowing that already it may be too late. He turned to the detective at the desk. "Call the hospital. Pull the search team from Highley's office and have them start looking for Katie. Tell them to look everywhere— every room, every closet. Get all the hospital personnel to help. Every second counts."

Without waiting for instructions, the younger investigator ran to start up the car. "Come on, Richard," Scott snapped.

Richard grabbed Katie's file. "We have to know what-all he's done to her." For an instant he looked at Edgar Highley's body. They'd been seconds too late preventing his death. Would they be too late for Katie?

With Scott he hunched in the back of the squad car as it raced through the night. Highley had given Katie the heparin over an hour ago. It was fast-acting.

Katie, he thought, why didn't you tell me? Katie, why do you feel you have to go it alone? Nobody can. Katie, we could be so good together. Oh, Katie, we could have what Molly and Bill have. It's there waiting for us to reach out for it. Katie, you felt it too. You've been fighting it. Why? Why? If you'd only trusted me, *told* me you were seeing Highley. I'd never have let you go near him. Why didn't I see that you were sick? Why didn't I *make* you tell me? Katie, I want you. Don't die, Katie. Wait. Let me find you. Katie, *hang on.* . . .

They were at the hospital. Squad cars were roaring into the parking lot. They ran up the stairs into the lobby. Phil, his face drawn into deep lines, was commanding the search.

Bill and Molly came running into the lobby. Molly was sobbing. Bill was deadly calm. "John Pierce is on his way over. He's the best hematologist in New Jersey. They've got a reasonable supply of whole blood on hand here, and we can get more from the blood bank. Have you found her?"

"Not yet."

The door to the fire stairs, partly ajar, burst open. A young policeman ran out. "She's on the floor in the morgue. I think she's gone."

Seconds later, Richard was cradling her in his arms. Her skin and lips were ashen. He could not get a pulse. "Katie. Katie."

Bill's hand gripped his shoulder. "Let's get her upstairs. We'll have to work fast if there's any chance at all."

◆ 80 ◆

She was in a tunnel. At the end there was a light. It was warm at the end of the tunnel. It would be so easy to drift there.

But someone was keeping her from going. Someone was holding her. A voice. Richard's voice. "Hang on, Katie, hang on."

She wanted so not to turn back. It was so hard, so dark. It would be so much easier to slip away.

"Hang on, Katie."

Sighing, she turned and began to make her way back.

◆ 81 ◆

On Monday evening Richard tiptoed into Katie's room, a dozen roses in his hand. She'd been out of danger since Sunday morning, but hadn't stayed awake long enough to say more than a word or two.

He looked down at her. Her eyes were closed. He decided to go out and ask the nurse for a vase.

"Just lay them across my chest."

He spun around. "Katie." He pulled up a chair. "How do you feel?"

She opened her eyes and grimaced at the transfusion apparatus. "I hear the vampires are picketing. I'm putting them out of business."

"You're better." He hoped the sudden moisture in his eyes wasn't noticeable.

She had noticed. With her free hand she gently reached up and brushed a finger across his eyelids. "Before I fall asleep again, please tell me what happened. Otherwise I'll wake up about three in the morning and try to put it together. Why did Edgar Highley kill Vangie?"

"He was experimenting on his patients, Katie. You know about the test-tube baby in England, of course.

"Highley was far more ambitious than to simply produce in vitro babies for their natural parents. What he set out to do was take fetuses from women who had abortions and implant those fetuses in the wombs of sterile women. And he did it! In these past eight years he learned how to immunize a host mother from rejecting an alien fetus.

"He had one complete success. I've shown his records to the fertility research lab in Mt. Sinai Hospital, and they tell me that Edgar Highley made a quantum leap in blastocyst and embryonic research.

"But after that success, he wanted to break new ground. Anna Horan, a woman he aborted, claims that she changed her mind about the abortion, but that he knocked her out and took her fetus when she was unconscious. She was right. He had Vangie Lewis in the next room waiting for the implant. Vangie thought she was simply having some treatment to help her become pregnant with her own child. Highley never expected Vangie to retain the Oriental fetus so long, although his system had become perfected to such a degree that the race issue was really not a consideration.

"When Vangie didn't abort spontaneously, he became so fascinated by his own research that he couldn't bear to destroy the fetus. He decided to bring it to term, and then who would blame him if Vangie had a partly Oriental child? The natural mother, Anna Horan, is married to a Caucasian."

"He was able to suppress the immune system?" Katie remembered the elaborate charts in college science courses.

"Yes, and without harm to the child. The danger to the mother was much greater. He's killed sixteen women in the last eight years. Vangie was getting terribly sick. Unfortunately for her, she ran into Highley last Monday evening just as she left Fukhito. She told him she was going to consult her former doctor in Minneapolis. That would have been a risk, because a natural pregnancy for Vangie was a million-to-one shot, and any gynecologist who had treated her would have known that.

"But it was when she mentioned Emmet Salem's name that she was finished. Highley knew that Salem would guess what had happened when Vangie produced a half-Oriental child, then swore that she'd never been involved with an Oriental man. Salem was in England when Highley's first wife died. He knew about the scandal."

"And now," Richard said, "that's enough of that. All the rest can wait. Your eyes are closing again."

"No. . . . You said that Highley had *one* success. Did he actually transfer a fetus and have it brought to term?"

"Yes. And if you had stayed five minutes longer at Molly's last Thursday night and seen the Berkeley baby, you could guess now who the natural mother is. Liz Berkeley carried Maureen Crowley's baby to term in her womb."

"Maureen Crowley's baby." Katie's eyes flew open, all sleepiness gone. She tried to pull herself up.

312

"Easy. Come on, you'll pull that needle out." Gently he touched her shoulder, holding her until she leaned back. "Highley kept complete case histories of what he did from the moment he aborted Maureen and implanted Liz. He listed every medication, every symptom, every problem until the actual delivery."

"Does Maureen know?"

"It was only right to tell her and the Berkeleys and let the Berkeleys examine the records. Jim Berkeley has been living with the belief that his wife lied to him about artificial insemination. You know how Maureen felt about that abortion. It's been destroying her. She went to see her baby. She's one happy girl, Katie. She would have given it out for adoption if she had delivered it naturally. Now that she's seen Maryanne, sees how crazy the Berkeleys are about her, she's in seventh heaven. But I think you're going to lose a good secretary. Maureen's going back to college next fall."

"What about the mother of Vangie's baby?"

"Anna Horan is heartbroken enough about the abortion. We saw no point in having her realize that her baby would have been born if Highley hadn't murdered Vangie last week. She'll have other children."

Katie bit her lip. The question she'd been afraid to ask. She had to know. "Richard, please tell me the truth. When they found me, I was hemorrhaging. How far did they have to go to stop the bleeding?"

"You're okay. They did the D-and-C. I'm sure they told you that."

"But that's all?"

"That's all, Katie. You can still have a dozen kids if you want them."

His hand reached over to cover hers. That hand had been there, had pulled her back when she was so near to death. That voice had made her want to come back.

313

For a long, quiet moment she looked up at Richard. Oh, how I love you, she thought. How very much I love you.

His troubled, questioning expression changed suddenly into a broad smile. Obviously he was satisfied at what he saw in her face.

Katie grinned back at him. "Pretty sure of yourself, aren't you, Doctor?" she asked him crisply.